The

A. A. Chaudhuri is a former City lawyer. After completing a degree in History at University College London, she later trained as a solicitor and worked for several major London law firms before leaving law to pursue her passion for writing. She lives in Surrey with her family, and loves films, all things Italian and a good margarita!

Also by A. A. Chaudhuri

She's Mine
The Loyal Friend
The Final Party
Under Her Roof
The School Gates

A.A. CHAUDHURI

The School Gates

hera

First published in the United Kingdom in 2025 by

Hera Books
Unit 9 (Canelo), 5th Floor
Cargo Works, 1-2 Hatfields
London SE1 9PG
United Kingdom

Copyright © A. A. Chaudhuri 2025

The moral right of A. A. Chaudhuri to be identified as the creator of this work has been asserted in accordance with the Copyright, Designs and Patents Act, 1988.

All rights reserved. No part of this publication may be reproduced or transmitted in any form or by any means, electronic or mechanical, including photocopy, recording, or any information storage and retrieval system, without permission in writing from the publisher.

A CIP catalogue record for this book is available from the British Library.

Print ISBN 978 1 80436 983 8
Ebook ISBN 978 1 80436 984 5

This book is a work of fiction. Names, characters, businesses, organizations, places and events are either the product of the author's imagination or are used fictitiously. Any resemblance to actual persons, living or dead, events or locales is entirely coincidental.

Look for more great books at www.herabooks.com

Printed and bound in Great Britain by Clays Ltd, Elcograf S.p.A.

This is an uncorrected proof. Please note that the text has not yet been finalised and is subject to change.

If you wish to quote from this book, please contact us to confirm the final wording.

Trusting is hard. Knowing who to trust, even harder.

Maria V. Snyder

Prologue

The pain had been relentless.

At one point, terrifying. Like nothing she'd felt before. An all-consuming, merciless pain that surely no mortal being should be able to withstand. It had come on quite suddenly, after she'd been doing OK for some hours. Wondering to herself what all the fuss was about, why people made such a big deal out of it. But she'd spoken too soon, had been too cocksure, and like a tidal wave that had seemed to come out of nowhere, it had hit her, subsumed her. Making her regret her words and feel like her entire body was being ripped apart. The pain had seemed to go on forever, but she knew this was not the case. The sheer intensity just made her feel like it was never-ending. But within an hour, it was over. And when she gazed down at her beautiful baby boy, she knew why they said it was the best kind of pain. And why, as soon as she saw her newborn child, that pain was forgotten.

He was the most precious, most exquisite, most perfect little thing she had ever seen. A true miracle of life she fell instantly in love with. All thoughts of the horrors that came before, all the sadness she had endured, were pushed to the back of her mind. They were no longer significant compared to the angel lying in her arms, nuzzling at her breast.

And at that moment she also knew that she would do anything to protect her child, come hell or high water. She'd move mountains for him. Kill for him. From now on, he was the number one priority in her life. Nothing else mattered. And she'd sooner die than let any harm come to him.

She needed to get away, though, and fast. Somewhere she and her precious baby boy could start anew. She didn't want him raised so close to where her nightmare had started. The place that had caused her so much heartache, and very nearly broken her. If she stayed here, it would feel like he was tainted with that same sorrow, same misery. He deserved to be happy.

Plus, she had no idea if she'd be placing him in danger by staying here. That was her biggest fear. That *he* might return, seek her out. Harm her child.

No, it was best that she started afresh. Just like the person whose opinion she valued above all else had advised her to. Some place new where she was no longer Elizabeth Mosley.

But someone else entirely.

From now on, she was Lola Martinez.

Chapter One

Lola

Friday, December 15th 2023

'Joy's looking lovely tonight. That colour really suits her, compliments her skin tone beautifully.'

Nothing. Not a word, nor so much as a glance in response to my perfectly pleasant, honest observation. That's pretty much how it's been the entire evening as I've tried my best to make small talk around the dinner table at the Reception parents' Christmas do. Forcing down the expensive three-course meal I've already paid for despite every bite being an effort. I've known these women for over a year now, spent many a heartfelt moment with them. Or so I thought. Yet tonight has felt a thousand times more awkward than the day we first met.

It was bad enough back then, when they eyed me with pity, despite making a vain attempt not to show it. But now all I see in their eyes is contempt. A sentiment they've made no effort to hide. In fact, they seem to be delighting in it and that's so much worse. Makes me feel sick to my stomach.

'B, let's go dance with Joy and Dee,' Clarissa nudges Bianca in her side, 'show them how it's done.'

Another snub.

It's like I don't exist. Or worse, am some kind of social leper. I want to cry. For the ground to swallow me up.

And it's then that I feel the tears amass in my eyes. My insides burning with a mixture of hurt and anger. I bite my lip, will my tears not to spill over my lids and make me feel even smaller than Clarissa's already done in blanking me so cruelly.

Finally, a sly sideways glance my way, most likely to confirm that I am feeling as humiliated and unwanted as they're clearly so desperate to make me feel, whereupon I self-consciously pick up my wine glass and put it to my lips as a means of distraction, even though the last thing I need is more booze. And then, to my dismay and relief, both her and Bianca are up on their feet, linking arms and giggling like goofy teenagers as they stumble away from the table and make their way towards the dancefloor where an equally inebriated Joy and Dee are swaying along to 'Dancing Queen'.

In truth, I should have trusted my gut and never have come here tonight. Not with the alcohol flowing and holiday emotions running high. It was a mistake, and you'd think I'd know better considering how tense things have been at the school gates recently. And, more importantly, in light of the messages I've been receiving. Messages threatening my life. My son's life. Scaring the hell out of me. Turning me into a nervous wreck. The kind of person I swore never to be when I moved here. Just at the thought of those messages I instinctively pull out my phone from my clutch. OK, so it's been a while since I received one. Yet, I can't help fearing that another one might have come through while I've been here. To my relief, there's nothing. Still, I find myself wondering if one of *them* here this evening could be behind them. I hadn't wanted to accept that possibility, despite their recent cold behaviour towards me and, more importantly, what the last message said.

But thinking about the way they've treated me tonight, like I'm no better than the dirt beneath their shoes, I'm starting to wonder if I was being naïve. That they are, in fact, capable of things I hadn't thought possible. Perhaps having somehow learned the truth. All the secrets I've been keeping from them. Including one thing I'm deeply ashamed of.

Perhaps the person I trust most in this world was right all along?

The fact is, I've always felt like an outsider amongst the parents at St Xavier's Primary. I've never quite fitted in, despite me desperately wanting to. For my child — Luca's — sake more than mine. And thinking back I feel a little foolish for having thought I'd finally become part of their circle, having spent the best part of a year trying to forge friendships with these women. Because the way they've treated me tonight has only proved just how out of place I really am. Simone is my only true friend in the nest of vipers I've found myself entangled in. But she's at home with the kids this evening, her husband three hundred miles away on business, no grandparents around to babysit. She doesn't trust anyone else with her kids. And I can't say I blame her. Strangers are dangerous, no matter how nice they might seem on the outside.

Simone warned me not to go this evening. Said Luca and I should come over to hers for a sleepover, and that once the kids were in bed we could chill out with a bottle of wine and a movie. But I didn't listen. I put my own shallow desires — the chance to patch things up with *him, but also walk in here with my head held high and prove to everyone I deserved to have fun as much as anyone* – above friendship, what truly matters. Even though he's been so cruel towards me lately. Has made his feelings frighteningly clear. And now it seems that I am paying the price for my superficiality, my pettiness, even. OK, so it's true he led me on, but that doesn't excuse my behaviour. I'm a grown woman, and he's a married man. I should have known better, and yet I behaved like some stupid schoolgirl with an obsessive crush. I can't help feeling so pathetic, so ashamed. So sick with regret. But perhaps that's exactly how I deserve to feel.

Simone confronted me about it some time ago, when I'd gone round to hers for coffee. She warned me not to go there. Said I was asking for trouble, that his wife would make it her life's mission to destroy me if anything physical ever happened between us. That she'd slaughter me in front of the whole school without a moment's hesitation. She said I'd be crazy to risk everything for the sake of wild, mindless passion, and deep down I know that she's right. But it's not that easy. I'm not the kind of person who can switch my feelings on and off like a tap. I was forced to do that a long time ago, and it's something that's haunted me ever since.

–

Tonight, as I entered the room, where everyone was mingling with a welcome glass of champagne, they looked at me as if I was the enemy. A pack of hungry wolves baying for my blood.

Feeling awkward, I'd ended up chatting with a few of the other reception parents – some of whom I'd never exchanged more than a smile or brief hello with – before we all sat down for dinner at beautifully decorated tables indicative of the joyful festive occasion it should have been. But as I stood there making small talk, I couldn't help wondering if word had spread further than our little group. Whether the entire year-group of parents knew my secrets, were perhaps gossiping about my private life at that very moment. Whether, in fact, every wife and mother amongst them considered me a threat to their families.

Me, the young, single mum.

The outsider.

The home-wrecker.

It's kind of ironic when I think about it. After all, I moved here to start over, forge a new life for me and Luca. Where no one knew me, least of all my secret, the ghastly truth I've been hiding all these years. But far from achieve the anonymity I craved, it seems I'm the one everyone's talking about, due to my own stupidity. How the fuck could I have allowed things to go so badly wrong?

I realise now it was all just a game to the women I've tried so hard to become friends with. I was naïve and foolish to think I could be one of them. Slot easily into their complicated lives like the missing piece of a complex jigsaw. I was a novelty at first, an amusing plaything to distract them from their dull existences, their deep insecurities, frustrations. Fears.

Their demons.

Someone they felt sorry for because I didn't have their seemingly perfect lives. They had charmed me with their saccharine smiles and false pleasantries. Seduced me with their weekly coffee mornings, lavish dinner parties and wine-fuelled nights out. But I guess it was only a matter of time before they showed their true colours.

I am not one of them. I can never be. And now I realise I need to leave before I say something I regret. Because the fact is, I know all their secrets, every last damned dirty one of them. I could easily spill the beans, make a scene, shame them all with the dirt I have at my fingertips. If only to get back at them for humiliating me tonight. For blanking me at the school gates without having the decency to explain why. In my heart I know it's probably karma for what I did. But they can't possibly know the truth, can they? Even though I'll admit it's a thought that's crossed my mind lately.

Despite my humiliation, I don't want to betray their secrets. Don't want to be that kind of person. I promised myself and Luca that I'd never stoop that low. Yet another poisonous parent who delights in spiteful gossip. I promised *her* that too.

It's just after 11:30 p.m. and I realise I need to get out of here fast. It's like I can't breathe. My head spinning with a rollercoaster of emotions that are making me dizzy. I'm not sure how I lasted this long, to be honest. I hurriedly pick up my silver clutch and skirt the edge of the dancefloor. Deliberately avoiding eye contact with anyone. I hear several familiar voices call after me – one male, two female – as I stride away from the dance floor, the familiar chorus of 'Come on Eileen' fading into the background. But I don't look back. It's too late for them to feel guilty about the way they've treated me. I keep going, my head muzzy from too much champagne, my stomach churning with trepidation. Out of the function room I scurry, before I race down the hotel corridor and stop at the cloakroom to grab my coat. I wouldn't bother if it wasn't for the fact that it's below zero outside. The muffled voices of wasted partygoers linger behind me in the distance, George Michael's 'Last Christmas' coming on but failing to drown them out.

My heart is pounding furiously now as I rummage around in my clutch for my coat ticket. As usual, it's crammed with too much stuff. I've never been the most organised of people. I'm relieved to find it wedged beneath my compact and a tube of nude lip gloss. My hand is unsteady as I fish it out, then hastily uncrumple it, conscious that I need to get out of here quick sharp.

I hand it over to the kindly looking attendant behind the counter. Tell him to hurry because my cab is coming even though that's a lie because I haven't even had the chance to search for one yet on my Uber app, simply because I dashed out without thinking things through. Desperate to escape. To avoid their questions. I glance back in the direction of where I came from, am relieved to see no one has come after me. A little hurt too. I guess they really don't give a shit about me. The attendant gives me a look of understanding, sensing my discomfort, that something's not right, and assures me he'll be back with my coat asap.

While I wait, I pull out my phone and see that I have a new text. It's from Simone.

> Hey, honey, how's the party going? Hope it's been fun in the end and that Bianca's not been too much of a bitch. Let me know the goss when you can. Watching Love Actually for the millionth time, wish you were here, S xx

I almost want to cry reading Simone's message, knowing that right now I could be curled up under a blanket with her, warm and safe, rather than feeling hurt and alone, with no clue as to how I'm going to get home. I should have listened to her. Why the hell didn't I? I should have listened to my only other true friend too. She warned me to stay away tonight, but I thought I knew better.

Simone also urged me to pre-book a cab home. But again, I didn't listen. I said I'd play it by ear, see how the evening went. That I was used to walking, at any rate, so it wouldn't be the end of the world if I ended up doing the same this evening. What the hell was I thinking? It's December and frigging freezing out there! Simone had looked at me like I was mad, and who could blame her?

I open the Uber app, go to my saved addresses and press the one at the top of the list. 5 Jacinda Court, Kingston. The two-bed second floor riverside flat where I live with my son, who right now is being cared for by his doting grandparents. I feel an overwhelming surge of love as I picture Luca sleeping at this moment, tucked up in his racing car bed, cuddling his precious bear, Snowy, who he's had since birth for comfort. Those long black eyelashes of his tickling his soft almond skin. The way he twitches his nose when he dreams. As I think on this, I feel sick at the thought of any harm coming to him. I shouldn't have left him this evening. OK, so there've been no messages lately, but that doesn't mean the person threatening my son's safety has gone away. It was selfish of me to put my own needs first, even though Mum said I needed a break, needed to let my hair down. She's in the dark about everything, though. I didn't want to upset or scare her. I knew that if I told her about the texts she'd go straight to the police. Something that can never happen, simply because it's too dangerous. For all of us.

Damn, no Ubers! I guess I shouldn't be surprised. It's a Friday night in mid-December; the party season in full swing. Spur-of-the-moment cabs are as rare as hen's teeth. I curse myself for not pre-ordering one like Simone advised me to. It was unbelievably dumb of me. I seem to be making stupid decisions left, right and centre lately. I can't hang around, though. I need to get home quickly, make sure that Luca's safe. Get as far away as possible from all of *them*.

I fling on my coat and dart out into the freezing night. It's nearly a quarter to midnight and the biting air takes my breath away, piercing my petite frame like a frozen arrow, my freshly pedicured bare toes already starting to lose sensation. I'd be a fool not to keep to the well-lit main road the whole way, but I'm suddenly desperate to get back to Luca and I'm conscious that halfway along there's a short cut down to the river path which will get me back faster. I wait for a safe moment to cross the road, but just as I'm standing there I hear my phone ping a text. It can't be Simone again, she only just messaged. Maybe it's Mum, wondering how I am, when I'll be home. She still worries about me getting home safely despite me being a grown woman. It doesn't annoy me. Rather, I feel lucky, blessed. Grateful to have a mother who cares about me so much. I pull my mobile out of my clutch, go to my messages. My legs nearly give way when I read the text:

> You think you can slink away like that, you filthy slut. Shy away from who you really are, from your past. You don't get to do that. I warned you not to talk, but you did. Even though you thought I wouldn't find out. Your son will be so much better off without you. You don't deserve Luca. Don't deserve to be a mother.

Fuck. Is it him? The person I fear most. Has he been watching me? But for how long? I'm suddenly choked with fear, wondering whether I'm right, that my tormentor is back and means me real harm. Or perhaps it's someone else playing with me? Taunting me with their cruel yet empty words. I know I should go back to the hotel, ring for a cab, however long it takes. But I just can't face those women again. I hurry to the other side as best I can in my four-inch heels. For pity's sake, why didn't I bring trainers or sandals to change into? I practically live in them when I'm not working.

I keep walking, and at the same time instinctively look over my shoulder for any sign of company. It's eerily quiet, spookily still, making the slightest sound seem that much louder. There's no one about, just the odd car whooshing by. I feel a strange mix of relief and dismay. Afraid of, and yet at the same time craving, company. Still, it's not like I'm in some dodgy area of Kingston. It's Surbiton. Known for being a safer, more affluent part of town. I tell myself I'll be OK, then I quickly text Simone back, tell her she was right, that I shouldn't have gone to the party, that it had been a nightmare because they all hate me and I had to get away. I tell her I'm walking home, taking a short cut along the river path to save time because there are no cabs. That I prefer walking in any case. At this I get an almost immediate response:

> WTF, are you fucking crazy?? I know you like walking, but it's pitch-black dark, it's not safe. Go back to the hotel now, I'll call you a cab. S x

I smile at her concern, again inwardly chide myself for being so shallow in choosing the chance to see *him* over spending time with my best friend this evening. I text Simone thanks but explain that I need to get back to Luca, lie that I'm nearly home anyway so it makes sense for me to keep on walking. She messages me back, tells me I'm a nutter, but that I should text her as soon as I'm home safe and sound. I tell her of course, then focus on the task at hand, by now feeling chilled to the bone. Before long, I'm at the slope leading down to the river path. I hesitate, my head urging me to keep going along the main road, particularly given the creepy text I just received, my heart assuring me it will all be OK and that this way I'll get home faster to Luca and my warm bed. I inhale the cold crisp air, feel it catch in my throat like lethal shards of glass, then I take the plunge and venture down towards the river's edge. I guess I should be thankful it's not raining or blowing a gale, despite my earlobes and fingers having lost all feeling.

It's about a ten-minute walk in trainers, fifteen in these ridiculous heels. Still, I totter along the path as fast as I can, every now and again glancing left at the tranquil water. It looks so still it might as well be frozen over. In the daytime, this part of the Thames is invariably dotted with kayaks and pleasure boats, ducks and swans merrily gliding along and occasionally swimming to shore in the hope of finding food. But now it's empty and soulless. The sanctuary of the dead, not the living. I keep going, despite the fact that my toes are in agony with the arctic temperatures. It's nearly midnight. I figure I am perhaps five minutes away from our flat set in a three-storey block on Riverside Walk, a paved piazza of thriving pubs, bars and restaurants. I could have rented somewhere away from the river, a small semi-detached house on a quiet suburban road, for example. But somehow I feel safer here in a modern gated block where there are always lots of people about and a porter on site. I can already hear the muffled voices of late-night revellers in the distance. It buoys me. Hopefully, before long I'll see a friendly face, possibly even a neighbour or two.

I reach the only café along this stretch, shortly before the path becomes wider leading to the main piazza. The café's closed now, the immediate vicinity deserted. But that's when I hear a noise coming from behind me. I don't think it's an animal; the movements seem wrong for that, heavier, more pronounced. More human-like. Fear strangles me, a myriad of thoughts rushing through my head. *Why did I leave the party? I should have stayed and faced the music. How could I have been so stupid to walk alone at this time of night? I of all people should know better. This is all my fault; I should have listened to Simone! I should have been truthful with my parents.* About everything...

At least two people know the truth. If the worst happens, I can rely on them to tell it. Protect Luca. It's just as I'm thinking this that my phone starts ringing. I know I shouldn't answer, that I should focus on making a run for it. But the urge is too great. I tell myself I can at least call on the person's who's ringing for help, and in doing so perhaps scare away whoever's following me. I pull my phone out from my coat pocket, upping my pace at the same time, my feet in serious pain, panic bulldozing through me.

Maybe it's Simone, or Mum, I think to myself, trying to remain hopeful. But it's not. It's an unknown caller, a realisation that only serves to intensify my fear. Yet, once again the impulse to answer the call overwhelms me. I press the green button, and when I hear what the person at the other end of the line has to say, I find myself rooted to the spot, unable to believe the bombshell I've just been told.

How could this be?

And then I hear my name spoken. I want to scream, make a run for it, but I can't. My voice and legs are anaesthetised by sheer unbridled terror.

Before I know it, I feel a gloved hand across my mouth, a potent, sweet smell invading my nostrils. I try to struggle, to put up some kind of a fight. But it's useless, the fight swiftly going out of me.

And then everything descends into darkness.

Chapter Two

Detective Inspector John Banner

Saturday, 16th December 2023

I watch Frank Daily – the pathologist recently called to the scene – lean over and meticulously examine the young woman's body. Around us, a team of crime scene investigators led by Philip Newman, all kitted out from head-to-toe in white protective clothing, studiously set to work combing the area for evidence. Yellow tape cordons the entire zone off from the general public, the spectacle already attracting the curiosity of pedestrians observing the riverbank from the main Portsmouth Road above. Some of them have had to take detours to reach their destinations. It's only 7:45 a.m., so still early, but before long news will have travelled far and wide and the press will descend on the scene like vultures and demand a statement.

Violence, theft, sexual offences – they are all sadly common in my patch. But not murder. This is shocking news, sure to strike fear into the hearts of the community, dampening the yuletide cheer.

'She's been dead at least six or seven hours, I'd say.' Frank looks back at me over his shoulder. 'Body is approaching full rigor mortis.' He pauses, his eyes steadfast. 'I'm also pretty sure this was no accident and that she was murdered.'

An early morning jogger had spotted the woman's body on the riverbank around 7 a.m. Her face is hauntingly pale, damp strands of jet-black hair clinging to her ashen cheeks. She's maybe in her late twenties, early thirties, and despite her sickly pallor and blue-tinged lips she has a continental look about her. Very beautiful. Petite too. Judging by the way she's dressed underneath her sodden grey belted wool coat – she's wearing a strapless green sequin dress and silver peep-toe stilettos – I'm guessing she'd been on her way home from a Christmas party when the bastard attacked her. Perhaps he killed her on the main pathway before rolling her body over the edge and fleeing. It's hypocritical of me but I find myself saying a silent prayer to a God I long ago stopped believing in that this woman is single and childless, and that I won't have to deliver the worst news imaginable to any kid of hers. Particularly at this time of the year, a time which should be filled with love, hope and laughter. Not the kind of horrors that could scar a child for life.

I crouch down alongside Frank, my thighs still aching from overdoing it in the gym yesterday morning. 'Why are you so sure she was murdered?' I ask. 'And that it wasn't an accident or overdose of some sort.' I think I already know the answer to my question, but I want Frank to confirm my thoughts all the same.

'Well, the autopsy will verify my initial findings,' Frank says, 'but it looks like she's been suffocated. See here.'

Frank points to the woman's bloodshot eyes, as well as some bruising around her nose and mouth. All tell-tale signs of suffocation. I nod. Just as I thought. There's no blood that I can see, nor any signs of strangulation. Neither is there any vomit to indicate alcohol or drug poisoning.

'Perhaps denoting that her killer was male, sir?' DC Peter Wild, who was first on the scene and is standing beside me, observes. 'You'd need to be pretty strong to pin someone down long enough to smother them to death, wouldn't you?'

'Not necessarily,' I say. 'Particularly if the victim was taken unawares from behind or heavily intoxicated. It would have been dark, and she'd been out partying by the looks of things.'

'The postmortem will tell us more, like I said,' Frank says. 'For example, whether there were any drugs in her system, making her more vulnerable and easier to over-power.'

I nod again. 'Thanks, Frank. Let me know as soon as you've completed the autopsy.'

'Of course.'

Wild and I walk over to where Philip Newman, the Crime Scene Manager, is standing, his team painstakingly recording, collecting and securing potential evidence in clear plastic slips. Two of them are taking photographs and physical measurements of the scene, all in the hope that it will shed some light, offer some clue, however small, as to what happened here.

'Do we have an ID yet?' I ask him.

'Yes. Victim's clutch bag contained various cards and a driver's licence. One Lola Martinez. Twenty-nine years old.'

'Married, kids?'

I pray not.

'Not married.'

I inwardly sigh with relief.

'But we believe there's a child.'

Jesus, even worse. The poor mite may very well now be an orphan if there's no father.

'Any idea as to the child's age?'

'Judging by the photo she carried in her purse, maybe six or seven. Could have been an old photo, of course.'

My stomach heaves. But I also wonder why whoever was looking after the child hasn't reported Lola missing if they expected her home last night? Or, at least, by the early hours of this morning. Where a child's involved, you'd expect them to, even though we don't typically act on missing person's cases until after 24 hours has passed. Unless she was supposed to be staying over at a friend's place? Or a lover's? In that case, why hasn't the friend or lover done the same? And what the hell was she doing walking along the river path by herself at such a late hour? Even if she lived nearby, it would have been more sensible to take the main road.

'No mobile phone?'

'No.' Newman shakes his head.

Meaning either she misplaced it last night, or the killer took it. But why would they do that? Because this wasn't some random attack, and her attacker knew something that could potentially incriminate them was on Lola's phone? It would explain why no money or credit cards were taken.

I turn to face Wild. 'Check all CCTV in the area, and do a background check on Lola Martinez asap. We need to find out where she lives, who her son is, and break the news to any other existing family. Hopefully they can tell us more about Lola's whereabouts yesterday evening. We'll need to gather a forensic team to comb her place for any potential clues as to who might have wanted her dead. And if she was at a party, there'll be a whole host of potential witnesses we need to talk to. One of them may even be her killer.'

Chapter Three

Lola

Before
September 2022

Of all the mornings for Luca to throw a tantrum, it would have to be today. Although, when I think about it, I guess I shouldn't be surprised. Starting primary school is a big deal for any child, but especially for a boy like Luca, who's spent most of his life being taken care of by either me or my parents. Aside from spending three mornings a week at a local nursery, he's been cosseted in our tight-knit cocoon since the day he was born. Snugly wrapped up in our safe bubble of love; a bubble I've been determined to keep intact until now. If anything, I am to blame for his reluctance to start school. Even though I knew this day was unavoidable and that I'd have to let go sometime.

'Come on, Luca. You don't want to be late for your first day, do you?'

I'm standing in our narrow hallway, my five-year-old lingering at the nearby kitchen door, rooted to the spot. I know exactly what's going through that smart little brain of his. He's wondering if he can catch me unawares and zigzag past me into his bedroom where he'll lock the door and refuse to come out. But I'm ready for him. My eyes shoot left and right, primed for any stunt he might try and play.

He stomps his foot. 'Don't want to go.'

He looks at me with serious eyes, his expression steadfast. A look I'm all too familiar with. It's both aggravating and adorable. Not for the first time, I fleetingly wonder if his particular form of stubbornness is genetic. He certainly doesn't get it from me. If anything, I'm too easily persuaded. Too congenial, to the point it's got me into trouble in the past. His big brown eyes laser through me, and I know I have my work cut out. I really don't need this, and I want to be mad at him, but it's impossible. He's far too cute and he knows he has me wrapped around his little finger. I'm also fully aware I should be stricter with him in general, but I can never bring myself to enforce the *tough love*, like Mum says I need to once and a while, just so he won't grow up to be a *spoilt brat who thinks he can get away with murder*. Her words, not mine. Words that fill me with unease for more reasons than she could ever know. For one, I feel too guilty that he has no father figure in his life. That's not my fault, but I can't help feeling the way I do. And two, I simply can't bear to upset him. It hurts too much, because he's everything to me, and I could never do anything to cause him pain. I of all people know what a cruel, terrifying world it can be, and because of this I'm petrified of driving him away. Desperate to keep him close. Protected.

'Luca, aren't you excited to make new friends? You're going to have so much fun. Teddy will be there. And Lilly, who you met on induction day. Remember?'

Teddy is a friend from nursery. Annoyingly they're not in the same form, which would have made life a lot easier in terms of coaxing Luca to go willingly today. Each class is being phased in over two days. Teddy's first day was yesterday, and according to Jill, his mum, he loved it. I just hope and pray that Luca loves it too.

'Teddy had a blast yesterday,' I say excitedly. 'He told his mummy that there was so much fun stuff to play with. You don't want to let Teddy down, do you? He'll be so disappointed if you're not there today.'

It's a bit of a low blow, using emotional blackmail to get around my five-year-old. But needs must. We literally have two minutes before we need to make tracks to catch the bus and avoid being late. I already expect to feel like a fish out of water; I don't need to add insult to injury by being the last one to arrive.

Luca appears to think on this. He frowns. Scrunches his nose. 'But Teddy's not in my class,' he says eventually.

I had a feeling that was coming. Like I said – he's too smart.

'So? You'll still see him in the playground. And at lunchtime. You don't want Teddy to make new friends and forget about you, do you?'

Despite feeling guilty about my methods, I pray this does the trick, conscious of time ticking away. The last thing I want is for Luca and I to make a bad first impression on his teachers. Thankfully, it works.

'OK.' Luca relents with a little shrug.

I smile broadly. 'Great! Now pick up your satchel and let's get going!'

Without giving my son the opportunity to change his mind, I whisk him out the door and into the carpeted corridor, slamming the door behind me. Then I march us both towards the lift a little way down. Miraculously, it's already parked on our floor, and in no time at all has delivered us to the ground level of our apartment block.

As we race out of the building, my hand wrapped tightly around Luca's tiny palm, I pray to God that the number 418 bus, which will take us to the bottom of the road St Xavier's Primary is located on, arrives on time.

It's a Tuesday in early September and we're in the throes of an Indian summer, the temperature warm and sultry, more like mid-July than the beginning of autumn. There's still that air of hopefulness and vitality, people going about their business with a spring in their step, rather than being weighed down by colds and inclement weather. I'm dressed in a floaty floral summer dress with a sweetheart neckline, sleeves that go down to my elbows, and a skirt that settles mid-calf. The colours complement my olive skin, a hue I've been blessed with courtesy of my Spanish mother. I never like to wear anything too short or revealing, and normally I'm happier in jeans, but it's far too hot for denim, so this is the next best thing. I don't know how Luca's not sweating buckets in his green V-neck jumper which he insisted on wearing despite the school saying he'd be OK in his white shirt and grey shorts on account of the unseasonably hot weather. Secretly, I think he's proud of it, and wants to make a good impression.

Thankfully, the bus turns up just as we reach the stop, unsightly damp patches forming under my arms, my heart beating a little too fast with both stress and physical exertion. But by the time we've reached our destination, I've managed to calm myself, while Luca's practically jumping up and down in his seat, itching to get out and start his new school. All the way there he'd gabbled on about what he might do today, who he'd meet, what snack he might be given, whether there'd be cars and sand to play with. I should feel relieved at his sudden enthusiasm after our earlier stand-off. But in truth, it's a bittersweet moment. I want him to make friends, be happy. Have fun, live a normal life. More than anything I do. But I also can't bear to let him go, or to think that one day he'll leave me and find a life of his own. I tell myself to snap out of it. That I'm being dramatic as usual. He's only just starting reception; we've a long way to go before I'm waving him off to university.

The bus comes to a standstill and I usher Luca off before me. A few other parents do the same with their children, some bursting with excitement, others wearing more reticent expressions. 'Good luck, young man,' the uncharacteristically friendly bus driver calls after Luca.

At this, Luca swivels his head around and gives the man a wide grin. Right now, he looks all the more adorable having lost his two front teeth. 'Thank you!'

I give the driver my thanks too. 'No problem,' he says. 'That's a sweet boy you have there.'

I nod, my heart almost melting with love for my son.

Standing on the pavement, I take Luca's hand, cherishing the feel of his small soft fingers wrapped in mine, a part of me never wanting to let go. We trot up the hill towards the school entrance gates, a throng of parents and children making their way inside, incessant animated chatter filling the air around us. My heart flutters with anticipation as I watch them, wondering what kind of people they are. Hoping they'll be nice, that we'll get along fine. But most of all, that Luca will be happy at this school. That he'll make friends and won't get teased or bullied. I take a deep breath, praying that everything will be OK for me too, rehearsing in my mind what I'll say when I'm inevitably asked questions about Luca's father.

The same story I tell everyone, I guess. Even my own parents.

I gaze down at Luca as he takes in the scene with wide eyes, his green school satchel almost as big as him pressed against his tiny waist, wondering if he's about to have another meltdown. But he doesn't. Instead, he tells me to hurry and then, before I know it, we've walked the short path up to the playground and are waiting in line behind the orange lollipop, as instructed in the welcome email sent out to parents back in July. There's a similar line of parents and children queueing alongside us behind a blue lollipop.

There must be around fifteen kids in front of us, with more joining behind. Most of them are accompanied by both parents, but a few have only one or the other. My stomach burns when I think about having to lie to them all. The way I've lied to Luca from the moment he was born.

'Hi, what's your name?'

All of a sudden, a pretty little blonde girl standing in front of us swivels around to speak to Luca. She's dressed in the school's prescribed green and white checked dress. Her wavy hair is tied up in neat bunches with matching green coloured ribbon, and she has the biggest bluest eyes imaginable.

'Luca. What's yours?' my son asks.

'Jess.'

'Hi, Jess. This is my mummy.' Luca looks up at me, and I smile at the little girl.

'Hello, Jess.'

'Hi, Luca, hi Luca's mummy, this is my mummy.'

Jess tugs on her mother's hand. She appears to be on her own, and at this moment locked in lively conversation with some parents gathered in front of her, but she immediately turns around at her daughter's touch. As we make eye contact, I can't resist sneaking a peek at her hand, the selfish part of me hoping to see that her ring finger is bare. But it's not. Rather, it's adorned with the most exquisite-looking diamond I've ever seen. A diamond-studded platinum band compliments it beautifully. She smiles. It's a broad open smile, revealing pristine white teeth, her pale blue eyes equally warm despite having a certain melancholy about them. Her ash blonde hair is swept away from her face in a ponytail, accentuating her high cheekbones, while she's dressed in a mid-calf strappy cotton dress, teamed with denim mules. Very elegant, but not in an intimidating way. In fact, everything about her radiates warmth.

'Hi, I'm Simone,' she says, still smiling. 'Looks like our two have hit it off, doesn't it?' She gives her daughter a playful nudge.

'It does,' I say, glancing down at Luca and Jess, who are now busily chatting away about their favourite Paw Patrol characters. 'I'm Lola.'

'Lola, what a pretty name,' Simone says, her eyes lighting up. 'Quite unusual too.'

I shrug my shoulders nonchalantly. 'I guess.' At the same time, my beloved grandmother's face appears in my head. She, who died when I was fifteen, and whose name I assumed five years ago.

Although I've been trying my best to hide them, Simone picks up on my nerves. Truth is, I've never been great at disguising my feelings. Sometimes I wish I had a thicker skin. 'Big day, isn't it. Do you have older kids? I don't think I've seen you before in the playground.'

'No, just the one.' I gaze down at Luca, who's still locked in animated chatter with Jess.

'Jess is my second, I have another in Year 2,' Simone explains. 'There're a few of us with older ones.' She looks back over her shoulder, and I can see that the parents she was talking to are now gathered in a larger huddle. Mums and dads who've clearly known each other since their older kids started in Reception and are presumably old hats at this game. I feel the butterflies in my stomach. I bet all their little ones live with both parents. Or at least have both a mum and dad in their lives. Being a single mother shouldn't be an issue in this day and age, but the fact is there'll always be those who'll judge and look down on me, perhaps even consider me some kind of social pariah. It's why I chose St Xavier's over St Agatha's, despite St Agatha's only being a five-minute walk from home. And, more importantly, Catholic. I was born and raised a Catholic, and my faith is important to me. But there's no way I'd have been able to face the parents at St Agatha's as a single mum. I can only imagine the comments I'd have got behind my back, possibly even to my face. The looks, the stares, the endless gossip.

With the only other school on my list having a bad reputation for bullying and a low Ofsted rating, and having talked it through with the person I trust with all my heart, I realised St Xavier's was my best option. I count myself lucky that I had that choice, what with London schools typically being oversubscribed. Usually, a parent has no option but to send their child to the nearest school. Still, it helped that Luca and I became regular attendees at St Xavier's Church (which has strong links with the school) before I submitted the school application form, famili-arising ourselves with the kind and understanding vicar there. I confided my fears in her about being ostracised by other parents, while ensuring Luca participated regularly in Sunday school. Slightly cheeky, I know, but it's not like I'm the only parent who does this. And, unlike a lot of the parents who suddenly turn religious and become regular churchgoers to get their kids into school, my faith is important to me. I just pray to God that after all the sacrifices I've made, I've made the right choice.

'Don't look so worried; they're all lovely,' Simone assures me. 'I'll introduce you if you like. They haven't forgotten about being newbies, and what a big step it is when your first starts school.' She chuckles. 'It's nerve-wracking. More so for us parents than the kids, I think! I mean, I was a mess. Liam, my husband, thought I was insane. But that's men for you, isn't it? They don't feel things so keenly, the way we women do.'

I'm sure she's right. Only I don't have a Liam around to test that theory myself. Even so, she's being so nice, I figure it's easier to agree and move on. 'Yes, that's true.' I nod.

I'm about to ask how long it took her first child to settle in when the bell rings. A violent protracted clang that almost makes me jump out of my skin. All at once, the excitement and noise levels shoot up a notch. Kids screaming, parents trying desperately to calm them down and arrange them in an orderly line.

'Mummy, is it time to go in?'

Luca looks up at me with those big dark eyes of his and I feel the tears gather in my own. I always knew this day would come, but I hadn't imagined it would be quite this hard. I tell myself to hold it together, for his sake. But it's easier said than done. Aside from the three mornings a week at nursery he's attended since the age of three, he's always been under my watchful eye. For five years, I've protected him like a lioness defending her cub, forever looking over my shoulder for fear of my past coming back to haunt me. But now things are different, and I have to face the fact that I can't control everything.

I blink back the tears, give him a broad smile. 'Yes, darling it is. Excited?'

He appears to consider this for a second or two. 'Think so.' He looks at Jess, as if for reassurance.

'Luca, it's time, it's time!' Jess squeals, star-jumping on the spot. 'We're going to have so much fun. Penny said we are, didn't she Mummy?' Jess looks up at her mother and I catch Simone's eye, as if to seek clarification.

'Penny's her older sister,' she explains. 'Jess has been doing drop-offs and pickups with me for the last two years. She's been itching to start school, having had daily updates from Pen on how much fun it is.' She looks down at Jess, caressing her cheek with the palm of her hand, and all at once I recognise in her gaze that same fierce, all-consuming love I feel for Luca. 'Isn't that right, sweetheart?'

Jess nods eagerly. 'I wish Daddy was here! Why does he hardly ever come to school, Mummy?'

Simone bends down to kiss her daughter on the forehead. 'Darling, you know your daddy works hard all day. He earns the money so we can go on nice holidays and buy you lots of pretty dresses and ballet shoes.'

Hearing this, I feel a tug of jealousy. But also guilt, when I see Luca's mournful expression. I know what he's thinking. *Why don't I have a daddy like Jess? Why am I the odd one out?*

As much as I try to be there for Luca, to be two parents in one, there'll always be a void in his life. A part of him that will never feel complete. And that's something that breaks my heart.

'Hello, boys and girls, we're ready to go in now. Say goodbye to your mummies and daddies.'

Both form tutors have appeared. I recognise them from induction day. Miss Day, Luca's teacher who's perhaps in her mid-twenties, and Mrs Robson, who looks about ten years older and just addressed the kids.

I crouch down in front of Luca. 'Enjoy your morning, sweetheart. Be good, make lots of friends, and I can't wait to hear all about it.' I smile, bravely suppressing my tears, but when Luca wraps his arms around my neck and squeezes me to him so tight I can barely breathe, telling me how much he loves me, I can't stop one from escaping and rolling down my cheek.

And then, just like that, he loosens his grip, and I watch him skip off behind Jess, pausing at the lollipop to turn his head and give me one last smile, before racing into the reception playground and disappearing inside his classroom.

Out of sight. Out of my reach. Out of my control.

Now what? It's only a morning session for Luca's class today, so I need to be back for 12:15 p.m. to collect him. I plan on taking Luca to McDonald's for lunch as a treat. He doesn't know it yet and I can't wait to see the look on his face when I surprise him. We don't make fast food a regular habit; it's strictly reserved for special occasions, but, luckily for him, today falls firmly into that category. I look at my watch and see that I have three hours to kill. I work two mornings a week as a receptionist at a GP's surgery, as well as doing some freelance copywriting work from home. Both jobs help pay the bills. The receptionist position didn't require any set qualifications, only good literacy, numeracy and IT skills, all of which I have. I enjoy it for the most part. It's a small, friendly practice, and I get on well with everyone there. Perhaps rather fancifully, the copywriting work offers me some level of comfort that my English Literature degree hasn't gone to complete waste, even though it's far from the high-flying publishing career I'd originally envisaged for myself. Today I cleared my schedule for Luca. I couldn't risk anything getting in the way. Maybe I'll go home and tidy. Or treat myself to a good book while having a relaxing bath. It's too hot to go for a run, my usual form of stress relief other than reading. I need to do something, though, to make the most of having some free time again. But all I can think about is how much I'm going to miss Luca.

As if she has sensed the ache in my chest, Simone places a hand on my shoulder. 'It's OK, Lola,' she says soothingly. 'You'll be fine. The first day is always the worst. Come have a coffee with us.'

Lost in my thoughts, I'd failed to notice the crowd that's gathered around me and Simone. Three women and two men. I feel their eyes on me, sizing me up, all kinds of theories and speculations doubtless raiding their minds.

'Ladies, this is Lola. Her son's in orange class, like ours.'

They all smile and say hello in unison.

'Lola? That's different. Like the showgirl?' I feel my face flush, my cheeks suddenly burning with embarrassment. The comment was made by a woman, maybe an inch shorter than me at five foot three, who appears to be in her early forties, with shoulder-length auburn hair and a husky tone of voice. Almost as if she smokes too much. She's attractive, but her dark brown eyes are hard and I feel instantly ill at ease in her company. One of those people who you can sense, right from the first, that you're never going to be bosom buddies with. The other women, except for Simone, chuckle along with her. I'm not sure it's because they found her comment genuinely funny or because they're too scared not to.

'Bianca, stop being such a cow, you're embarrassing poor Lola,' one of the men says.

'Oh, for fuck's sake, Damien, lighten up will you, it was just a joke.' Bianca rolls her eyes at him. He's tall, tanned and athletic-looking, as if he sees the inside of a gym regularly, a pair of Oakleys perched on the top of his head, wedged into a thick head of dark brown hair. In fact, looking at him more closely, he reminds me of someone I once knew. Only an older version. Bianca's beady eyes drill through me, perhaps noticing where my line of vision is directed. I'm guessing they're a couple, and, as if reading my mind, she confirms this with a snigger: 'Husbands, who needs them?'

I give a faint smile in return, while thinking she has no idea that she's directing her remark at the wrong person.

'Hi, I'm Damien. The *husband*.' Damien offers me his hand with a wide grin and I shake it gratefully. He then turns to his wife and answers her question, despite it having being rhetorical. 'Well, you do, my dear, for a start. Unless you'd like to put a stop to those fortnightly manicures and New Year ski trips? I don't suppose you fancy selling the villa in Majorca either?' Unlike his wife, his eyes are warm and welcoming, his manner easy, his voice soft, although right now it has a patently mischievous edge to it. I mean, I may be wrong, but something tells me he's not that much bothered about the trappings of wealth he's just alluded to and that they're mainly designed to placate his high-maintenance wife. Bianca looks fit to burst, but somehow reins in her anger, doubtless not wanting to lose face in front of me, the new kid on the block. Evidently, from what Damien just said, they're loaded, and I can't help wondering why their kids aren't in private school. I know I've only just met her, but Bianca seems like the type who'd fit right into that privileged environment.

'Lola, this is Deidre and Joy,' Damien continues with a twinkle in his eye, basking in the glory of shutting his wife up. I exchange hellos with both women, who seem friendly enough. More chilled and less intimidating than Bianca, at least.

'And I'm Stephen, Deidre's husband.' The other man, shorter and stockier, with receding grey hair and steel-frame glasses, offers his hand. 'You'll see me more of me at the gates than you will Dee.' He glances at his wife and I feel a spark of tension.

'Everyone calls me Dee, so please do the same,' Dee says, ignoring her husband's gaze. 'Everyone except my parents,' she clarifies. 'Always hated Deidre myself, but my father insisted on naming me after an aunt he doted on.' She winks. 'Irish side of the family.' She pauses briefly. 'Anyway, you'll see me on Fridays, generally. I work in London Monday to Thursday. Not off getting manicures, just to set the record straight, in case that's what Stephen implied.'

'I meant nothing of the sort, darling,' Stephen says.

Dee gives him a raised eyebrow in return.

'Who's your child?' Bianca demands to know, breaking the awkwardness. 'He's not called Charlie, is he?' She gives a chuckle, as if amused by her own wit in alluding to a popular kids' TV programme, then glances at the other women, who this time look mildly uncomfortable. I swallow my anger. It's not like I haven't been asked that one before.

'Luca.'

'Luca and Lola, how sweet.' Her tone couldn't be more patronising, but I manage a smile. I catch Damien shooting daggers her way. 'Are you Italian?' she carries on. 'Also, forgive me for saying so, but you look super young. Not washed-up crones like the rest of us, ha ha. You must have been barely out of your teens when you gave birth.' She gives a bitter laugh, catching the others women's eyes again.

'Hey, speak for yourself.' Joy nudges her in the side.

'Well, obviously not you, hon. With your black genes you're loaded up on natural oils. Not a wrinkle in sight.'

Joy laughs, apparently not in the least bit offended. I'm gobsmacked, but I'm guessing she's used to it.

'My mother's Spanish, actually,' I say. 'My father's English.'

'How exotic,' Joy says.

'Yeah, because being half Cuban, half Zimbabwean is sooo run-of-the-mill, Joy,' Dee says rolling her eyes.

Joy grins. 'Point taken. Still, I love Spain. Which part is your mum from, Lola?'

'Madrid.'

'Nice.'

'I prefer Barcelona actually,' Bianca pipes up, 'I find it a bit friendlier.'

How ironic.

'Did Simone mention we're going for a coffee in Surbiton, Lola? Do join us,' Damien smiles, quashing his wife's catty remark.

'Actually, why don't we all go back to mine?' Simone says. 'It's so close, makes much more sense. We can sit out in the garden, hang out as long as we want. Surbiton's going to be rammed on such a beautiful morning – we might not even get a table.' She's probably right about that. It's partly why I prefer Kingston to Surbiton. Surbiton's a lovely area, no question, close to the river with a speedy commute and good schools. It's why so many couples with kids on the way move there, also to have more space, a garden, and because it's slightly more affordable than central London. But being a young, single mum, I feel like I stand out more in Surbiton than I do in Kingston. I often joke with Mum that it seems to be chock-full of yummy mummy stay-at-home mums and their hedge fund husbands. OK, so I might be stereotyping a little there, but that's the general feel of the place. To me, at least.

Everyone nods their approval at Simone's suggestion. All except me. 'How about it, Lola?' Simone says kindly. 'Do come.'

A part of me is desperate to make my excuses, a little voice inside me saying that I am better off keeping myself to myself. That I don't belong around these people, all of whom have doubtless shared numerous drunken nights out, and know each other's foibles, life histories, secrets. While here I am, a complete stranger to them. I'm not sure I have the energy or the will to try and ingratiate myself into their clique. But then, when I think of Luca, about the fact that he'll be making friends with their children, I tell myself to get a grip and at least give it a shot. It's not like I have anywhere better to be. And really, it's only Bianca who seems off. The others seem nice enough.

I smile. 'Sure, that would be nice.'

'Great,' says Simone. 'Is Clarissa joining us?' She looks at Bianca.

'She had to dash for a doctor's appointment,' Bianca replies. 'I'll text her the change of plan.'

Seeing my quizzical expression, Simone explains: 'Clarissa's another mum, with Erin in Year 2 and Molly in Reception. She's been class rep two years running and knows everyone. You'll love her. If there's anything you want to find out about St Xavier's, she's the person to ask. There's nothing that gets past Clarissa. Nothing.'

Shit, I think to myself. That's all I need. I just hope and pray I prove to be the exception where Clarissa's concerned, and that she never discovers what I'm hiding.

Only one person knows the truth. Someone I trust implicitly. It's how I intend to keep things. Just because it's safer for everyone.

Chapter Four

Detective Inspector John Banner

Sunday, 17th December 2023

It's been less than a day since Lola Martinez's mother learnt of her daughter's murder, but in that short time Elisa Mosley appears to have aged by a decade. I can tell she's barely slept or eaten. Her skin is sallow, her cheeks drawn, the dark puffy circles beneath her eyes the most telling. She's unsteady on her feet too as she leads DC Wild and I through to the spacious living room of her and her husband's terraced house in Berrylands – one of the more peaceful areas of Kingston-Upon-Thames, and a five-minute drive from the heart of Surbiton – and I worry her legs might give way at any second. Her grieving husband, Don, sits stock still in a black leather armchair, his complexion as wan as hers, his expression vacant, as if he's still in shock.

Yesterday, Elisa told Paula, the family liaison officer who broke the tragic news to her and Don, that Lola had texted her around 12:25 a.m. saying she'd decided to crash at a friend's house which was a short walk from the hotel where the Christmas party she'd gone to was being held, so they shouldn't worry about waiting up for her. Apparently, there was nothing about the style or phrasing of the message which suggested anyone but Lola had sent it. She said she'd call in the morning to say when she'd be coming home. It explains why neither Elisa nor Don called the police to say their daughter hadn't come home on Friday night. They went to bed believing her to be safe and well, and had told Luca as such when he woke up yesterday morning.

But given the likely timing and location of Lola's death, it seems probable that her killer sent the message to stop Lola's parents from worrying and calling the police, and that Lola was in fact already dead by the time it was delivered. I've yet to make this point with Elisa and Don, but I will in due course. I also make a mental note to ask everyone at the party whether any of them had offered to have Lola overnight, despite my gut telling me otherwise.

Just then, Elisa swivels round to look at me, still with that glazed look in her eyes. 'Oh, I'm sorry,' she says, her voice frail and monotone, 'where are my manners, I should have asked if you'd like some tea or coffee?' Despite Elisa being born to Spanish parents, there's no trace of an accent. Her Northern twang is as distinct as her husband's, and so I'm guessing she was born and raised in this country, presumably up north somewhere. Either that, or she moved to the UK when she was very young.

I hold up my hand, give Wild a quick glance. 'No, really, that's very kind of you to offer, but we're fine, we just had one at the station.'

'Luca's sleeping,' Elisa explains as she invites us both to sit on one of two matching floral-patterned sofas. Glancing around, I see there are several religious paintings adorning the walls, the most striking being a framed canvas of Jesus on the cross taking centre stage over the mantlepiece. On the mantlepiece itself, I spot several framed family photos, including one of Lola standing between her parents when she was a little girl, another taken with her on her graduation day. They look so happy, so proud of their daughter. I can't imagine how hard this is for them, to have lost their only child, and I feel sure Luca is the only thing that's keeping them going right now. After all, to lose a child is every parent's worst nightmare, a fear that often keeps me awake long into the night. A fear that's only exacerbated by my job, and by the pain, loss and grief I encounter time and time again.

Wild and I park ourselves on the sofa nearest to Don, while Elisa perches tentatively on the other. Right now, they both look so fragile, like pieces of broken china that can never be fixed. No glue strong enough to mend the indelible crack in their hearts. Elisa goes on: 'Luca was up for most of the night, crying out for, for...' Poor woman, she can barely get the words out. 'I'm sorry, I – I just can't. It's too much. I still can't believe it. Keep thinking that any minute now Lola's going to walk through the door and it will all have turned out to be a hideous nightmare.' She retrieves a handkerchief from her skirt pocket and dabs her eyes. Just then, her husband gets up from his chair and sits beside her, wrapping his arm around Elisa's shoulder, before drawing her close. Then they both start sobbing uncontrollably.

It's awkward, incredibly so. Up there with some of the most difficult moments I've faced throughout my career. Moments that still haunt my dreams at night; moments that no amount of sparring at my local gym can obliterate. I know they'll be with me till the day I die. Tragedies born from human nature at its darkest.

'Luca's not processed his mother's death yet,' Don explains between sobs. 'It's too much for a six-year-old. He keeps asking when she's coming home.'

I think of my own son, Michael, barely a year older than Luca, and it's like my heart has been crushed with a thousand bricks when I imagine something happening to me or Jo, my wife. How lost and alone Mikey would feel. How terrified and confused. How such a tragedy could ruin his life. It's something I confided in Jo last night, not long after I'd got home and slumped on the sofa with a beer, feeling spent by the day's events. As ever, she tried to be strong, but I know it's something that frightens her too. I hope and pray that by some miracle, Luca comes through this. Elisa and Don seem like good people who adore their grandchild. Somehow, they need to find it in themselves to be strong for him; they cannot allow their grief to swallow them up the way I've witnessed grief consume people in the past.

'Of course, it's only natural,' I say gently. 'I assume Paula told you about the grief counselling services we can provide? I know of several brilliant child counsellors, all very experienced in their field.'

'Yes.' Don nods. Both he and Elisa have stopped crying, but Elisa remains silent, as if she hadn't heard me, her head buried against Don's chest. 'Thank you. Someone's coming to see Luca later.'

'And the both of you should speak to someone too,' I add. 'It's vital that you do. I know you feel you have to be strong for Luca, and you're right, you do. You're his flesh and blood and he needs you now more than ever. But you're also only human, and you need professional help to get through this as much as Luca. There's no shame in it. If you don't look after yourselves, you'll be no use to him.' I rest my gaze on Don, thinking he's my best option right now to understand the logic of what I'm saying. He seems to. Gives a slow nod.

'Good. I assume Lola named you both as Luca's legal guardians in the event of her death?'

'Yes,' Don says faintly.

'You need to find the bastard who did this to my child!' Elisa suddenly blurts out, her tone much harsher than before. 'What are you doing about that? What have you found? Anything? Anything at all!'

Her eyes have gone from being vacant to rabid, mad with grief and rage, and God only knows what other dark emotions. I've no doubt that given the chance she'd thrust a knife through Lola's killer's heart without a second's hesitation. And, secretly, I wouldn't blame her. If it were my child, I'd want to do the same.

'There's a forensic team analysing all the evidence we've collated from the scene as we speak,' I explain. 'And I have other officers making door-to-door enquiries, as well as speaking to everyone at the party on Friday night – hotel staff too – to see if they can shed any light on who might be responsible for Lola's murder. Also, a forensic team will be searching Lola's apartment for any possible clues. Unfortunately, there's no CCTV on the section of the river path where Lola was found and most probably attacked, which may have helped us identify her killer quicker. We are, however, checking the CCTV on the main Portsmouth Road to see if anyone suspicious was seen walking in the immediate vicinity around the time she was attacked. They could have come from either direction, of course.' I lean forward. 'In the meantime, it would be really helpful if you and your husband would be kind enough to answer some questions.'

Elisa fiddles with the silver crucifix adorning her neck, then gives a slow nod. 'OK. Go ahead.'

'So, we know Lola was at a Christmas party on Friday night.'

'Yes, that's right. It was a parent social. A drinks reception and formal sit-down dinner, from what Lola told us, followed by a disco. The rep for Luca's class – Clarissa, who I've met on several occasions – organised it. They're a pretty tight-knit bunch, go out a lot. Drink a lot. Too much, I'd say. It's not healthy. They're parents, after all, not twenty-somethings just out of university.'

Elisa's tone is scornful, disapproving. I think of my own son's classmates. Their parents are a mixed bunch. Mostly pleasant, but a few are nothing short of pains in the necks, always bragging about their kids' achievements or complaining endlessly on the WhatsApp chat about the school. Jo and I often use my work as an excuse not to go to parent meet-ups. As much as they can be a burden, the unsociable hours I keep can come in handy sometimes. 'Do you know the rep's surname?' I ask. 'It's important we speak with her and everyone who was at the party on Friday night. Particularly those Lola was particularly friendly with.'

'Why?' she shoots back. 'Isn't it likely this was just a random attack? Some junkie or tramp looking for money? I mean, you said you don't think she was sexually assaulted.' She puts her palms together, looks briefly up to the ceiling. 'Thank heaven for small mercies. That's right, isn't it?'

Elisa glances at her husband as if seeking reassurance, the veins on her neck taut with anxiety, her eyes wide and starry. The idea that her little girl might also have been violated understandably too much to bear.

I shake my head. 'No, we don't believe she was sexually assaulted, although the postmortem will confirm this. It will also hopefully provide some valuable insight as to whether Lola's murder was random or premeditated. The thing is, her purse wasn't taken. Unlike her mobile. Assuming she hadn't lost her phone, this indicates to me that her killer didn't want us to find it; also, that money wasn't the goal.'

'Are you saying Lola's killer took her phone because they believe it may have implicated them in some way?' Don looks horrified.

'Yes.'

'So, if that's the case,' Elisa says, 'you think that maybe Lola's killer sent me that text, saying she was staying over at a friend's place, so I wouldn't get worried when she didn't come home? I did think it odd Lola didn't name the friend. I also don't remember her mentioning anyone living that way. At least, not the mums she was friendly with.'

'Yes. But that's why it's important we question all of Lola's friends and acquaintances, to rule out her agreeing to stay over at any of their houses. I suppose it's possible she may have agreed then changed her mind. But it seems unlikely given the timing of the text, which doesn't accord with her approximate time of death. They also might be able to tell us if she ever mentioned being threatened by anyone. Or falling out with them.' I pause. 'Can either of you offer any insight there?'

Elisa shakes her head vigorously. Don does the same. 'No,' he says, 'she never said anything like that to us.'

'OK. But if you do remember anything of that nature, please let me know. It's really important.' I hold their gazes to emphasise my point, because I cannot be sure how much either of them is taking in at this moment. Don gives a gentle nod.

'So, getting back to the class rep…' I start to say.

'Yes,' Elisa interjects, 'you wanted the surname. It's Hilton. Clarissa Hilton. I've met her several times as I mentioned – a real bossy busybody, in my opinion. They all are, except for Simone. She's lovely; Lola had a soft spot for her. And they became very close. She was her only real friend at that school. The others were so full of themselves. And such gossips.'

'Do you know Simone's surname?'

'Loxley. Nice husband too. Liam. Not like Clarissa's. She's married to some banker in the City with pot-loads of money. The show-off type. Never at home, never has time for his kids, from what Lola told me. Buys their affection to assuage his guilt. You know the type I mean?'

I give a nod, while glancing at Wild, a signal to note down some names on the pad he's holding.

'I've met a few of the mothers at St Xavier's, actually,' Elisa says. 'Because I do drop-offs and pick-ups twice a week, while Lola works…' Elisa falters again. 'Sorry, I keep doing that. While she worked part-time as a receptionist at a local GP practice.'

'That was her only employment?'

'No, she also did some freelance copywriting work from home. It allowed her to get by. We helped Lola out financially too. As best we could. She studied English Literature at university, you see; had wanted to get into publishing, but then Luca came along and her plans changed. The copywriting work allowed her to feel she was making some use of her degree.' She glances at Don. 'We're strict Catholics, and Lola was also very true to her faith. Abortion wasn't an option.'

So, Luca was born out of wedlock. That much is clear. But why does Lola have a different surname to her parents if she wasn't married? And what happened to the father? Neither Elisa nor Don have mentioned him so far. Again, why? Clearly, they don't consider him a danger to Lola, else they would have mentioned him, told me to look into his whereabouts. There's only one explanation I can think of, but I decide to give it a while longer, then raise the subject if they don't. I also can't help thinking how it's not always that simple a choice for some women as far as abortion is concerned, no matter how strong their beliefs: women who don't have loving parents like Lola's to support them.

'Of course, Lola was fortunate in other ways too,' Elisa continues.

I cock my head. 'How do you mean?'

'Not long after our grandson was born, Lola was informed of a trust that had been set up for Luca. To run until he turns eighteen, at which point he'll assume control of the money.'

'A trust? Do you know who's behind it? Who contacted Lola about it?'

Don shakes his head. 'We have no idea who's behind it, and neither did Lola. It was some lawyer based at a firm in Scotland who contacted her. Made it clear that their client, the benefactor, wanted to remain anonymous. Lola felt very uncomfortable about taking the money at first. We did too. But we were going through a bit of a tough patch at the time, financially speaking, and we ended up convincing her to go along with it.'

'You really have no idea who might have set it up?'

Although by no means unheard of, secret trusts certainly aren't commonplace, and I tell myself it might well warrant further investigation.

'No, not really. I asked my brother, Rafael, who's single and lives in Madrid,' Elisa says, 'if he was behind it. He's always been on his own and was fond of Lola. But he categorically denied it. He's a very secretive man, though, so I wouldn't be surprised if it was him. He was devastated to hear about Lola, obviously. Asked if there was anything he could do to help.'

'I see. OK, so getting back to the parents at Luca's school,' I say. 'You mentioned Clarissa and Simone. Any others I should speak to?'

'Well, Lola had some of them round for tea once. One of them stood out in particular – Bianca. Can't think what her surname is. I tend to stand apart in the playground, can't bear the gossip. Bianca sticks in my mind, though, because she made some rather underhanded comments about Lola's flat. Even though it's a perfectly nice flat and suited Lola and Luca fine.' She pauses to wipe another stray tear. 'Really up herself, that one. Like she believed herself to be better than Lola. I hate to say it, but I think it was because Lola didn't have a husband. They looked down on her. But in the same breath, I think they secretly envied her freedom. Were jealous of her being that much younger and, dare I say it, more attractive than them.' Elisa gazes up at the mantlepiece and a framed photo of Lola in her school uniform. She looks about sixteen. 'She was beautiful, our Lola, but beauty's not always all it's cracked up to be. It can be a curse as well as a blessing.'

'You think they were *all* jealous of her?'

'Absolutely. It's human nature. Plus, women can be so catty, can't they? Maybe not Simone. But definitely that Bianca. She seems to be the ringleader of their little group, from the little I've seen. Lola intimated as such on several occasions. There's always one, isn't there? The one the others flock around because it makes them feel like they're part of a special group, and they can't bear to be left out. The mouthy intimidating sort who likes to take control because inside they're deeply insecure and crave attention. Adulation. Lola was never like that; she was an individual. She didn't feel the need to suck up to people to feel included.' She pauses. 'They're a poisonous bunch if you ask me. But Lola chose to be friends with them for Luca's sake.'

I think I know what she's getting at, but I seek clarification all the same. 'How do you mean?'

'She's a — sorry — she *was* a single mum, like I said. It was hard for her. Not financially, but emotionally. She felt guilty about Luca not having a dad. Wanted him to fit in, be popular and not get picked on. She was secretly a little self-conscious too. She sensed that the likes of Clarissa and Bianca looked down on her, despite pretending not to. Just from the subtle comments they made. She told me they would occasionally sneak in questions about Luca's dad, even though she told them what happened.'

'But to your knowledge, she never had any major disagreements with any of the mums at school?'

Elisa shakes her head. 'No, nothing like that. Not to my knowledge, at any rate. I'd tell you if that was the case. Having said that, Lola was such a kind and thoughtful soul, there's every chance something may have happened but she chose not to tell us. So we wouldn't worry.'

'I understand.' I pause, take a moment, before I decide to bite the bullet and ask: 'So, what did happen to Luca's father?'

Elisa is silent. It's like she's had her fill of questions for now, any remaining energy sapped out of her. Or maybe the answer is too painful for her to articulate, which explains why she and her husband have held back thus far.

'He died in a car accident up in Scotland when Lola was only a few weeks along. A month before she graduated,' Don explains. 'She refused to talk about it after it happened. Said it was the only way she felt able to deal with it, and that if we loved her, we shouldn't ask her any questions. We didn't even know they were together; never even knew his surname. She was only twenty-two at the time, in her last few weeks at Edinburgh uni when it happened. She even forbade us from mentioning it when we went up for her graduation. Not to her friends or tutors or anyone. Like I said, no one knew about the pregnancy at that stage because she wasn't far gone.'

'Isn't that a little strange?' I say. 'Asking you not to mention what happened to any of her friends?'

Don nods. 'Yes. I mean, we did think it a little odd at the time. And I can't say it didn't make us curious to find out a bit more about the chap and what happened. But he wasn't a student so I'm not sure her friends really knew a great deal about him. She met Ben in a bar in Glasgow, you see – where he lived – one night when she was out for a friend's birthday. He was a bit older, training to be a chef. That aside, Lola was so fragile at the time. We saw no benefit in pushing it or disrespecting her wishes. She was desperate to move on, and we wanted to help her do that as best we could.'

Don and Elisa exchange a look of understanding.

'I see.' There's a brief silence, then I ask, 'Why Edinburgh uni? It's a long way from here, and I get the feeling Lola was very close to you, being an only child.'

'Yes, she was,' Elisa says. 'But we're not from these parts originally. We're from Durham. You can probably tell from the accent.'

I give a faint nod.

'Lola was desperate to go to uni, but somewhere close to home. Durham was too close – she wanted some freedom – but she also wanted to be able to commute back on weekends.' Elisa gives a sad smile. Glances at Don. 'Mainly to do her washing, I think.' It's the kind of glance that tells me Elisa would give her right arm to be able to do something as simple and mundane as Lola's washing again. 'Anyway, Edinburgh seemed like the perfect choice. And it was. She loved her time there. Well, up until Ben died. At first, when she told us she was pregnant, we thought Luca was probably the result of some drunken one-night stand because we'd never met Ben, even though Lola never did that sort of thing – sleep around, I mean – at least, not the Lola we knew.'

'At first?'

'Yes,' Don says. 'But then she told us that her and Ben had been seeing each other secretly for six months and were madly in love. That's what made it all the more heartbreaking. The fact that she'd envisaged a life with him. I remember she cried like a baby that night. Sobbed in Elisa's arms.' Don glances at Elisa, whose eyes have filled with tears again. 'I just can't understand why she kept him a secret all that time. We'd have welcomed him with open arms, despite his background. It was tragic. The poor boy's whole life was tragic, actually.'

'How so?'

'His parents died in a fire when he was a small boy,' Don explains. 'He was brought up in foster care, apparently. I think that, along with his difficult childhood, perhaps caused Lola to worry we wouldn't approve. That we'd think he wasn't good enough for her. Anyway, after the accident happened and she managed to graduate with a 2:1, Lola came back to live with us, all thoughts of pursuing a career in publishing pushed to the back of her mind. She was a mess, and at one stage we were afraid she might do something stupid. She rarely left the house, only for check-ups and such like. Elisa barely left her side.'

'It was a hard labour,' Elisa says. 'But she came through in the end; naturally, I mean. And then she surprised us the morning after Luca was born, with the announcement that she'd decided to change her name and was moving down south. Her name was Elizabeth before. Elizabeth Mosley.'

My ears prick to attention. At last, an explanation for Lola's name being different to that of her parents. 'Why would she change her name?' I ask.

Elisa shrugs. 'She refused to give us a proper explanation, just claimed that a fresh start in a new city required a fresh name. Initially, we thought she might be suffering from postpartum depression. But unlike when she was pregnant, locking herself in her room all day, barely engaging with the world around her, the moment Luca was born she had a new energy about her. She didn't appear disconnected with Luca; she was eating OK, didn't seem depressed as such. In fact, she barely left Luca's side, was reluctant to hand him over to us so she could take a break and get some sleep. When she changed her name, we were somewhat baffled, and not a little hurt, to be honest. But she assured us she was fine in herself and that the name change had nothing to do with anything we'd done wrong. That more than anything she loved us and wanted us to move down south with her. The fact that she took my late mother's maiden name softened the blow. She also said that we should never under any circumstances mention Ben's name again. Not to her or to anyone. Nor mention her real name to any new friends she might make. We agreed and didn't hesitate to go with her. Don found some work down here, and I got a job at the library. Truth is, Lola's our – sorry – she *was* our only child, and it went without saying that we wanted to be near her and help look after our only grandchild. Even though…'

'Even though what?'

'Even though it was clear that Lola was hiding something from us. About Ben, and the reason she changed her name. I still think she was. She claimed it was simply the case that she needed to start over. That by almost becoming a different person, this was her way of moving on from Ben's death.'

'But you didn't buy that?' I ask.

'No.' Elisa shakes her head. 'Not deep down. Like I said, we felt she was keeping something from us. It would explain how protective she was over Luca. I mean, as mothers we all like to protect our children, but it was more than that with Lola. It was almost obsessive. I should have questioned her more, why she felt the need to relocate more than 300 miles away from her childhood home. But she'd been through so much, and she was our only child. More than anything, Don and I just wanted her to be happy. She'd always been a sensible girl, and I guess we trusted there was a good reason for all the upheaval.'

There's a moment's hush as Elisa's words hang in the air. All I can think about is why Lola changed her name. Why she moved nearly 300 miles away from her childhood home. The place where Luca was born. Also, who is this mysterious benefactor Elisa mentioned? Not that I think he or she had anything to do with Lola's murder, necessarily. But if they cared enough to be providing for her child, they may also have kept track of her movements and therefore may potentially know something helpful.

I simply don't accept Lola wanting to change her name for the sake of a fresh start after her child was born. Nor moving across the country. No one takes such a drastic step without good reason, especially if they're on good terms with their parents. Her boyfriend dying doesn't feel like a plausible reason, somehow. It makes me think that Lola was scared. That she was hiding from someone. Elisa and Don must have suspected the same, but it's clear they trusted their daughter's judgment and were perhaps afraid if they pressed her too much, they'd drive her and Luca away for good. Something they couldn't chance.

But who was Lola hiding from? And why?

More pressingly, did she tell anyone?

Chapter Five

Lola

Before
September 2022

HERETOCHAT.ORG
Chat Now in confidence. We're here for each other

Lola: Luca's first day at school went pretty well. He didn't want to go initially, then he got there and made a friend and came out all smiles and full of stories. I was a bit of a mess when I watched him walk off, and I felt a bit embarrassed. But one of the mums was lovely. She's called Simone and invited me back to hers for coffee with some of the other parents in his class.

Tracy: That's nice. And please don't be so hard on yourself, Lola. It's a big day for any parent, a massive milestone in Luca's life, and you're bound to be emotional. Particularly given all you've been through. I told you how my ex's sister was when her son started. Tom, her other half, called her a nutter. But he was just being a typical bloody man. No heart. Really glad you made a friend, though. Simone sounds lovely. It's important you make time for yourself, and have some adult company. You're still young, you need to enjoy yourself, have a life. Plus, it's not like you have to worry too much financially. Luca's sorted with that trust, so you can afford to spend a bit more on yourself.

Lola: Yeah, I know, and I will. I felt so pathetic crying, though. None of them were crying. Mind you, the ones I met all had older ones in Year 2 like Simone. Guess it didn't feel so momentous for them.

Tracy: Exactly. And they won't know what you went through. Why keeping Luca safe is so important to you. How can you not be emotional? It would be unnatural not to be.

Lola: Thanks, that helps. You always make me feel better, don't know what I'd do without you, I'm such an emotional basket case.

Tracy: For God's sake, don't call yourself that. You're just someone who's had a lot to deal with, and you've been through some really tough times. Like me. But that's what I'm here for, to listen. We're here for each other, right?

Lola: Thanks. And yeah, course. Sometimes I really wish we could meet. So I could thank you in person. I mean, you're like my best friend.

Tracy: That's sweet, but you know that's not the way this site works. The whole point is that it's anonymous, so we can say whatever we want in confidence. A safe setting for anyone in need to spill their secrets, worries, fears and so on. But if we meet, we'd be crossing a line and jeopardising that. You get that, right? I don't want to spoil things. Besides, you might be disappointed, ha ha!

Lola: No, that's not possible! But yeah, I know. And I'm so grateful to you for listening. The other day, I had such an urge to tell Mum and Dad what happened when I was at uni. I think it was partly the result of my emotions getting the better of me, what with Luca starting school and it being such a big milestone. But I know that I can't tell them, because I'd potentially be putting their lives at risk. You and I both know that. But it's not the only reason stopping me. It's also because I feel they'd be disappointed in me. Too much time has passed and I've told too many lies. I'm not sure they'd see me as the same person if they knew the truth.

Tracy: That's where you're wrong. They love you, no matter what. Sometimes it's just easier talking to someone neutral with no pre-conceived ideas, no expectations of you. That's why you joined this site in the first place, right?

Lola: Yes, exactly.

Tracy: You know it's why I joined. I couldn't deal with Mum's cancer; no one seemed to understand what I was going through, and it's not like I had a sibling to talk it through with. Or a boyfriend. Being with Jeff put me off men for life. And Dad was broken, so I didn't want to lay it all on him.

Lola: Oh hon, I get that.

Tracy: But like I told you before, my buddy was a godsend because she'd been through something similar. She understood me. Didn't judge me. It's why I wanted to give something back to this site by becoming a 'buddy' myself. It's what brought us together, Lola.

Lola: I know, and you've done so well. You should be proud of yourself. I'd love to help someone who's struggling with similar issues, the way you've helped me. But I'm not sure I'm there yet. That I'm as strong as you.

Tracy: That's not true. And hey, I still have my bad days. I mean, I know I'm the one who's meant to be helping you, but it's not like I don't have the occasional moan. You listen to me too. You know you do.

Lola: Aww, thanks. And don't be daft, it's the least I can do. I want to be there for you. I guess for me, at first I signed up because I was struggling at uni, drinking too much, and I didn't want to disappoint Mum and Dad by failing. You know how I felt such intense pressure. It was weighing me down. So much so I couldn't sleep, couldn't breathe at times. It doesn't help me being an only child, I guess. You of all people get that.'

Tracy: I do, believe me.

Lola: It all falls on me, to be this perfect daughter. No sibling to take the heat off, not even for five seconds. It feels smothering at times. Even though a lot of that's probably on me. Anyway, I didn't think that six years later we'd still be chatting. But I'm so grateful for it. You saved my life. God only knows what Dad would say, he's such an old-fashioned northerner, as much as I love him to bits, bless him. Men certainly don't cry where he's from. Or talk about their problems.

Tracy: Well, he's from a different generation. Anyway, I want you to know I'll always be here for you, to listen and advise, just as I hope you'll always be there for me. And yeah, with both of us being only children, I think that's why we clicked from the outset. But you also need to know that you're stronger than you give yourself credit for. You made a new life for yourself, have a happy healthy child. That's a lot to be proud of.

Lola: Thanks, that's true, I guess. But again, it's largely thanks to you giving me the confidence to make that move. Do you think he is safe, though? Luca, I mean. I just worry so much. I lie awake in bed sometimes, imagining he'll find me, steal Luca.

Tracy: That's not going to happen. You changed your name, moved 300 miles away, made a fresh start. Plus, you're barely on social media, and never post pics of Luca. It's all good, I'm sure of it. How would he know where to look? Why would he? He may be in prison by now for all you know. He may even be dead. I wouldn't be surprised. Scum like him usually get their comeuppance.

Lola: I can't stop thinking about what he whispered into my ear, though. It never leaves me. It's always there, nearly six years on. Tell anyone, and I will find you and hunt you down, and everyone closest to you.

Tracy: But you haven't told anyone. And it's getting on for six years, like you said. Don't worry, you're safe as houses. Just focus on making friends with the other parents. You have babysitting on tap, don't make excuses, you need to put yourself out there, make time for you.

Lola: I'm scared.

Tracy: Of what?

Lola: Of being hurt by a man.

Tracy: Just because it happened once, doesn't mean it will happen again. I mean, I know I'm a bit of a man-hater, but they're not all bad. You had the most hideous experience, but all that is in the past. Done and dusted. You have so much to look forward to, don't waste your time dwelling on the past. Look to the future. On finding happiness. How did coffee go by the way? You didn't give me any details.

Lola: It was good. Simone's lovely, and Dee and Joy seem OK. Clarissa's a bit on the bossy side, it has to be said, but friendly enough. She's the class rep and on the PTA. But one of them seems like a bit of a bitch – Bianca. I could tell she didn't like me. Her husband was nice, pretty gorgeous actually. God knows how she bagged him. He's much more down-to-earth than her.

Tracy: Don't go there. Big red flag.

Lola: I know, I know, I won't. I'm not stupid.

Tracy: Meet any other dads?

Lola: Simone's husband, Liam, was working, but if he's anything like her, I'm sure he's lovely. Didn't meet Clarissa's other half, or Joy's, but Stephen, Dee's husband was there. Apparently, he teaches languages from home. She's the main breadwinner, though. Barrister in the City, only at the gates on Friday.

Tracy: Well, they certainly sound like a mixed bunch. Never a dull moment at the school gates I bet!

Lola: Yeah, but I can't imagine becoming best friends with any of them. Especially Bianca. I can tell she looks down on me, being a single mum. She comes across as such a privileged try-hard.

Tracy: So don't become best friends with them. You said Simone's nice, though. Stick with her. Just learn to get along with the rest, use them for a bit of fun, but don't spill your secrets.

Lola: Thanks, that's true. And I won't, don't worry. I hate playing these games, though. I've always been happier having one or two close friends; I've never slotted easily into big groups. Some women seem built for cliques, like they get a kick out of it. Desperate to be one of the cool gang. That's never been me. I wish I was made that way sometimes. Maybe then I'd feel like less of an outsider.

Tracy: You're doing it again. Giving yourself a hard time.

Lola: But it's not easy for me, especially being a single mum. And I'm worried they'll discover the truth.

Tracy: How? No one knows. Except me. Right? You've never gone to the police.

Lola: Nope. Never.

Tracy: And I'm not going to tell. He's certainly not going to. If he's even still alive, that is. Which only leaves you. And I'm pretty sure you're not going to say anything. Unless you get so plastered it all comes out.

Lola: That's why I never drink too much. It's too dangerous.

Tracy: Good. So there you go then, you'll be fine. Just stick to your normal story, and all will be well. Trust me, it will. No one will ever discover you were raped. And that you have no idea who Luca's father is.

Chapter Six

Detective Inspector John Banner

Monday, 18th December 2023

'You were good friends with Lola?'

It's been over forty-eight hours since Lola Martinez was found murdered. The postmortem confirmed that she was knocked out with sevoflurane, a fast-acting anaesthetic inhalant, presumably from behind via some sort of cloth put to her mouth, before being asphyxiated. The bruising around her nose and mouth being evidence of this. It's also clear the killer used gloves because there was no foreign DNA present. Her blood alcohol was 0.16, so high, but not shockingly so. There were no other drugs, neither prescription nor illegal, found in her system. No foreign DNA or fingerprints elsewhere on her person, again indicating the murderer used gloves. CCTV footage covering the main Portsmouth Road heading north from the party venue towards Kingston town centre has thus far brought up nothing suspicious. Apart from a couple walking hand in hand, along with a group of teenagers perhaps on their way back from the pub – both of whom stuck to the main road rather than take a detour down to the river path – no other pedestrians were spotted on camera between the time Lola left the hotel and was killed. That's not to say the culprit couldn't have been lying in wait for her on the river path already when she ventured down that way. But we have no way of checking that. Right now, another detective – DI Golding – and a forensic team are combing every inch of her apartment, including her laptop and landline, for anything that might offer some insight into her comings and goings, any quarrel she may have had with a friend or lover or family member. Her murder could still be a random act of violence, of course. But the fact that she didn't have her mobile on her and neither can we trace it, plus no money or cards were taken from her purse, is telling, and I'm more and more convinced with every passing minute that this brutal and vicious attack was planned. Whether it's linked to her decision to change her name six years ago and move to the other end of the country, I can't say right now. But something tells me there is a link. I just need to find out what it is.

'We were friends, yes,' Clarissa Hilton confirms. She's a tall, imposing woman, with a commanding, schoolmistressy tone of voice, her dark blonde hair pinned high with a claw clip, a pair of black-framed reading glasses perched on the end of her nose. 'But I wouldn't say we were *good* friends, as such. I mean, I liked her well enough, welcomed her to the school with open arms – I always do, the newbies, I know how intimidating it can be. We'd chat in the playground, at parent socials, and so on. I even had her round to the house on several occasions. But I never really *knew* her, if you know what I mean. She kept her cards very close to her chest.'

'I see. So, just to confirm, you didn't offer to have Lola stay over at yours on Friday night?'

Clarissa wrinkles her nose, causing her glasses to slide down a touch. She pushes them back up. 'What? No, why would I do that? Besides, it makes no sense, I'm completely in the opposite direction to where she lived. Why do you ask?'

I describe the text Elisa received from Lola.

She raises her brow. 'Oh really, how strange. Well, as you can see, I don't live within walking distance of the party venue. And as far as I know none of the others offered to have Lola over either. Despite Bianca living close by, admittedly. Besides, Bianca left alone, sometime after Lola, I seem to recall. Her husband, Damien, was at home with the flu.'

We're seated around a rectangular oak dining table in the slick island kitchen of the Hiltons' six-bedroom family home. Located on a private gated estate just off Kingston Hill Road, one of the most desirable roads in the Kingston area. Everything about it screams money, but not in a gaudy way. Even the Christmas decorations dotted around the house have a sophisticated feel to them. I think of my own Christmas tree, just about every inch of it covered in baubles and tinsel, on Mikey's insistence. Looking around, the furnishings are classy and minimalist, from the plush cream carpets and parquet flooring to the sleek nutmeg sofas, to the quirky pieces of modern art scattered around adding a splash of colour to the generally neutral tones. It's surprisingly tidy too, considering the Hiltons have two children, not a muddy shoe or stray toy in sight. But I already get the feeling from her tone and manner that Clarissa rules the roost with an iron fist. Plus, she no doubt has a cleaner to keep the place spick and span.

'It's a lovely place you have here,' I observe.

'Thank you, I'm very fortunate and I won't be shy about it. I think it pays to be upfront about something that's a fact. Why deny it? Yes, we have money. Yes, my husband is a millionaire by birth. But he also has a day job and works extremely hard, so it's not like he doesn't do his bit, and pay his taxes. We could put our kids in private school if we wanted to, but we believe in an equal education for all.'

'What does your husband do?'

'He's a banker in the City.'

Not exactly an honest day's work, then. I hold my tongue. Suppress memories of my father working gruelling sixty-hour weeks as a long-haul truck driver just to put food on our table.

'And may I ask, do you work?'

She gives a light chuckle, then throws her head back dramatically as if I've just made the most outrageous joke. 'Gosh, no, I don't have time, with two children under ten, a prominent role on the PTA and being class rep for both my children's forms. It's a full-time job, I'll have you know! Never a spare moment. I'm really not sure how I cope sometimes, it can be very stressful, very time-consuming indeed, but you'd be surprised how few people step up to the job. Always some excuse.'

Like work, perhaps? Once again, I bite my lip.

'But I don't mind,' she waffles on. 'I've always been efficient, good at taking the lead. And a people person. That's very important in any leadership role. I'm sure you'd agree, Inspector. More coffee?'

She offers up the cafetière of fresh real coffee she made for us when I first arrived, having pointed out that it was organic and made from the finest Peruvian coffee beans. The diamonds on her ring finger glimmer under the kitchen's skylight as she does so. It's a blindingly sunny day, despite the sub-zero temperatures, and I imagine this room must feel like a greenhouse in the height of summer.

'Thank you,' I say, at which point she proceeds to top up my mug.

'So, you said Lola left the Christmas party alone, and quite suddenly. Did anything happen?'

There's a moment's hesitation on Clarissa's part, her usual decisiveness abandoning her.

Why is that? I wonder.

'Happen? How do you mean?' She removes her glasses and gives me a quizzical look, one that feels a bit too forced.

'I mean, did Lola quarrel with anyone, or seem upset? It would explain her taking off so suddenly. The cloakroom attendant confirmed she left alone, and that she seemed quite distressed.'

More hesitation. Then: 'No, there was no quarrel, Lola seemed fine to me. To all of us.'

She's lying. Again, why?

'It's why we were all so horrified to hear the news,' she carries on. 'One minute, we were at the table, laughing and joking, having a good time, the next she'd upped and left. I seem to recall Dee, Joy and Stephen calling after her. But she just kept going. It really is quite the mystery. Baffling, really. But one I hope you'll solve. For that poor child's sake, if nothing else. I assume you found Lola's phone? Maybe she received upsetting news.'

'There was no phone on her.'

Clarissa's eyes pop open. 'Oh dear, that's unfortunate. I definitely saw her look at it during the evening.'

'Yes, so did the cloakroom attendant.'

'Do you think her killer took it?'

'Quite possibly.'

'Why?'

'Because there may have been something incriminating on there.'

'Oh, I see, that makes sense. I guess she could have dropped it on the way home, though.'

'My team have combed the area thoroughly, and there was no sign of a phone. They've also tried tracing it. But again, nothing.' I pause for a second, then say, 'You didn't think to go after Lola when she rushed out? To check she got into a cab safely?'

Clarissa's face turns a shade of crimson. 'Look, Inspector I'm not her mother, and as I said before, we weren't *that* close. But I'll be honest, we were all a bit squiffy by then, not really thinking straight. Plus, we girls were having a good boogie on the dance floor. I do remember Bianca speculating that maybe Lola got her period or something, or perhaps Luca was sick. I feel bad, though, when I think of that poor boy left without a mother, and now an orphan. But there was no malice behind our leaving her to it. You have to believe me.'

Why am I not so sure of that?

She sighs. 'I only wish I had gone after her, in hindsight; made sure she got a cab like you said. Convinced her not to walk home. I can't think what could have possessed her to do that.'

'And what time did you leave the party?'

Clarissa takes a protracted sip of her coffee, as if she needs time to ponder this.

'To be honest, it's something of a blur. Robert and I had a bit of a row and he left before me.'

'What did you row about?'

'Oh, nothing much, I can't even remember now. He got the bus home because he couldn't find a cab. Made me laugh, just because I'm not sure Rob's taken the bus in some twenty years!'

'Was this before or after Lola left?'

'After.'

'And you? How did you get home?'

'I left around the same time as Joy. Like me, she'd sensibly pre-booked a cab. She lives in New Malden, not too far from here, just off the A3.'

'Is Joy married?'

'Yes, to Gavin, but he was at home with the kids. They always struggle to get babysitting. Plus, Gav's a bit on the quiet side, not one for big social gatherings.'

'And who else did you say was on your table that night?'

'Bianca, as I already mentioned. She lives just off the river road, in Thames Ditton. Her husband, Damien, was at home with the flu like I said, so she was there on her own and, like Joy, had pre-booked a cab, left shortly before us. I don't even remember saying goodbye to B. The only other people on our table that night were Deidre, or Dee as she likes to be called, and her husband, Stephen. They live in Ham, the other side of Kingston, so you'd have to ask them how they made it back.'

'OK, Mrs Hilton, thanks for your time, you've been most helpful.' I down the last dregs of my coffee then get up.

Clarissa smiles, then rises from her chair herself. I can't help noticing how relieved she looks that the conversation is over. 'Not at all, I'm glad to have been of some assistance.' She walks me to her front door.

'I may be in touch with more questions,' I say, 'but for now, enjoy the rest of your day.'

'Thank you, Inspector. I just hope you find the monster responsible, and get justice for that poor little boy. I for one won't rest easy until you do.'

I walk away from Clarissa's front door, and as I do I can't help feeling that she's not been entirely truthful with me, despite saying all the right things to my face.

Something happened at the party on Friday, I'm more convinced than ever of this. Something that could well be connected to Lola's murder.

Chapter Seven

Lola

Before
September 2022

Simone wasn't kidding when she said her place was only a short walk away from St Xavier's. We reach there in less than ten minutes, she and I taking the lead, while the others lag behind. It's an elegant four-bedroom double-fronted detached house spread over three stories. On the way, she explained how she and her husband, Liam, who's a GP, bought it eight years ago, having had their first child and decided to move out of London. 'We couldn't afford a house with a garden in Queen's Park where we lived in a nice, but small, flat. A junior GP's and nurse's salary combined didn't hack it, I'm afraid.' She pauses, then adds, 'The schools were also pretty dire.'

'Is that how you met?' I ask. 'Through work?'

Simone laughs. 'You'd think, but no, we were actually set up on a blind date. I wasn't long out of a bad break-up, feeling low and sorry for myself, and my friend, Beth, thought I needed to get back in the saddle, have some fun. She'd just got engaged to this guy called Jim, a medical school mate of Liam's. Liam was a workaholic – he still is, to be honest, although not as bad – and Jim told him he needed to get a life, so he and Beth decided to set us up.'

'How romantic,' I say.

'Well, sort of, I guess. It was a bit awkward to start with, I'd never been on a blind date before. I mean, the idea of internet dating freaked the hell out of me, just because I'm so wary of strangers. I mean, you get all sorts of dodgy people on the web, don't you? And a blind date seemed almost as bad. You can probably tell I'm not an extrovert like Bianca. I'm quite shy and not good at putting myself out there or making small talk. But Liam instantly made me feel so relaxed, and it was like we'd known each other forever. Plus, he was bloody gorgeous, so that helped. As shallow as that makes me sound!' She giggles like a lovestruck teenager. It's clear she's still head-over-heels in love with her husband.

I smile, feeling genuinely happy for Simone, only because she seems like such a nice person. But at the same time, I wonder if I'll ever find that sort of happiness with a man. I had it once, and then I lost it. One of the most painful episodes of my life. I know I need to put myself out there. But I guess I'm too scared. Petrified of falling hard for someone, only for them to reject me once they discover how Luca was conceived. Or worse, they turn out to be a scumbag like his father. Neither could I live with myself, much less be happy in a relationship with a man I respect, if I kept the truth from them. The deceit would eat me up.

There's a tall imposing woman standing at Simone's front door when we arrive. She's wearing a white blouse matched with a long blue pleated skirt and flat tan sandals, her blonde hair pushed back with oversized designer sunglasses.

'What took you all so long?' she bellows.

I'm guessing this is the infamous Clarissa.

The women all rush up and bear-hug Clarissa like they've not seen her in years. I hang back with the blokes, feeling awkward and hugely out of place.

'That's Clarissa,' Damien whispers in my ear. My insides burn as he does so. The woody smell of his aftershave fills my nostrils. What the hell's wrong with me? I tell myself to get a grip. He must be at least ten years my senior and completely off limits, but there's something incredibly attractive about him I can't seem to shake. That cheeky smile of his reminds me of someone who was once very special to me. And, although I may be imagining things, there's a definite spark in his eye when he catches mine. It kind of shocks me. Just because it's a feeling I've not experienced in a long time, and I'm almost not sure what to do with myself.

Even so, I try to play it cool. Say with a smile: 'I figured.'

The women all break away from Clarissa.

'How the hell did you get here so fast, woman?' Bianca says. I can immediately tell that she and Clarissa are close; there's a palpable easiness between them that speaks volumes.

'I'm superwoman, you know that!' Clarissa grins. Then she winks. 'But also, my GP's around the corner.'

Just then, she locks eyes with me. As if seeing me for the first time, even though I get the feeling she doesn't miss a thing, like Simone mentioned earlier. She steps forward and gives me a warm smile. 'Hi, I'm Clarissa. My kids are Erin and Molly. Molly's in orange class. I assume your child is too?'

'Yes, that's right,' I say with a smile in return, thankful to her for breaking the ice, despite me feeling intimated by her larger-than-life persona. 'I'm Lola, and my son is

Luca. Simone kindly asked me back for coffee with you guys. Hope that's OK.'

What the fuck? Why am I asking for this woman's permission to have coffee? I guess it's a combination of her commanding presence and the fact that the other women all seem to worship her.

'Course it is, the more the merrier. It's always nice to have a newbie join the gang.' She turns to Simone. 'Come on Simi, let us in so we can give Lola here a good grilling. Could do with some new blood to spice things up. Life's become so boring and predictable.'

She chuckles and everyone laughs along with her, but I feel my stomach churn. The thought of being grilled by these women fills me with alarm, but right now there's not much I can do about it. I'm trapped, and I can see no way to avoid the interrogation.

Before long, we're gathered in Simone's slickly designed pale blue kitchen. The units are all the same shade, while the worktop has a smooth white finish.

'Simi, I just love this worktop,' Bianca gushes, running her fingertips over the laminate gloss. 'Damien, we need to redo ours, it's looking so tired.'

'It's not even a year old, don't be fucking ridiculous.'

She doesn't bat an eyelid at Damien's harsh response. It's almost as if she's used to it, and this is normal banter between them. Damien looks at me and winks. Not in a creepy fashion. Rather, it feels more flirtatious. I can't help smiling back, then quickly stop myself when I catch Bianca shooting daggers my way. Shit. I'm not sure she liked me much to start with, but now I think I may have made myself an enemy for life.

'Coffee, tea, something cold?' Simone looks at each of us in turn.

'Got any vino?' Bianca grins, then raises her eyebrows impishly. She looks at the other women, as if to get them onboard. It's ten in the morning, and I do my best to disguise my shock.

'You are bloody incorrigible, woman,' Dee says. She places an arm around Bianca's neck, then kisses her on the cheek. 'Much as I'd like to get shit-faced, I've got two witness statements to draft later, and I need to be stone cold sober. As it is, I'm losing half a day's work just being here, so I need to work faster.' I notice Stephen roll his eyes at this remark. 'Coffee for me please, Simi.'

Bianca yawns loudly. 'Boring.'

'Plus, I'm not sure Miss Downes would approve,' Joy says. 'That woman's got the nose of a bloodhound; she'd smell the booze on our breaths a mile away. Being headmistress is wasted on her – she should work for MI5, I reckon.'

Everyone laughs. 'I bet she chucks it back in secret,' Dee says, running her hand through her striking red curls. 'Probably a bloody alcoholic. Clarissa, care to tell us anything?'

Clarissa adopts a look of surprise. 'Moi? Why should I know anything? I'm not BFFs with the woman.'

'But you are on the PTA, so you know all the goss. Who's a secret boozer, who's unhappily married, whose kid beat up who.'

'Who's having an affair.' Bianca glares at Damien, but I sense it's more of a warning than an accusation.

He doesn't rise to the bait in any case. I'm guessing he's used to her theatrics and has heard it all before. 'Coffee for me please, Simi,' he says calmly.

Bianca gives a little huff.

'I'll have a tea please,' Stephen says. 'Just some milk, no sugar.'

'Honestly, I have no idea about the head's personal life, other than the fact she's a lesbian,' Clarissa maintains.

'Well, we all know that,' Joy says. 'I saw them out having dinner once. They were very cute, I have to say. Tea for me too, hon, three sugars.' She winks. 'But don't tell Gav, he's been on at me to cut down.'

'It's nice Miss Downes has a life outside St Xavier's,' Simone says. 'And I think it's lovely she's so in love. Makes her a bit more human.' She claps her hands. 'Anyway, let me make the drinks. I'm gasping.'

I offer to help, and before long we're seated on wicker chairs around Simone's oval glass-topped garden table, a plate of M&S luxury shortbread biscuits lying in the centre, a vast umbrella shielding us from the sun.

'So, Lola, is your other half working today?' Joy asks before grabbing a shortbread.

I knew it was only a matter of time before the question was asked. In fact, it's a miracle it's taken this long. Even so, it doesn't make answering any easier. I feel my palms go sweaty as seven pairs of eyes lock on mine.

I take a jittery sip of my tea. My pulse accelerates as I place the mug back down on the table and start picking at the skin around my nails the way I always do when I'm feeling nervous or uncomfortable.

'Actually, it's just me and Luca,' I say. 'No husband, or partner. Just us. He's all I need, actually.' I give an awkward smile and pick up my tea again, slyly gauging everyone's reactions over the rim of my mug.

There's an uncomfortable silence, the tension filling the air suddenly more stifling than the heat. Everyone is clearly trying their best not to look shocked, but they're failing miserably. I see the fleeting looks that pass between them, their brains in overdrive, wondering what the story behind my singledom is. Whether it's juicy, scandalous even. There's no brushing this under the carpet, and I know I need to explain more, if only to break the awkward hush. More importantly, so we can all move on. But Bianca beats me to it. I might have guessed she'd be the first of the bunch to speak. No doubt she'll view me as even more of a threat now that she knows I'm not tied down by marriage or a long-term partner like the rest of them. She glances at her husband. He gives her a look as if to say 'no' but I can tell by her expression that she's planning on doing the exact opposite. I should have gone home to tidy after all.

'Do you mind me asking what happened to Luca's father? If it's not too intrusive a question, that is.' She's chomping at the bit, itching to know the truth, I can see that from the hungry glint in her eye. I imagine single mums aren't that common at St Xavier's. It's so middle class and normal. Everyone coupled up with two point four children. I'm a novelty, a scandal waiting to be unpicked. Shaking up their run-of-the-mill lives.

'Jesus,' Damien says through clenched teeth.

'Bianca, it's none of our business,' says Simone, looking equally horrified. She glances my way apologetically.

'I agree, it's not,' says Clarissa. '*Unless* Lola wants to tell us, of course.' She casts her eye around the table. The all-seeing oracle of the group. 'I mean, you're absolutely right, Simi, it is none of our business.' She eyes me gravely. 'And we certainly don't mean to pry. But please don't think you can't be open with us. We're here to listen, not to judge. I, for one, want you to feel comfortable around us. That you can tell us anything. We have no secrets between us.'

I'm grateful to Clarissa for saying this so kindly, but I don't for one minute believe her spiel. Even so, I can't avoid answering the question. My single status is out now, and if I don't give them more of an explanation, I could end up making life difficult for Luca at school. It shouldn't have to be this way; people should mind their own bloody business. But the fact is, I need to swallow my pride and do whatever it takes to ensure the love of my life is happy.

'Thank you, I appreciate that,' I say. 'Basically, I was seeing this guy up in Scotland when I was at Edinburgh university, and we were pretty serious. I got pregnant, but he died before Luca was born.'

Once more there's a deafening silence. Shocked expressions all around. Even Bianca appears lost for words. I can tell it's not what she expected or, indeed, was hoping for.

'Oh, Lola, I'm so sorry, that's so sad,' Simone says, placing her hand on mine. Everyone takes turns to express their condolences, and not for the first time I feel like the shittiest person alive for pretending Luca's dad is dead. I mean, I hope he is dead. I hope he's in hell where he'll rot for all eternity. But it's still a shitty lie. I'm still deceiving people. Even though this is the best way. Because if I tell people he's dead, that's it, end of story. There's no comeback for him, no possibility of our being in contact, of him appearing in Luca's life, or at the school gates. And it's why I tell Luca the same lie, because I need to protect him. Protect his feelings. Not give him hope that one day his father might appear. Or put ideas into his head that at some point in the future, when he's older, he might try searching for him.

'Thank you, it was a car accident,' I say, pre-empting the question I know is racing through their minds. 'He was going too fast, they think. The car skidded, veered off the side and plunged into a river.'

Joy instantly gets up from her chair and comes round the side of the table to hug me. Her citrusy perfume filling my nostrils, her elegant braids brushing against my cheek. 'I'm so sorry, Lola, that's unbelievably tough. I can't imagine what you went through.' Once more, the guilt shoots through me, but I continue to play the game, knowing that once I get over this first hurdle, we can all move on, the hard bit done and dusted.

Everyone echoes her sentiments, Bianca included. 'Poor Luca, that must be so tough on him,' she says. 'Not having a father around. I mean, every child needs a father in their life.'

Another little dig. Why? What's the point? Why does she have such a large chip on her shoulder? I feel the anger rise up in me, but I keep my cool. 'It is, but he's never known any different,' I say. 'It's why I moved away from Durham, where I was raised, when Luca was born. To make a fresh start.'

'Makes sense,' Dee says. 'Do you have help?'

'Yes, Mum and Dad moved down here from Durham with me. I'm an only child, so they have no other kids or grandkids to worry about. They've been lifesavers actually; not sure how I'd have managed without them. The one thing Luca's not been short on is love.' I blink back tears when I think about how true my words are. How I'd have been lost without my parents, especially in those initial days after Luca was born. I was a mess. I didn't know what I was doing, had no clue how to manage a newborn baby. It was bad enough being a single first-time mum. I was also plagued with nightmares of that night, of how Luca was conceived, and yet still consumed with an overwhelming love for my baby that I hadn't thought possible.

'That's great,' Simone says. 'As much as my mother gets on my nerves sometimes, I couldn't do without her. It's the same with Liam's parents, although his mum helps out more. His dad's not quite as hands-on. Not sure how parents without grandparents around manage, to be honest.' She stops short, looks at Joy, her face reddening. 'Oh, my goodness, I'm so sorry, Joy, that was incredibly tactless of me. I didn't think.'

Joy, still crouching down next to me, shakes her head. 'Don't sweat it, Simi, I know you didn't mean anything by it.' She turns to me and explains. 'My parents died a few years ago. Dad had a heart attack, and Mum passed away six months later. Gav lost his folks when he was in his mid-twenties.'

'Oh my God, I'm so sorry,' I say.

'It's OK. It was some time ago now, as I said, and that's life, isn't? I mean, don't get me wrong, my siblings and I were devastated. But the world around you doesn't stop because your life goes to shit, does it? You have to find a way to be strong, move on. For the sake of your children. They're what's most important. I'm lucky I have a brother and two sisters to support me, like you have your parents.'

I admire Joy for being so strong and accepting of the terrible tragedy she suffered so young. I only wish I was that strong. That I didn't feel the need to take a razor to my upper thighs to escape the emotional pain and feelings of worthlessness and self-disgust that plague me night and day. I gently stroke my finger over the fabric of my dress, conscious of the ugly scars concealed beneath it.

My parents aren't aware I self-harm. I'm too ashamed to tell them. And I'm careful to keep it from Luca. It's why I'm always sure to lock the bathroom door, or wear clothes that cover my thighs. Swimming's trickier. But Luca takes lessons and on the rare occasions when I do go in the pool with him, I'll either say I have 'my mummy problems' and wear a swim-skirt, or cover it with a plaster and say I cut myself shaving.

Only Tracy knows. Signing up to Here to Chat six and a half years ago was the best decision I've ever made. Aside from choosing to keep Luca, of course. I've always been a perfectionist, but being that way is not without its drawbacks. I started suffering from panic attacks at university when the pressure of exams, of performing well, got to me. I couldn't afford to see a trained therapist, so I did a search for online support groups, and that's when I came across Here to Chat. A free, friendly, anonymous chat group which offers subscribers support for all sorts of issues, ranging from grief to depression to anxiety and so on, and sees them matched with a suitable 'buddy'. Someone who's experienced similar issues to your own, who will hear you out, help you talk through your problems in confidence, and ultimately make you feel better and able to face the day. Anxiety was my main issue at the time, and having clicked on the appropriate tab from the drop-down menu, all I had to do was specify in a bit more detail the kind of 'buddy' I'd be looking to chat with, i.e. male or female, age range, only child and so on, and a few more specifics of the stuff I was struggling with. My search presented me with a number of possible 'buddies' for me to pair up with. I guess I clicked on Tracy's profile because the problems she'd faced seemed to match mine the best, plus she wasn't much older than me, not long out of uni. She'd experienced panic attacks the way I had after her mum got sick with cancer. Also like me, she was an only child and prone to putting herself under pressure. I liked the fact that I didn't have to go anywhere physically to meet someone. That it was anonymous. Talking to someone online also meant there was no chance of me being spotted going to see a 'shrink', and this potentially getting back to Mum and Dad, or word spreading around campus and me consequently gaining a reputation for being the campus 'nutjob'.

Tracy never judges me. I trust her implicitly to keep my secret. After all, besides my parents, I've known her longer than anyone, plus she's been through so much with me over the last six-and-a-half years. But as I sit here with these women, I can't ever imagine confiding in them. OK, so we've only just met, and Simone seems nice enough, more normal, more discreet. But the others – Bianca and Clarissa especially – I wouldn't trust them as far as I can throw them. It's clear they're all about appearances. When Clarissa urged me to open up to her just now, it wasn't out of genuine concern as far as I could tell; it's because she enjoys a bit of salacious gossip. I've no doubt she and the others would be shocked if they knew the truth. That they'd drop me without a second's thought. Label me some kind of pariah. It's too chancy opening up to any of them. The only way I can keep Luca and I safe is by keeping my secret to myself. And Tracy, of course. She is my confidante. But a faceless one. Something she says is for the best. I know that she's right, even though I'm sometimes desperate to put a face to a name. There are occasions when I lie in bed at night, imagining what she looks like, what her voice sounds like. The colour of her hair, her eyes, her skin tone.

I'm sure she's nothing like the way I picture her.

But that's OK. Because it's what's on the inside that counts.

That's all that ever matters.

Chapter Eight

Detective Inspector John Banner

Monday, 18th December 2023

'I'll just get Simone; she's been lying in bed all morning. Hasn't touched any breakfast, not even managed a cup of tea.'

It's midday. Around ten minutes ago, Wild and I arrived at the home of Simone and Liam Loxley. Having been greeted at the door by Liam, who offered us both refreshments which we declined, we've taken a seat on a sofa in their living room, which has sliding doors leading out to their patio and the garden beyond.

'I'm sorry to hear that,' I say. 'I understand that she and Lola were close; her death must have come as a huge shock.'

Liam nods gravely. He's a handsome fellow, with a thick head of dark brown hair and equally dark expressive eyes. 'Yes, it has to us all. I was away in France on a drug medical conference when Simone texted me the news on Saturday afternoon.'

'You're a drug rep?'

Liam shakes his head. 'No, I'm a GP. Famco Pharmaceuticals was hosting the event on the outskirts of Paris, trying to promote their new drug to a bunch of doctors like me. They do something similar every year, but not always at the same venue. I'd been umming and ahing about whether to go. I wish I hadn't now.'

'When did you get back?'

'Very late on Saturday evening. I was meant to get the Eurostar yesterday morning with my colleagues, but Simone was in such a state, I changed my ticket.' He strokes the five-o'clock shadow shrouding his jawline. 'Haven't even had time to shave. I got a locum to cover my patients this morning so I could do the school run because Simi wasn't up to it. Our girls asked me what was wrong with mummy. I couldn't lie, I had to tell them, but I don't think they really understood. How's Luca by the way? Poor little lad must be in shock. Thank goodness he has such great grandparents. I've met them a couple of times. Lola seemed very reliant on them.'

'Yes, he's extremely fortunate to have such devoted grandparents who appear to be in reasonably good health too. Still, it's obviously hit them hard and they are going to need time to process and come to terms with their daughter's death.'

Liam nods. 'Yes of course, I can't even imagine what they're going through. If Simi and I can help out in any way, have Luca over from time to time, we'd be only too happy to lend a hand. He's a good lad.'

Liam turns and leaves the room. I hear his footsteps trudge up the stairs, and before long I vaguely make out voices filtering through the ceiling above us, followed by the shuffling of feet – I'm guessing Simone has yet to change out of her night clothes – and then, shortly after that, footsteps padding back down to the ground floor.

Liam appears first at the living room door, closely followed by his wife. She's wearing fleecy grey jogging bottoms and a black turtleneck jumper, her blonde hair tied up in a scruffy bun. No make-up that I can see, but she's still very attractive without it, despite her pale complexion and the almost haunted look in her eyes. I immediately get up and extend my hand, Wild following suit. 'Hello, Mrs Loxley, I'm Detective Inspector John Banner, and this is DC Peter Wild.'

Simone shakes my hand, her own feeling like ice, as if it's lacking in circulation, then she does the same with Wild. I'm guessing she's not eaten much to speak of since learning of Lola's death. I notice the dark shadows beneath her eyes, which are red-rimmed, presumably from crying. 'Has Liam offered you both something to drink?' she says, her voice flat.

I hold up my palm. 'We're fine, really. We just need to ask you a few questions and then we'll leave you in peace.'

She gives me a jaded smile then takes a seat next to her husband on the other sofa. He takes her hand in his, clasps it tightly, as if to bolster her.

'I know this must be very hard for you,' I begin. 'I spoke to Clarissa Hilton earlier, and she said how close you and Lola were. As did Lola's mother, in fact.'

Simone nods. 'We were. I still can't believe it. I mean, I only texted her on Friday night.'

I instantly straighten. 'You did?'

She nods. 'I messaged her a little after 11:40 p.m. to ask how the party was going. I couldn't go because Liam was abroad and we didn't have babysitting. My parents were away on a cruise, Liam's dad isn't well, and his mum had a medical appointment yesterday morning that she couldn't change. Liam's sister's also got young kids of her own, and has enough on her plate. Bit like my own sister, Ruby. Anyway, Lola messaged me back, maybe ten minutes later, saying she'd left the party and was walking home, taking a short cut along the river path to save time because she couldn't get a taxi. She claimed she preferred walking, but I know she only said that to stop me worrying. I told her she was crazy. That she should go back to the hotel and wait for one, however long it took. I even offered to call one for her. But she wouldn't have it. Said she needed to get back to Luca and that she was nearly home anyway.'

'I see. Did she say why it was so urgent that she got back to Luca? Given the fact that he was safe and sound with his grandparents.'

'No.' Simone shakes her head. 'I couldn't understand it. But there was clearly no point in trying to talk her out of it. I could tell she'd made up her mind.' She hangs her head, then wipes her nose with the back of her hand.

'Did she say anything else in her text? I'd like to see the messages if that's OK.'

Simone hesitates. Looks at Liam nervously. It's clear she's hiding something. Almost as if she's too afraid to speak up.

'What is it, Simone?' I urge. 'Please, you must say what's on your mind. The cloakroom attendant at the hotel said Lola seemed upset when she left. Do you know anything about that?'

Again, Simone glances at Liam, as if for reassurance.

'Go on, darling,' he says. 'You must tell the inspector. He'll only find out anyway.'

'Find out what?' I ask.

Simone inhales deeply. 'Wait. I'll get my phone. It's on charge in the kitchen.' She gets up from the sofa, disappears from the room, and in no time at all is back, her mobile phone in her right hand. I watch her scroll through her messages, before she looks back up at me.

'Lola did say something else.' She turns the screen around for my benefit. 'See.'

I read Lola's message.

> Hey hon, thanks for the message. You were right. I shouldn't have gone to the party. It's been a total nightmare, they all fucking hate me and I had to get away. No cabs, so I'm walking home. L x

So Clarissa *was* hiding something. She point-blank lied to me when she said everything had been fine at the party. 'By *they*, she meant the other mums?' I say.

Simone nods. 'Yes. I felt so angry on Lola's behalf. I told her to message me as soon as she got home.'

'So she didn't say she was crashing at a friend's house?'

Simone frowns. 'No, I told you, she was desperate to get back to Luca. Why on earth would you ask that?'

'Lola's mother received a text from Lola around 12:25 a.m., so after she messaged you, saying she'd decided to stay over at a friend's. It's why Elisa didn't raise the alarm when Lola failed to come home. Apparently, she would always wait up for her.'

Simone looks puzzled. 'What? But that's crazy.'

'You didn't think to phone the police when Lola didn't text to say she'd arrived home safely, like you asked her to?'

'But that's just it, she did text.' Simone scrolls through to another message, her eyes focused on the screen. 'Or at least, someone did. At the time I had no reason to think it wasn't Lola. I mean, it sounded like her; she always called me hon, always signed off with L and a kiss.' I think of Elisa, who also confirmed there was nothing about Lola's text which suggested she hadn't written it. Indicating that her killer knew her well, or was at least familiar with her style and therefore confident in replicating it. 'But I guess now we know that's not the case,' Simone carries on. She hands me her phone. Showing a text from Lola sent to her at 12:30 a.m. Some five minutes after Elisa received a message sent from Lola's phone.

> Hey, hon, reached home safely. Thanks for caring, love you lots. Will call tomorrow. Lx

I glance at Wild and we exchange knowing looks. This second text from Lola's mobile gives us conclusive proof that her killer messaged both Elisa and Simone after murdering her, so that both women would think she was safe and well and wouldn't raise the alarm.

I look directly at Simone. 'Why did you tell Lola not to go to the party?'

Simone glances at Liam.

'Go on, hon, tell DI Banner,' Liam urges, squeezing her shoulder. 'This is our friend we're talking about. We need to get justice for Lola. And for poor Luca.'

Simone gives him a sad yet grateful smile. I watch her inhale deeply again. I get the feeling she feels torn between telling the truth for Lola's sake and being loyal to her other mum friends. 'Lately, things have been rather strained at the school gates. Horribly so, in fact.'

'Strained? How do you mean?'

'In the sense that the other mums in our circle have been giving Lola the cold shoulder. And although they've not said anything to me, I get the feeling they've been talking about her behind her back.'

'Why would they do that?'

Simone shrugs. 'I don't know, really. Maybe because she's... sorry, she *was* different, I guess. A single mum, young and attractive. You don't really get that combination at St Xavier's. I think they felt threatened by her. Although, having said that, she seemed to be getting on with most of them fine up until September. But there was like this sudden shift in behaviour towards her when the kids started back this term. It was weird.'

'Did you question any of them about it?'

'Yes, I did. I asked Dee and Joy, only because they're more chilled than Bianca and Clarissa. But they said I was imagining things. I wasn't, though. It was obvious the way they blanked Lola at every opportunity. Not just at the school gates, but on social occasions like the Year 1 class drinks we went to just before half term. I asked Lola if she'd done anything to upset them, but she said she hadn't. Couldn't think what was up with them all. Poor thing was so upset, and I felt so cross with Bianca and Clarissa because I was sure it was their doing, I still am.' She stops talking, looks up at Liam. 'Wouldn't you say that's fair? The way they'd been treating Lola, that is.'

Liam nods. 'Well, obviously I don't do the school run much, but on the occasions when we've all been together – the half-term drinks, for example, like Simi mentioned – I've definitely noticed some of them being off with Lola. Not the dads, more the mums. Usually these things pass me by, like they bypass most men. But there's been some definite tension, I agree.' He shrugs. 'Then again, Bianca's always been difficult.' He stops talking abruptly. 'Shit, sorry, I shouldn't have named names.'

'Why not?' Simone says harshly. 'You said we needed to get justice for Lola. It's true, she's a bloody cow, she always has been. She treated Lola unfairly right from the first day we met her, acted like she was beneath the rest of us, when in fact Lola had more class in her little finger.' Simone stops talking, but the tears are now streaming down her cheeks.

'It's OK, Simone,' I say. I look up at Liam. 'I assume you're talking about Bianca Radcliffe?' He nods. 'Please don't feel bad for naming names. This is a murder investigation and there's no room for protecting people or holding back. Not if we want to find Lola's killer.'

'OK, thanks. It's just that we're a pretty tight circle, as Simone said, and I don't want Jess and Penny, our daughters, to suffer the consequences of any aggro between the adults.'

Simone lowers her eyes. 'It's why I didn't press the point with Dee and Joy, as much as I'm ashamed to admit it. It was cowardly of me. I should have stood up for Lola more, demanded to know why they had such a problem with her.'

I shake my head. 'It's OK, you mustn't beat yourself up about it. Playground politics is hard, I understand that completely being a father myself. And don't worry, Liam, I'll be discreet when I speak to Mrs Radcliffe and her husband.' Liam gives me a grateful smile, at which point there's a short pause, before I say, looking at Simone, 'So, I take it you were friends with the other women in your friendship circle before Lola joined? What with you all having older kids, I mean.'

'Yes, that's right.' Simone nods. 'Me, Clarissa, Bianca, Joy and Dee – we all hit it off and became this core group, doing everything together. I expect we've earned a bit of a reputation amongst the other parents, when I think about it. I met Lola in the playground the day our younger ones started in Reception. She looked really nervous. But our kids took an immediate shine to each other and we got chatting and I really liked her. She was like a breath of fresh air. We'd all planned to have coffee that morning after dropping off the kids and I asked her if she wanted to join.'

'And how did the others feel about that?'

'They didn't object, but I could tell they weren't keen on her infiltrating the gang. It's pathetic really. I mean, we're grown adults. Bianca kept making snide comments, particularly when Damien, her husband, was nice to Lola. I think she was jealous. Damien's a bit of a flirt, you see. But then, when Lola explained how Luca's father died in a car accident when she was at university, I think even Bianca felt sorry for Lola. We all did. And for a couple of months things were OK, and I thought they might get along. But then, around November of the same year, there was a bit of an incident in the playground, and Bianca made it pretty clear that she and Lola were never going to be friends.'

Chapter Nine

Lola

Before
November 2022

I'm sitting behind reception at the GP surgery in Kingston where I work two mornings a week when my mobile phone lying on the desk in front of me starts to vibrate. I always keep it on silent but close by, in case of an emergency. Not just with Luca in mind. Mum and Dad are in their late sixties now and although they're still pretty fit, I constantly worry about something bad happening to them. I've always been a worrier, a trait that perhaps stems from being an only child and having relied on my parents so much over the years. Being close to them is both a blessing and a curse, I've come to realise. A blessing because, sadly, not all children have such loving relationships with their parents, but also a curse because in being so reliant on them, there are literally times when I'll lie in bed panicking that I won't be able to cope without them when they're gone. I know I need to grow up, to learn to stand on my own two feet, but it's easier said than done, especially after all I went through.

It's nearly lunchtime and I'm approaching the end of my shift. It's deathly quiet in the waiting area, only one patient left to be seen by the doctor, and once she's been through, I can go home for a couple of hours before I have to venture out again to collect Luca from school.

I pick up my phone, and my heart instantly accelerates when I see who's calling: St Xavier's. All at once, a torrent of possible scenarios ranging from mildly concerning to downright hideous fly through my head: Luca has head-lice, has pooed himself, or worse thrown up and/or has a high temperature. Or, worse still and my ultimate fear – an intruder broke into the school grounds and kidnapped him. This last possibility is completely irrational, I know that. But it's always there. Simply because I live in a constant state of the unknown. Not knowing if my rapist, his father, is still out there. Whether he's watching me, like he intimated. Whether he knows about Luca, despite me trying my best to hide and become a different person. I live in perpetual fear of crossing paths with him again. But what's worse is that I have no idea what he looks like, making the whole scenario even scarier. *He* knows what I look like, but I could walk right past him on the street and have no clue if I'd just crossed paths with the man who attacked me. Violated me. He has the upper hand, and it scares the shit out of me. That night, nearly six years ago now, when I'd been walking back from the library to my digs in Edinburgh, it had been sheeting down with rain, barely a soul about. I should have left earlier, but I was stressing big-time about failing one of my modules, so I stayed late to study more. Tracy had said it was the only way to conquer my fears. 'If you put the work in, give a hundred per cent, you know you've done everything you possibly can, and anything more is in the lap of the gods. That was my mentality, anyway, and it paid off.' I knew she was right. After all, she graduated with a high 2:1 in

English and went on to become a teacher at a top fee-paying school. When I thought about it, what she said made sense, and I realised that's all I could do. And, after a time, by focusing on my studies, immersing myself in them, it stopped me stressing about failing.

But then that godawful night happened. The night that changed the course of my life. The night I was attacked. The scumbag had worn a mask. Pounced on me panther-like from behind. I remember being utterly terrified – I couldn't even speak, my entire body paralysed from head to toe. Before I knew it, he'd pushed me into a deserted side alleyway and shoved me up against the wall. Finally, I found my voice, begged him not to hurt me. I said if he let me go, I wouldn't tell a soul. But that's when he threatened me, threatened my parents, said if I didn't play along like a nice girl, he'd hurt me, hurt my mum and dad. He was strong, I remember that. But that's all I can recall about him. Nothing else that would enable me to identify him in a line-up if it ever came to that. I've racked my brain over and over to see if I can recall the sound of his voice. But I can't. Only the words he said to me, which are seared into my brain for all eternity.

Is it any surprise that all this time later, that terrifying night still haunts my dreams. Why I shudder every time I hear a strange noise at night. Why, whenever I see the school's number pop up on my phone, I can't help thinking the worst – that he's back. Knows about our child. That he'll take him away from me, or worse, harm him. My paranoia isn't helped by something I read in the newspaper last week. An article in *The Times* said that the police are looking into the possibility of a serial rapist being responsible for attacks on women in their late teens to early-twenties over the last seven years, the latest being in September of this year. Until now, they hadn't made the link, but a chief inspector in Oxford recently came up with the theory, based on the fact that all the victims were around the same age, all undergraduates, highly attractive and of a similar height and hair colour and, most importantly, only children. All that, despite there being no obvious geographical link; the attacks having taken place all over the UK. The article suggested this was intentional, designed to throw the police off track, so they wouldn't make the connection, the last two attacks having occurred six months apart in Birmingham and Devon.

I know I'm probably overthinking things, that the police aren't necessarily right and even if they are, it doesn't mean I was targeted by the same bastard who hurt those poor women. But what if I was, and he's still out there? Attacking women. Only children like me who he perhaps sees as being more dependent on their parents than those with siblings. Watching them, watching me. Waiting to strike again. But, more importantly, waiting to hurt my sweet boy. Since reading the article I can think of little else. Simply because I do fit the profile of the other victims. Even though, as I said, it could still be a coincidence. A part of me feels guilty for not going to the police at the time and speaking up. But it's too late now, so much time has passed, why should they believe me? Plus, it's not like I have any means of identifying him. And, like I said, back then I was simply too scared. Scared he'd make good on his threat and come for me and my parents. Punish those I love the most. And I guess a little part of me worried I'd be accused of making it up. That somehow the police would find out I'd been struggling at university and therefore conclude I fabricated the whole story as a cry for attention. Looking back, it sounds crazy, but I wasn't in a good place mentally, and my self-confidence was rock bottom. How was I to know back then that my attacker was quite possibly a serial rapist?

Anyway, it's had me sick with worry and more protective than usual over Luca. Something Mum is bound to pick up on, but which I can never bring it upon myself to open up to her about. Too much time has gone by and the lies have become too big, despite the guilt I feel about lying to her and Dad, the two people I love most in this world besides Luca. It's like there's this tug of war between the fear and guilt that torments my brain every second of every day. The fear of what will happen if my secret gets out, and yet the guilt I feel about not being truthful with those who care the most about me.

I've yet to talk to Tracy about the article I read, but I plan on doing so later, because it's torture keeping this to myself, and she's always so good at calming me down and reassuring me it's going to be OK.

Lost in my thoughts, I focus my attention back on my phone and the fact that someone from St Xavier's is ringing me. Fretfully, I pick it up, but remain fearful of answering, of learning yet more unsettling news. Finally, I pluck up the nerve. 'Hello,' I say tentatively.

'Hello, Miss Martinez, this is Laura on reception at St Xavier's Primary. Don't worry, Luca's fine and well' – I inwardly sigh with relief, having held my breath since she started speaking – 'but I'm calling to say he got into a fight with one of the other children in his class today, and it would be great if you could come in for a chat with his form tutor after the school day finishes. Say, 3:45 p.m.? Luca is welcome to sit outside the classroom while you're speaking with Miss Day.'

I'm beyond relieved that Luca's OK, but at the same time I'm stunned to hear he's been in a fight. Luca's been at St Xavier's over two months now, and never once got into trouble. Neither were there any incidents at his nursery before. In fact, the teachers there had always praised his impeccable behaviour and kindness towards other children. That made me so proud. I know I'm biased, but he really is one of the gentlest, kindest souls I know, despite his innate stubbornness. The kind of boy who'd sidestep an ant because he couldn't bear to hurt it. For obvious reasons, I've always impressed on him the need to be kind and thoughtful and that violence is never the answer. So I'm somewhat alarmed to hear he's been physical with another child. And I can't help worrying if it's genetic, even though I know I'm getting ahead of myself as usual.

'A fight?' I say, my stomach churning. 'With who? What happened exactly?'

'I think it's best if you come in and discuss it with Miss Day. The other child's parents will be present too.'

I swallow hard, while summoning up the courage to ask my next question, just because I'm so fearful of the answer: 'Can I ask who the other child is?'

It seems like an age before Laura replies. Finally, she says, 'Summer Radcliffe. I think you know her parents.'

Shit, of all the kids, it had to be Bianca's child. The worst possible scenario. I say thank you, then put down the phone and sit in silence, imagining how things will play out later.

All I can think is that I'm screwed. This is going to give Bianca even more reason to dislike me.

Chapter Ten

Detective Inspector John Banner

Monday, 18th December 2023

It's 2 p.m. and Wild and I have just parked up in front of the Radcliffes' home just off the river road, having not long made tracks from the Loxleys'. Simone still seemed fragile when we left her sitting on the sofa, cupping a mug of tea, yet barely drinking it. It's clear that Lola's death has hit her hard, a blow that's going to take her some time to recover from. The two of them had shared a close bond, Liam told me in a low voice as he showed Wild and I to the door. He explained how Simone had been drawn to Lola's gentle, easy-going manner, in contrast to some of the parents at St Xavier's who could be highly-strung. He feared for his wife's mental health, having never seen her this delicate. 'Simone has a very soft centre,' he said. 'She doesn't have the hard skin that some of the mums at St Xavier's do, and I worry what this might to do her in the long-term.' I didn't doubt Liam's words. And, of course, he was speaking from a medical point of view as well as that of a loving husband. At that point, I suggested to Liam that Paula come round to talk to Simone, and perhaps recommend a number of counsellors who deal with situations like these, and who therefore might be able to help Simone through this difficult time. He'd given me a grateful nod, said he'd like to take me up on that. I also did something I rarely do, and gave him my card. Told him to tell Simone she should feel free to call me if she remembered anything else that might prove helpful to the case. Being Lola's best friend, someone Lola confided in and socialised with on a regular basis, I can't help thinking she's the person most likely to have pertinent information. But what stuck in my mind as we drove away from their home was Simone's clear animosity towards Bianca Radcliffe, who we've just this minute come to see. Evidently, there was no love lost between Lola and Bianca, particularly after the playground incident between their children last year. So, it'll be interesting to hear Bianca's version of events.

My stomach growls as I switch off the ignition. I've not eaten anything since the meagre bowl of granola I shoved down my throat at 6:30 a.m. and it feels like my intestines have started to feast on themselves. Still, it's important I strike while the iron's hot and speak to the women in Lola's friendship group at St Xavier's as soon as possible. Even though the term 'friendship' doesn't quite feel appropriate, having spoken with both Elisa and Simone.

'Do you think one of the women at St Xavier's could be a credible suspect, sir?' Wild asks.

I shake my head. 'It's too early to say, but we can't rule it out. Clearly, from what the Loxleys said, there was a fair degree of animosity between Bianca and Lola, plus things had generally been tense at the school gates lately.'

'Yes, but murder, sir? What possible motive could any of them have?'

'You'd be surprised what ordinary people do when they've had a bit too much to drink and there's existing ill-will between them. Doesn't take much to set them off, especially if they're on the hot-headed side. Plus, this time of the year can be the worst for break-ups and violence, you know that. Like a pressure cooker coming to the boil. Not only that, it's evident something happened on Friday evening at the party, no matter what Clarissa Hilton said. We know that from Lola's text to Simone.'

'Couldn't the killer have sent that, sir? A red herring to mislead us.'

'No, I don't think so. I'm pretty sure Lola sent that one before she was attacked. It fits with the timing.' I unbuckle my seat belt. 'Anyway, let's see what this infamous Bianca has to say for herself. I've got a feeling we'll have our work cut out for us where she's concerned.'

The Radcliffes live in an impressive four-bedroom detached Victorian house arranged over three floors with a loft conversion and sizeable garden. I take the lead as we stroll up to the front door, before ringing the bell. Thirty seconds or so pass before it opens, a woman perhaps in her early forties standing there. She's dressed in black leggings and a zip-up purple fleece top, no make-up, her auburn hair tied up in a bun.

'Yes, can I help you?' Her sharp tone is a marked contrast to the genial reception we received from Clarissa Hilton and the Loxleys. As is the hostile expression she's wearing. I called ahead, so she's definitely expecting us. Her acting like she doesn't know who the hell we are therefore seems unnecessary, and not a little irritating.

Still, I politely introduce ourselves, and allude to our earlier telephone conversation.

'Oh, yes of course,' she says, yet still with the same haughty dismissive tone. She pokes her head out of the door, looking left and right, then quickly ushers us inside as if she's afraid someone might be watching. My gut tells me it's not because she's scared of someone, but rather she's worried about her reputation with the neighbours being tarnished.

'You rather caught me at a bad time, just back from my yoga class, so please excuse the state of me.'

'Not at all.' We follow Bianca inside. Despite both Wild and I declining, she insists on making us both a cup of oolong tea, whatever that may be, then guides us through to the smaller of two reception rooms where we take a seat on a black leather sofa. Bianca plonks herself on the matching sofa opposite, crossing one leg over the other, her mug resting on her knee. I know from what Simone told me that Bianca is a full-time mum, and tends to spend a lot of her free time (i.e., when the kids are at school) at the gym or taking long lunches. Her husband, Damien, is a director of The Radcliffe Group, a successful IT company started by his father, John, whose offices are based in the exclusive area of Wimbledon Village.

'So how can I be of help?' Bianca says, her eyes lasering through me as if *she's* the police officer doing the questioning, rather than me.

I go over the circumstances of Lola's death, but at this point don't mention my conversations with Clarissa or the Loxleys'. Or, indeed, Elisa.

Bianca makes a tutting noise. Then shakes her head gravely. 'It really was so stupid of Lola to walk home from the party in the dark like that, and on the river path of all places. I mean, if she had any sense, she would have at least taken the main road all the way, which is well-lit. What on earth could have possessed her?'

Her lack of compassion is hard to swallow, and it's a fight to suppress the anger rising in me. This woman is a mother and you'd think she'd have more empathy knowing a little boy in her child's class has lost his mother under horrific circumstances. Not only that, he has been orphaned overnight. You'd have to have ice running through your veins not to feel heartbroken for the poor mite.

'People do these things when pushed,' I say. 'Out of love.'

Bianca cocks her head, her eyes wide. 'Pushed? Not following, how do you mean?'

'Well, for one, she couldn't get a cab, what with it being a Friday night and the height of the party season. But we also understand something happened at the party. Forcing her to leave early and walk home. Not only that, she was desperate to get back to Luca.'

Bianca gives a forced chuckle. 'Happened? What on earth is that supposed to mean? Other than the fact that we all got absolutely trashed, I can't think what you're getting at.'

'Lola texted Simone Loxley while she was walking home. Told her she should never have gone to the party. And in her own words, "*it was a nightmare*" and "*they all hate me*". By this, I can only presume she meant the parents in her friendship group at St Xavier's. You being one of them.'

I maintain a deadpan expression, as does Wild, while Bianca looks stunned, her face having gone beetroot red. In the short time I've known Bianca, she doesn't strike me as the kind of person who's normally lost for words, but at this moment her voice appears to have escaped her.

'Any idea what Lola could have meant by that?' I say.

Bianca manages to recover her composure, putting on her best smile. 'No, I don't, Inspector, and I'm being completely honest with you when I say that. I hate to speak ill of the dead, but Lola had a very active imagination and, dare I say it, a bit of an inferiority complex. I think she was paranoid.'

I frown. 'How do you mean?'

'Look, I am all for single mothers. I champion them, in fact. The way Lola raised that little boy all by herself – admittedly with the help of her parents – was more than admirable. I, for one, wouldn't have been able to manage it. But it was obvious to all of us that she didn't feel as if she was as good as the rest of us. You know, in not having a husband or a partner. We welcomed her with open arms, but it was never enough. She envied our lives. Our complete families.'

What a pompous condescending thing to say. As well as Bianca having the gift of the gab, it also hasn't taken me long to reach the conclusion that I don't trust the words that come out of her mouth for a second. But for now, I don't let on. I simply say, 'I see, so what are you saying? That she made it all up, lied in her text. Her "inferiority complex"' – I do the air quotes thing – 'therefore has nothing to do with you and the other mums giving her the cold shoulder in the playground of late?'

Bianca visibly flinches. 'What? No! Wherever did you hear that?' She narrows her eyes. 'Was it Simone?'

I stay silent.

'Simone is such an old softie,' she goes on. 'She gets taken in by people, can be so easily influenced. Lola wanted her sympathy, that's all. I'm not saying she was deliberately manipulative. All I am saying is that Lola took offence unnecessarily. Read too much into things. I don't know, maybe I was locked deep in conversation with a mum in the playground and didn't notice Lola standing there, and then Lola assumed I was ignoring her, when I wasn't. It's so easy to get the wrong end of the stick, particularly for someone like Lola, who wasn't the most naturally self-assured. The rest of us can be, well, quite in your face, I suppose. We were pretty drunk on Friday night, taking cracks at one another across the dinner table, and I think Lola felt a bit left out. I'm sure that's why she took off so quickly. And, of course, Simone, who she's close to, wasn't there.'

'So do I also take it that you don't believe her leaving in a hurry had anything to do with the fact that she was anxious to get back to Luca?'

Bianca gives an uneasy chuckle. 'Luca? Why would she have been anxious about getting back to him? As I understand things, her grandparents were babysitting Luca that night.'

I nod. 'Yes, that's correct.'

'So why would she have been worried? Having said that, she was rather overprotective of that little boy.'

'How so?'

'Well, to not put too fine a point on it, she mollycoddled him. She wouldn't leave him at people's houses for a playdate, for example. Except for Simone's house, of course. She'd always stay to help supervise. Like she didn't trust us with her child.'

'He's only six, five when he started school, I can understand that. Some children don't like to be left alone until they're at least eight or nine. My son was the same for his first two years of primary.'

'Yes, I get that. But the thing is, we could all see that Luca was happy for her to leave him by himself, at birthday parties and such like. But she stuck to him like glue. I felt for the boy, I really did. She smothered him.'

'I see. Do you think there was a particular reason she was so overprotective?'

'Well, the father died in a car crash, so I guess that may have contributed to it, causing Lola to always fear the worst. Although, and I know it sounds a bit harsh, I have my doubts about that story, if truth be told.'

I lean forward. 'You do? Why?'

She shrugs her shoulders. 'I don't know, I just do. The others felt it too. Like she was holding back.'

Something tells me there's more to Bianca's doubts than a mere 'feeling', but for some reason she's being deliberately sketchy. 'They did? Are you sure it's just a feeling? Or did someone find something out about Lola's past?'

Bianca sips her coffee, her eyes boring through mine over the rim, like she's biding her time, trying to concoct a response in her head.

'No,' she says eventually. 'It was just a feeling, like I said. But I guess now we'll never know.'

It's clear she's not going to budge on that one, so for now I change tack. 'Tell me, is it true that you and Lola had a falling out November before last? Because of something that happened at school between Luca and your daughter, Summer? Perhaps that's why Lola became so overprotective?'

Bianca's cheeks redden once more. 'What? How do you know about that, and what's a minor playground scuffle got to do with anything?'

'Please answer the question, Mrs Radcliffe.'

'What? No, I will not answer the question. I'm not under arrest; this is preposterous. Whether or not Lola and I had a bit of a disagreement over a year or so ago has no bearing whatsoever on her being anxious about her son last Friday. Or, indeed, being overprotective in general. There may have been a whole host of reasons why she was worried. Reasons we may never know about.'

She has a point; we don't know for sure why Lola was so anxious to get back to Luca. And she won't be the first parent to rush back home from a social event for their kids. Some parents even use their children as an excuse to leave because they've had enough. I've done it myself. Elisa and Don have also both confirmed there was nothing wrong with their grandson that night, so on that basis it can't have had anything to do with his health. But what if Lola wasn't just being overprotective? What if she genuinely feared for Luca's safety? If that's the case, it begs the question, *why?*

'What time did you leave the party, Mrs Radcliffe?' I ask.

Bianca cocks her head. 'Erm, when was it now, around 12:15, I think.'

'So, not long after Lola?'

'No, I don't suppose it was. But I took a cab, despite living close by. Unlike Lola, I made the sensible decision of pre-booking one, even though I can walk to my house in fifteen minutes from the hotel.'

'I see. Do you have a receipt for that?'

She frowns. 'No, I don't have a receipt. Do you get a receipt every time you get a cab?'

'And your husband was at home when you got back?' I carry on, ignoring her.

'Yes.'

'What time was that?'

'I don't know, around 12:25, I guess.'

'Was he up?'

'I don't know.'

'You don't know?'

'I slept in the spare room.'

'So you don't know if he was at home?'

Bianca plays with her bun. 'What? No, I mean I didn't physically see him, but I jolly well hope he was there as he was meant to be minding the kids!'

'Why did you sleep in the spare room? Had you been fighting? Is that why he wasn't at the party? Because you'd had a falling out?'

Bianca gives a little huff. 'Absolutely not. He's been suffering from a bad bout of the flu, so I didn't want to disturb him. Neither did I wish to contract it myself.'

I look around. 'And yet he was well enough to look after your children. And presumably well enough to go to work today. That's some recovery.'

Bianca fiddles with the zip on her fleece. 'Yes, he's much recovered, thankfully. As for my daughters, Summer and Tilly, they're not babies anymore, they're very self-sufficient these days, being *girls*.'

I smile. 'I see. Pleased to hear he's feeling better. So, you didn't see your husband until the next morning?'

Bianca hesitates. Then nods. 'Yes, yes that's right.'

'Tell me, is it true your husband flirted with Lola?'

To her credit, Bianca doesn't appear fazed by my question. She simply rolls her eyes. 'Damien would flirt with your grandmother, Inspector, given the chance. Lola was nothing special, I'm quite certain of that.'

Despite her apparent nonchalance, there's a definite trace of bitterness underlining Bianca's last comment.

'So his flirting had nothing to do with your falling out in the playground? There was never anything more between them?'

Bianca's eyes grow steely. 'No, never. I told you, that playground scuffle between our kids was nothing. It was water under the bridge. My marriage to Damien is rock solid. I trust him completely. He'd never cheat on me. He knows his life wouldn't be worth living if he did, because I'd take him to the cleaners and he'd never be able to set foot in this house again.'

I don't doubt this last part of Bianca's response to my question. But it does make me wonder as to the lengths she'd go to make sure things never got that far. I wrap up the interview and Wild and I take our leave, not feeling in the least bit convinced that Bianca Radcliffe has been entirely honest with us.

Chapter Eleven

Lola

Before
November 2022

HERETOCHAT.ORG
Chat Now in confidence. We're here for each other

Tracy: Hey lovely, how you doing?

Lola: Not great, if I'm being honest.

Tracy: Why? What happened? I thought things were going well.

Lola: I had a bit of a run-in with one of the mums at school.

Tracy: Argh. Don't tell me, Bianca?

Lola: Yes, how did you guess?

Tracy: Just based on what you've told me about her. She doesn't exactly sound like a piece of cake. Although you did say the other day you were getting on better.

Lola: We were. But Luca got into a fight with her daughter this morning, and we got called in for a chat after pick-up. I felt like the naughty kid myself being brought before the teacher.

Tracy: Luca got into a fight? He's never done that before, has he? You always say he's the gentlest of souls.

Lola: He is! That's why it was so upsetting. At first, I was worried he might be showing his true colours, that he'd got his genes.

Tracy: Lola, that's so daft. You know how daft that is, surely?

Lola: Is it? There's something to be said for nature.

Tracy: There's also a lot to be said for nurture. Luca's been raised in a non-threatening, loving environment. There's no reason he should have adopted his father's violent tendencies.

Lola: I guess. Truth be told, when I heard what happened, I couldn't blame Luca.

Tracy: Why? What did happen exactly?

Lola: Luca pushed Summer and she fell and hit her head in the playground.

Tracy: Oh no! Why did he do that?

Lola: He wouldn't say in front of the teacher, or Bianca and her husband, Damien. But when we got home, he said it was because Summer called him a mummy's boy. And that he didn't really fit in their class as everyone else had a mummy and daddy, just like his mummy, i.e. me, didn't fit in with the other mums and dads because I didn't have a husband.

Tracy: That's awful. What a little so-and-so Bianca's child is. I can understand why Luca lashed out like that. Poor thing.

Lola: Yep. I'm so angry – clearly all that came from Bianca. Gossiping at home in front of her kids. Luca was so upset when he was telling me all this, and it broke my heart. He feels different enough as it is, surrounded by kids who have a mum and dad, and this has only gone and made him feel more insecure. I can't help feeling it's my fault for exposing him to this kind of crap. I told him it was wrong of Summer and that he should have told his teacher, but I think he was too scared. In case the other kids turned on him for telling on her. Even at this age, they're scared of ratting on one another.

Tracy: Understandable. You should tell his teacher, though. She needs to know what really happened, that Luca had a good reason and wouldn't hurt another kid for the sake of it. She must know what this Summer is like, more especially what her mother is like. I bet you this isn't the first time this sort of thing has happened. She sounds like a bit of a precocious child. I'm betting Bianca thinks the sun shines out of her arse and she can't put a foot wrong, though.

Lola: Haha, you made me laugh out loud. Thanks for bringing a smile to my face. Yes, I guess I should tell the teacher. I'm desperate to tell Bianca as well, just so she knows what a spiteful daughter she has, but there's no point. She'll only deny it, accuse me of making up stories or Luca of being a liar and then he'll end up being ostracised at school or something. Fuck, the world is so unfair. I hate playing these mind games, but Bianca rules the roost in that place, I don't have a sodding chance against her. God knows what her husband sees in her. He's way too good for Bianca. She must have tricked him into marriage or something.

Tracy: Does someone have a crush on someone? I told you not to go there.

Tracy: Lola, are you there? Seriously, don't go there, it won't end well, and you'll only make things worse for Luca.

Lola: Sorry. Yeah, I know. God knows how she bagged him, though. She's so awful.

Tracy: What did Bianca say when you met with the teacher?

Lola: It was horrendous.

Tracy: Ahh, it's OK, you don't have to tell me.

Lola: No, I want to. It's always good to talk, let it all out. So, I left work...

Chapter Twelve

Lola

Before
November 2022

I take a seat outside Luca's classroom and tell Luca to sit beside me. He does so silently, his expression sheepish, his movements tentative. In short, the poor child looks broken, and it breaks my heart to see him so vulnerable and sad. When I collected him in the playground, he could barely look me in the eye, his little face shrouded in guilt. I tried to hug him, like I always do, but instead of reciprocating my embrace with a customary fierce hug of his own, he stiffened at my touch, perhaps not thinking himself to be worthy of my cuddles because he'd pushed Summer to the ground at morning break time. Apparently, she hit her head hard, became somewhat dazed before throwing up en route to see the nurse, and, having been swiftly informed by the school office, a panicked Bianca had collected her daughter within thirty minutes and rushed her off to Kingston A&E. I know all this from Simone, who heard it from Clarissa whom Bianca had texted from the hospital. Goodness knows what Bianca said about me and Luca in her text; I can only imagine the number of expletives. She's probably bad-mouthed me to the whole group by now. No doubt they're debating the entire affair via a newly formed WhatsApp group as I sit here worrying. I just pray it all blows over and that this one mistake on Luca's part won't lead to him being ostracised by the other kids in his class. It would crush him. He already feels different as it is.

I consciously stood apart from the other mums and dads in the playground while I waited for Luca to appear. Simone included. I avoided eye contact with everyone by staring at my phone, at nothing in particular. But I've come to realise that in a school like St Xavier's, once you're part of a clique like the one Clarissa heads up, it's next to impossible to keep yourself to yourself. I could feel their eyes boring through me as I stood there, doubtless itching to know my side of the story, excited by the prospect of some playground shenanigans to gossip about. Waiting for the kids to be dismissed had felt like an eternity, my insides doing somersaults, my cheeks burning with shame. I might have known Clarissa would be the one to make the first move.

'Hi, Lola, darling, how are things? I heard Luca and Summer had a bit of a spat earlier today. I wouldn't worry too much about it; kids will be kids. You'll be pleased to know Summer's OK. Bianca called to let me know. Just a bit of a bump, but that's a good thing, it's when there's no swelling you have to worry. Poor B was beside herself because Summer was apparently very listless in the car.' She'd looked at me gravely at that point. Thought she was being clever, trying to appear kind and yet her last comment was clearly designed to make me feel guilty. But I told myself I needed to remain calm. If I retaliated, I knew I'd only make things worse. They'd doubtless assume Luca got his temper from me, the news spreading like wildfire, and Luca suffering in the process. I needed to act like everything was under control, that *I* was in control and that it was no big deal, even though I was far from sure if that was the case. I still don't. Luca has barely spoken a word to me since being dismissed. I just pray he had a good reason for the way he behaved, even though this in no way condones his aggression.

'I'm glad Summer's OK,' I said with a smile. 'Can't think what could have come over Luca. He and Summer have always got on well. Must have been some silly misunderstanding, I reckon. You know kids. I'm sure Miss Day will sort it all out.'

By then, Joy and Simone had appeared. Dee too, what with it being a Friday and her day off. All listening in intently, their senses on high alert.

'Yes, no harm done, nothing to fuss over,' Dee said in her usual lawyerly matter-of-fact manner.

'Still, you have to nip it in the bud at an early age,' Clarissa said with a shake of the head.

'Nip what in the bud?' I asked.

'Aggression. If you don't, before you know it, he'll be an unruly teenager on drugs, doing graffiti, getting into knife crime, and you'll be powerless to stop him.'

At this point I'd looked at Simone and, bless her, she came to my rescue. If she hadn't, I'm not sure I'd have been able to control my tears, or my temper, despite having made a pledge to stay calm only minutes before.

'Clarissa, I think you're going a bit over the top,' Simone chided. 'Kids this age have squabbles in the playground all the time. It doesn't mean they're going to turn to drugs or become vandals as teenagers. You're getting ahead of yourself and blowing things out of proportion. And it's not as if Luca's always getting into fights.' She'd looked at me and smiled. 'He's always as good as gold when he comes round to our house. I can't think of a better-behaved child.'

I could have kissed her at that moment. It did the trick, Clarissa backtracking instantly. 'Oh yes, yes, of course,' she nodded vigorously. 'Sorry, Lola, I didn't mean to alarm you, I'm just looking out for little Luca, that's all. I'm sure it will all be fine.'

'Course it will,' Joy said. 'Jeez, if you could have seen some of the fights I had with my siblings at the age of five you'd have been shocked. I still have the scars to show for it.' We'd all chuckled at this, but as the bell rang and we ventured towards the orange lollipop, waiting for our kids to appear, I prayed Joy was right and that Luca's behaviour was normal rather than a sign of things to come.

Just now, as Luca and I continue to sit outside Miss Day's classroom, I hear footsteps approaching. The same sick sensation I felt earlier when I received the school's telephone call swirls in my guts because I think I know it can only be one person.

'Hello, Lola.'

Bianca.

Damien is with her. Her tone is hostile, her beady eyes drilling through me. My cheeks are suddenly on fire with shame. I start subconsciously picking at the skin around my fingers. I want nothing more than for the ground to swallow me up at this precise moment. Damien gives me a weak smile, and I return the gesture with a feeble smile of my own.

'Hi, Bianca, hi Damien. How's Summer?' I ask, hating how timid my voice sounds.

Bianca glares at Luca, and now I can literally feel him shaking alongside me. More than anything I want to take him in my arms and squeeze him tight. Tell him everything's going to be OK and that I love him more than anything in this world. I know he wouldn't have pushed Summer for no good reason, I just wish he'd pluck up the courage to tell me what happened.

'She's with my mother. Has a nasty bump on her head, and a ghastly scrape on the back of her leg, no thanks to Luca here. Honestly, when I think how much worse her condition could have been' – she shudders – 'well, it doesn't bear thinking about. You need to get your son under control. Attacking a vulnerable little girl like that.'

I feel a rage burn through me as she says this and I'm on the verge of blowing my top when Miss Day appears. She gives us all a warm smile, then hands Luca (who's on the brink of tears) a copy of *Charlie and the Chocolate Factory*. She tells him to read it while she speaks to the adults in her office. He nods obediently, bravely fending off the tears.

I bend down and kiss Luca on the top of his head, tell him to behave and promise that I won't be long, before following Bianca and Damien inside Miss Day's classroom. The tension is almost unbearable as we take a seat across from her desk in the far corner. Thankfully, she's brought some adult chairs in, so it doesn't feel like she's looking down on us like we're three naughty school children here for detention. Looking around, it's such a joyful classroom, the walls adorned with the children's colourful pieces of art, the current theme being Bonfire Night, but right now all that is lost on me, and I want nothing more than to be able to get out of here and take Luca home.

Of course, Bianca is all smiles for Miss Day. Sucking up to her big-time. 'I can't thank you enough for acting so quickly and calling me, Miss Day,' she gushes. 'If you hadn't applied the ice to Summer's head, I dread to think what might have happened.' She shakes her head dramatically, while cutting me a sly sideways glance, and I feel myself recoil. 'Thankfully, she's much better, you'll be pleased to know, but it's obviously been very traumatic for our little girl. Hasn't it, Damien?'

Bianca eyeballs her husband, and I notice him squirm in his seat, while giving me an uneasy, almost apologetic look. 'Damien?' she urges.

'Well, it's never nice getting a bump on the head,' he says congenially, 'but she'll bounce back in no time. Kids are so much more resilient than us oldies. By the morning, she'll have forgotten all about it.'

At this, Bianca gives him her classic death stare.

'I'm sure that's right,' Miss Day says kindly. I like Miss Day. Her voice is calm and soothing, yet has an underlying authority to it. 'However, we obviously want to avoid anything of this nature happening again. I spoke to both children and neither was very forthcoming.'

Bianca tuts. 'I think it's perfectly clear what happened. Luca pushed Summer because she's so popular and he wanted to gain some attention.'

'What?' I gasp. 'Why on earth would he do that? Luca's never done such a thing in his life, why would he start now? I can only think that Summer must have said something to provoke Luca. He's normally such a placid child.'

Bianca's mouth opens in apparent shock. Her eyes agog. 'Never! Summer has a heart of gold, and has been nothing but kind to Luca, inviting him over for playdates and her birthday party recently, as you well know. Clearly, Luca is jealous.'

I'm on the point of erupting when Miss Day catches my eye – a signal for me not to go there – then she says, 'Mrs Radcliffe, did you ask Summer what happened?'

'Of course,' Bianca huffs. 'She said Luca just pushed her out of the blue while a bunch of them were playing tag.'

I shake my head. 'Again, I refuse to believe Luca would do that without good reason.'

'Well, you would say that.' Bianca scowls.

'Bianca!' Damien admonishes. 'Take it easy, for goodness' sake.'

'OK, we all need to calm down,' Miss Day says firmly, looking at each of us in turn, 'as any stress on your part will only filter down to the children, and that's not what we want here.' She eyes me directly. 'I've told Luca that pushing or any kind of physical aggression is completely unacceptable. He was very sorry, and assured me he'd never do it again.' I nod meekly. Bianca mutters something under her breath, but I count to three in my head, willing myself not to rise to the bait. Miss Day keeps her gaze on me. 'I'd also like you to have a chat with Luca when he gets home, see if there's anything bothering him. He might open up to you in the home environment. Is that OK?'

I nod again. 'Yes, I will do, thank you.'

Miss Day looks at Bianca. 'We really need to put this behind us now. It's important the children get along in my classroom and I would urge you, the adults, to do the same.'

Bianca gives a heavy sigh. 'Yes, OK, I understand.'

'Absolutely,' Damien says more brightly. He grins, gives a light chuckle. 'Are we dismissed?'

I can't stop a grin from creeping up on me, too, and have to fight the urge not to burst into fits of laughter.

'Yes, thank you for coming in, I do appreciate it,' Miss Day says. She gets up, then ushers us all to the door, shaking each of our hands in turn, before opening it.

'How's the book going?' she says to Luca.

'Good,' he says, not daring to look Bianca's way.

'Take it home with you – be a shame not to finish it now that you've started. It's one of my favourites. Maybe your mummy will let you watch the film sometime.' At this, Luca's eyes light up and I could hug Miss Day for finally putting a smile on my boy's face.

'I need the loo,' Damien whispers in Bianca's ear. 'Meet you at the car.'

Bianca eyes her husband warily. 'Fine. Don't be long though. Thanks again, Miss Day.' She gives me a brief glance. 'Bye Lola, see you tomorrow I guess.'

I inwardly sigh with relief, having thought she was about to walk off without saying goodbye.

'Bye, Bianca, have a good evening.'

'You too.' She glares at Damien again. 'Be quick, Mother needs to get home.'

'Yes, darling.'

Miss Day disappears back inside her classroom while I help Luca with his coat. I'm conscious Damien hasn't left yet despite professing to need the loo, and I feel his gaze on me.

'Listen, I'm sorry about all this. Sorry B was coming on so strong in there. Summer is fine. Believe me, she's a chip off the old block.' He grins and I grin back.

'That's OK, Luca shouldn't have pushed Summer.'

'I'm sure he had his reasons. Hopefully you'll get to the bottom of it once you're home.' He leans in, then whispers in my ear: 'My child is no angel. Let me know what Luca says; you have my number, I think.' His lips brush my earlobe, making me tingle all over. He pulls away and meets my gaze and I'm sure I'm not imagining the heat between us. A sensation I've not experienced in a long time. So much so, I'd almost forgotten how delicious it feels. Sure, I've been on the odd date since Luca was born, but none of them turned into anything serious. Not just because of what happened to me, or the fact that I'm afraid of opening up to a man, but because none of the guys I've been out with have had the effect Damien seems to have on me. More than anything, I wish it wasn't so. But at the same time, I love how it makes me feel, how it gives me such a rush. A rush I don't want to come down from.

'Yes, I do,' I say, my body suddenly warm all over.

'Great, well I'd best be making tracks, else I'll be in the doghouse. Again.' Another boyish grin, and then he takes off, leaving me standing there wondering what the hell just happened.

'Mummy, can we go now?' Luca tugs at my coat. 'I'm so hungry.'

I look down at him, my stomach still fizzing with excitement. 'Yes of course, sweetheart, let's go. I'm starving too.'

Waiting for the bus, I tell myself to snap out of it, that Damien's just an incorrigible flirt and I'm reading too much into things. In any case, I can't go there. No matter how tantalising it is. It would be wrong. Plus, Bianca hates me enough as it is. If anything were to happen between Damien and I, she'd kill me.

I have zero doubts about that.

Chapter Thirteen

Detective Inspector John Banner

Tuesday, 19th December 2023

It's 7 a.m. and I've not long arrived at Kingston police station. Having just sat down at my desk, I'm about to bite into a moreish Danish I picked up on the way in, when the phone on my desk rings. The caller ID tells me it's DI Golding, the officer leading the forensic search at Lola's flat. I sigh, trying my best to ignore the inviting aroma of fresh pastry pervading my nostrils as I place my breakfast down on the paper bag it came in and answer the call.

'Golding?'

'Yes, sir. I just wanted to give you an update on what my team's found at Lola Martinez's flat so far.'

I straighten, the urgent tone of Golding's voice telling me he finally has something of note. 'Yep, tell me.'

'Lola kept a diary for 2023. And it appears to contain some interesting stuff.'

My pulse quickens. 'Like what?'

'Sir, I think you need to read it for yourself.'

I know he means well, is just being respectful, but I can't wait for that. I'm eager to hear the gist of it now. 'Just give me a brief overview. I'm about to go and interview another couple of potential key witnesses who attended the same party as Lola on Friday night. Whatever you found may affect my line of questioning.'

'I understand. OK, looking at my team's notes, in a November entry Lola mentioned receiving some threatening messages.'

'Threatening how?'

'As in threats to her and her son's lives.'

That perhaps explains her telling Simone she was anxious to get back to Luca on Friday. Did she receive another threatening message that same night? It would make sense.

'Go on.'

'She said she felt guilty for not telling her parents about the messages but didn't want to put them in danger.'

'Danger?'

'Yes, because, and here's the biggie, she said she worried it might be the same person who attacked her all those years ago at university. The same "evil shit" who may have attacked the other women she's read about in the papers. Who told her if she didn't keep quiet about what happened that night, he'd come for her and her parents.'

'Christ. You don't think she's talking about…'

'The Campus Prowler. Yep, that's what I was thinking.'

In November of last year, a DCI based in Oxford came up with the theory that the same man was responsible for attacking a string of female students over the course of the previous seven years, and that he was getting away with it because there was no obvious geographical connection, and because the attacks were well spaced out. He further based his theory on the fact that all the students were petite, slim and attractive with dark hair and eyes and appeared to have come from loving stable upbringings, but were also extreme perfectionists and, more importantly, only children. He came to this conclusion following interviews with the victims who had come forward, along with their parents and loved ones. However, since the article first appeared in the newspapers, leading the press to unhelpfully coin the accused 'the Campus Prowler' and make him something of a celebrity, no further attacks have been reported, the potential suspect perhaps choosing to lay low having realised the police were onto him. Could it be that Lola was raped by the same man? That he's the one who sent her threatening messages about Luca. Could Luca, in fact, be his son? Meaning Lola fabricated the story about Luca's father dying in a car accident because her attacker had threatened her parents' lives and it was best to pretend that he was dead? The timing fits, and it would explain why she was so keen to move down south and change her name. Also, why she's so protective over Luca. Perhaps he murdered her on Friday night because he found out she told someone about him, thereby breaking her promise? Or am I overthinking things? Making too big of a leap here? I know I can't ignore other possibilities, that one of the guests at the party may have had something to do with Lola's death, because clearly something happened on Friday night, causing Lola to rush off and tell Simone it had been 'a nightmare' and that she 'should never have come', no matter what Clarissa and Bianca claim. Plus, there's Lola's run-in with Bianca last year to consider, not to mention Simone's claim that things had been tense in the playground lately. Perhaps my upcoming interviews with Joy Grainger and Deidre Walton will shed further light on this. Even so, I make a mental note to look into car accidents in the Glasgow area in April/May 2017, when Lola would have been in her final term at university and newly pregnant. I hadn't thought to do so before because I had no reason to doubt what Elisa and Don told me, plus we had more pressing issues to deal with. But this new information has changed things. Now there's a chance Lola made up the whole story to protect her parents and I need to confirm if this is true.

'Thanks, this is good stuff,' I tell Golding. 'Anything else?'

'As I said, my team is still going through the diary, and Lola's laptop is also being looked over by digital forensics. There is one other thing worth mentioning for now, though.'

'Yes?'

'In her diary, Lola refers to the mums at school giving her the cold shoulder since around the second week of the autumn term, so around September time onwards.'

'Yes, I'm aware of that.'

'But were you aware it was because she was worried it was because they knew she'd kissed Damien Radcliffe?'

'Christ alive.'

Simone said Bianca's husband was a flirt, Bianca admitted it herself, but it seems he took things a lot further than that. But more's the question – did Bianca know?

'Any idea if they slept together?'

'No, no mention of that.'

'Right. Is that it then?'

'For now. Like I said, I think you need to read it.'

'I will. Keep it under seal and I'll get to it later.'

I hang up, my stomach stirring. Not because it's craving my yet untouched pastry, but because finally we have something. Something solid that could potentially help us catch the monster who killed Lola.

Chapter Fourteen

Lola

Before
December 2022

'Are you sure you're OK to watch Luca? It's a big ask, on top of minding your girls. I feel bad.'

I've not long arrived at Simone and Liam's house. It's a Friday night in early December, and Clarissa is having a festive gathering at her place. Girls only. After what happened with Bianca at school, I was in two minds whether to accept Clarissa's invitation, but Simone pointed out that Bianca's been OK with me since, and that I shouldn't let her rule my life or spoil my chances of having fun.

'Besides, I need you there,' she'd said as we sat having coffee at mine not long after Clarissa had sent the invite on the WhatsApp group chat. 'You know how overbearing they can be, but you're my partner in crime, and we need to stick together.'

When she said this, it made me feel special, and I couldn't say no. I love spending time with Simone. She's so kind and warm, but she also has a cracking sense of humour when it's just us, and we're not being overpowered by the others in the group. There's a certain fragility about her too, one that I recognise in myself. I often wonder if there's something in her past she's hiding, something painful. But I don't want to pry in case she takes offence and I ruin what we have. I wouldn't want her to put me on the spot about my background, so what gives me the right to ask the same of her? Anyway, to be honest, it's really only Bianca who I feel the most uncomfortable around. Clarissa's not so bad on her own but the two of them together are a formidable pair. I know Bianca hates my guts. Goodness knows what she'd think if she knew I'd been texting her husband. He messaged me a couple of days after our chat with Miss Day; asked me if I got anything out of Luca about his fight with Summer. He said Summer hadn't opened up to him, but that he suspected she'd done something to rile Luca. I was in two minds about whether to tell him the truth, but in the end, I did. After pressing send, I felt so anxious, worried he might take offence and accuse me of making up horrid lies about his daughter to protect my son. But he didn't. He was so nice about it. Said how sorry he was, and that he hoped Luca was OK. He also assured me that this would never happen again.

Lately, I've caught myself thinking about him a lot. His mellow voice, his kind eyes, the way his lips had brushed my earlobe outside Miss Day's classroom. I know I shouldn't have such wicked thoughts, and that I need to banish him from my mind, but I can't seem to help myself. I've not felt this way about anyone in a long time. I just hope no one picks up on the chemistry between us. Simone included. She's the only one of the group who hangs out regularly at mine for coffee or a glass of wine. The one occasion I had them all over it ended up being the most humiliating experience. One I vowed never to repeat. It was a couple of weeks before Luca and Summer had their spat. I'd basically been invited to all their houses by then, and I wanted to return the gesture, even though I couldn't help feeling embarrassed by how tiny my place was, especially compared with Clarissa's and Bianca's massive houses.

'Well, isn't this just delightful,' Clarissa had said. 'Reminds me of my student flat at uni.' There was nothing obviously wrong in what she'd said, and her tone had been affable enough, but to me it sounded patronising, and not for the first time it made me feel like a fish out of water. That I didn't quite fit into their middle-class yummy mummy group. As usual, Bianca had been her passive aggressive self, agreeing that my flat was charming but that she couldn't imagine keeping her girls under control in such a confined space and that it was such a shame Luca missed out on a garden to kick a ball around in, as all boys yearn to do. Mum was there, and I had to make wide eyes to stop her from giving Bianca an earful. I could see she was on the brink of erupting. She has my grandmother's fiery Spanish temperament. It's why I didn't tell Mum about what happened in the playground between Luca and Summer. I ended up bribing Luca to keep quiet about that too, as guilty as my actions made me feel, promising him McDonald's once a month if he kept 'our special little secret' from Nana.

Ordinarily, I'd have asked Mum and Dad to babysit this evening, but Mum's down with a horrendous cold, poor thing, and Dad's looking after her. He said he'd still be able to watch Luca but, for one, I didn't want to overtax him and secondly, the last thing I need is Luca catching Mum's germs and getting ill before Christmas.

Anyhow, when I mentioned to Simone that I'd be hard-pressed to make Clarissa's Christmas soiree she said she was sure Liam wouldn't mind watching Luca with their girls.

'Are you kidding?' Liam gives me an astonished look when I suggest it might be too much for him to handle Luca on top of his girls. 'For once I won't be outnumbered in this house!' He grins at Luca, who's still clutching my hand and looking slightly apprehensive. He's never had a sleepover before, aside from staying at Mum and Dad's, and so I can't blame him for being a little anxious, despite getting on well with Penny and Jess. Both of them are currently engrossed in *Beauty and the Beast*.

'You see what I have to put up with, little man?' Liam points to the television then gives Luca a playful punch on his shoulder. 'But maybe you and I can turn the tables, introduce the girls to *Star Wars* or something? You like *Star Wars*?'

Luca nods eagerly.

I smile, grateful to Liam for his kindness.

'Great! Who's your favourite character?'

Luca's eyes light up. 'Luke Skywalker,' he says, his voice animated. 'I have his lightsaber.'

'Well, what do you know, he's my favourite too!'

'Argh, Daddy, *Star Wars*!' Penny groans.

'Boring!' Jess backs her big sister up.

Simone rolls her eyes. Then grins. 'Look what you started now.' She leans over and whispers in my ear. 'He's in his element. Liam always wanted a boy and now he gets to live that dream for the night.'

'Heard that,' Liam says. He winks. 'And by the way, I'm all for trying for another one.' He pulls Simone close, plants a kiss on her cheek, at which point she blushes and pushes him away, even though I can tell she loves it when he does that. Truth is, she's as besotted with Liam, ten years on, as he is with her. Consummate soulmates, a concept I know is often met with cynicism. But not by me. Because I found my soulmate once. Someone I totally and utterly connected with. Only I went and lost him.

'You must be joking, that ship has sailed!' Simone says. 'Back off, mister!' Just then, she checks her phone. 'Uber's a minute away.' She turns to me. 'We'd better go – see you lot later.' She kisses Liam on the lips. 'Good luck, darling.'

Liam looks down at Luca and high-fives him. 'I don't need any luck, I've got my wingman here.'

At this, Luca grins from ear to ear and immediately lets go of my hand and tells me I am free to leave. 'Have a nice time, Mummy, don't get too drunk.'

We all burst into fits of laughter. The girls pause their film and kiss Simone goodbye.

'You too, Mummy, have a nice time.'

'I will, my darlings.' Simone kisses them in turn. 'Be good for Daddy.'

Simone and I head out, grabbing the wine and flowers we bought earlier for Clarissa on the way. Before long, we're in the cab heading to her house.

'It's really good of Liam to have Luca,' I say, turning to Simone.

Simone smiles. 'Yeah, he's so good with kids. It's one of the reasons I knew he was the one.' She grins. 'Apart from him being a dreamy doctor, of course.'

I chuckle. 'Yeah, that helps.'

'I've always wanted a family. And I was upfront with Liam from the start about that. Thankfully, he wanted the same. I saw how brilliant he was with my sister's kids, and I knew he'd make a great dad. I think when your parents bicker a lot when you're a kid, which was the case with Liam's mum and dad, it can go one of two ways. It can either put you off marriage and kids for life, or make you determined to do things differently. Lucky for me, Liam chose the latter. As did his sister, Jen.' Just then, Simone stops talking. A look of alarm sweeping across her face. 'Shit, sorry, I'm being so tactless. You lost the love of your life before he even had a chance to be a dad. What was I thinking!'

I reach over and take her hand in mine. Clasp it tightly. 'Really, it's fine. You can't tiptoe around my feelings. What happened to me was crap, but I can't begrudge a friend for finding happiness. And I *am* happy for you.'

Simone smiles. Squeezes my hand back. 'Thank you. I hope you find love again.'

In an ideal world, I wish that too. But Simone doesn't know the truth. Doesn't know I've been lying to her from the start. It's bad enough that I've lied to her, someone who I've gradually come to regard as my best friend. But having to lie to someone I love romantically, who I'd want to spend the rest of my life with – that would be torture. As would their rejecting me if I chose to tell them the truth.

So, I simply smile at her and say, 'Yes, I hope so too.'

It's a twenty-minute drive to Clarissa's. Hidden away within an impressive gated estate, I always feel out of place coming here. It's not like I was brought up in poverty. Mum and Dad worked hard and we lived in a pleasant but average three-bed semi-detached in Durham with a reasonably sized garden. It did us fine, the neighbours were nice, and we were happy. But it's like entering a whole other world visiting Clarissa's estate, and, although I love my flat, coming here only illustrates the disparity between her world and mine. Still, I tell myself to try and enjoy myself this evening. I'm normally so restrained where alcohol's concerned, but with Luca staying over at Simone's tonight I might go a bit wild, if that's what it takes to relax me and have fun. Especially in Bianca's presence.

Our cabbie has a quick word with the porter via the intercom, at which point the barrier opens to let us through, and in no time at all we're standing outside Clarissa's front door. Simone presses the bell. As we wait, freezing our arses off because it's so damned cold, I hear a cacophony of laughter, voices and music coming from inside. Clearly, the party is already under way and I give Simone a look as if to say as much.

'Don't worry,' she says. 'It'll be fun. Just relax. Have a drink, take an interest in their lives, pander to them. They love that. Bianca especially. It's what she craves. Attention. Being made to feel special. *Loved.*'

I roll my eyes. 'It's exhausting, though, isn't it? Pandering to them, I mean. Try as I might, I don't ever feel completely relaxed in their company. Her, especially. I can be myself around you. With them, I feel like I'm walking on eggshells, always trying to think up something to say. Even worse, wondering if it's the right thing to say.'

Simone's about to respond when the door opens. 'Darlings! Where the fuck have you both been? We're already got through a bottle of Bolly, come on in!'

Clarissa ushers us inside into the warmth of her hallway, Kylie blaring in the background, then bear-hugs us both before taking our jackets and depositing them in her massive built-in coat closet. She eyes us up and down. I'm wearing my customary jeans teamed with a red long sleeve satin blouse, while Simone's in a shimmery green one-shoulder dress cut to mid-thigh. She has a stunning figure, more like she's in her late twenties than approaching forty. But I also know that, unlike the others, she takes care of herself: exercises religiously, eats the right foods, and doesn't overdo things where the booze is concerned. It's not just down to genes, but hard work.

'Wow, looking hot, ladies, too fucking hot for my liking,' Clarissa says. 'You trying to show us fatties up?' She says this playfully, but there's a palpable hint of bitterness veiling her comment, while I'm sure I'm not imagining the look of envy in her eyes.

And suddenly I wonder if coming here tonight was such a good idea after all.

Chapter Fifteen

Detective Inspector John Banner

Tuesday, 19th December 2023

'I'm sorry for the mess, Inspector. What with the horrendous news about Lola, I've not had the time or the will to clean and tidy the house. With two kids, you can imagine that by the end of the weekend it's in something of a state.'

I'm sitting across from Joy Grainger in her living room. Wild is working another case, so I'm flying solo today. Unlike Clarissa's and Bianca's, Joy's home, where she lives with her two children and husband, Gavin, is a modest three-bed semi-detached in New Malden, similar in size and layout to my and Jo's place, located on a quiet road just off the main busy high street. On the drive over, my mind was still buzzing with Lola's shocking disclosure in her diary that she kissed Damien Radcliffe. I now have something concrete from Lola's own thoughts to put to the other mothers in her group in terms of the hostile treatment they'd recently been giving her. I just hope Joy will be more forthcoming than Clarissa and Bianca were yesterday. She certainly seems more agreeable in nature, and now I have this added leverage to help prise the truth from her.

'Nothing to apologise for,' I say. 'I have a young son of my own, so I can completely empathise.'

Joy smiles. 'Thank you.'

'No problem. And thank you for agreeing to speak with me. I hope I'm not keeping you from work.'

She shakes her head. 'Not at all. I work from home. Gavin – my husband – and I, have our own events planning business. He's out visiting a wedding venue at the moment.'

Joy is around five feet nine and not a small lady from any angle. Standing alongside her, I can imagine she must have dwarfed Lola's slender five feet-four frame.

'Sounds like a fun job.'

'Yes, I love it, and it gives me flexibility with the kids. But it does mean I sit on my butt for much of the day and don't do nearly enough exercise. Which isn't good news, because I love my food too much. My late mother's family recipe for fried beef and pineapple flan especially.' She grins. 'Mum was Cuban. Not good for the cholesterol, I know!'

I smile and murmur my agreement, while thinking I also need to cut down on the chocolate bars. Easier said than done in a job where a quick sugar hit is often all I have time for.

'Gavin used to work in advertising,' she goes on, 'and his hours were pretty long, so it's nice the kids now get to see us both, plus we can share the load.' She pauses. Then says, 'So, are you any closer to finding out who murdered poor Lola?' All of a sudden, there's a sad look in her eye. 'I can still scarcely believe it. It feels so odd saying those words out loud.'

I nod. 'We're working on it.' Then I explain why I believe Lola's murder wasn't random, but rather, premeditated, on account of the texts both Simone and Elisa received, and which we now know Lola can't have sent. On hearing this, Joy appears horrified. 'You were good friends with Lola, I take it?' I then ask.

She nods. 'Yes, I'd like to think so. We're quite a close-knit bunch at school, as you might have heard. Lola only came on the scene in September of last year, but she fitted right in.'

'She did? Despite her being considerably younger, and a single mum?'

Joy frowns. Fidgets in her seat. 'Yes, why? Have you heard otherwise?'

'Lola's mother gave me the impression that Lola was desperate to fit in, but that she was always made to feel like the odd one out. More so by certain people in your group. I also spoke with Simone Loxley. She said there's been a fair amount of tension at the school gates recently.'

Joy starts fiddling with her wedding band. 'Tension, how do you mean?'

'Like your little group had been giving Lola the cold shoulder. Perhaps it's something that's been brewing for a while, since Lola's son pushed Summer Radcliffe to the ground in the playground in November of last year?'

'You know about that?'

I nod. 'Yes. We also know that Lola sent Simone a text message soon after leaving the party on Friday night saying the evening had been a nightmare and that she believed you all hated her.'

Joy looks aghast. 'No! She did? Why on earth would she say that?'

'That's what I'd like to find out, Joy. Were you aware that Lola kept a diary?'

She shakes her head nervously, her eyes suddenly anxious. 'No.'

'In a recent entry she talked about being given the silent treatment by all of you in the playground, and at class events. Thereby corroborating what Simone told me yesterday.'

Joy shakes her head again, now looking markedly flustered. 'I really don't know what Lola was talking about, or Simone. We were always nothing but nice to Lola. I mean, apart from Bianca's minor spat with Lola over Luca and Summer's fight when there was some fleeting tension, I'll admit, we all got on like a house on fire. We always included Lola in things: dinners, spa days, the lot.'

Joy's lying. But why? Because she herself has something to hide? Or because she's been told to keep to the same story by Clarissa and Bianca, who clearly rule the roost in the clique these women have going on? Maybe both? It's clear I need to break one of the group, though, and having learned from Simone that Deidre's a barrister and as tough as old boots, instinct tells me Joy is my best bet.

'So you weren't aware that Lola and Damien Radcliffe had kissed?'

Joy squirms in her seat. The guilt is written all over her face. Her silence telling.

I go on. 'Lola mentions kissing Bianca's husband in her diary. Since diaries are a record of people's innermost thoughts, warts and all, I'm inclined to think she was telling the truth. So, let's start again: has there been some animosity in the playground recently, and did this animosity perhaps come to a head on Friday night at the Christmas party?'

Joy gives me an incredulous look. 'Are you trying to imply that one of us had something to do with Lola's murder because of some silly playground squabble or romantic dalliance?'

I remain poker-faced. 'You tell me. People have been murdered over a lot less.'

Joy briefly looks away, still looking decidedly uncomfortable. 'OK, Bianca's going to kill me if she finds out I told you this, but yes, it's true, she did find out Lola kissed Damien.'

Bingo.

'How?'

'Back in September of this year, she received an anonymous text message.'

I lean forward. My curiosity piqued. 'What did it say?'

'It said, "*She's not to be trusted.*" Attached was a photo of Lola and Damien kissing in Canbury Gardens, by the river. It was sent from an unregistered phone, because when she tried calling the number back, the line was dead, and neither could she trace the call.'

'I'm guessing Bianca told you all immediately?'

'Yes. She created a separate WhatsApp group, circulating the photo to everyone. Well, everyone bar Simone.'

'Why not Simone?'

'Because she knew how close Simone and Lola were and didn't want it getting back to Lola.'

'Why wouldn't she want it getting back?'

Joy hesitates.

'Why?' I say sternly.

'Because she wanted to punish Lola. By giving her the silent treatment. She wanted to make Lola suffer, in not knowing what she'd done wrong. Tormenting her. Blanking her from the group.'

It's like *Mean Girls* for the over-40s.

'Did Bianca confront her husband about the kiss, do you know?'

'Yes, of course. She told him she'd take him to the cleaners, and humiliate him in front of his father, who he hero-worships, if he didn't put a stop to whatever was going on. He categorically denied sleeping with Lola, but who knows.'

'Was Damien really ill the night of the Christmas party?'

Joy shakes her head. 'No. Bianca couldn't bear seeing him and Lola in the same vicinity. There was a definite spark between them. We could all feel it. I'm certain Simone did too. I don't think Bianca trusted him, and she was jealous of Lola, because she was young and beautiful.'

'And having learned about that kiss, how did it make you feel towards Lola? Did it change your opinion of her?'

'I'll admit, I saw her in a different light after that. That the sweet innocent image she presented to the world was perhaps fake, and that she couldn't be trusted.'

'That seems a bit harsh. After all, it takes two to tango and I hear the Radcliffe's marriage isn't a bed of roses.'

Joy shrugs. 'So, what marriage is? It didn't give Lola the right to seduce someone else's husband. They have kids. It was wrong, wicked in fact! We felt sorry for Lola after hearing what happened to Luca's father, and we welcomed her into our group. But that's how she repaid us. By betraying us. Betraying our trust.'

I study Joy for a moment. See the fire in her eyes. A look of anger. I feel certain there's something else bothering her. 'Repaid you? We were talking about Bianca just now. Did Lola upset you personally in some way?'

A flash of alarm sweeps across Joy's face. 'What? No, of course not. I was just upset for Bianca, that's all. She's been a good friend to us all for the last three years since our older ones started in Reception, so of course it affected me personally. As it did Clarissa and Dee.'

'I see. So, how were things on Friday night? Tense, I'm guessing?'

She nods meekly. 'Yes, I won't lie, they were tense. We'd reserved our table back in the summer, before Bianca received the photo of Damien and Lola kissing. Things were inevitably strained. None of us talked to Lola, and it was clear she was disappointed Damien didn't show. I'm amazed she stayed that long to be honest. I noticed her chatting to some other parents in Reception class for a bit, before we all sat down to dinner and everyone was mingling in the bar. Obviously I don't know the ins and outs, but I'm sure Lola must have been wondering why Damien had suddenly gone all cold on her. Bianca told him no more texts or communication with Lola whatsoever.'

'But there wasn't some big falling out as such? No major scene?'

'No, Bianca's too clever to make a scene in a public place. Just serious silent treatment like I said, and some subtle digs by Clarissa and Bianca, to the point that I don't think Lola could take much more. When she suddenly took off, when we were all on the dance floor, Dee, Stephen and I called after her, just because we felt a bit guilty – she looked like she was on the verge of tears – but she didn't turn back.' She sighs. 'I feel so bad now, and I regret not chasing after her. I should have done more. But I'd had too much to drink, and then Bianca called after us, told us to let her be, and that she wasn't worth it.'

'Did you leave before or after Bianca?'

'After. Same time as Clarissa. We were the last of the group to leave. Gavin was at home with the kids. Parties and discos aren't really his scene, and it saved on babysitters. We don't have parents to watch the kids, you see.'

I nod. 'OK, I think that's nearly everything for now. Just one more thing, did Lola ever mention being frightened of anyone?'

Joy frowns. 'No, how do you mean?'

'I mean someone from her past?'

She shakes her head. 'No. All I know is that Luca's father died in a car crash when she was pregnant and that she moved down south for a fresh start.'

'And did she ever show you a photo of Luca's father?'

'No, she didn't. To be honest, I always had the feeling there was more to that story than meets the eye. Like she was holding something back. We all felt it. Even Simone. You might want to ask Dee, though. She'd be your best bet.'

'Why's that?'

'I think Lola told Dee something in confidence once. Dee wouldn't tell us what it was all about; she's very loyal like that. Perhaps it comes from being a barrister and being bound by client privilege. Even after we found out about Lola kissing Damien, she wouldn't tell us what they discussed. Despite her being mad with Lola.'

'When was this?'

'I seem to recall it was back in February of this year. When we were all over at Dee's place. So well before Bianca found out about Lola and Damien. I remember Bianca made some sarcastic comment about Lola's flat not long after, while we were having coffee in town, and Dee shot her down when Lola went up to the counter to get more drinks. Told her she had no idea what Lola had been through, that she'd had it tougher than most, something Bianca didn't know the meaning of, and that Bianca needed to stop being such a bitch. Bianca was startled. We all were. But it made me wonder if it was something to do with Lola's past, and what happened to Luca's father.'

Chapter Sixteen

Lola

Before
December 2022

HERETOCHAT.ORG
Chat Now in confidence. We're here for each other

Tracy: Hey, how did the dinner party go?

Lola: Fine. Sort of. Well, actually it was a bit uncomfortable.

Tracy: How so? Not Bianca again? Thought you two had made up.

Lola: No, not her. Well, not really. I mean, it was nothing awful she said to me in particular. As expected, everyone was pretty tipsy when Simone and I arrived.

Tracy: That's nothing new! They're a bunch of lushes, right?

Lola: Haha. True. I even got a bit pissed myself.

Tracy: Oh God, you didn't let anything slip, did you?

Lola: Not that I know of. I'm sure I'd have heard from someone by now if I had. Simone would definitely have said something.

Tracy: Phew. So how was it uncomfortable?

Lola: Clarissa got really wasted, like completely off her face. It was so unlike her. I mean, she likes a drink, but normally she's in control. But it was obvious something had happened to upset her, and that she was using drink as a crutch.

Tracy: Did anyone get to the bottom of it? Ask her if anything in particular was up?

Lola: No, no one asked her directly. But then, when I left the table to use the loo, I overheard Bianca and Clarissa chatting, and I couldn't believe what I heard. It really shocked me.

Tracy: What was it? Actually, scrap that. You don't have to tell me, I'm here to talk through your problems, not other people's.

Lola: Yeah, I know I shouldn't be discussing other people's private stuff. It's just that, well, it really touched a nerve. Got me thinking. Particularly given all the stuff that's been in the newspapers recently.

Tracy: What, you mean about the Campus Prowler?

Lola: Yep.

Tracy: OK. If it makes you feel better to tell me, then do. You know what we discuss here is in complete confidence. I know I can tell you anything. For Christ's sake, you know all about my friend Phil and his affair, not to mention my alcoholic headmaster. You'd never tell anyone about those things, would you?

Lola: Course not! How could you even think that?

Tracy: I don't, I trust you. And you can trust me with anything you say.

Lola: I know that. OK, so we'd all sat down to dinner…

Chapter Seventeen

Lola

Before
December 2022

'God, I'm so glad you made this evening a girls only night, Clarissa, it's way more fun! Shall I go grab us another bottle?'

It's just gone 8:30 p.m. and we're all seated around Clarissa's stunning bespoke dining table. As we all sat down, she gushed about how she and Robert had bought it from Hadley Rose and that it was made from carefully selected oak timbers. I hadn't dared mention I'd never heard of Hadley Rose and that my kitchen table where Luca and I eat all our meals was IKEA's finest. I can't deny it's not beautiful, though, like something out of *Homes and Garden* magazine. Not that I've ever read *Homes and Garden*, but I've seen it on the stand in the newsagents and can imagine a lot of the homes in there are like Clarissa's, with posh custom-made furniture, 56-inch TVs and immaculately maintained gardens. I wish more than anything that Luca had a garden to run around in, but the park's not far away and we have the river to look out on, so it's not all bad. He can also go round to Mum and Dad's any time he pleases, and their garden is more than adequate for his needs.

After demolishing two more bottles of Bollinger between us in Clarissa's massive kitchen-diner, she ushered us through to the dining room, and shortly afterwards served up a delicious first course of smoked salmon tartare with organic walnut bread she bought from some specialist deli. Clarissa explained that it's rare they eat in the dining room as a family except for special occasions like Christmas or New Year, so it was something of a treat to be entertaining us in here tonight. The walls are adorned with eye-catching pieces of modern art, a crystal drop chandelier hovering above us, adding to the grandiose feel of the room. She's even brought out the best china and silverware, which made me laugh inside on account of the fact that my crockery is from Sainsbury's, my cutlery Lidl's finest. Not for the first time, sitting here I feel a huge disparity between Clarissa and me, a chasm I feel certain I'll never be able to bridge. And I'm not just talking about our material differences. It's the fact that we have nothing in common, period. Not even politically, despite her professing to vote Labour. The hypocrisy of champagne socialists like her and Bianca astounds me, but I keep tight-lipped because I don't want to get into an argument. It's simply not worth it.

'Oh, yes, darling, do grab another bottle of the Chablis, and the Barolo – I can see Dee will need some more red – you know where it is!' Clarissa says in response to Bianca's offer to fetch more wine. Bianca gets up from her seat – or more like staggers – then makes for the door, stumbling slightly as she does. She's so pissed. Everyone is, save for me and Simone. We've been taking it easier than the rest of the crew, interspersing glasses of water with our wine in a bid to avoid a raging hangover tomorrow. I'm conscious that I have to pick Luca up in the morning from Simone's place, then take him for a swimming lesson at our local leisure centre, and I can't bear to feel like death warmed up when I do. The noise in there can be deafening, the humidity intense and far from ideal when you've had too much to drink the night before.

'That duck was delightful, you must give me the recipe,' Dee says, before chucking back her fourth glass of red. I didn't mean to keep tabs on her as such, but I've always liked watching people. Observing their habits. Not in a creepy way, I just find it interesting. I think perhaps it harks back to my childhood. I always accompanied my parents to their friends' houses for dinner parties and so on. I'd sit quietly at the table while the adults talked. Only speaking when spoken to. Not having a sibling meant there were no distractions, and it forced me to behave and sit still. Like a mini adult. Their friends used to comment on me being the perfect child, but in truth, I had nothing better to do than sit there, listen and observe. Much of the time I was bored stiff. Itching to go home. Tracy says she can tell I'm a good listener, even though we've never met. She is too. It's why we get on so well, I guess. We're very alike, being only children, and we understand each other.

'Since when do you cook or follow a recipe, Dee?' Joy playfully prods Dee in the side, before throwing back her own wine.

Dee cuts Joy an unimpressed look. 'And what's that supposed to mean?'

'What she means is, Steve does all the cooking in your house, and you know it. So, it's him Clarissa should be passing the recipe on to, you crafty bitch.' Bianca has suddenly appeared with another bottle of white and red. I look at my glass, virtually untouched after two and a bit glasses of fizz, which is more than I usually drink these days. I've never been good with wine, and I think I might vomit if I touch another drop. So much for going wild this evening, but it's probably for the best. I might say something I regret.

'Yeah, fair point,' Dee chuckles, apparently not in the least bit offended at having been called a crafty bitch by Bianca. It's normal repartee between these women, something I'm not sure I'll ever get used to. They're so loud, so in your face, and it's not me at all. I think that's why Simone and I clicked. Like me, she's quiet, and I don't think I've ever heard her swear. Sometimes it's hard to believe she ever became friends with these women, they seem so different.

'At least Steve's good for something, I guess,' Dee sulks.

All of a sudden, there's an uneasy silence as Bianca sets the wine down on the table. We all eye each other warily, no one knowing quite what to say in response to Dee's remark. It's not like we all haven't noticed the tension between her and Stephen. I noticed it the first day I met them in the playground. But because she's never openly raised the issue of them having problems, no one's ventured to say anything. At least, not when I've been around. She also strikes me as being a very practical person, not the emotional type who likes to air her problems and cry on people's shoulders, but rather, someone who prefers to keep her troubles buttoned up inside. Perhaps that's what makes her a successful criminal barrister. In her line of work, dealing with all kinds of horrible cases, I can imagine you'd go insane if you allowed yourself to get emotionally attached.

'It's OK, you don't have to go all silent on me,' Dee says bluntly, looking at each of us in turn. 'Steve and I are going through a rough patch, as I'm sure you've all picked up on. Here, pass the Barolo, B.' Bianca hands the wine to Dee who pours herself another full glass of red. I know she's out at client events at least three times a week. Small wonder she has such a high alcohol tolerance. Perhaps it's also why her marriage is on shaky ground.

'Oh, honey,' Simone says, 'I just think you guys need to spend some quality time alone. You have to admit you're out at work dos an awful lot. Liam and I always try to carve out time for each other. I'm not talking about going out necessarily, that's not easy with kids, but when they're in bed, ask each other about your days, watch a movie or something. Do you ever do that?'

'Schmoozing with clients comes with my job, Simi, I don't have a fucking choice. It's how we afford the mortgage and family holidays.'

'That's what Damien tells me,' Bianca rolls her eyes, while I feel a shiver of excitement at the mention of her husband's name. I tell myself to snap out of it. Focus on Dee. 'Always out at some client function or other. I swear he spends more time networking than actually working. Can't complain, though, it's paid for Courchevel next month. Can't fucking wait.'

'I get it, Dee,' Simone says softly, ignoring Bianca, who's somehow managed to make the conversation about her. 'But he's a man, and maybe, what with you being the main breadwinner, he sometimes feels a bit, well…'

'Insecure, neglected?' Joy chips in.

'Well, yes,' Simone says.

'Simi and Joy may have a point,' Clarissa says, waving her wine glass around precariously. 'I mean, look at them, for God's sake. They both have bloody perfect marriages!'

'I think you're exaggerating!' Joy says. Simone smiles shyly.

'I'm not. It's bloody sickening,' Clarissa goes on, before banging her wine glass back down on the table. She's seriously drunk, even more so than Bianca, in fact, which is saying something. I don't think I've ever seen her this pissed or loud.

'Jeez, thanks, Clarissa,' Joy looks around the table grinning.

'Clarissa's bang on,' Bianca says. 'Joy and Gav, I mean, you guys are so similar, you're like the left arm to his right. Not many couples could work in business together, and from home, where there's no escape, but you've clearly got it sussed.'

Joy shrugs. 'What can I say, we're both creative. He's super organised and I've always loved a good party. Event planning seemed like a no brainer. He bugs the hell out of me sometimes, I won't lie, but I wouldn't want to work with anyone else.'

'You see!' Bianca then turns to Simone. Jabs her finger at her. 'And you, you especially make me want to vomit, with your perfect dishy doctor. I mean, why can't you act like a proper sex-starved middle-aged couple who've been together far too long and hate each other's guts, as opposed to acting like you're horny as hell on honeymoon the whole fucking time. Does anything about Liam get on your nerves? I could write a whole page of A4 when it comes to the stuff Damien does that gets on my tits.'

'Amen to that!' Dee and Clarissa say in unison.

I glance at Simone and instantly feel for her seeing the uncomfortable look on her face. I'm on the brink of speaking up and telling them she's just being kind and they should stop giving her a hard time, when Dee says bluntly, 'Steve's having an affair.'

Silence. Thirty seconds of it. An awkward toe-curling hush.

'For fuck's sake, someone say something,' Dee bawls, knocking back more wine.

'Oh, Jesus, Dee, are you sure?' Joy places her hand over Dee's.

Dee breaks free from Joy's grasp, then runs her hand through her hair. 'Yes, I'm sure. I saw the texts. He was in the shower when it buzzed and I couldn't resist.'

'Fucking bastard,' Bianca scowls. 'I'd fucking rip Damien's heart out and cook it in on a spit if I caught him cheating.' She gives me a brief, yet hard look, and I feel my face flush. Thankfully, no one but Simone seems to notice. I guess they're all too shocked by Dee's news. The thing is, even though her and Steve appeared to be having problems, Steve is the last person you'd think would cheat. Short, balding, a bit boring if I'm being honest, in truth I'd have pinned my money on Dee being the one to stray, not him. I mean, she's super intelligent, attractive, has a wicked sense of humour; I can imagine she'd have her pick of men in the City to embark on an illicit affair with.

'Who is she, do you know?' Joy asks.

Dee shakes her head. 'I don't know much. Only that her name is Anna. Could be a false name, of course. And before you ask, there's no chance they're just friends. Because although I didn't see her face, I did see her boobs and crotch. Even worse, she wasn't a heifer, she was bloody thin. No love handles or stretch marks in sight.'

Clarissa tilts her head. 'No, don't know any Annas. Know some Annes, but no Annas. Did you note down the number? Maybe she's a hooker? I can't think why else she'd be screwing Steve, no offence.'

'That did occur to me, and yes I did screenshot the number.'

'Called it yet?' Joy asks.

'Nope.'

'Why the hell not?' Bianca says.

'Because it's too fucking humiliating, that's why.'

Tears are now streaming down Dee's cheeks, a sight I never thought I'd witness, only because she always acts so tough. Joy immediately pulls Dee's head to her shoulder and softly strokes her hair.

'I tell you, all men are absolute pigs,' Clarissa says. 'Want me to call her? I'll fucking do it now!'

'No!' Dee says. 'I'm going to confront him first.'

'When?' I ask. It's the first word I've uttered in ages.

Everyone looks at me. 'Oh, she speaks – I almost forgot you were here!' Clarissa chuckles. Bianca laughs too.

'Clarissa!' Simone scolds, as I feel my eyes well up. It's stupid, really. I mean, I'm a grown woman, I shouldn't get upset. But the way she just talked down to me, it made me feel about three feet tall.

'Sorry, angel,' Clarissa says to Simone. She looks at me. 'Sorry, Lola, I'm a bit pissed, not myself, take no notice. No offence meant.' I catch Bianca giving Clarissa a concerned look. Their eyes settle on one another a fraction longer than necessary, an almost knowing look, and it makes me wonder if there's something Clarissa's not telling us. Sure, I've seen her pissed before, but today she's acting off the rails.

'To answer your question, Lola,' Dee says, 'after Christmas.'

'After Christmas!' Joy exclaims. 'That's another three weeks or so.'

'Yes, I'm aware of that.' Dee rolls her eyes. 'But I can't spoil things for the kids.'

'But won't they already be spoiled? I mean, it must be hard to act normally around Steve,' I say.

'It is. Every time I see him, I want to slap his face. Better still, grab his tiny scrotum and squeeze it so tight he passes out with pain.' At this, we all can't help but giggle. It makes Dee chuckle too.

'And lying next to him in bed, well, it's a wonder he wakes up alive. It's bad enough having had to live with his snoring all these years, I can't tell you how tempted I am to put a stop to it permanently while he's having his dirty dreams.'

'So tell him, you silly bint,' Bianca says. 'There's no way in hell I'd be able to keep it from Damien. Not for one bloody second.'

That, I can believe.

'I can't. If he tells me he's in love with her, then I won't be able to get through Christmas, period. At least this way, in blind ignorance, I can force myself to do so by drinking my way through our wine rack.'

'A-fucking-men to that!' Clarissa hoists her glass up unsteadily again.

'Darling, don't you think you need to slow down?' Bianca leans in towards Clarissa.

Clarissa turns her head, then raises her eyebrow. 'That's a bit rich coming from a lush like you.'

Bianca doesn't take offence. 'Come on, let's go get that lovely lemon tart you made.' She looks around the table. 'We'd all like some, wouldn't we?'

Everyone nods. 'Absolutely,' Simone smiles.

Bianca helps Clarissa up. 'I'm fine, I'm not some old granny!' Clarissa barks crossly.

Her out-of-sorts behaviour makes me wonder if she and Robert are having problems too. I've only met him twice. Once at a school assembly, the other time at half-term drinks Clarissa organised. He seemed OK, but a bit of a show-off. He spent most of the time talking about his recent business trips to China and New York, and how he couldn't understand why anyone would choose to fly economy. I was desperate to point out that for the majority of people this wasn't a choice, but in the end I held my tongue, as I thought it best not to get on his wrong side. I'm not sure his kids see a lot of him either and I can't help wondering if Clarissa busies herself with class repping and the PTA because she barely sees her husband and it helps fill the time. They met through a mutual friend, apparently, marrying four years later, at which point she stepped back from a high-paid job in PR to become a full-time mum.

We watch in awkward silence as Bianca guides Clarissa out of the room.

Finally, once it's clear they're in the kitchen, only because we can vaguely make out Clarissa chuntering away, Dee speaks up. 'Jesus, what's that all about. Something's up with Clarissa, that's for sure. I mean, I've seen her pissed a hundred times before, but always in a jolly way. She seems so melancholy.'

'Agreed,' Joy says. 'I'm worried about her.'

'Me too,' Simone says. 'I'm sure B will get to the bottom of it. She's closest to Clarissa.'

I'm suddenly bursting for the loo. I've sort of needed to go for ages, but now I can't wait any longer, even though

I realise it's bad timing, what with Bianca and Clarissa possibly having a heart-to-heart in the kitchen.

'I need the ladies,' I announce. 'I'll go upstairs; where is it again?'

'First door on the left,' Joy says.

I say thanks, then get up and leave the room. You have to pass the kitchen door to reach the stairs, and, just as I do, I'm conscious of whispering coming from inside. It's wrong of me, I know that, but I can't help myself. Maybe it's the champagne, the fact that I'm not entirely sober, but I instinctively put my ear to the door and try to listen to what's being said.

'I think you need to talk to someone, see a therapist,' Bianca says.

'No, I'm not one of those women, I'm not crazy. My sister went in for that kind of malarky and look where that got her.'

'Why would anyone think you're crazy? People don't see therapists because they're nuts. Well, not in the majority of cases. They see them because they're having a difficult time and they need to talk it through with a professional. Someone neutral, who you can trust to keep whatever you say to them confidential.'

I'm shocked. Shocked that Clarissa appears to be going through something so traumatic that Bianca is advising therapy. She always seems so in control, the mother hen of the group. Just like that, she feels more human, more approachable. More like me. And there was me thinking we had nothing in common.

'OK, maybe I will. But you cannot tell the others. It's so embarrassing.'

'Course I won't. But you know they'd understand. Why on earth should you be embarrassed?'

'Because it's a sign of weakness. They won't respect me in the same way.'

'That's fucking bullshit, but it's OK, don't worry, I won't say anything. But seriously, hon, if they knew about your little sister, what that arsehole did to her, they'd understand, really they would. Her suicide, her rape, that's too much for you to live with in silence – it's been seven years! They'd be heartbroken for you. Particularly now we know the bastard is most probably the same guy they've been talking about in the newspapers. I mean, that's what's triggered all this, isn't it? Understandably so.'

My heart jerks. Unable to believe what I just heard. I didn't even know Clarissa had a sister.

'Yes, and I know you're right. But still, I can't face rehashing it all.'

'I get it,' Bianca says in an uncharacteristically soothing tone. 'How's your mum?'

'Same. She'll never come out of that place. Dinah's suicide broke her. Broke Dad. It's another reason I can never seem to move on, despite so much time having passed. Despite her and Dinah clashing, she was always their favourite, being the baby – a "nice surprise" as Mum used to tell people.'

That place? Her mother's in a care home? Yet it sounds like more than a care home. Possibly some kind of psychiatric ward. Clarissa's always maintained her parents moved to the US after they retired, and that her mum suffers from severe arthritis, which is why they never come over to the UK. She's been lying all along, it seems, but on hearing what happened to her sister I can understand why. Plus, I'm the last person who should be judging people when it comes to lying. All of a sudden, I'm seeing Clarissa in a totally different light. Hiding a pain, a frailty, behind the cheery confident façade she presents to the world. Not for the first time, I feel a tug of guilt for having never gone to the police. But I still can't bring myself to, despite it being apparent that Luca shares the same DNA as the bastard who raped both me and Clarissa's sister. Plus countless other women. It's just not something I can bring myself to do. I simply can't put Luca through that, let alone myself. It would tear me apart, possibly scar him for life.

'I'm sorry, Clarissa,' I hear Bianca say.

'I just pray they catch that fucking bastard.'

'So the police think it's most probably the same guy they've been talking about in the news? This Campus Prowler?'

My pulse accelerates again.

'They're not sure. Dinah doesn't quite fit the bill. She wasn't an only child, for a start.'

'But she was a student at the time, had the same hair and eye colour as the others? Petite?'

'Yes. She was gorgeous too, not to mention a bloody perfectionist. The officer I spoke to said the other victims, at least the ones they're aware of, were like that.'

I can hardly believe I'm hearing this. The fact that Clarissa's sister and I may well have been raped by the same sicko. I'm so torn, on the one hand desperate to tell Clarissa about what happened to me, to empathise with her, but, on the other, fearing that if I do, it won't be long before word gets round and my parents will know I've been lying to them for the last five years or so.

The fact is, I can't trust Clarissa to keep her mouth shut, despite the pain she's clearly going through over her sister's death. For now, I need to act as if nothing's changed, even though keeping this a secret is going to be one of the hardest things I've ever done.

Chapter Eighteen

Detective Inspector John Banner

Tuesday, 19th December 2023

When we arrive at Deidre Walton's house, her husband, Stephen, explains that she's popped out to collect a prescription from the chemists, but will be back shortly. It's a little after 3 p.m. and I'm eager to hear what Deidre has to say following my interview with Joy. Her being convinced that Lola told Deidre something significant about her past has had me chomping at the bit ever since. Stephen guides us through to their living room and I take the opportunity to ask him what he thought of Lola.

'She was a lovely girl,' he says. 'I say *girl*, just because she was so much younger than the rest of us.' He smiles. 'But she was a great mother to young Luca, I could tell that from the first. Doted on the boy, that much was clear. It's so sad, poor lad. I still can't believe it. Why do bad things always happen to good people, Inspector?'

He has a bookish look about him, his tone nasally, yet not unfriendly.

'Believe me, if I had a pound coin for every time I've been asked that, I'd be very rich,' I say. 'It is a tragedy, but we're determined to find Lola's killer, I can promise you that.'

He gives me a sad smile. 'Good. Lola's death really cut Dee to the quick. It's why she's home this week. Couldn't face work, which I can tell you is most unlike Dee.'

'She works hard?'

Stephen nods vigorously. 'Harder than anyone I know. I mean, it helps that she's brilliant at her job, and very well-respected by both her clients and her colleagues. But it's not just that. She's built that way. A natural grafter. Determined.' He chuckles. 'The opposite of me.'

'And may I ask, what do you do?'

'Well, I used to be a recruitment consultant. Now I teach French and Spanish online.'

'I see, quite the change.'

'Yes, I guess. I loved languages at school, and my degree was in French, but I somehow fell into recruitment, did that for fifteen years. But a few years ago, when Dee got made partner and her hours went up, I jacked it in. For the kids' sakes, really. I appreciated my mother always being there after school for me, and I wanted the same for our kids.'

'And it works well?'

Stephen pauses, a flicker of apprehension in his eyes. 'Yes, for the most part. I'll be honest, we went through a bit of a tough time a year or so ago. I guess it was a hard adjustment for me to make relying on Dee to pay the mortgage, harder than I thought it would be, plus I barely saw her, but Dee and I are back on track now.'

Just as he says this, we hear the front door slam. 'Ah, that's Dee now. Dee!' he shouts out.

'Coming!'

A few seconds later, a tall, statuesque woman with striking scarlet hair appears in the doorway.

'Darling, this is Inspector Banner,' Stephen explains. 'He's investigating Lola's murder.'

Deidre strides forward as I rise from the sofa, then shakes my hand firmly. She has a strong grip, and makes direct eye contact with me at the same time. She has barrister written all over her, both in her demeanour and her authoritative tone of voice.

'It's good to meet you. How is the investigation progressing?' she asks.

'Slowly, but we've got some interesting leads to go on in the last twenty-four hours, so that's something.'

Deidre nods her head. 'That's good. In my profession, I know how slow criminal investigations can be, and I'll do anything to help. Anything at all that can help bring this animal to justice.'

'Thank you.' We all sit down. 'Can you tell me how Lola seemed to you last Friday night, at the Christmas party, I mean.' As with the other women, I go on to explain what we know so far, including the fact that Lola left suddenly, and appeared upset, along with her subsequent text message exchange with Simone.

Deidre sighs. 'I think Simone is overegging it a bit.'

Where have I heard that before? 'Really? Why's that? I've seen the message. It was obvious from what Lola told Simone that you all made her feel deeply uncomfortable, and that she regretted going along that evening. Less than an hour later, she's dead. Coincidence, or not?'

Deidre lets out a huff. 'Christ, you're not suggesting one of us had something to do with her murder, are you? Steve and I left well after Lola, in a cab, I might add.'

'Clearly there was a lot of animosity towards Lola, and I'm trying to find out why.'

Deidre gives a heavy sigh. 'We were all really pissed, and when that happens we can get a bit lairy. Christ, Bianca calls me a crafty bitch all the time, but I don't take offence, it's just how things are between us. No malice intended. I think Lola felt a bit overwhelmed because Simone wasn't there. They're close, and Simi's on the quiet side, like Lola was.'

'So there was no ill-feeling towards Lola?'

'What? No!'

'None whatsoever, despite her having kissed Damien Radcliffe. Something Bianca discovered courtesy of an anonymous text. Something she told the rest of you about.'

At this, Deidre's face drops. She glances at Stephen, who's now looking deeply uncomfortable himself. 'How would you know about that?'

'The kiss? Lola mentioned it in a diary she kept. A diary I'm guessing none of you ladies were aware of?'

Deidre shakes her head. 'No.'

'Joy Grainger, who I spoke with earlier, has also confirmed that after learning of her husband's kiss with Lola, Bianca notified you all immediately via a secret WhatsApp group Simone was purposely excluded from.'

I watch Deidre swallow hard, having realised she's been caught red-handed. The confident barrister facade I encountered when we first met swiftly crumbling.

'OK, I didn't want to say anything because it felt like I was betraying Bianca. We promised to keep it a secret.'

I lean forward. 'That's what Joy said. But Deidre, you're a criminal barrister, you're the first person who should be alive to the dangers of withholding potentially crucial information from the police, and the last person I'd expect to be guilty of that.'

'She was just being a good friend, Inspector,' Stephen interjects crossly.

Deidre looks at him tenderly. 'Thanks, love, but he's right, I should know better.' She pauses, as if working herself up to tell a difficult truth. 'It's true, our opinion of Lola changed when Bianca told us about her and Damien kissing.'

Same thing Joy said.

'Do you have any idea who could have sent Bianca that text?'

Deidre hesitates, then says, 'No, no idea. It could have been anyone.'

'Anyone from your group?'

'What? No! If any of us had seen Damien and Lola kissing, we would have told Bianca to her face, not sent her some creepy anonymous message. Poor B, she was devastated. I mean, granted, she can be hard work, but I have no doubt she loves Damien.'

'Loves Damien, or loves the lifestyle he provides?' I say provokingly.

'That's unfair,' Deidre says. 'I mean, yes, she loves the lifestyle, but if all she cared about was him keeping her in the lifestyle to which she's become accustomed, why should she give a toss if he messed around? He's never going to leave her, not with two young kids and a reputation to protect.' She shakes her head. 'No, she was hurt. Hurt badly. B can be a flirt herself, but she would never cheat on Damien.' Deidre cuts Stephen a sly look. 'Having said that, we women are the more loyal of the species. More able to resist acting on our urges.'

I can't help thinking this was a blatant dig. Did Stephen stray too? Looking at him, I find it hard to believe, but perhaps that's what he was referring to earlier when he mentioned they'd been through a rough patch.

'So, if you're saying she loves Damien, and that she knew he was messing around with Lola, surely this would give Bianca a clear motive to do Lola harm, wouldn't you say?'

Deidre makes wide eyes. 'What! No! Absolutely not!'

'It's true they never hit it off, isn't it? Her and Lola, I mean. I know about Luca pushing Bianca's daughter to the ground.'

'That was long forgotten and way before Bianca found out Lola kissed Damien. I even think she was starting to like her. But then she got that text message, with a photo of them snogging, and it broke her. She told us to stop talking to Lola, to blank her in the playground. In all honesty, I'm amazed Lola turned up on Friday. I can only assume it was because she was hoping to see Damien. I get the feeling she was a bit obsessed with him.'

'Why would you think that?'

Another guilty look. Then she says quietly, 'Damien told me. Maybe around six weeks ago.'

'He did?'

'Yes, one Friday afternoon at pick-up. When Bianca had gone to see her mum in hospital, after her hip operation. Thankfully, Lola's mother was picking Luca up that day. Damien knew Bianca had told us all about the kiss between him and Lola, and he told me in confidence that Lola messaged him all the time, asking if they could meet, if she'd done anything to upset him. After Bianca got that text and laid down the law, he was terrified. Damien's a bigwig at his father's company and petrified of displeasing his dad. Of clients getting wind of his infidelity. He told Lola not to bother him anymore, blocked her. That's why

I'm certain B had nothing to do with her death. It was nothing more than a kiss, and Damien's turned over a new leaf since.'

'Did he tell Bianca about Lola's texts?'

'No, he was too scared. He told me not to tell her, and I promised I'd keep my word. Which I did. I always do.'

I study Deidre for a few seconds, digesting all she's just said while trying to decide whether I believe her. Being a barrister, she has so much to lose if she's caught lying. My gut says she's telling me the truth, but I've also learned from experience that the most unsuspecting of people can turn out to be the best liars.

'Why do you suppose Damien confided in you?' I ask.

Deidre shrugs. 'I don't know. Because I was there at the time. And because we've known each other for some time now.'

'But perhaps more so because of what you do for a living? He feels he can trust you to keep a secret. Client privilege and all that.'

Deidre shrugs again. 'Yes, I suppose so.'

'Is that why Lola confided in you?'

Deidre recoils in her chair. Looks taken aback. 'Lola? Confided in me?' She glances at Stephen, who looks equally startled by my remark. 'I think you're mistaken as to how close we were,' she says. 'If Lola confided in anyone, it would have been Simone.'

'So I'm told. But your friend, Joy, seems to think otherwise.'

Deidre gives a nervous laugh. 'She does, does she? It seems Joy's had a lot to say for herself lately. Remind me never to confide my secrets in her. How's that, then?'

I explain what Joy recounted to me. About Deidre reprimanding Bianca for being rude to Lola one time when they were all out having coffee, insinuating that she'd been through a lot, and had had it tougher than most.

I watch Deidre swallow hard. She looks at Stephen.

'Did Lola tell you something, love?' Stephen says.

Deidre sits back in her chair with a heavy sigh, a resigned look sweeping across her face.

'OK, yes, she did. Something she felt deeply ashamed of. Even though it was by no means her fault.'

I wait with bated breath for her to continue. I'm almost certain I know what Lola confided in her, but I'm also hoping Deidre knows other details that elude me.

Details which might help shed light on who wanted Lola dead.

Chapter Nineteen

Lola

Before
February 2023

It's Friday. St Xavier's breaks up for half term today, and to mark the occasion, Dee's asked us round for coffee and cake.

Earlier this week we had snow, which the kids were all madly excited about, running around like lunatics in the playground, firing snowballs left, right and centre. I never tire of seeing the look on Luca's face when he wakes up to a blanket of white, but dealing with the trek to school and lugging myself to work is nothing short of miserable. In all honestly, I feel worn out, and I'm so glad I have a week off work and the school run to look forward to. Time to chill out with my little man.

'So, what's everyone up to for half term?' Dee asks as we sit around her kitchen table, cradling mugs of steaming tea and coffee, a plate of homemade carrot cake Simone rustled up lying in the centre. She's so good at baking, while I'm positively awful. No matter how hard I try, I either undercook or burn things. 'I have a trial starting next week,' Dee goes on, 'but Steve's OK with it. He's taking the rugrats to Center Parcs so I don't feel too guilty, knowing they're going to have fun. I'll miss them though, I have to say.'

It's lovely to see Dee looking brighter. It was Simone's birthday around a month ago, and we all went out for dinner. Towards the end of the evening, Dee's tongue loosened, and she told us she'd confronted Steve after New Year and he admitted to exchanging flirty texts with some woman at the gym, but that nothing physical had ever happened between them. His excuse was that he'd been bored, that he felt like he was invisible to Dee and consequently sought his kicks elsewhere. Like a typical man, thinking with his penis. Apparently, the photos had been deceptive, in that although the woman had a good body, she looked way older than her forty years, and spoke like an extra from *Eastenders*. Dee's exact words. This had made us all giggle. Steve had begged for Dee's forgiveness, and now they're attending couples therapy once a week.

Bianca opens her mouth to speak in response to Dee's query as to our plans for half term. 'All except you, B,' Dee cuts her off. 'Yes, we know you're off skiing, you've only been telling us that for the last six bloody months.'

Everyone yawns their agreement.

Bianca shuts her mouth. Puts on a wounded look. Then grins. 'You bitches are all just jealous.'

'She's right,' Clarissa sighs. 'At least, I know I am.'

Ever since I overheard Clarissa and Bianca discussing what happened to Clarissa's sister last December, I can't seem to look at Clarissa without feeling sad for her. She lives in a mansion, runs the roost at school, is super popular with two beautiful children and a millionaire husband, but there's a hole in her heart that will never be filled, no matter how much money she has, or how popular she is. So many times since that night I've wanted to reach out to her, to share my experience, a little part of me – as selfish as it might sound – also thinking it might be a way of getting closer to her. To bridge the social divide between us. But on every occasion I've stopped myself. Having confided in Tracy about it, even though she was devastated for poor Clarissa, she convinced me that no real good can come of it. I'd only be making life hard for myself and my parents, she said. The bastard who raped me made it clear that if I told a soul I'd be as good as dead, as would my loved ones. Tracy's right. I can't trust Clarissa to keep it between us. I can't tell anyone, period. It's too dangerous, and I'd be placing everything I have in jeopardy. Neither can I bear to see the look on my parents' faces if they discovered I've been lying to them all this time.

'Rob's buggering off to New York Wednesday to Friday, so as usual I'll be flying solo for much of the week,' Clarissa says bitterly.

I'm half tempted to offer to meet up with her and her kids, but, in truth, I'm looking forward to it just being me and Luca. Plus, whatever Clarissa ends up doing with her two, it's bound to cost a fortune. I simply don't have money to burn like she does.

'I'm not working Thursday and Friday,' Joy says. 'Let's do something. KidZania at Westfield, maybe?'

Knew it. That place costs an arm and a leg.

Clarissa's face brightens. 'Thanks, darling, I'd love that. And so would the girls. It's a date. We can sneak in some retail therapy too.'

'Absolutely!' Joy winks. 'I've been working like a dog these past few months, I deserve a treat. Maybe we can fit in a quick make-over at the Charlotte Tilbury counter in John Lewis as well?'

'Now you're talking,' Clarissa smiles.

'How about you two?' Bianca looks at Simone, then me. Why does it always feel like an interrogation with her? The moment her demon eyes laser through me, I feel my insides seize up, my mind under pressure to come up with a satisfactory response. Or maybe it's my guilt talking? The fact that I can't seem to get her husband out of my head. Or the fact that we're still texting each other, and that I can't help wishing for more.

'We're going down to Devon for a few days, same place we normally stay in,' Simone says. 'It's such a cute cottage, we love it.'

'Won't it be frigging freezing?' Dee comments with a frown.

'Yes, but it's peaceful. We'll wrap up warm, take long walks, come back to a roaring fire and some hearty food. Stuff our faces with scones and clotted cream.'

Bianca puts her finger down her throat. 'Urgh you and Liam are so sickening, how do you do it? Maintain that spark I mean.' She looks at the rest of us. 'I think we're all curious to know what your secret it. It's not normal after ten years of marriage.'

Simone blushes. Like she's in the first throes of love. I hate to admit it, but Bianca's right. I mean, I'm no expert on marriage, but I know from what Mum's told me that marriage is hard work. She mentioned that even she and Dad, who are devoted to one another, have had their tough patches, and that when kids come along things change. But they don't seem to have changed for Simone and Liam. And, like Bianca, I can't help wondering what their secret is.

Simone shrugs. 'I don't know, he's just really attentive. He listens, and we make time for each other, try and do some of the things we did before the girls came along.

When he returns from a boys' trip or medical conference, he always brings me something back, tries to make up for the time away. He's always been caring; it's why I fell for him.'

'And his Brad Pitt face has nothing to do with it, I take it?' Joy laughs.

'Or his smoking hot bod?' Bianca cuts in.

'OK, maybe those things have something to do with it,' Simone giggles. 'He is very good at taking care of himself. Goes to the gym regularly. It's why I go, because I don't want to feel frumpy next to him.'

'Not like Rob,' Clarissa sighs. 'Too many rich client dinners and not enough exercise has led to him developing that classic middle-aged paunch. I mean, we're the ones who gave birth to their kids, we have an excuse, but men, they have no excuse for the excess flab.'

'I bet Liam's good in bed too, with a body like that.' Dee nudges me in the side, while winking at Simone.

Just then, Bianca catches my eye. 'And what are your plans, Lola?'

I'm sure she knows I have nothing exciting planned. Principally because I can't afford it. On that basis, I can't decide if she's simply trying to include me, or show me up. Whatever her motive, I can't not reply.

'Not much, just spending time with Luca. Might go see a movie.'

'Exciting stuff.' Bianca widens her eyes. For Christ's sake, does she always have to be such a cow? I tell myself to rise above it.

'I think it's lovely,' Simone says, smiling at me. 'Those moments won't last forever. When they want to spend time with us, I mean. We have to make the most of them being little. Before we know it, they'll be off to uni, and all we'll be good for is doing their dirty laundry.'

'So, no change there then?' Joy laughs. Everyone appreciates the joke, bar me. Just the thought of Luca going off to uni and leaving me behind makes my heart sink, even though I realise how selfish that sounds. By then, he'll have access to the trust fund his secret benefactor set up for him. Every day I wonder who his Good Samaritan can be. I just wish I knew, so I could thank them in person. Particularly as just before Christmas they made a rather large injection of cash.

'Lola,' Dee says, perhaps noticing my discomfort, 'I was going to ask you if Luca might like a couple of jumpers and trousers Oscar has grown out of. It's not charity, OK, before you think that. It's just that he's barely worn them, and I'd like to see a friend make use of them.' She smiles at me. 'They're Zara, size eight.'

While Esme, Dee's youngest, is in Luca's class, Oscar, her older child, is in Year 2. He's very tall for his age, so I'm not surprised he's not fitting size-eight trousers anymore.

'Sure, that'd be great,' I say.

'Great, come upstairs and let me show you.' Her gaze lingers on me, and I get the feeling there's more to her asking me to accompany her than looking at Oscar's hand-me-down clothes. After all, she could have easily shown them to me down here, in front of everyone.

'Sure,' I say, while catching the quizzical look on Clarissa's face. I swear that woman never misses a thing.

I follow Dee upstairs to Oscar's bedroom. We go inside, whereupon Dee shuts the door behind her. 'Here they are.' She picks up a large Sainsbury's bag nestled in the corner of the room and brings it over to the bed. Plonks it on top of Oscar's *Avengers* duvet.

She fishes out the trousers and jumpers and hands them to me. 'What do you think?'

'They're great, Luca will love them,' I say, while looking through the various items. 'You sure I can't pay you for them?'

'Don't be silly, are you kidding! You're doing me a favour taking them off my hands.' She folds them again neatly and places them back inside the bag. Then she pauses, turning to look at me, concern etched across her face. It throws me, and I can't help wondering what she's about to say.

'Lola, are you OK?'

I swallow hard. 'Yes, why?'

'It's just that, recently, well, I've noticed some burn marks on your wrists, and I was concerned.'

My stomach heaves. Fuck. And there was me thinking I'd been so careful. 'Oh, that was just me being clumsy getting food out of the oven,' I stutter.

She looks at me gravely. 'It's not just that. When we went for that day spa a couple of weeks ago, I noticed…'

'You noticed what?'

'Some cuts on your thighs. When we were in the sauna.'

I feel my face flush. I hadn't wanted to go that day, but Simone persuaded me to. Said I deserved a treat. I told her I didn't have the money but then she mentioned it secretly to Mum who ended up giving me half the cash. She said she agreed with Simone that I should treat myself. In truth, I think she was still angry with Bianca for looking down on my flat and wanted me to prove to her that I was their equal.

'You've been watching me? What the hell, Dee, that's kind of creepy! What are you insinuating?' I say crossly.

She's entirely on the money though, and the defensive nature of my response probably tells her that. Recently, the cuts on my thighs became infected, and so I got a bit worried. I couldn't go and see the doctor, for obvious reasons, so I decided to give the cutting a break, and started giving myself little burns. I just can't seem to stop myself, as horrid as I know it is. How ashamed it makes me feel. Talking to Tracy should be enough, but it isn't.

'Lola.' Dee places her hand on my shoulder. 'I know self-harming when I see it. I've had clients who self-harm. I want to help – please tell me what's wrong. It's not good for you. It's not good for Luca. You must know that. You could do yourself serious damage one day.'

I feel the tears well up. My bottom lip trembling. 'I know, but I can't seem to stop myself.'

Dee urges me to sit next to her on the bed. 'Why? What happened? Is it to do with Luca's father dying in that accident?'

I badly want to tell her, to open up to someone other than Tracy about my past. About the terrible secret that's been weighing me down for the past six or so years. A secret that's been consuming me once again after hearing about Clarissa's sister and the fact that my rapist might be the same man responsible for Dinah's suicide and a whole series of other attacks on young women. But it's not that easy. All I can hear in my head is *his* voice, warning me to keep my mouth shut. Threatening my parents' lives.

'I can't tell you. It's too risky.'

'Too risky? Listen, love, I'm a barrister; anything you tell me in confidence will stay between us, I give you my word.' She pauses. Then says, 'OK, just to prove you can trust me, I'm going to tell you something none of the girls downstairs know about. Something I am deeply ashamed of. Something even Steve doesn't know about. Can I trust you not to tell them, or anyone, if I confide my secret in you?'

I'm gobsmacked by Dee's kindness, and at the same time I can't help being intrigued to hear what her secret is. It sounds serious. I find myself nodding. 'Yes, you have my word. I promise.'

She inhales deeply, then says, 'When I was 17, I was involved with a boy called Josh who was bad news. I knew he was trouble, but I guess I'd always been a sucker for the bad boy. He was so handsome and cool and I was besotted. My parents couldn't stand him, but I was a typical teenager and thought I knew best. One night, we went to a party. Everyone was drinking and doing drugs, Josh included. He'd taken coke and had been downing vodka. He'd also driven us there.' At this point, Dee looks down, and I'm on tenterhooks wondering how her story ends.

She looks up again, meets my gaze, her eyes filling with tears. 'Josh drove me home, but he was completely off his face. Going too fast on some narrow roads.'

I think I know what's coming but I don't speak. Simply wait for Dee to finish.

'There was a teenage girl crossing the road. He didn't see her, was going way too fast, and he hit her.'

I cover my mouth with my hand in shock. 'Oh, Jesus.'

Tears are now streaming down Dee's cheeks. 'There wasn't a soul about, and no CCTV. I told him to stop, that we had to report it, but he said he'd kill me, kill my parents if I dared breathe a word.' She pauses once more. Then continues. 'I shouldn't have listened to him. I should have been stronger, braver, and come forward. That girl's parents deserved to know what happened, and

Josh deserved to be punished. But I was young and scared. And I've kept the truth to myself all these years.'

'Is that why you became a prosecution barrister?' I ask.

'Yes.' Dee nods. 'It was largely about me wanting to make up for what I'd done. To get justice for victims like that girl. But it's never enough. The guilt never leaves me.' She pauses. 'And I guess it's why I married Steve. He was the complete antithesis of Josh. At least, I thought he was, until I caught him cheating.'

'Yes, but that's all good now, isn't it?' I say soothingly. 'He explained it meant nothing.'

Dee nods. 'Yes, I know. And I realise I'm partly to blame. I neglected him, because I am a workaholic. But he doesn't know why I work so hard, and sometimes the deception eats me up. If the Bar Council knew what I'd done, that I'd failed to report a serious crime, I'd be disbarred. So you see, Lola, I've really risked my neck telling you all this. Because I recognise someone in pain, and I want to help, if I can.'

I see the compassion in Dee's eyes and I can't help feeling touched. She's confided her darkest secret in me, and it tells me I can trust her to keep mine.

I squeeze her hand, take a deep breath, then tell her everything.

Chapter Twenty

Detective Inspector John Banner

Tuesday, 19th December 2023

'So you've known the truth about Luca's father since February of this year?'

'Yes,' Deidre admits with a faint nod, glancing at Stephen, who's looking shocked.

'And Lola was self-harming?'

She nods again.

'Why would she tell you all that? If her rapist had threatened to kill her and her family if she talked, I mean. Why would she take such a risk?'

Deidre shrugs. 'I guess because I'm a barrister, and she trusted me to keep it a secret.'

I don't buy it. Something doesn't add up. It doesn't make sense that Lola would tell Deidre something so big, so personal, and not tell Simone, her best friend. The only explanation I can think of is that Deidre told Lola something about herself. A secret she perhaps can't afford to get out, and therefore omitted from the exchange with Lola she just recounted to me and Stephen.

'And what was your reaction when she told you she was raped? That Luca's father hadn't died in a car accident.'

'I was devastated for her. But in some ways, I wasn't surprised. Because of the self-harming. I've prosecuted my fair share of rape and child abuses cases, and it's not uncommon for the victims to self-harm.'

'Did you encourage her to get help?'

'I did. I told her she needed to speak to someone, see a therapist.'

'You did?'

'Yes. But she said she already had someone to talk to. Someone she'd been speaking to since before she was raped.'

'Since before she was raped? Why was she already seeing a therapist?'

'It wasn't a professional therapist, as I understand things. More of an online "buddy" to chat to. Lola told me she got very stressed at university. Suffered from severe panic attacks. She explained how she'd been terrified of failure, of letting her parents down, despite being close to them, so she felt the need to talk to someone neutral about it. She couldn't afford to see a professional, but it wasn't just about the money. She also didn't want anyone at university finding out that she was struggling, which would have been a risk had she physically gone to see a therapist in Edinburgh.'

'Do you know the name of the online site she used?'

'No, she wouldn't say. I get the feeling it was more of a chat forum, where people could talk to others who'd been through similar experiences. She did say this person had been a godsend, and had encouraged her to move away after Luca was born, to start a new life. Had even suggested Kingston might be a good place to start over.'

This is big. I need to find out who Lola was speaking to. Who knows what she told them about her rapist, or what was going on at school. Whoever this person is, they may hold the key to unlocking the mystery of who murdered her.

'You weren't tempted to tell the other mums the truth about Luca's father after Bianca received the photo of Lola and Damien kissing? Clearly, she was a very troubled young woman. Desperate for affection.'

Deidre's eyes grow cold. 'No, I made a promise to Lola. I knew the potentially serious consequences of me not keeping my promise. Besides, what happened to Lola back then doesn't excuse her kissing Damien. That was unforgiveable. They are two separate things.'

Again, I get the feeling Deidre's holding back, in the same way I felt it with Joy. That it wasn't just Lola fooling around with Damien that incited both women's hostility towards her. My gut tells me Lola must have done something else to anger them. Something personal. And I can't help wondering if that's a mystery Lola's online friend can help me solve.

Chapter Twenty-One

Lola

Before
February 2023

HERETOCHAT.ORG
Chat Now in confidence. We're here for each other

Tracy: Lola, I thought we agreed it's too dangerous for you to tell anyone else the truth about Luca's father. I can't believe you've gone and endangered yourself like that.

   Lola: You're mad with me, aren't you? I feel bad. Like I've let you down.

Tracy: No. I'm not mad. I'm concerned. Concerned you've gone and put yourself at risk. Your parents too. Not to mention little Luca. I mean, it's pretty clear from what you've told me that these women aren't the most discreet. It's why you didn't open up to Clarissa. What if Dee tells one of them?

   Lola: She won't.

Tracy: How can you be so sure of that?

   Lola: I can't say, I'd be betraying her trust.

Tracy: Her trust? Oh, I think I get it. She's told you a secret about herself, hasn't she? Still, it can't be anywhere near as awful as what happened to you.

Lola: Well, it's different. And it is pretty bad. Potentially pretty serious for her if it gets out. I really feel for her. She's been carrying such a heavy burden for years, and it's eating her up. I know what that feels like. To hide something huge from those you love the most. It consumes your thoughts, day and night.

Tracy: Oh. Well, I'm sorry to hear that. That's terrible. Poor Dee. But why did you tell her in the first place? Did she ask you if something was up? Or find out something about you? It makes no sense that she would have asked you out of the blue, with no good reason.

Lola: OK, yes, she did find something out about me, but it's not what you think.

Tracy: What is it? You know you can tell me.

Lola: I don't want to. Not this. Please don't be offended. I know you're worried about me, but I trust Dee not to tell a soul. I can't tell you the details but all I can say is that if what she told me ever came out, she'd be disbarred. It's that serious. She can't afford to tell anyone my secret, she'd be risking everything.

Tracy: OK. No worries, I understand. And was she sympathetic towards you?

Lola: Yes, very. She understood that I'd been going through a particularly bad patch after reading about the Campus Prowler in the newspapers.

Tracy: Did she think there was a connection? That it might be the same person? I'm guessing she must hear some stuff in her line of work.

Lola: She wasn't sure. She agreed I seemed to fit the bill in terms of the other victims. I badly wanted to tell her about Clarissa's sister at that point. But I kept it in. It wasn't my secret to tell. I shouldn't even know about it, and she may not trust me to keep hers if I let on that I'd eavesdropped on Clarissa and Bianca's conversation.

Tracy: That's a very good point. Anyway, how's the little man?

Lola: Aww, he's fine. It's been so amazing spending time with him over half term. I wish he had another week off. We've not done a lot, made some cupcakes, watched DVDs, gone for walks, but it's been nice.

Tracy: Good. You don't have to spend money to have fun, just being together is what matters. How's the football going?

Lola: God, he loves little league! I can tell I'm going to be one of those mums standing on the sidelines freezing my arse off on Sunday mornings.

Tracy: Probably! But he'll appreciate it, for sure.

Lola: Yeah, I know. Right, I'm going to sign off for now. Thanks for listening, as ever.

Tracy: Always, that's what I'm here for. Whenever you need me.

Chapter Twenty-Two

Detective Inspector John Banner

Wednesday, 20th December 2023

It's 5 a.m. and I can't sleep, having tossed and turned all night. My wife, Jo, is lying next to me, locked in a deep slumber. I turn on my side and take a few minutes to study her face. As beautiful to me as on that first day I laid eyes on her at a friend's thirtieth-birthday drinks. I never believed in love at first sight before that night, and my mother was certain I was doomed for perpetual bachelordom. But Jo proved us both wrong. One smile in my direction and I was putty in her hands. My love for her was sealed by the fact that she had the kindest heart imaginable. I was in awe of the work she did as an addiction counsellor. She looks so peaceful right now, and I wonder to myself what she's dreaming about. If at all. I never sleep well. It comes with the territory, I guess. My sleep perpetually disturbed by ghastly images from previous cases I can never seem to expel from my mind no matter how hard I try. And the knowledge that any minute the phone might ring.

Quietly, I unwrap myself from the duvet and tread softly to the door. I haul on my dressing gown, which is hanging on a hook, before securing the belt firmly around my waist and creeping out of the room. I tiptoe past my son's bedroom, then pad quietly down the stairs, silently praying that I don't wake him up. Thankfully, I don't, and I breathe an inward sigh of relief when I reach the bottom step.

This case is slowly consuming me. So much so I've barely spent any time with Mikey over the last few days, much to my shame and regret. So many questions are plaguing my mind, Lola's murder proving to be far more complex than I could ever have imagined. I can't help feeling that the mums in Lola's immediate circle are holding back. It grates at my soul, angers me even. After all, she was a mum of young kids like them. Has left behind an innocent child. You'd think they'd be more forthcoming, more eager to help me solve this case. And it makes me wonder why they're holding back. What it is they're not telling me? Having said that, there's no denying Lola was keeping secrets of her own. Despite being incredibly close to her parents, she hid the truth behind Luca's paternity from them. It tells me I can't just focus on her mum friends, and whatever it is they're hiding. I have to look wider, consider other possibilities. Other angles.

Last night's team briefing didn't help my frustration. The CCTV we've looked at so far hasn't picked up anything useful, while Wild confirmed to me that the various door-to-door enquiries he's made – speaking to Lola's neighbours and other parents at St Xavier's – have proved similarly fruitless. Small wonder I can't sleep. That when I look at my own son, I can't help seeing Luca and feel like I'm failing him.

I open the kitchen door and switch on the light. Fill the kettle, then wait for it to boil, my mind going over the last few days, and what we know so far. I haven't yet had the chance to read through Lola's diary. That's this morning's job. I'm also hoping to hear what digital forensics have found on Lola's laptop. After speaking to Deidre, I called DI Golding, told him to get on the phone to the officer leading the digital trawl, and tell her to look out for evidence of this chat group Lola appears to have frequented. It also occurred to me that Lola may have told whoever she was speaking to about the threatening texts she'd been receiving and who she suspected might be behind them.

The kettle comes to the boil and I make myself a black coffee, then take it through to my tiny study and sit at my desk, before opening my laptop.

I go to Google and type in 'Campus Prowler', but also the terms 'female, student, rape, university', hoping to find something useful in what's been reported so far, even though I'm pretty sure I've already read everything there is to find online. The same results I've seen before appear – mainly interviews with the Oxford DCI – Jack Kane – who came up with the theory, along with a few victims who spoke up, and details of the areas of the UK the rapist is said to have operated in. But then my eye catches something I hadn't previously spotted on page three of the search results. Something that makes me sit bolt upright. A piece in The *Liverpool Echo* from six years ago, reporting the funeral of a local MP's daughter who killed herself following a vicious attack the year before at Bristol University. I click on it, and can hardly believe my eyes when I see the accompanying photo. It shows Dinah Caffrey, with her parents – Michael and Stephanie Caffrey – and older sister, Clarissa, accompanied by her husband, Robert. Apparently, Michael Caffrey had been stationed there only seven years before, following an application by himself, having been a lifelong Liverpool FC fan. It would explain why Clarissa doesn't have an accent. She was brought up in Barnes, and there appears to have been an eighteen-year age gap between Clarissa and Dinah, meaning Clarissa's parents can only have been in their early twenties when they had Clarissa.

Christ. This means Clarissa's sister was also raped as a student within the timeframe outlined by DCI Kane. But she doesn't fit the profile. All the other victims were only children. Just as I'm thinking this, my mobile rings. I rush to pick it up, conscious of Jo and Mikey sleeping soundly upstairs.

It's Golding. 'Sorry, John, I know it's early but you said to call if digital forensics found anything significant.'

I straighten. My pulse accelerating. 'Absolutely, what is it?'

'They've confirmed that Lola had been a subscriber to a site called Here to Chat, and that her last visit to the site was last Thursday. The day before she died.'

'And is it some kind of informal online help group, as Deidre Walton suggested?'

'Yes, it appears so. Similar to Mumsnet, only more geared towards people wanting to chat with others who've gone through similar issues, like depression, grief, and so on. There are both open and private one-to-one chat forums you can set up and which can only be accessed with a password. You can also key in certain terms which allows you to narrow down other users who fit your profile and have experienced similar problems. From there, there's the option to message them, see if they'd be up for chatting privately.'

'Is there a way to access Lola's private chat?'

'Yes, well, sort of. Luckily her password was automatically saved so all the team had to do was click on it to access the chat, but once they were in, they found all the previous chat was blank. Like it had been deleted. No record of what her and her buddy had been discussing.'

'Would that happen automatically?'

'I doubt it.'

'But did you get a name?'

'Yes. The username was Tracy. But that doesn't mean it was her real name. There was no surname, apparently.'

'Tracy,' I mumble out loud. 'So you think this Tracy with whom Lola was chatting deleted all the chat between them? Perhaps after learning of Lola's death?'

'It's possible.'

Why, I wonder? Because Lola had previously told her she was frightened that she'd been receiving threatening messages, and then, having heard about her murder, Tracy was scared of being the next victim? Perhaps she's an only child like Lola, and shares traits similar to the other victims?

'Can we recover the chat?'

'We might be able to, but it'll likely take a bit of time. Do I have your authorisation to contact the owners of Here to Chat, to see if they can help? It should be in their archives.'

'Yes. And while you're there, find out how it works; whether there's any way of identifying where this Tracy individual is based.'

I hang up and am thinking about going for a shower when my phone buzzes. A text. It gets my pulse racing once again, because once I read the message, I realise it can only be from one person.

The person we've just been talking about. Tracy.

You don't know me, but I was a friend of Lola's. The only person she could trust. You need to know that those women are toxic. All they care about is themselves, their image. And the men aren't much better. They're tainted with their wives' selfishness. If I were you, I'd be speaking to them all again, particularly Damien Radcliffe and Deidre Walton. Because they all had secrets. Secrets Lola came to know about. Secrets I know about and which makes me scared for my own life. Secrets they'd do anything to protect. Image is everything to them, Inspector. Don't believe what you hear or see. It's all a lie. One big toxic façade.

Chapter Twenty-Three

Lola

Before
June 2023

It's Friday, a beautiful warm summer's afternoon, and Simone suggested we all take the kids to the park after school. I'm feeling the most at peace with myself than I have done in a long time. Having that heart-to-heart with Dee back in February really helped. The fact that she cared enough to confront me with her suspicions about my self-harming, and was prepared to risk her career by telling me something so huge about her past, made me feel special, that she valued me as a friend, and that she trusted me to keep her secret. A secret no one else knew about, not even her husband. And even though I still don't feel completely comfortable in Bianca's presence, I tell myself that's OK, that she's just one person. What matters is that I finally feel like a proper part of the group as far as the others are concerned. That I *belong*. Being part of their circle makes me feel, well… normal, I guess. Stronger. Knowing I'm not alone in this parenting business, despite not having a husband or partner. I feel like the future is looking up and that I'm finally on the right track.

Dee convinced me to see a trained specialist about my self-harming. I realised she was right, and that I needed to see a professional, because it was getting out of hand and if I didn't put a stop to it soon, one day the consequences might be fatal. I can't risk doing that to Luca. He's the most precious thing in the world to me, and the thought of him being left without a mother because I was too scared to face up to my demons is unbearable. Doctor Sanders, the GP I work for, was so kind when I asked him for a referral. He confessed that he suspected I'd been hurting myself, and was relieved I was finally confronting my problems. The consultant I've been seeing has also been brilliant, teaching me various coping mechanisms: deep-breathing and meditation techniques, for example. He also encouraged me to join a mutual support group where I can talk in confidence with fellow sufferers. Dee said she was proud of me when I mentioned to her the other day how well I was doing. Now and again she and I meet for coffee, chat about how I'm doing, how the therapy's going. It's nice to have made another friend I feel close to, can confide in, other than Simone. Even though I'll always consider Simi my best friend. I told Dee the progress I was making was all thanks to her, and promised that her secret was safe with me. That I would never in a million years betray her confidence.

'That looks like a good spot,' Simone says as we enter the park. 'There, just under that big oak tree.'

What with it being such a warm afternoon, we decided to venture to Canbury Gardens, which lies adjacent to the river path and is conveniently only a ten-minute stroll from my flat. The area is teeming with parents and kids, picnic blankets spread out everywhere, footballs being passed back and forth, dogs going crazy at the sight of so much commotion and wanting to join in the fun.

We all agree with Simone's suggestion and, before long, have spread out the various blankets we've brought between us under the tree, along with some nibbles and drinks we picked up along the way from a local Tesco Metro. The children soon decide they want to play hide-and-seek and before they scurry off I tell Luca not to venture too far. He nods obediently before zooming off with the other kids.

'You really are the classic helicopter mum, aren't you?' Bianca suddenly pipes up.

I feel my face flush. She has such a nerve saying that. If I'm a helicopter mum, then she's the classic lawnmower parent. I know that's a term, because I've read about it on the internet. As far as I can tell, she micromanages every aspect of Summer and Tilly's lives. The poor things do every after-school club under the sun, and I know for a fact that Bianca's constantly emailing the teachers about their academic performances, asking for special treatment, interfering in every aspect of her girls' education even though they're only in primary school. She has no idea why I'm so protective of Luca, that it has nothing to do with me wanting to manage every area of his life, and everything to do with keeping him safe from the evil fuck who raped me. I catch Dee's eye and she gives me a look as if to say 'calm down, she's not worth it', and it helps.

Because the fact is, she's right. Bianca's not worth it. More's the point, she's not as self-assured as she makes herself out to be. For one, she's desperate for her daughters to be the best at everything to make up for her own failings. That's what Damien's intimated to me, anyway. And because of this I somehow feel less intimidated by Bianca, less afraid to stand up to her. Having said that, I need to be careful with my response. Otherwise she might grow suspicious I've been talking to her husband, which is the last thing I need. 'No, I don't think so,' I say calmly. 'I just worry about his safety. There're a lot of weirdos about. You never know who's around, preying on innocent kids.'

'Lola's right,' Simone says. 'I read only the other day in the paper about a child who got abducted from a busy park, despite his mother keeping close tabs on him. She turned her head for a few seconds, and he was gone. Devastating.' She shakes her head. 'It gives me a sick feeling in the pit of my stomach.'

Bianca rolls her eyes. 'Sure, I guess. I'm sorry. Is it because of what happened to Luca's father? Did that make you more anxious, do you think?'

I catch Dee's eye again. Swallow hard, take a breath.

'Yes, I guess so. When something as awful as that happens, it changes you. I hope you never have to find out the hard way like me.'

Bianca doesn't respond, perhaps not expecting my passive aggressive response. I glance at Dee and I can tell she's impressed with how I managed to keep my temper in check, but at the same time knock Bianca down a peg or two.

'I can understand that,' Clarissa says. She gives Bianca a knowing look. 'There *are* a lot of creeps out there, and you can never be too careful. Lola's right to be cautious. We all should be, we should never take the safety of our loved ones for granted.'

'Amen to that,' Joy says.

Bianca gives Clarissa a guilty look. I badly want to console Clarissa, tell her I know she's speaking from personal experience and that we have far more in common than she could ever realise. But I hold my tongue. The fact is, I shouldn't have been eavesdropping that night, and now that I finally feel a part of the group, I don't want to jeopardise that.

A little later, Simone and I are pushing Jess and Luca side by side on the swings. In some ways, I feel like I'm betraying our friendship in not telling her about what happened to me at university, when I've gone and confided in Dee. I consider Simone to be my best friend, and if anyone should know the truth, it should be her. But then I tell myself I'd never have opened up to Dee if she hadn't confronted me. Also, more importantly, told me her devastating secret. It's best I keep the ugly truth to as few people as possible, like Tracy said. So far, following that mantra has kept me safe. It's why I've still not gone to the police, despite other victims having been so brave in coming forward. Luca's safety is paramount. I can't risk it, no matter how guilty I feel.

'Liam said he'll do a BBQ tomorrow afternoon. Do you want to come over with Luca? The girls would love it. It's going to be twenty-six degrees according to the BBC.'

I smile. 'Yes, I'd love that. *We'd* love that. Luca always has such a good time at your place. Liam's so lovely with him; it's so nice to see him kick a ball around with a guy. I try my best, but I'm so useless at sports. Luca's too sweet to say anything, but I know he'd much rather play footie with Liam than his flat-footed mum.'

Simone chuckles. 'Ahh, don't be silly, that boy is lucky to have a mum as devoted as you. He doesn't care if you're crap at football. He just wants to spend time with you. I see the way he looks at you. You're everything to him.'

I smile, grateful for Simone's reassurance, while giving Luca another push. There's so much noise around us, I'm pretty sure he's not paying attention to what Simone and I are saying. At least, I hope he's not.

'I guess so. I just feel guilty sometimes that he doesn't have a father figure around. To do the stuff only a dad can do best.'

Simone shakes her head. Then whispers, 'Some kids have dads who are terrible fathers. Alcoholics, wife beaters, child abusers. It's better to have one loving parent than two where the dad's the scum of the earth. Luca is happy and loved. That's all that matters.'

I smile, reach out and touch Simone's arm. 'Thanks, Simi.' At the same time, she has this woeful look in her eyes and it makes me wonder if she's speaking from personal experience. She always talks highly of her parents, but I know her dad was in the Army and away a lot. Also, that he was strict with Simone and her sister when they were kids.

'It's my pleasure,' she says. 'And whenever you need Liam to kick a ball around with Luca, he'd be only too happy. You know he feels outnumbered in our house anyway.' She grins mischievously, then we both giggle.

'Simi, Lola, come quick!' Our carefree moment is interrupted by Dee's frantic shouting.

We look over in alarm to where she's standing, waving hysterically at us. Realising that something bad must have happened, we urge the kids to get off the swings before rushing over to her.

'What's happened?' Simone says, her eyes anxious.

'It's Joy,' Dee says, her eyes brimming with tears. 'She's collapsed.'

Chapter Twenty-Four

Detective Inspector John Banner

Wednesday, 20th December 2023

It's a little after 8 a.m. and I'm sitting in a break-out room at Kingston Police Station, the shutters down, Lola's diary lying on the table in front of me in a sealed evidence bag. There's normally a constant stream of people bursting in and out of my office, the phone ringing incessantly, so I've come here for some peace and quiet. Carefully, I remove the diary from the bag and open it to the first page, my latex gloves making those simple steps that much trickier than would be the case with my bare hands. But this is potentially vital evidence, and I'm conscious that it needs to be handled delicately. And read carefully. My team did a good job spotting some crucial entries by Lola, but I can't afford to miss anything. For example, if Lola mentioned 'Tracy' anywhere. I find it odd that she wouldn't. Clearly, Tracy played a key part in her life, which is why I need to go through everything with a fine toothcomb.

The anonymous text I received a few hours ago keeps turning over in my brain. I tried texting back, then calling the number, but there was no dial tone. Evidently the sender used an unregistered phone before disabling it. *Why?* Because they're scared and fear for their own life?

Because they can't risk being identified? That's certainly what they inferred in their message. It has to be Tracy, because I can't think who else Lola would have shared such intimate details with. Elisa didn't mention any other friends she was close to, aside from Simone, so it seems the logical conclusion. Whoever it is, it would appear that Lola disclosed her deepest fears and most painful secrets to them. But the text insinuates she revealed her friends' darkest secrets too. I need to speak to her mum friends again, put them on the spot, press harder. I'm certain Joy and Deidre were holding back when they said their opinion of Lola changed purely because she'd kissed Damien. If Deidre knew Lola was chatting to someone online, was she worried that Lola had perhaps revealed Deidre's secret to them? But why would she think that? The chat between Lola and Tracy was private and password-protected, so Deidre could never have known what they talked about. I'm missing something. Some key piece of information that for now eludes me. I'm determined to find out what it is. But first – Lola's diary.

I start reading, and as I do, Lola's guilt for hiding the truth about Luca's father from her friends, but even more so from her parents and Luca, is evident, despite her feeling that she couldn't risk their lives by coming clean. I wonder to myself how it must have felt, living in constant fear like that. Never being able to relax completely, always on guard and alive to every strange noise she might hear after turning the lights out at night. How her mind must have been in perpetual turmoil, wondering if she and Luca were ever truly safe.

I painstakingly plough through the first six months of this year. Scanning every word, hoping to find some clue as to who may have killed Lola. There are normal day-to-day entries. She records funny things Luca had said or done, how he was doing well at school. She talks about her work, how a few of the patients at the GP surgery could be difficult to handle. How she enjoyed a relaxing February half term with Luca. I learn about Deidre's husband's dalliance with a woman at his gym (this explains the cutting comment she made in his presence yesterday), but how they worked things through and got over the worst. Lola also mentions her chat with Deidre, and how because of Deidre's kindness, Lola sought help for her self-harming and by the summer appears to have stopped hurting herself completely. All this Deidre had told me yesterday, confirming that she was telling me the truth about what Lola had disclosed to her. Lola describes spending a lot of time at the Loxleys'. How Simone was a good friend, how Liam was a star with Luca, and how sad she sometimes felt when she watched them kick a ball around that Luca didn't have a permanent father figure in his life.

But there are other more significant details. Details that make me sit up straight and cause all sorts of theories to hurtle through my mind. Like a trip to the park in June where Bianca had accused Lola of helicopter parenting, but how Clarissa had defended her, no doubt because she knew the pain of losing a loved one herself. It's clear from her entries that Lola somehow found out about Clarissa's sister's suicide, and had badly wanted to console Clarissa and share her own terrifying ordeal, but felt that she couldn't risk taking that step because she was scared that Dinah's rapist was the same scumbag who had raped her, and was also worried that Clarissa couldn't be trusted to keep it to herself. It's also clear to me that the day Lola told Deidre the truth about Luca's father, Deidre confessed a secret of her own. Lola doesn't mention what it was, but I feel sure it's something big. And it explains why Lola trusted Deidre to keep her secret. It was a quid pro quo of sorts, confirming my initial instincts, despite Deidre claiming Lola trusted her simply because she was a barrister.

I keep reading, and am shocked to discover that Joy Grainger suffered a minor heart attack that same June day in the park when Bianca labelled Lola a helicopter mum. All the women had rallied round, taking her husband, Gavin, and their kids, meals while she was recuperating. But interestingly, in the same entry, Lola describes how she discovered something about Joy when she went round to her house not long after Joy was discharged from the hospital. Something that shocked her. Again, she doesn't disclose what it was, but it's evident that Lola found the burden of keeping it to herself a heavy one. What could it have been? And did Joy confess it of her own volition or did Lola find out inadvertently?

Lola's increasingly unhealthy obsession with Damien Radcliffe also stands out like a sore thumb, corroborating what Deidre told me yesterday. She describes how she thought about him constantly, would imagine him making love to her, how she wished more than anything he and Bianca would break up, how he was too good for her. It's funny: in so many ways, Lola comes across as a mature, kind and level-headed young woman, putting her son first and having compassion for others. But as far as Damien Radcliffe is concerned, she seems to have lost all sense of reason. A classic case of fatal attraction that could only ever end in heartache. Having said that, it's also clear it wasn't some one-sided obsession on Lola's part. Rather, Damien led her on, complaining to Lola about Bianca and her constant demands, that nothing he ever did was good enough, that she was obsessed with their children being overachievers, while neglecting him and his own needs. And, more significantly, he told Lola that she was unlike anyone else he'd ever met; kind and compassionate and the only one who really listened to and understood him. Classic cheating husband lines if ever I heard them. It riles me. The way he manipulated her. Took advantage of her kind nature, presumably to massage his own bruised ago. But I know I have to stay calm. Getting angry with Damien won't do me any good.

I keep flicking through the pages, hoping to find a reference to their kiss. And before long I do, in an entry Lola wrote in late August of this year, not long before the new term started. The timing makes sense, based on the anonymous text sent to Bianca in the first week of September, attaching a photo of Lola and Damien kissing. But it's also clear to me that Lola didn't know about the photo, and in subsequent entries she writes about being confused and hurt by Damien's radical shift in behaviour towards her, that she had no idea why he was blanking her, or what she'd done wrong to upset him. She talks about messaging him, but how he blocked her number; how she then tried emailing, and eventually, when that didn't work, she turned up at his office, whereupon Damien became angry and threatened to get a restraining order against her if she didn't back off.

I place the diary down on the table for a moment. Sit back and think. It's essential I speak to Damien, hear his side of the story, without his wife around. I need to ask him about that kiss, about the photo sent to his wife's phone and what Bianca said to him the day she confronted him about it. But, more importantly, I need to ask him how Lola's threats made him feel. Angry, I'm guessing. But angry enough to kill her?

I pick the diary up again. Scanning more pages, I find Lola refers to frightening messages she started receiving in October, as Golding previously mentioned. Messages threatening her and her parents' lives, as well as Luca's safety, and which carried on through to the beginning of December, but which then stopped abruptly. Again, I wonder if she received another disturbing message at the party, causing her to rush home to Luca, fearing for his safety.

Finally, Lola talks about feeling hurt by the other mums' dismissive behaviour towards her. How she wondered if it was because they'd somehow found out about her kiss with Damien, but that she couldn't think how, because she was certain no one he or she knew had been around at the time.

I close the diary. Sit back again. It's clear from everything I've read so far that whoever texted me this morning was telling the truth – Lola knew intimate secrets about the other mums. Not only that, she was infatuated with Damien, and had angered both him and Bianca with her obsessive behaviour. Everyone had a possible motive to want her gone. On that basis, does this mean that the scumbag who raped her is nothing more than a red herring diverting my attention from the real culprit? After all, it happened nearly seven years ago, and he got away scot-free. Why re-enter her life now?

Again, I'm curious as to why Lola doesn't mention Here to Chat, nor more specifically Tracy, in her diary. Clearly, Tracy was an important part of her life. Was she trying to protect her identity? Was Tracy hiding from someone too, and Lola therefore felt an instinctive need to protect her?

I just hope and pray that digital forensics are able to retrieve Lola's conversations with Tracy. Right now, they feel like my best shot at nailing her killer.

Someone who I'm starting to believe murdered Lola to keep her quiet.

Chapter Twenty-Five

Lola

Before
June 2023

It's Wednesday morning, five days on from Joy's heart attack in the park, and I've just turned up at her house with a Tupperware box containing a healthy Mexican bean stew I made last night. After undergoing numerous tests and being closely monitored for three days, Joy was discharged yesterday and is now hopefully on the road to recovery. She hadn't told anyone she'd been suffering from mild chest pain and shortness of breath. She also thought the excessive sweating she'd been experiencing was due to the hot weather coupled with her African skin, which tends to perspire more. The tests revealed that she was suffering from type 2 diabetes, high cholesterol and high blood pressure, conditions that were partly genetic, but also down to the high sugar and high fat content of her diet, and the fact that she did little exercise. Apparently, Gavin had been on at her to lose weight, to get some exercise, but she'd fobbed him off. She's also someone who apparently avoids the doctor like the plague, perhaps because both her parents died from heart attacks and she didn't want to face reality.

Gavin greets me at the door. The poor guy looks shattered, his face drawn, dark circles underlying his eyes, as if he hasn't slept a wink since all this occurred. I can't even begin to imagine the stress he's under. Clarissa had been the one to call for an ambulance that horrendous afternoon, and once the paramedics arrived and stabilised Joy, Dee phoned Gavin, telling him what had happened and that he needed to make his way to Kingston Hospital quick sharp. Trying to console Joy's hysterical girls was something that will forever stick in my mind. All our kids were freaked out, to be honest. Once they took Joy away, Dee having ridden in the ambulance with her while Clarissa offered to watch both their kids, we parted ways. Everyone's mood was sombre, shell-shocked that something like this could have happened to one of our friends. Someone so young and seemingly full of life, and who only minutes before had been laughing and joking with us all. It made us think about how precious life is, how every moment counts. How vital it is we don't waste a second of it, and that we take care of ourselves. On the walk home, Luca kept asking me if Joy was going to be OK, and all I could say was that I hoped so. Later, as I tucked him up in bed, he made me swear that nothing so awful would ever happen to me. I assured him it wouldn't, that Mummy was fine and not going anywhere. But I felt like the biggest fraud, making such a promise to him. Because, of course, none of us know what's around the corner; none of us could ever have foretold that something so terrible could happen to our forty-two-year-old friend. Life is cruel, unpredictable, fragile. All we can do is live it as best we can and take things one day at a time. But that's too much for a boy who's just turned six to comprehend. And later, when I curled up in bed, I couldn't stop the tears from falling, knowing I won't always be around to protect my little boy.

'How are you holding up, Gav?' I say as I step inside the hallway, handing him the stew.

'So-so, I guess. The last few days have been rough, I won't lie.' He looks down at the stew. 'Thanks for this.'

I smile. 'It's the least I can do. And of course, I can only imagine how tough it's been. I still can't believe it happened. She's so young.'

Gavin shakes his head. 'It's frightening. I just wish she'd listened to me. She's been a bit breathless of late, you see, and I've been on at her to get some exercise, watch her diet. She told me to stop nagging, that I was stressing her out. They've put her on blood thinners, medication for her diabetes and a strict low-fat, low-sugar diet. Less meat, less fried food, more veg and pulses.' He pauses, then grins. 'You can imagine how happy that made her.'

I grin back. 'Yeah, I can. She does love her sugar and fried foods. Still, if it saves her life, it has to be done. For your and the kids' sakes, if not hers.'

Gavin nods, his eyes glassy. 'Don't know what I'd do without her.'

I massage his shoulder. 'She's going to be OK now, you'll see.'

He gives me a grateful smile. 'Thanks, I hope so.'

'I *know* so. So can I see the patient?'

'Sure.' He lowers his voice. 'One thing you should be aware of — they put her on a short-term dose of anti-depressants, just to get through this tough period, so she might seem a little out of it.'

I smile. 'No problem, I'll bear that in mind.'

Gavin nods his appreciation then takes me through to their living room where Joy is resting on the sofa.

She instantly looks up and gives me a big smile, appears brighter than she did a couple of days ago when I visited her in the hospital. Although it could be the antidepressants, of course.

'I'll take this to the kitchen,' Gavin says, gesturing to the stew I made. 'Can I get you a drink, Lola?'

I shake my head, tell him I'm fine, at which point he leaves us to it, and says he's going to take a nap upstairs.

'Nice to see you, lovely,' Joy says, her speech a little slurred, her eyes mildly glazed. It's hardly surprising they put her on tablets after what she's been through. I'm sure I'd be the same. 'I'm so frigging bored,' she goes on. 'Gav is driving me crazy fussing over me like a mother hen.'

I kiss the top of her head, then take a seat on the armchair opposite.

'And with good cause,' I chide. 'You scared the life out of him. Hell, you scared all of us. You need to do what the doctors say, OK? Nice healthy low-fat stuff. And get some exercise.'

She sighs. 'Yeah, I know. And I guess I should know better given my family history. I suppose I was in denial, plus I love my Cuban food too much. But I promise I'll turn over a new leaf.' She pauses, her face clouding over. 'The kids were terrified; I couldn't put them through that again.'

I nod. 'Our kids are our worlds. And seeing them suffer is the worst pain any parent could bear. It's our job to protect them for as long as we can.'

At this, Joy starts crying. Fat tears stream down her face.

'Oh no, Joy, what is it?' I ask. 'Sorry, I shouldn't have laid it on so thick, not when you're only just recovering.' Guilt pummels my insides. Poor Joy. She's heavily medicated, her emotions all over the place. Yet here's me making matters worse. *Think, Lola!* I scold myself inside.

She shakes her head. 'No, it's not you.'

'It's not?' I say. 'What is it then?'

Another shake of her head. 'Really, it's nothing.'

I get up from my chair and kneel down beside her, place my hand on her shoulder. 'It's OK, you can tell me. It's not good for you to keep things inside; you need to let it out. Trust me, I know that more than anyone.'

She looks at me with grateful eyes. 'You're talking about Ben, aren't you? Losing him in that car crash.' I swallow hard, the guilt tugging at my insides. Here I am imploring Joy to open up to me, to be honest, and yet I'm point-blank lying to her face.

'Yes,' I say, feeling like a fraud. I hand her a tissue, and she dabs her eyes. 'What is it?' I urge. 'You can tell me.'

Her eyes travel to the door.

'It's OK,' I assure her. 'Gav's upstairs, taking a nap. He won't hear us.'

I watch her inhale then exhale deeply. Like she's Atlas with the weight of the world on her shoulders. 'OK, so, I know I always make out how wonderful my parents were.' She pauses. Then says, 'But they weren't.'

'They weren't?' I say gently.

'No, my dad, my dad, well, he, he, was cruel. He sexually abused me when I was a child.'

I gasp in shock. 'Oh, Joy, I'm so sorry.'

The tears are now falling hard and fast. It's as if her near-death experience has driven Joy to expel all the pain and suffering she's clearly kept bottled up inside for a long time. 'It went on for years, until I was old enough to fight back. I tried to tell my mother, but she worshipped my father, wouldn't hear a bad word against him. Plus, he hit her too. And my younger siblings. But the sexual abuse was only reserved for me. I'm not sure why, perhaps because I was the oldest. I never told my sisters and brother about it; they had enough to cope with. I can't tell you how relieved I was when I finally moved out.' The words are pouring out of her fast and furiously now. Both the shock of nearly dying along with the antidepressants she's on are perhaps propelling her to confess her inner demons and make a clean slate. I can understand that. I've been there with Dee. It's cathartic, liberating. She goes on. 'And then, when I married Gav, I was so happy to have found a good and decent man. Dad of course acted like he'd never done anything wrong, and I was too ashamed to tell Gav what went on in my childhood. I also knew he'd kill Dad if he learned the truth. I figured it was in the past, and that I needed to move forward. But then we had Darcy, and I noticed the way my dad would look at her, from around when she turned four. When she was dressed in a pretty dress, or was paddling naked in the pool at home. I recognised that look and it frightened me. And I felt so alone because, of course, I couldn't tell Gav, and Mum was a lost cause.'

'Oh, Jesus, Joy, I can't even begin to imagine how that must have felt,' I say, a sick sensation swelling in my gut.

'I felt sick, sick with disgust and rage. It was like you said, the thought of my child being in danger, of suffering, it was all-powerful, and it consumed me. Made me crazy. I knew I'd never be able to rest easy until I was certain he could never hurt her.' She pauses, looks into my eyes, and I almost can't bear to ask my next question.

'What happened, Joy? What did you do?'

My heart is in my mouth as I wait for her to respond, wondering what manner of sin she's about to confess. I watch her chew on her bottom lip, guilt enveloping her face. Then she says, 'I killed the son of a bitch. I killed my own father.'

Chapter Twenty-Six

Detective Inspector John Banner

Wednesday, 20th December 2023

'No, it can't be true.'

I've not long arrived at the Mosleys' home. Having learned the shocking truth about what happened to Lola at university, and received confirmation from Wild that there were no fatal car accidents in Glasgow around the time Lola would have been newly pregnant with Luca, I didn't think it fair to keep either from her parents a second longer, even though, at the same time, I feel like I've gone and broken their hearts all over again.

'Are you sure?' Elisa says. Her face is a canvas of pain. Don looks frailer than ever.

I nod gravely. 'Yes, I'm afraid so.'

Elisa starts crying hysterically, and in my mind I'm thankful to Simone and Liam for agreeing to have Luca over to theirs while I speak freely with his devastated grandparents. Earlier, I called Elisa and Don, warning them that what I was going to discuss was sensitive, so if they were able to arrange child care that would be best. St Xavier's breaks up for the Christmas holidays this afternoon, so right now Simone and Liam are able to give Luca their undivided attention, before their daughters are home.

'Oh my poor, poor girl. Why wouldn't she have told us?' Elisa says forlornly. 'To have kept something so hideous to herself, and fabricated that story about Ben and the accident, it's – it's unbearable to think how much pain she must have been in. What she went through. We – we weren't bad parents. She knew how much we loved her, how she couldn't have done anything to upset us. What did she think we'd say if she told us the truth? That we'd turn her away? Of course we wouldn't have done! Oh, my darling girl, to think what she suffered. To think that Luca… the poor child. Is that why she wanted to move down here, change her name? Why didn't I press her more?' She looks at Don. 'Why didn't we? We knew something wasn't right with her explanation. We should have asked her more questions, we should have been better parents!'

The words rush out of Elisa's mouth like a bullet train. She's in a state of disbelief, understandably so. Tears fill her eyes. Don's too. I nod. 'Yes, I think so. She wanted to get as far away as possible from Edinburgh. Where there were no reminders of what happened to her. Please, you mustn't for one second imagine Lola thought you wouldn't support her. Besides, her wanting to move away and change her name wasn't just about her needing to make a clean break after being raped.'

'It wasn't?' Elisa says between sobs.

'No,' I say gently. 'The man who attacked Lola threatened her. Threatened both your lives, if she went to the police, or told anyone, in fact. She couldn't risk it, couldn't bear the thought of anything bad happening to you. Besides Luca, you were all she had.'

'Oh, sweet Jesus,' Don says, putting his face in his hands. He comes up for air, his tormented eyes piercing mine. 'That's why she was so protective of Luca, wasn't it?'

I nod.

'Was she scared he'd come back and find her, take Luca?' he asks.

'Yes.' I nod. 'I believe so.'

'How do you know all this, Inspector?' Elisa asks.

Once again, I'm about to hit Elisa and Don with more shocking truths. About how their beloved daughter had feared for her life. It's beyond tough, and as a parent I can only imagine the agony they must be in. But I plough on all the same. Because I have no choice. I need to solve this murder. Get justice for Lola.

'Lola kept a diary. More recently, she describes how she'd been receiving threatening messages these past couple of months, and feared it might be the same man who raped her. She was too scared to tell you, because she was afraid you might go to the police and, in doing so, put your own lives at risk.'

'Oh, poor love,' Elisa shakes her head.

We sit in agonising silence for a few seconds, then I force myself to broach another difficult topic. 'Do either of you remember reading about the Campus Prowler in the newspapers a while back? Around November of last year.'

Don nods. 'I do recall reading an article of that nature.' His brow creases. 'You think the same man attacked our Lola back at university?'

I nod. 'She seems to fit the victim profile.'

'So there's a chance *he* killed Lola?' Elisa says.

'Yes, there's a possibility based on the fact that we know he threatened her at the time. But I'm not convinced. It's been nearly seven years since the attack. And if anything, he appears to have been laying low since the articles appeared. I checked, and Lola never reported being raped. So why come back into her life now? What motive or gain did he have from killing her? I see none.'

'Do you have another theory then?' Don asks.

'Possibly.'

'Possibly? I don't understand.'

I have to tread carefully here. Elisa made it clear during our first meeting that she didn't have a lot of time for Lola's mum friends, and had a particular disliking for Bianca. If I tell her and Don there's a chance one of them may have had something to do with Lola's death, she'll be banging on their doors before anyone can stop her. More's the point, I don't have any solid evidence right now. And the last thing I need is to open myself up to an accusation of slander.

'Right now, I can't disclose the details. It's all conjecture, and I hope you can understand my position.' Neither of them say anything. I can see that they're not happy with my response, but they must surely understand where I'm coming from. I move on. 'I'm guessing you also weren't aware that Lola subscribed to an online help group called Here to Chat?'

Both Elisa and Don shake their heads dejectedly. 'No, we had no idea,' Don says. 'But then it seems our daughter was hiding a great deal from us.' His tone isn't bitter. Rather, it's sad, regretful.

'What kind of help does it give?' Elisa asks.

'It's basically a forum which allows people to share and talk about their problems anonymously, covering issues like depression, panic attacks, grief and so on. As I understand things, Lola suffered from panic attacks at university. She didn't want to go and see a professional therapist in person – I'm guessing that was too expensive – so she went online and discovered Here to Chat.'

Elisa looks at Don. 'Good Lord. We had no idea. No idea she felt so much pressure at university. She acted like she was in her element.'

Don shakes his head. His face full of anguish. 'She always was a bit of a perfectionist, but we thought she thrived on pushing herself. How can we have been so blind? Why on earth go on some anonymous chat forum when she could have talked to us? The people who loved her most.'

I sympathise with Don's pain, but I have to motor on all the same, as harrowing as this must be for him. 'The last time Lola went on Here to Chat was the night before she died. It appears she made one special friend on there – a "buddy" – as the site refers to those who've experienced similar problems. Someone called Tracy, who Lola confided in about the pressure she felt at uni, and later about the dreadful thing that happened to her. It seems this Tracy advised her to move away after the rape, citing Kingston as a good place to make a fresh start.'

Don frowns. 'How do you know all this? From her diary?'

'No, Lola didn't mention the chat forum in her diary. We think perhaps she was nervous about naming Tracy, and therefore keen to respect her privacy. We initially found out about Here To Chat by looking at Lola's laptop. Unfortunately, the chat appears to have been deleted, but we're working on retrieving it. The details I just relayed are from another source.'

'What source?' Elisa says with a frown.

'I can't say right now.'

I fear this won't go down well. Elisa is on the verge of responding, when Don interjects. 'So, are you thinking Lola might have told this Tracy character about the threatening messages she'd been receiving? Including who she thought might be behind them?'

'Yes.' I nod.

'So you need to get access to that chat!' Elisa states the obvious.

I keep my voice calm. 'Like I said, my digital forensics team are trying their best to retrieve it. I'll keep you posted as and when I hear more.' I hesitate. 'There's something else, though.'

'What?' Elisa asks irritably. Almost like she can't bear to hear anymore.

'I received an anonymous text message this morning. I believe it was from Tracy.'

'Why would you think that? What did it say?' Don asks anxiously.

'Well, the sender said they were a friend of Lola's, someone Lola could trust. They also mentioned some things about the mums in Lola's friendship circle at school. Things that weren't too favourable, shall we say.'

Elisa's eyes grow hard, her tone bitter. 'That, I can believe.'

'What are you implying?' Don says. 'That one of them might have had something to do with Lola's death?'

I shake my head, even though in my mind I can't help considering the possibility. 'Absolutely not. And I can't stress enough how important it is for you not to go jumping to such conclusions. We need to keep our cool here.'

'Our daughter is lying in a morgue, and our six-year-old grandson has lost his mother, and you're asking us to keep our cool!' Elisa's eyes are wide, the veins on her neck taut with tension.

'I'm sorry, but yes. We have to, if we're to get to the bottom of this. I know it's hard, but right now I'm exploring a number of theories, and we can't go making accusations without solid evidence. OK?'

Elisa nods reluctantly.

I continue. 'Lola made it clear in her diary that she learned some things about these women. Intimate secrets they wouldn't want getting out.'

'What secrets?'

'Lola didn't say specifically. I was hoping she might have mentioned something to you, even in passing. But I can see from your reaction that she didn't.'

Elisa shakes her head. 'No, she didn't.' She sighs heavily. 'That was our Lola, she had such a kind heart. Loyal to the core.' Hearing her say this, I can't help wondering what Elisa's and Don's reactions would be if they knew Lola had kissed Damien Radcliffe, and that a photo of them kissing was sent anonymously to Bianca Radcliffe's mobile phone. A photo Bianca shared with all the women bar Simone. It's not something I plan on telling them for obvious reasons.

Just then, Elisa looks at me sharply, as if something's only just occurred to her. 'You're not thinking Lola betrayed one of their secrets and paid the price for it, are you? I wouldn't put it past the likes of that Bianca to go to such lengths, she's vicious.'

I shake my head. 'No. I'm not saying that at all. Just because Lola's knew some of their secrets doesn't mean that any of them were responsible for her murder. Far from it, and I can't stress that enough. They all left the party well after Lola, and took cabs home.'

'That's what they told you.' Elisa says. 'But how do we know for sure they got cabs? Did you see the receipts? The CCTV? How do we know they're not all in this together and backing each other up?'

She makes a good point, and my failure to respond is perhaps telling.

It also makes me wonder if Damien Radcliffe was at home all night, like Bianca insisted he was. Despite her acknowledging that she didn't see her husband until the following morning.

It's something I plan on asking him to his face when Wild and I pay him a visit this afternoon.

Chapter Twenty-Seven

Lola

Before
July 2023

It's the second Saturday in July, and I've just arrived at school with Luca for St Xavier's annual summer fete. Aside from the Christmas fair, it's their biggest fundraiser of the year, open to the public for a fiver per adult ticket, half price for kids. I'm on the cake stall at 11 a.m., giving me an hour to kill with Luca who, like most kids here, is keen to spend his pocket money on all kinds of tat he doesn't need. It's a beautiful day, so the footfall is higher than average, with the queue to get in running all the way down the hill. We stand in the boiling sun for about fifteen minutes before finally reaching the front entrance, where Clarissa and a few other mums are sitting behind a table taking money and handing out coloured wristbands in return.

'Hi, Lola, hi, Luca, so lovely to see you!' she exclaims, almost as if she's surprised we're here, even though she's the one who assigned me to the rota. I return the sentiment with a smile and ask if she's seen any of the others in our group.

'Bianca's on the tombola in the assembly hall, I think. Not sure if Joy or Simone are still here as they had the

9.30 a.m. shift on pin the donkey, but I've not seen them come back this way, so I assume they are. They might be outside near the bouncy castle, I guess. I think that's where Dee planned on taking her two after she finished her face painting shift, which is out on the main lawn.'

At the mere mention of a bouncy castle, Luca's face lights up.

'Mummy!' He pulls at my hand, nearly dislocating my arm from its socket. 'I want to go on the bouncy castle! Can we go there first?'

I look down at him and smile. 'Sure, sweetheart, course we can.' In my mind I'm hoping Simone's still there as she promised to watch Luca while I do my duty on the cake stall.

'Have a good time, make sure your mummy spends lots of cash!' Clarissa winks at Luca, before giving me a mischievous raised eyebrow. Looking at Clarissa right now, so full of get-up-and-go and cheerful self-assurance, you'd never imagine the pain she's hiding. I've wondered many times since last December if she took Bianca's advice and went to see a therapist. I hope so. No one should have to endure that kind of torment alone. All it does is eat away at you. I know that only too well.

Luca and I hustle our way through the swarms of people. The main hall is chock-full with stands of all varieties. I scan the hundreds of faces, hoping to spot Damien, even though I know it's unlikely he'll show up to something like this. I remember him saying that school fairs were his idea of a nightmare, and that he'd rather spend the morning working. I can't say I blame him. Looking around, there are definitely more mums than dads. In some respects, that's comforting because I feel less like a fish out of water. I spy Bianca on the tombola stall at the far end of the room. She's with a mum I vaguely recognise from the other class, and who right now is looking incredibly bored while Bianca appears to be running the show and in her element. Thank God I'm not with her. It would have been the longest thirty minutes of my life.

We battle our way outside onto the sizeable expanse of grass where there's a bouncy castle and various other stalls ranging from name-the-teddy to Nerf gun target shot to fortune telling.

'There's Jess, Esme and Erin!' Luca shouts. Before I know it, he's let go of my hand and sprinted towards the massive green and yellow inflatable castle, screaming out his friends' names, causing Simone, Dee and Joy to simultaneously turn their heads in my direction. They wave and I wave back, before I start walking towards them. As I do, I get an uneasy feeling in the pit of my stomach when I catch Joy's eye. It's nice to see her out and about again, looking so well, but I can't get her confession out of my head. The fact that she admitted to injecting her father – a type 1 diabetic – with an overdose of insulin, causing him to go into cardiac arrest one afternoon when he'd been napping at home and Joy's mother was out. The coroner ruled it an accidental overdose, apparently, something that can happen from time to time. Joy had worn gloves, and of course, her father's fingerprints were all over the reusable EpiPen. Dee's confession was shocking enough, but Joy's trumps hers by a mile. Cold, pre-meditated murder, rather than an accident at someone else's hands. How can I keep something so huge to myself, let alone act normally around her, knowing what she's done?

But then, when I look at our children, so innocent and vulnerable, when I think about someone hurting or abusing Luca, I know I wouldn't hesitate for one second to do the same as Joy. And because of this, I have this insatiable urge to protect her.

I can't give her up. Not after she begged me to keep quiet. 'Fuck, I shouldn't have said anything. It's unfair of me to lay this on you, it's the meds, they've loosened my tongue, made me blurt out things I shouldn't. Please, Lola. Please promise me you won't tell a soul,' she'd said. 'I can't let this get out, can't lose my kids. The scandal would damage them for life, and it would break Gav. I can't do that to them. Can't ruin their lives. What we have. Please, promise me, Lola.'

I saw the tears glistening in her eyes, and promised her there and then that her secret was safe with me. That I'd never do anything to jeopardise her freedom or her family's.

Luca's already bouncing up and down alongside his friends by the time I reach the girls. It's still baking, but looking up at the sky there's a bit more cloud coverage than earlier, taking the edge off.

'You OK to watch Luca while I do my shift on the cake stand?' I ask Simone.

She smiles. 'Of course, no probs.'

'Ugh, you're so lucky getting cakes,' Dee says. 'Face painting is the worst, principally because I'm shit at art, and can't even apply my own make-up. God knows why Clarissa lumbered me with that. Think she was having a laugh.'

'For Christ's sakes, Dee,' Joy chuckles, 'it's only kids' face painting, you're not making up the cast of *The Lion King*.'

We all chuckle with her. 'Fair point.' Dee holds up her hands.

'Ladies!'

All at once we swivel round to see Liam, Stephen and Damien coming towards us. My heart skips a beat at the sound of Damien's voice, and I immediately feel overcome with awkwardness. Simone notices. She briefly catches my eye, a look as if to say '*Are you insane?*', but thankfully Dee and Joy appear oblivious to my discomfort.

'You mums not having a go?' Damien gestures to the bouncy castle, a twinkle in his eye. He fixes his gaze on me, and I feel my insides bubble with excitement. I just can't help the way he makes me feel, I only wish I could. None of this is my fault; he's the one doing the flirting. If only he ignored me, avoided direct eye contact, I'm sure I'd get over him before long. But clearly, he revels in the undeniable attraction between us.

'No, it's for kids only. Which means you guys are all eligible,' Dee says with a grin. We all laugh.

'Good one,' Damien says.

Just then, the children jump off the bouncy castle and come bounding towards us.

'Hey, little man!' Liam scoops Luca up in his arms and starts spinning him around. Luca giggles uncontrollably and it makes me smile seeing him so happy.

'Do it to us!' the girls all say in unison. Liam puts Luca down and one by one swirls each of the girls around.

We all laugh along. All except Simone, who seems vacant all of a sudden. 'What's wrong?' I whisper.

She looks at me nervously. The others are all laughing and locked in animated conversation, as they watch Liam entertain the kids, so I'm certain they won't hear us if we keep our voices low.

'It's nothing,' she whispers back.

'What? No, it's not, I can tell. What's wrong?'

'I'm worried Liam's having an affair with his receptionist.'

I look at her, stunned. 'What? No way! Liam adores you! He would never in a million years cheat on you.'

'I'm not so sure.' She shakes her head. 'He's been working late a lot recently. I've seen Siobhan. She's gorgeous, and she flirts bigtime with him, something he's admitted to me himself.' As I look into Simone's eyes, I see the tears forming.

'I don't believe it, not for one second. Why don't you ask him?'

She shakes her head vehemently. 'No way, he'd go ballistic.'

'Liam? Why?'

'Because I've done this before. Accused him of having an affair.'

'You have? Why?'

'Because he's smart and gorgeous and a doctor, and I still can't believe he picked me.'

'But you two are so happy. How can you even think he'd stray. You're bloody gorgeous too.'

Simone gives me a shy smile, then a little shrug. 'I don't know. I guess I've never had a lot of confidence. Dad was so harsh on my sister and me. And Mum, although I love her to bits, she was very critical of the way I looked growing up. She'd tell me to lose weight if I put on a few pounds, criticise what I wore or the way I styled my hair as a teenager.'

'She did? Well, more fool her. You take no notice, you're stunning and smart and Liam's lucky to have you. I can one hundred per cent guarantee he's not having an affair. If anything, he should be worried about you straying!'

Just then, Liam happens to turn around and look our way. He catches both our eyes and gives a big grin. Then lets his gaze settle on Simone. His intense look of longing speaks volumes. She smiles back shyly.

'See?' I say. 'If a man looked at me that way, I'm sure I'd think I was the most beautiful woman on earth.'

Another coy smile. 'Yes, I guess you're right,' Simone says. 'I just get so jealous sometimes, when I see the way women look at him.'

'It's normal,' I say. 'I bet Liam gets jealous of the way men look at you. I've noticed it when we've been out.'

Simone sighs. 'He does get jealous, that's true. Too jealous sometimes.'

I'm about to ask what she means by this when Dee looks our way and tells us the kids all want ice cream. 'Come on, let's go,' Simone says, 'I could do with cooling down myself.'

I follow Simone's lead, and at the same I can't help wondering whether her last comment had a double meaning to it, given what we've just discussed.

Chapter Twenty-Eight

Detective Inspector John Banner

Wednesday, 20th December 2023

It's 3 p.m. and Wild and I have just arrived at the offices of The Radcliffe Group in Wimbledon. A family run affair started by Damien Radcliffe's father, John. According to the website, it offers premium IT support services to small and medium-sized businesses based in Wimbledon and central London, and prides itself on providing friendly, efficient and personal service for its customers. Here's hoping Damien keeps up that friendly persona when I drop the bombshell that I know about him kissing Lola.

Wild drove us here, my conversation with the Mosleys occupying my thoughts for pretty much the whole journey, the shock and disbelief on their faces having learned that Lola was hiding such a terrible secret for so many years hard to shake. I hadn't had the heart to tell them about the self-harming. I decided no good could come from breaking that to them. And besides, Lola had stopped hurting herself by the summer thanks to Deidre's help, despite the threatening messages she'd been receiving, along with the cold treatment directed towards her by those in her immediate circle at school. Two things that could have sent her spiralling again. I know this because the postmortem turned up no evidence to suggest she had regressed.

We've been asked to take a seat by Damien's PA in the slick, shiny waiting area, and the man himself soon appears, offering us a warm smile and a confident handshake. He's a handsome guy, looking much younger than his forty-four years, and I can see why someone like Lola might fall for his charms. He asks his PA to bring some coffee through to his office before ushering us inside and closing the door behind him.

It's an impressive space, as glossy as the waiting area, not to mention Damien himself. Damien's desk is set against a vast window overlooking Wimbledon Village, an expensive-looking black leather couch and matching armchair, along with a tasteful glass-topped coffee table, nestled in the far right corner. Damien directs us towards the couch, while he perches on the adjacent armchair.

'Thanks for seeing us at such short notice,' I say.

Everything about Damien exudes confidence, from his open hand gestures to his assertive tone of voice, to his radiant smile. But I wonder if it's all an act. Whether, in fact, he suspects why Wild and I are here, and inside he's shitting bricks. The fact is, some people are better than others at putting on a face, but you can be sure that even the most carefully constructed façades are penetrable.

'My pleasure,' Damien smiles. Just then, his PA appears with a tray of coffee. She lays it down on the table in front of us, before Damien thanks her and says he'll take things from there.

She leaves and he starts pouring the coffee. 'So, how can I help? You mentioned there'd been some developments regarding poor Lola's murder. That's good to hear.

I can still hardly believe it myself. That poor child of hers. No father, and now no mother. It's so sad, so terribly sad.'

I can't help feeling he's overegging it a bit, but that doesn't necessarily make him a murderer. I tell myself to keep an open mind.

I fill him in on the threatening texts Lola had been receiving since October, about the messages she'd exchanged with Simone before she was murdered, and about the cold treatment his wife and the rest of their circle at St Xavier's had been giving Lola.

For the first time, Damien looks unsettled. 'Really? Gosh, I had no idea, that's awful. Why would they do such a thing? I wasn't there at the party that night, of course. I was at home sick, and doing my best to look after the kids.'

His response tells me that neither Joy nor Dee have told Bianca about my recent conversations with them. It follows that Damien won't be aware of Lola's diary, or the fact that I know Bianca forced him to stay home last Friday because she didn't want him anywhere near Lola.

I don't waste time enlightening him. 'We know that's not true. The being sick part, at least.'

Damien gives an uncomfortable chuckle. 'What? How do you mean? I *was* sick.'

'No, you weren't. Your wife ordered you to stay home because you kissed Lola.'

At this, Damien's face turns scarlet. 'What? That's absurd.'

'We know about the photo sent to your wife's phone, Damien. There's no point denying it. Lola also kept a diary, in which she described your kiss.'

'Jesus,' Damien mutters. He fiddles with his tie. 'OK, you got me, I wasn't ill. And you're right, Bianca forced me to stay at home. But that's where I was all night. I swear it.'

It's hard to know if he's telling the truth as far as his whereabouts are concerned, but I leave that for now and move on.

'Tell me what happened between you and Lola. How things panned out when you told her the kiss couldn't happen again.'

Damien sighs then leans back in his chair. The confident façade has all but vanished, and suddenly he's just like any other man. Vulnerable. Fallible. Human.

'Lola was a beautiful girl. She had a lovely personality too. Kind, caring. Warm-hearted. I love my wife, but she's not the easiest of women. She can be very demanding, very self-centred at times, not to mention judgmental. Bianca wasn't particularly nice to Lola when Luca joined the school and her attitude pissed me off. I made a point of being friendly, and sure, yes, I am a natural flirt, and I could tell she fancied me. I hold my hands up, it felt good to have a beautiful, younger woman like Lola, fancy me; it was flattering, made me feel good about myself, reassured me that I still had that effect on women, and I couldn't help but indulge that, particularly as Bianca and I were going through a bit of a dry spell – sexually.' He pauses. 'Jesus, I can't believe I'm saying this out loud.'

'It's OK, it's best you're honest,' I say. 'Please, continue.'

'Anyway, I'm sure you heard about the playground squabble between my daughter, Summer, and Luca?'

I nod.

'Well, again, and I know I shouldn't say such things about my wife, but the fact is Bianca was a real bitch to Lola when we got called in, and it angered me. Particularly when I then learned from Lola that Summer had taunted

Luca about not having a father. I knew where that came from and I confronted Bianca about it. I was mad at her for filling our daughter with spiteful thoughts. And like I said, things weren't exactly rosy between me and Bianca at the time. I texted Lola back, reassured her it was all Summer's fault, that Luca was a good child, and that he'd never have intentionally hurt Summer. I sensed that's what she was most worried about. About Luca having violent tendencies or something.' He chuckles uneasily. 'I think all parents get a bit freaked out when their kids get into a fight, and just want reassurance it's nothing to worry about long-term. Wouldn't you agree, Inspector?'

More's the point, Lola feared him turning out like Luca's father, I think to myself. Still, I don't voice this out loud, because based on Damien's response it's pretty clear he's in the dark on that score. I nod. 'Yes, I think that's fair.'

'Anyway,' Damien continues, 'we started texting pretty regularly – telling each other things about our days, funny things the kids had done. I'd sometimes talk about work, and so would she.'

'And your wife never found out?'

'No, she doesn't have my passcode. I convinced myself I wasn't cheating on the basis that it was just texting, conversation. But I knew deep down it was more than that. It was serious flirting. And when we saw each other at school, or at parent drinks, there was undeniable sexual tension, and I'll admit, I enjoyed it. It was exhilarating, exciting. It always is, isn't it? Forbidden fruit.'

I don't comment. Tell him to go on.

'Anyway, after the kids broke up last summer, B and I spent a month or so at our apartment in Majorca. I didn't see Lola for a while, and the texts were less frequent.

But towards the end of the summer, just after the August bank holiday, I bumped into her along the river path, near Canbury Gardens. I'd gone for a run, and she was walking home from work. Luca was at Lola's place with his grandparents. I'll admit, it was lovely to see her, and I suggested grabbing a drink. I shouldn't have done, it was stupid, and it gave her totally the wrong impression. But she looked so pretty, and I could tell how pleased she was to see me, and it was a huge boost to my ego, I'm ashamed to say. Just the night before, B and I had rowed and slept in separate beds.'

'I see. Go on.'

'Anyway, we grabbed a drink in the Boaters pub. Two drinks, actually. It was nice and there was definite flirting going on. We were both a bit tipsy and when we came out of the pub, there was a moment.'

'A moment?'

'Yes. She looked at me, I looked at her, and I couldn't help myself. I leaned in, and I kissed her. I guess it had been a long time coming.'

'And then?'

'And then I stopped myself, quickly broke away. I felt so ashamed, especially to have kissed her in such a public place. It was the booze, I guess, it loosened my inhibitions, but I was lucid enough to know what a bad idea it was and that I was risking my family all for the sake of some minor infatuation and pathetic ego boost.'

'So that's all Lola was to you, some minor infatuation?' I say.

Damien's cheeks colour. 'Yes, I'm afraid so. But Lola took my rejection badly. She told me in her texts that she was in love with me, that she thought about me all the time and that she knew I felt the same. I tried to let her down gently, but she had a major crush on me, I guess, couldn't see reason. I told her our kissing had been a mistake.'

'I see. And what happened in the following days, weeks?'

'She kept messaging me, asking if we could meet, just to talk. But I blanked her. Also because of the message Bianca received. Bianca told me to have no more contact with Lola.'

'And what was Lola's reaction?'

'Not good. She became stroppy, told me I'd led her on, that I couldn't treat her like this. So I blocked her. But then she emailed me at work, and it scared the hell out of me. I mean, it was starting to feel like full-on Glenn Close *Fatal Attraction* style even though all we'd done was kiss. I told Dee about it, just because I felt like I had to tell someone, and I knew how trustworthy she is. I was too scared to tell Bianca.'

As I sit here listening to Damien, I feel saddened that such a beautiful, kind and intelligent young woman like Lola appeared to have lost all sense of perspective where he was concerned. It's not as if she was short on love from her parents, but maybe that wasn't enough, and she yearned for romantic love; was perhaps instinctively drawn to a secure, charming, successful family man like Damien. Someone she saw as safe, while appearing unhappy in his marriage to Bianca.

'Going back to the anonymous text message you mentioned Bianca received,' Damien goes on, 'the one attaching the photo of Lola and me kissing, that was perhaps a couple of weeks after we kissed, at the start of the new term. As you can imagine, she went ballistic. I told her exactly how it happened, begged for her forgiveness, and reassured her that nothing like that had ever happened before or since.'

'And did she believe you?'

'I really can't say for sure. I mean yes, I'd like to think so. I told her we should tell Lola, because it was creepy. Clearly, we were being watched by someone we knew, because why else take the photo? Why send it to Bianca? It's not like I'm famous, or we're multi-millionaires. I mean, yes, we're comfortable, but we don't have Clarissa and George's level of wealth. It seemed obvious to me that whoever took it wanted to cause us trouble.'

'Any idea who it might have been? Perhaps a client, or someone you work with?'

Damien shakes his head. Then he shrugs. 'I suppose it could have been, although I can't think who. Really, I've no idea at all who might have sent it.'

'Could it have been one of Bianca's mum friends?'

'No way, they'd never do anything like that to B! When B told them, they were shocked.'

'But Bianca wouldn't let you tell Lola about the photo?'

'No, she forbade me from having any more contact with her, like I said.'

'She wanted to make Lola suffer, didn't she?' I say. 'That's why she told the other mums to give Lola the cold shoulder but keep her in the dark as to why.'

Damien nods meekly. 'Yes. She was hurting. I understood why she did what she did.'

I allow my eyes to drill through Damien's. 'Do you think your wife killed Lola?'

Damien looks aghast. 'What? No, that's insane!'

'Is it? She was upset. Felt betrayed. Intimidated by a younger, dare I say it, prettier mum who her handsome husband fancied, but more importantly kissed. How could she be certain you wouldn't do it again? That you wouldn't take things further? You admitted yourself that you enjoyed the attention, the flirting.'

'Bianca may be hot-headed, but she's not a killer.'

'Everyone has the potential to kill, Damien, simply because we're all human. It just takes the right moment, and the right circumstances. You've heard the term "crime of passion"? You'd be surprised how many ordinary seemingly placid people in this world have killed over a loved one. The green-eyed monster is an ugly beast.'

Damien shakes his head. 'No, I don't believe it. Besides, she came home by taxi, after Lola left.'

'You know that for sure, do you? You saw her that night? When she came home?'

Damien starts to clam up again. 'Er, no, I was asleep, in the spare room. We didn't actually see each other until the next morning.'

'Why the spare room?'

Damien hesitates.

'Why?' My eyes bore through his again.

'Because we argued the night of the party. Before she left the house.'

'About what?'

'I told her she was being ridiculous in not letting me go. That she needed to trust me in front of Lola, and that I couldn't avoid these types of social situations forever.'

'And did she see reason?'

'Well, no. She accused me of being desperate to see Lola. Said she didn't trust me as far as she could throw me. She'd had a glass or two of wine already, so I guess she wasn't thinking straight.'

'I see. So she was aggressive, would you say? Out of control?'

'What? No! I didn't mean to imply she was drunk or mad enough to kill Lola. Bianca isn't stupid, she loves her life, she has too much to lose to do a thing like that.'

'And what about you? Were you at home the whole night?'

Damien frowns. 'Yes, of course, I wasn't going to leave the kids alone, was I?' He gives me a cross look, as if I've asked the most ridiculous question to which he takes serious offence.

Even so, there's something in his demeanour that tells me Damien's not being entirely honest with me. For now, though, I decide to let things be.

Relief floods his face when I tell him we're done. He shows us to the door and opens it, at which point I pause, and take one last look around the office. 'Impressive offices you have here. I'm guessing you're a whizz with computers?'

Damien gives a nervous chuckle. 'Well, yes, this is an IT business, I'd need to know something about them.'

'You wouldn't want to risk losing something you and your father have worked so hard to build up, would you?'

'What's that supposed to mean?'

I smile. 'Nothing. Not for now, at least. We'll be in touch.'

Wild and I leave. And as we do, I think I can hear the sound of Damien's racing heart.

What isn't he telling me?

Chapter Twenty-Nine

Lola

Before
November 2023

Why aren't my messages getting through to him? It keeps saying 'sent as a text message' rather than 'delivered'. Has Damien blocked me? The very thought makes me sick to my stomach. Like I'm a menace. Or a plaything that can be tossed aside with no thought to my feelings.

Why has he gone so cold on me? How could he be so cruel, so hurtful, as if I mean nothing to him? After all, he was the one who kissed me, not the other way around. OK, so I was thrilled to bump into him that balmy afternoon in late August. I hadn't laid eyes on him in over a month and we had barely exchanged a single text, though during term time I'd see him at least once a week at the school gates and we would message each other regularly. Even though I knew he could never be mine and that it was wrong of me to lust after a married man, seeing him lit a fire in me. I never thought I'd turn into that kind of woman, particularly after what happened to me. But right from that first day we met in the playground, when Damien came to my rescue, defending me in front of Bianca, making me feel so welcome, I couldn't help falling for him. There was just something about him I found impossible to resist. Something familiar. Empathetic. But I guess that's human nature, isn't it? There's no simple formula for it, no on or off switch. We can't choose who we fall for. If only it were that easy.

For so long, I'd lain in bed night after night, imagining his lips on mine, his body pressed against my flesh, dreaming about him making love to me, us being a couple. That magical time of the day when I can stop what I'm doing and close my eyes, block out reality and escape to my fantasy world. A world with no Bianca. No restrictions on our being together.

I know I didn't imagine the heat that existed between us from the first time we met; the unspoken desire that gave me the kind of natural heady high that leaves you walking on air. And I feel certain he felt it too. I saw the longing in his eyes when we ran into each other on the river path. I could tell he didn't want the moment to end, which is why he suggested grabbing a drink. Again, it was him who initiated things, not me. And when we talked, it was so easy, like we'd known each other forever, the simmering tension between us exhilarating and yet, at the same time, unbearable. After agreeing to his suggestion of a drink, I phoned my parents and told them I'd bumped into Simone and was having a catch-up. I felt so bad for lying to them yet again. But if I told Mum I'd gone for a drink with Bianca's husband, she'd only worry and draw the wrong conclusions. Or the right ones, I guess…

I didn't want our time alone together to end. But, of course, it had to, eventually. We stepped out of the pub into the sultry evening, our bodies warm and relaxed from the alcohol, then strolled a few feet away from the main entrance in the direction of the river path. And that's when

Damien took my hand and stopped me in my tracks. Told me how nice this had been, how I was so easy to talk to. I could tell he was miserable at home. That Bianca had trapped him in a loveless marriage. He deserved so much more than that. He was craving the love and affection I so wanted to give him. I'm sure I wasn't imagining that; I felt it in my bones. And that's when he leaned in and kissed me. I could feel the desire radiating off him. And the kiss was magical, exactly how I expected it to be. But then, just like that, he quickly broke away. Mindful of our surroundings. The fact that we were in a busy area, and that someone we knew might have seen us. Even though he'd already said that Bianca was at home with the kids.

'What's wrong?' I asked.

His eyes had immediately darted left and right, then over my shoulder. 'Sorry, this isn't right. I was wrong to kiss you, please forgive me.'

He didn't even give me a chance to respond. Just took off like a shot, tearing down the river path as if he was in danger. Is that how he thought of me at that moment? Dangerous?

I won't deny that it hurt. Him taking off like that. It hurt like hell, in fact. But I guess at that moment I understood, because we were in a public place and he was nervous we'd been seen.

Later that night, I texted him. Asked him if he was OK. His response had been brief. He said he was fine but tired and that we'd talk soon. But we haven't spoken since, despite me telling him in subsequent texts how I couldn't stop thinking about him, and that I was falling in love with him and was sure he was falling for me. I knew how unhappy he was, and I told him that more than anything in this world I wanted us to repeat our kiss, suggesting that we meet in private somewhere. But he never acknowledged my invitation. His responses continued to be brief, always with some excuse that he was busy, tied up at work or with the kids. And now his messages have stopped altogether. Leaving me with no choice but to email him at work, if that's what it takes to get a decent response out of him. He owes me that. He can't just flirt with me for a year, send me messages, kiss me, then not have the courtesy to explain his distant behaviour. I won't have it. Won't be made to feel like a worthless piece of shit again.

I was beside myself last night and couldn't help unburdening myself to Tracy. She was as patient and kind as ever, but I sensed how disappointed she was in me. She's warned me off Damien countless times. Said he's just playing with me. That he enjoys having his ego massaged because that's what men his age do. *Think of Luca*, she'd said. *Think of the scandal that would erupt if you got involved with a married man. Bianca would tear you to shreds, and your face would be mud at school. Because let's face it, the mistress always comes off worse. Don't go there. You can't let Luca suffer. He's suffered enough.*

Deep down, I know Tracy's right. That it can never be. Not in the real world, at least. Only in my fantasy realm.

I just want some alone time with him. I deserve that. I can't have a man treat me like crap again. Use me for his kicks, then toss me aside.

Respect, that's all I want. And if I have to resort to banging down his front door, then so be it.

Chapter Thirty

Detective Inspector John Banner

Thursday, 21st December 2023

'It's good of you to see me again, Simone. How are you doing?'

I'm sitting with Simone at her kitchen table. Looking at her, she doesn't appear much better than when I was last here on Monday. Her naturally pretty face remains drawn, her hair dishevelled, and I'm certain she's wearing the same outfit as before. I can make out food stains on her turtleneck sweater. Still, it's been less than a week since her best friend's murder; it's not something she's going to get over quickly.

'I'm OK, I guess,' she says wearily. 'I'm glad the kids have broken up; I can't face the school gates right now. I'm afraid I'll say something I'll regret.'

'So you've not been to school since it happened?'

She shakes her head. 'No. Liam covered the school run for me the first couple of days. My parents got back from holiday on Tuesday night, so Mum helped out yesterday while Liam took Luca to the playground when you were over at the Mosleys'. I felt bad for not going with him, but I couldn't face it in the end. The last thing I wanted was to break down in front of Luca; he needs to be surrounded by strength, not weakness.'

'That's very considerate of you, but grieving isn't a sign of weakness; it shows how much you cared for Lola.'

She shakes her head again. 'That's kind of you to say. But in truth, I wish I was stronger.'

'It's good you have family around to help out,' I say.

'Yes.' She nods. 'I don't know what I'd do without Mum and Dad. They were always strict with me and Ruby when we were kids, but I can't fault them for being great grandparents. It was the same for Lola.' Her voice catches. 'Poor Elisa and Don. They're such good people, how are they coping? I wanted to reach out and call them this morning, apologise for not helping out with Luca yesterday. But I wasn't sure if they'd prefer to be left alone.'

'They're not great, I won't lie,' I say. 'But they'll get through this, for Luca's sake. And I'm certain they won't mind you reaching out. They knew how close you and Lola were. To be frank, I think you were the only one they liked in your parents circle.'

Simone nods again. 'OK, I will then. I should probably get out of the house, when I think about it. Going a bit stir crazy inside. I'll go round later. See if they need anything. And you're right, they need to be strong for Luca. Having said that, Liam and I want to help them in any way we can. It's not easy looking after a child full-time at any age, let alone at Elisa and Don's ages. If they need us to have him anytime, we'd be only too happy to.'

I nod. 'That's kind, but they seem pretty fit. And one child is much easier to handle.' I give a light chuckle to briefly lighten the mood. 'That's what my wife tells me, anyway, whenever I broach the subject of a younger sibling for our son.'

She smiles for the first time. 'Your wife's spot on.'

There's a short pause, then I continue. 'Simone, I've now had the chance to speak with Clarissa, Deidre, Joy and Bianca.'

Her eyes narrow. 'Oh, yes, and what lies did they spout? I'm guessing they pretended to be heartbroken over Lola's death.'

'They professed to be upset, yes.'

'Naturally. And did you mention the text Lola sent me, saying how she couldn't wait to get out of the party on Friday? How it was a nightmare.'

'I did,' I say. 'Initially, they claimed to have no idea what Lola was talking about.'

Simone sniggers. 'Of course they would.'

'But since then I've come to discover the reason your friends have been giving Lola the silent treatment these past few months. And at the party.'

She looks up. Is that a glimmer of hope in her eyes? 'You have?'

'Yes. It appears Bianca ordered them to cut Lola off.'

She shakes her head. 'Can't say I'm surprised. She is the ringleader and never liked Lola from the start. But was there any particular reason?'

'Yes. She received an anonymous text message in early September attaching a photo of Lola and Damien Radcliffe kissing.'

At this, Simone's face drops. 'No, I don't believe it.'

'It's true.'

She runs her fingers through her hair in frustration. 'Oh, Lola, how could you have been so stupid! Why didn't she tell me? She promised me she'd leave well alone.'

I can't blame Simone for being frustrated that Lola failed to confide something so huge in her. And it's interesting that Lola chose to tell Tracy but not her best friend.

Clearly, she trusted Tracy implicitly. The prime reason I'm here is to ask Simone if she's thought of anything else that might be relevant to the investigation following our initial conversation on Monday. Specifically with regards to her comment that Damien had flirted with Lola. And it seems from Simone's reaction that there is more to tell. I can't help wondering why she held back before.

'Leave Damien alone, you mean?' I say. 'When we spoke on Monday you mentioned he flirted with Lola that day she first met you all in the playground. But now it seems like you're saying she was romantically interested in Damien, wanted something more to happen? Why didn't you say so then?'

Simone sighs. 'I guess I didn't think it was relevant to the investigation. Plus the last thing I wanted was to paint Lola in a bad light. Like she was some kind of conniving home-wrecker. She really wasn't like that. She was just a bit fragile, I guess. Desperate to find love. And Damien, well, he led her on from the start. He's such a bastard. I warned Lola not to go there, told her no good could come of it. Bianca must have given him hell for kissing Lola. And I can't say I blame her, for all her faults. Bloody men.'

I nod. 'Yes, she did give him hell. She forbade him from going to the party last Friday, and made him block Lola on his phone and from his email.'

'I can't believe Lola didn't tell me the reason they were blanking her. She acted like she had no clue. She made me ask them, for goodness' sake.'

I shake my head. 'Actually, I don't think she was hiding that part from you. As far as we know, Lola had no idea about the photo.'

'She didn't?'

'No. I mean, it's clear she had her suspicions Bianca somehow found out, but that's all they were. Suspicions. The women agreed to keep it between themselves, at Bianca's insistence.'

'She wanted to punish Lola by giving her the silent treatment? Make her feel like some kind of pariah?' Simone says. 'It's why they didn't tell me, I guess. They knew I'd go straight to Lola.'

'Yes, it would seem so.'

Simone creases her brow. 'You said it's clear Lola had her suspicions that Bianca found out about the kiss. How so?'

I pause. 'That's what I was coming to. Lola kept a diary.'

Simone looks at me curiously. 'A diary?'

'Yes. That's how I know she was worried Bianca had somehow got wind of the kiss. In it, she talks about her feelings for Damien and the kiss. How hurt she was that he rebuffed her. It was clear she was obsessed with him. Dangerously so. She even turned up at his work, after he blocked her on his phone. At which point he became pretty angry and threatened to get a restraining order.'

Simone looks aghast. 'Poor Lola. What else did it say?'

I look at Simone gravely. 'This is going to come as something of a shock, but I feel you have a right to know being Lola's best friend. It appears that Luca's father didn't die in a car accident.'

Simone frowns. 'He didn't?'

'No.'

'How did he die, then?'

'That's the thing. We don't actually know if he's alive or dead. Lola was raped at university. And Luca is the product of that.'

Simone instinctively covers her mouth in disbelief, her eyes wide with horror. I omit to mention that Deidre was the first person in their immediate circle to learn this shocking news. Right now, the other school mums in their tight-knit group aren't exactly in Simone's good books, and if she hears that Lola told Deidre such an intimate secret, I can only imagine Simone's reaction. She'll feel hurt, devastated even, and will doubtless go knocking on Deidre's door no sooner have I left her alone, demanding to know why Lola chose to tell her rather than Simone, her best friend.

'What? No, that can't be,' Simone says. 'How could she not tell me something like that? How could she have kept something so huge from me? Poor Lola, I, I just can't believe it. Is that why she was so protective over Luca? Did she keep it from her parents too? Surely not?'

I nod. 'Yes, she did. I broke the news to Elisa and Don yesterday, while Liam was watching Luca. As you can imagine, they're in bits.'

Simone looks stunned. Her silence speaks volumes.

'I know this is hard, but I'm afraid there's more. Lola wasn't her real name. It was Elizabeth Mosley. She told her parents not to question her decision to take her grandmother's name. She said she had her reasons and that they needed to let things be. I can't go into too much detail but we think she moved down south because she was scared her attacker might find her, possibly even abduct Luca.'

Simone shakes her head slowly, as if she's in a trance. 'She must have lived in constant fear.'

'Yes, it certainly seems that way from what she wrote in her diary.'

'So, do you think the man who raped her killed Lola? That he somehow tracked her down. But why would he do that? It makes no sense. She can't have been a threat to him, can she? Not all these years later?'

'Yes, I agree, and that's why I'm not convinced it was him who murdered Lola, even though it's one theory based on the threats he made and how terrified she was of him coming back into her life. Which brings me to something else.'

'What?'

'We've also come to learn that Lola was a regular user of an online chat forum called Here to Chat,' I say. 'It was like therapy, where she discussed her problems, fears, difficult stuff she'd been going through. Did you know about that?'

Once again Simone looks dumbfounded. Which tells me she had no idea. Her reaction is hardly surprising, I'm laying on the bombshells thick and fast. But I had to ask; she was Lola's best friend. She shakes her head. Has the same bemused look on her face, similar to how Elisa and Don reacted. 'No. It appears I didn't know a lot about my friend. Why would she have gone on some dodgy website when she had two loving parents and me to talk to?' Hurt creeps up on her face. 'Why talk to some stranger online? It sounds so dicey. I mean, do we even know who this person is?'

I explain how Lola's subscription to Here to Chat dated back to her student days. 'It appears Lola befriended someone called Tracy. She helped Lola deal with exam pressure, and later – the rape. We also believe she advised her to move away and make a fresh start, after Luca was born.'

'You got this from the diary?'

'No. Another source. That's all I can say at this moment.'

'Another source?' She looks at me quizzically. I can't blame her. I'm being cryptic. But I don't want to betray Deidre's confidence at this point. And again, I can't help thinking Simone will be jealous that Lola confided something so huge in Deidre, but not in her.

'Have you been able to track down this Tracy?' she asks.

'No, not yet. My digital forensics team are working on that.'

'I see. Do you think Lola might have told her about Damien? About Bianca and the others acting so coldly towards her after Bianca received the photo of them kissing?'

'Yes, I do, and not just because she trusted her. Yesterday, I received an anonymous text message from someone claiming to be the only person Lola could trust. I believe it was Tracy. She warned me that the mums at school were hiding some dark secrets and couldn't be trusted.' I pause. Then say, 'Do you know what she might have been referring to?'

Simone shakes her head. 'No, I don't. Genuinely. And as much as I want to believe this Tracy friend of Lola's means well, don't you think it feels a bit dodgy her messaging you out of the blue like that? Also, how do we know she's telling the truth, and not just making trouble for the others by pinning the blame on them? I've known these women for three years, and I'd like to think I'd have some inkling of any secrets they might be keeping. Besides, why would they tell their secrets to Lola, who was still fairly new to the group? It doesn't make a lot of sense to me.'

Simone has a good point, except in the case of Deidre, who I remain convinced confided something in Lola in exchange for Lola being honest with her. Having said that, Deidre made it clear to the others in the group that Lola had been through a tough time. Perhaps this, together with Lola being a single mum, made her seem more empathetic in the others' eyes. Vulnerable, trustworthy even, in being able to relate to their sufferings. In contrast, perhaps they deliberately erected barriers with one another, wanting to appear stronger and more together than they actually were. But of course, I can't tell Simone my theory, because then I'd have to tell her what happened between Lola and Deidre.

'Then again, maybe I'm wrong.' Simone shakes her head. 'I really don't know what to think or who to believe anymore. But one thing seems clear to me, which is that you need to find this Tracy person. She could be the answer to everything.'

Chapter Thirty-One

Lola

Before
Late November 2023

HERETOCHAT.ORG
Chat Now in confidence. We're here for each other

Lola: I did something bad.

    Tracy: What? Are you OK?

Lola: No, I'm not OK.

    Tracy: Why? What did you do?

Lola: I don't want to say – you're going to be so mad with me.

    Tracy: It's Damien, isn't it?

Lola: Yep.

    Tracy: Tell me, hon, it's OK, I won't be mad.

Lola: But you told me to steer clear after he blocked me on his phone.

    Tracy: Yes, and for your own good. It's not good for your mental health, or for Luca, obsessing over this man who clearly isn't worth it. He took advantage of you in the park. It was a one-time thing, you know that. If Bianca finds out, she'll make your life a living hell, and Luca's. You may have to pull him out of St Xavier's. And that will devastate him.

Lola: It might be too late for that.

Tracy: Why? What did you do?

Lola: I emailed him at work. Got pissed off when he didn't reply. So I went to his office and demanded to speak to him. He had no choice but to see me. He didn't want to cause a scene in front of his colleagues.

Tracy: Lola, no!

Lola: I couldn't help it. I just felt so cheap, so used, that I deserved an explanation. I really thought he'd fallen in love with me.

Tracy: Oh, Lola, how could you have shown up at his work? He's never going to leave Bianca; he has a reputation to protect and all you were was a boost to his ego. I'm sorry to say it, but it's the truth.

Lola: Thanks for that. Thanks for making me feel better.

Tracy: I didn't mean it like that. All I'm trying to say is that he's not worth it. How could you go to his office? You know how people gossip.

Lola: Because I was desperate. He couldn't just kiss me and then treat me like I was nothing.

Tracy: What did he say?

Lola: He said if I didn't stop harassing him, he'd file a restraining order against me and then Luca might get taken away from me. It scared the shit out of me. I never thought he might threaten something like that. So I left.

Tracy: Lola, you can't win this battle. You have to back off now, let it go. Move on. Focus on Luca. How can you be a proper mother to Luca when you're obsessing over Damien?

Lola: I know, and I will. His threat got me worried. He sounded so angry and it was a real wake-up call. And yet, and yet I still can't get him out of my head.

Tracy: For God's sake, Lola, you need to grow up!

Lola: You're angry.

Tracy: No, no, I'm not angry. I'm just worried for you. What if Bianca finds out?

Lola: He'd never tell her.

Tracy: You're sure about that? Maybe she knows already. Couldn't that be why she and everyone else at the school gates has been giving you the silent treatment?

Lola: Yes, I guess. Actually, no, I don't think that's the reason. She'd never be able to keep something like that to herself, and neither would the others. I'm certain at least one of them would have cracked and said something to me. There's something else that's got them riled, I'm sure of it. Something they think I've done or misled them about. I'm wondering if they know I lied about Luca's dad. Maybe Bianca did some digging, found out I made it up. I wouldn't put it past her. Maybe they think I'm sick in the head for making up something so horrific about my son's father.

Tracy: It's possible, I guess. But wouldn't Dee have set them right? Surely, she would have said something to justify why you made the car accident up, even if she didn't tell them the full story.

Lola: I guess. Yes, you're probably right about that.

Tracy: Has Simone said anything? Has she tried talking to them?

Lola: She asked them once and they fobbed her off, so I told her not to pursue things.

Tracy: Why?

Lola: I don't want her getting involved, taking sides. It's not her battle to fight.

Tracy: But it still makes things awkward for her, doesn't it? She's like piggy in the middle, trying to be friends with you and them at the same time.

Lola: Yeah, I know. And I feel bad for her. Just as well she can't make the Christmas party, I guess.

Tracy: You're not seriously still going, are you? After all that's gone on? What if he's there? How awkward is that going to be?

Lola: I've paid the deposit now.

Tracy: So what? It's only money. It's not worth it, particularly if Simone won't be there to give you company.

Lola: Mum said I should go, let my hair down.

Tracy: You mum means well but she has no idea you kissed Bianca's husband or that those women are blanking you. I'm sure she'd think differently if she did.

Lola: Yeah, I know, you're right. Simone offered to have me round to hers. Said we could have a sleepover, watch a movie.

Tracy: Sounds like a much better option to me.

Lola: You think I should give in to these women? Isn't that weak?

Tracy: That's not what I'm saying. I just think you need to think seriously about what you hope to gain from it. Luca should be your focus, not those women.

Lola: So I'm not allowed to have a social life because I have a son and I'm a single mum? I'm supposed to stay in every weekend till he's eighteen and buggers off and leaves me? Life has been so shit to me, I deserve more, to have a little fun, don't I? You have no idea about the loss I suffered. You think you know it all, but you don't! You don't know the half of it!

Tracy: What? No! What's got into you? You know that's not what I mean.

Lola: Sorry, I don't feel like chatting anymore. I'm signing off, have a good evening.

Tracy: Lola, wait, don't go, don't leave things like this.

Tracy: Lola, are you still there? Lola… talk to me.

Chapter Thirty-Two

Detective Inspector John Banner

Friday, 22nd December 2023

It's Friday morning, three days before Christmas. Mikey's school broke up yesterday and Jo's taken him to her parents in Richmond for the day. They're seeing a panto – *Peter Pan* – at the theatre there, and might end up staying overnight, knowing I'm likely to be wrapped up in Lola's case until late. I can't help feeling a tug of regret that I can't be with them, sad that I often miss out on family occasions like these, special moments in Mikey's childhood I'll never get back. Before I blink, he'll be a grown man, living his own life. Still, I became a police officer for a reason, and I know I'd never be content doing anything else. It's where I belong. I'll just have to make it up to Mikey when things calm down.

When I turn up at the Hiltons' house, I find Clarissa's two girls glued to the television watching *Frozen*, the smell of cinnamon candles and homemade mince pies filling the air.

I called ahead to let Clarissa know I needed to speak with her again, and although she wasn't rude, there was a definite note of irritation to her voice.

As before, we go through to the kitchen and she offers me a mince pie with my coffee. 'Go on, I made them this morning,' she urges. 'They're very good, if I do say so myself.'

'Sure, why not,' I say, despite having just had breakfast and not feeling in the least bit hungry. 'Is your husband at home?'

'No, he's in the office today, then he's off until the new year.'

'Ah, that's nice,' I say with a smile, while feeling slightly envious of the man. Clarissa doesn't comment, her expression deadpan, which makes me wonder if their argument last Friday is yet to resolve itself.

'So, how can I help you, Inspector? I told you everything I know when we spoke on Monday.'

From the confident glint in her eye, it's clear to me that neither Joy nor Deidre have told Clarissa about our conversations on Wednesday. In the same way they hadn't told Bianca. Given how close they all are, I find this surprising. On the other hand, perhaps they're simply too scared of these women to admit they broke their pact to keep things between themselves.

'I'm not sure that's true, Clarissa,' I say.

Her confident demeanour swiftly evaporates. 'How do you mean?'

'I know about Damien and Lola kissing. I know about the photo Bianca received and her subsequently ordering you, Joy and Deidre to freeze Lola out.'

Clarissa swallows hard. I continue. 'Silent treatment which had been ongoing since September and which perhaps got too much for Lola at the party on Friday, leading to her hasty departure.'

Clarissa fiddles with her lethally expensive-looking gold charm bracelet. 'How do you know all that?'

I tell her about Lola's diary, and my conversations with Deidre and Joy. She appears shocked at the first revelation, livid at the second. 'You mustn't blame Deidre and Joy,' I say. 'When I told them about Lola's diary, they had no choice but to come clean. As should you now.'

Clarissa bites her lip.

'I know you feel loyalty to Bianca, but you withheld crucial information.'

'Why is it crucial?'

'It explains why Lola left in such a hurry.'

'Yes, but it doesn't explain who murdered her as far as I can tell.'

'We don't know that.'

She frowns.

'The fact is, we don't know who killed Lola. It could very well have been someone at the party. Someone who bore a grudge against Lola. More than that, had come to hate her.'

Clarissa's expression grows angry. 'You're not suggesting Bianca killed Lola because of a kiss, are you? She made it up with Damien – they were OK, back on track.'

'Is that so? The way I hear things, Bianca ordered Damien to stay at home on Friday because she didn't trust him to be around Lola. Not only that, they were sleeping in separate beds. You told me Damien had a nasty bout of the flu, but Damien has admitted to me himself that this was untrue, so there's no point denying it.'

Clarissa swallows hard. 'I see.'

'Why say he was at home sick? Why not tell me the truth to save us all some time? What are you hiding, Clarissa?'

She bites her lip again. It's the most nervous I've seen her. 'I'm not hiding anything. I simply didn't want to paint B in a bad light. Didn't want suspicion being cast over her. She's been a good friend to me. Sure, she's not the easiest of women, but no one's perfect, and at least she doesn't pretend to be perfect. Unlike Lola.'

'What do you mean by that?'

'Lola made herself out to be this coy, butter-wouldn't-melt young single mum, who'd lost her son's father in a tragic accident. But she lied to us, betrayed us, after we welcomed her into our fold.'

There's that word again – betrayed. As with Deidre and Joy, it feels like Clarissa's not solely referring to the wrong done to Bianca. It feels more personal. 'How did she betray you, Clarissa? You're not just talking about Bianca, are you?' Clarissa's lips are quivering now. I press on. 'Did she discover something about you, Clarissa? Did she find out about Dinah and tell someone?'

Clarissa shrinks back in her chair. Her eyes wide. 'How do you know about Dinah? Why would that have anything to do with Lola?'

'Because I believe the man who raped Dinah, raped Lola.'

My words seem to reverberate in the air. The silence clanging in my ears. 'Lola was raped?' Clarissa murmurs. 'When? How do you know it was the same man?'

I tell her what I know. Describe the similarities between Lola and Dinah, despite Dinah not quite fitting the bill in not being an only child. Clarissa still doesn't speak, her face ashen. Eventually, she says, 'Why didn't Lola tell us the truth?'

I explain how Lola was too scared. That even her parents didn't know. But that she did confide in two people: Deidre and a friend she made on Here to Chat.

At this, Clarissa looks up sharply. 'Here to Chat?'

'Yes,' I say. 'Have you heard of it?'

She nods. 'I have.'

'How so?' I ask eagerly.

'Because Dinah was on it. She confided in someone called Tracy for around six months before she was raped.'

Chapter Thirty-Three

Detective Inspector John Banner

Friday, 22nd December 2023

'Dinah was on Here to Chat too?'

I'm stunned by Clarissa's revelation, particularly the fact that her sister confided in someone called Tracy too, all sorts of questions flying through my mind as I try to figure out what this might mean.

'Yes.' Clarissa nods.

'How do you know?'

'Because she told me a couple of months after she was raped, when I suggested that she seek professional help. Her mental health had rapidly declined and I could see how much she was struggling when I went to visit her in Bristol. She'd stopped going to lectures at uni. Stayed cooped up in her halls the whole time, too afraid to come out.'

'She didn't go home to Liverpool, to be with your parents?'

Clarissa shakes her head. 'Unlike me, Dinah was a bit of a wild child. She had a difficult relationship with my parents, my mother especially. They didn't see eye to eye. My sister and I also had a tricky relationship. She'd tell strangers who didn't know who her parents were that she was an only child, and pretend I didn't exist. Made out that she was the special one in the family.'

Could the Campus Prowler have been one of these 'strangers' Clarissa referred to? Maybe Dinah told him she was an only child, which explains why he attacked her. Then again, the guy we're looking at seems too methodical not to have done his research on his victims. Unless it was a spur-of-the-moment attack. But that seems unlikely, given how targeted his other attacks seem to have been. Something doesn't add up.

'Why's that?' I ask.

'Because I was so much older, I guess. I mean, she could have been my daughter. We never developed a sisterly bond. Never played together, never shared the kind of milestones that sisters normally do – boys, make-up, periods and so on. Plus, I always did things by the book. I never caused my parents any hassle, or gave them a hard time. Exams never stressed me out either, I shone in them, in fact, got a first from Oxford, a high-flying job in PR, married a millionaire, had two kids. My life took the seemingly perfect trajectory. Dinah, on the other hand, was always a bit prickly. Right from when she was a child. She hated exams, hated living her life along the straight and narrow. She dated the bad boys, the rebels, the dropouts. I think she felt suffocated in our family, and the pressure to succeed the way I had done was too much for her. And, of course, we had the added pressure of Dad being an MP and constantly in the limelight.' Clarissa pauses, her eyes filling with tears. 'It's why she pretended to be someone else. Called herself Michelle online. Claimed to have a loving relationship with her parents, but also someone who struggled with pressure. I think she was lonely, felt lost even. Which perhaps explains why she went on that chat forum to start with. She wanted the attention she felt I always got, even though I know how much my parents adored her. I blame myself; I was too wrapped up in my own life to pay attention to what was going on in hers. To realise just how much she was struggling.'

'Why seek help online and not see a qualified therapist in person, do you think?'

Clarissa sighs heavily. 'Like I said, Dinah could be a different person online, and no one would know. She didn't want to go and see someone in the flesh because of who our father was. Didn't want word spreading and the press getting wind of it.'

'I see. That makes sense. What did she tell you about the site?'

'She said she chatted with this woman called Tracy who she got on really well with because she'd also struggled with feeling the pressure at uni and therefore seemed to understand her.'

'So if Tracy was helping her, why did you suggest that Dinah needed to see a professional therapist after she was raped?'

Clarissa looks at me incredulously. 'For one, Dinah wasn't being wholly honest with this Tracy character as far as I could tell. I mean, she went by a different name, pretended to be an only child and close to her parents. Whoever this Tracy was, they weren't being given the full picture, only half-truths. How then, could they have truly understood Dinah, or helped her?'

It's a fair point. 'Did you say this to Dinah?' I ask.

Clarissa nods. 'Yes. But she fobbed me off. Said I was the one who didn't understand her. That Tracy made her feel better about herself, which is all that mattered.'

'I see.'

'But feeling the pressure at uni and being raped aren't exactly like for like, Inspector. I'm sure you get that. After the attack, Dinah became a recluse, wouldn't go out. It was as if she only felt safe when she was talking to this Tracy person on her laptop. That's all very well and good, but you have to face the outside world, don't you? It's not healthy to rely on someone you've never even met to make you feel better.'

'Did you have any inkling in the days leading up to her suicide that Dinah might take her own life?' I ask.

'Well, the last time I spoke with her she sounded very down. Apparently, Tracy told her she couldn't chat anymore.'

'Really? Did she tell Dinah why?'

'Not exactly. She just said she was dealing with something really big and had to take a break. I think it really upset Dinah. She'd come to rely on Tracy a lot, and it was a devastating blow when she was already so fragile. I think she felt like she'd been abandoned.'

Clarissa pauses, seemingly lost in her thoughts, the memory of her sister, along with the tragic circumstances surrounding her death, doubtless plaguing her mind. Eventually, she says, 'So, do you think Lola was speaking to the same woman? I'm guessing it would have been around the same time? Surely she can't have been, though? Because Dinah's Tracy told her she was taking a break from the site. Unless she was lying, of course.'

I shake my head. 'I don't know. If it was the same person, I agree it seems odd she told Dinah she was taking a break, but at the same time carried on speaking to Lola. Then again, the site has over a hundred million subscribers, and so there's bound to be more than one

Tracy on it. Even so, it's curious that both Lola and Dinah were students and victims of rape within a year of each other, and had been chatting to someone called Tracy around the time both attacks happened. I mean, we know Lola was still talking to Tracy right up to the day before she was murdered.'

I pause. I need to find out whether any of the other victims who've come forwarded were subscribers to Here to Chat and, if they were, whether they spoke to a Tracy. If not, it's most likely a coincidence as far as Dinah and Lola were concerned.

But if there's a pattern, then this is going to set some serious alarm bells ringing in my head.

Chapter Thirty-Four

Detective Inspector John Banner

Friday, 22nd December 2023

It's 6 p.m. Getting on for a week since Lola's murder and I'm still no closer to finding out who's responsible. It's vexing, and despite not being a religious man, I find myself praying for some answers soon. Right now, I'm sitting at my desk, having just got off a call with DCI Kane, the officer who kick-started the investigation into the Campus Prowler. He couldn't recall any of the victims he'd questioned mentioning being users of Here to Chat, but when I explained how both Lola and Clarissa's sister had subscribed to it within the timeframes the attacks were carried out, and had been targeted themselves, he said he would look into the possibility that other victims had done the same as a matter of urgency.

Just then, I get a call. It's DI Golding. I don't waste a second in answering, hoping he has good news with regards to recovering Lola's private messages with Tracy.

'Banner here,' I say.

'John Here to Chat were able to provide us with access to the deleted chat. I'm looking at it right now.'

My heart accelerates. 'Good work. Anything strike you at first glance?'

'Well, the chat dates back seven years; it's going to take days to go through it all.'

Exactly what I feared.

'But,' he goes on, 'looking at the more recent entries, it seems Lola and Tracy had a bit of a falling out towards the end of November.'

'They did?'

'Yes. But judging by their last exchange – which was, as you already know, the night before the Christmas party Lola attended – they appear to have made up.'

'What did they fall out over?'

'Tracy told Lola not to go to the party. This was after Lola explained how she'd gone to Damien Radcliffe's office and he'd threatened to take a restraining order out against her. It freaked her out, but she said she still planned on going to the party. She told Tracy she needed to live a little and that Tracy didn't know the half of what she'd been through.'

'That's a bit cryptic. Wonder what she meant by that?'

'Yes. Very cryptic, I agree. I have no idea. Tracy said Lola was asking for trouble in going, and that Luca would ultimately suffer for it.'

'But Lola didn't take kindly to that, I take it.'

'No, she didn't.'

'And then?'

'And then, after a two-week break, Lola came back on the chat and apologised to Tracy. Tracy had sent several messages in the interim asking Lola if she was OK, and that she was worried about her, but Lola didn't reply until last Thursday evening. The funny thing is, Tracy seems to have had a change of heart about the party at this point.'

'In what way?'

'She said she was wrong to advise Lola not to go, and that Lola shouldn't cower to the other mums. She called them bullies, said Lola shouldn't let them think they'd won.'

'Quite the about-turn. Anything else that grabbed your immediate attention?'

'Yes, there was something else. Tracy suggested one of the mums might be behind the threatening messages Lola had been receiving. Because Lola knew their *secrets*.'

'Interesting. But did Tracy know them, that's the question?'

'I don't know the answer to that yet, we've only just made a start on trawling through. It appears Tracy sent a message to Lola late on Friday night asking how the party went, and two further messages on Saturday morning, but obviously she got no reply. Then the messages stopped, presumably because Tracy got wind of what happened to Lola.'

'How would she have found out? It made the local news, but not the nationals.'

Does that mean Tracy is local? I wonder.

'Any luck tracing Tracy's location?' I ask.

'No, I'm afraid not. It appears she used a VPN. Here to Chat have no way of tracking the source.'

Damn. I tell Golding to keep me posted then hang up. Why use a VPN? It's not like they were doing anything illegal? Why would Tracy take such extreme lengths to maintain her privacy? It's also curious how she went from warning Lola not to go to the party to virtually encouraging her to. Was it because she felt guilty for upsetting Lola and didn't want to risk losing her friendship? Or because of some other reason? The same reason she used a VPN? Because she herself had something to hide? Alternatively, was she scared that the same person who murdered Lola, might come after her? Right now, I have conflicting theories about Tracy. On the one hand, it seems she really cared for Lola – Golding just said she messaged her three times Friday through to Saturday morning asking how the party went. But it still seems fishy that Dinah was also chatting to someone called Tracy within the same timeframe as Lola, and that both women were raped while at university.

Just as I'm thinking this, Wild bursts into my room. He's holding a photograph of some kind.

I look up with a start. 'Ever heard of knocking, Wild?'

'Sorry, sir, it's just that I thought you'd want to see this straight away.'

Wild hands me the photo. 'The guys trawling through the CCTV spotted it. Caught on camera at midnight last Friday night.'

I stare at the photo for a few seconds. I recognise the riverside location: on the main Portsmouth Road coming from the direction of Riverside Walk where Lola lived. I see a man dressed in a long black wool coat and a black beanie, trying to look inconspicuous, but not doing a good enough job. Because it appears that for a split second he'd looked up. Caught by the camera. His face as clear as day.

Damien Radcliffe.

Chapter Thirty-Five

Lola

Before
Early December 2023

It's 11 a.m. and my argument with Tracy the other day keeps turning over in my mind. We've never rowed before. Not in all the years we've been chatting. I'm so angry with myself when I think about the way I behaved. She's become like a sister to me, has been nothing but kind to me and so I feel like the most selfish person alive for ending our chat so abruptly, for cutting her off and then failing to respond to her messages. Messages full of concern, asking if I was OK, saying how sorry she was and that she hoped I'd forgive her. Truth is, there's nothing to forgive. I know she only means well, that I'm lucky to have a friend like her. But the way I behaved, I don't deserve her kindness. That's why I haven't responded. I'm too embarrassed.

In my heart, I know she's right about the party. I should steer clear, particularly as Simone won't be there. I mean, what's the point if the others are just going to blank me? It won't be any fun, it'll be torture. Dee's coldness towards me is the most upsetting, after we confided our secrets in each other. She helped me, comforted me. But now she barely looks me in the eye, like she can't stand the sight of me. It's killing me, driving me to the brink of insanity almost. I just don't know what to do anymore, and now I may have lost the one person who's stayed true to me all these years.

Anyway, having thought long and hard about things, I've come to my senses, and realised that Tracy is right. Going to the party probably is a bad idea. After all, Bianca will be there, watching me like a hawk. I want to be able to patch things up with Damien, just because I hated how things ended between us when I went to his office, but how will I ever get the chance to speak with him in private?

I keep thinking about the way he looked at me the last time I saw him, around a fortnight ago. Almost a look of hatred in his eyes.

'Keep your voice down, will you!' he whispered irritably, even though he made a point of shutting his office door and telling his PA to go and run an errand for him.

I hadn't just gone there to ask why he was treating me so badly; I was hoping he could explain why the other mums were avoiding me. 'We only kissed, for God's sake, it's not like we had sex,' I said.

'It doesn't matter. It was wrong. Stupid. If Bianca finds out, she'll kill me and she'll make your life hell,' he said.

'But that's just it, she already is making my life hell! I don't understand why. You didn't tell her, did you?'

At this point, he looked at me like I was crazy. 'Course I haven't – I don't have a death wish!'

'So why is she and the rest of her clique, except for Simone, behaving like total and utter bitches towards me? Something's happened, I know it has. I don't deserve to be treated this way, and I demand an explanation.'

Damien had then grabbed my wrist. 'You need to leave. Don't come to my office again.'

I stood firm, even though my heart was galloping at a rate of knots, my knees on the verge of folding. 'Tell me what's going on or…'

His eyes bore through me. 'Or what?'

I swallowed hard. 'Or your father might just get wind that his precious son has been fooling around behind his wife's back, jeopardising his hard-earned business.'

The look he gave me at that point, it was as if he wanted to kill me. It terrified me. And then his grip had tightened, making me wince. 'You so much as dare and I'll…'

'You'll what?' I said defiantly while fighting back tears, still unable to believe how cruel he was being.

'Don't test me, Lola. You need to let this go. If you don't, I'll have no choice but to file a restraining order.'

'What!? Are you serious?'

'Deadly. I know you love that little boy. Don't do anything to jeopardise his happiness. Or your relationship with him. You're playing with fire, and the last thing you want to do is fan the flames.'

He scared me at that point. I hadn't felt that scared in seven years, and when I looked into his eyes, I realised then that I didn't know the real Damien Radcliffe.

Chapter Thirty-Six

Detective Inspector John Banner

Friday, 22nd December 2023

'Inspector, what on earth! You do realise it's 7 p.m. on a Friday, three days before Christmas? Why are you here? I'm about to take the girls up for their baths.'

'I'm sorry to turn up unannounced like this,' I say to Bianca Radcliffe, who's looking decidedly pissed off – and who could blame her? – 'but I need to speak with your husband.'

I see a flicker of apprehension in her eyes, but she holds herself well. 'Damien? Why?'

'Please, it's important I speak with him now. I understand he left his office just after 5:30 p.m. so I'm assuming he's home.'

Reluctantly, she opens her front door wide enough to allow me access. I step inside, and can immediately hear the clitter-clatter of crockery coming from the kitchen, along with the sound of the television. Bianca guides me through to the kitchen, where Damien is busy pouring two glasses of red wine. The radio is on, playing Christmas songs, the smell of frankincense infusing the air. I'm guessing the kids are watching television in the living room.

Damien immediately looks up. His eyes are apprehensive. He's not stupid; he knows I wouldn't be here if I didn't have a good reason.

'Inspector,' he says with a half-smile, trying his best to maintain his composure. 'It's late. What brings you here?'

I glance at Bianca, the tension palpable. 'Can I speak privately with your husband? I'll let you get on with bathing your girls.'

Worry sweeps across Bianca's face. I can see she's contemplating putting up a protest, but then thinks better of it. 'Of course, I'll leave you to it.'

She leaves the room, shutting the door behind her. Damien turns off the music, nothing but a thunderous silence engulfing the space between us.

'Take a seat, Damien,' I say, gesturing to the kitchen table. We both sit, at which point I waste no time in pulling out the grainy CCTV image of Damien taken last Friday evening. I show it to him. His eyes fill with alarm.

'This is you, is it not? Captured by CCTV on the Portsmouth Road last Friday night, just before midnight.' He remains mute. Just stares at the image, almost as if the act alone might alter what he's looking at. 'You told me you were tucked up in bed, at home with your girls. But clearly, you lied. Not only does it appear that you jeopardised your children's safety by leaving them alone in the house, you've been caught on camera in the exact same vicinity where Lola took her last breath.' I let this sink in, at which point he turns white. I allow my gaze to motor through him, fleetingly pondering my next question. Despite the anonymous text I received, warning me that Damien can't be trusted, I'm by no means convinced Damien is our killer. It's why I haven't arrested him yet. I do think he's holding back, though. And I see no other way forward than to push him more. To the point he can't hold in whatever he's hiding a second longer. Because whatever he's not telling me, it could prove crucial to solving this case. 'Did you kill Lola, Damien?' I thunder.

At this, Damien leaps up from his chair, starts pacing the room manically while ruffling his hair in frustration. 'No! Of course not!'

'Then tell me why you lied? Why you were in the exact same area where Lola was murdered, around the exact same time? Given your history, the fact that she was clearly obsessed with you, to the point you threatened to get a restraining order against her, it doesn't look good.'

He stops pacing. Props himself up against the kitchen island. Let's out a heavy sigh. 'I got a message that night.'

'What message?'

'A message from Lola.'

'When?'

'Around 11:00 p.m. I was a bit confused at first, because it wasn't her normal number.'

'What did she say?'

'That she was using her mum's old phone because she'd lost hers the day before. She asked me to meet her in front of the River Café, just off the Portsmouth Road, at midnight. Said she wanted to talk, smooth things over, that the party had been awful and that she believed I knew why the other mothers were treating her so badly.'

'And you agreed to meet her?'

'She said if I didn't she'd kill herself and then I'd have her blood on my hands, and Luca would be without a father. She also threatened to send my dad an email telling him about our kiss – my clients too.'

'Show me the message.'

'I can't, I deleted it.'

'Of course, how convenient.'

'Did you really expect me to keep a message like that? How was I to know she was going to be murdered the same night?'

I study Damien hard. Given the fact that he's clearly a man who's good at putting on appearances, it's hard to know if he's telling me the truth. But for now, I give him the benefit of the doubt. 'So, what happened?'

'I didn't want to leave my girls, obviously, but I had no choice. I knew Bianca would be back soon, plus we'd already agreed I'd sleep in the spare room. I was banking on her being so pissed that she'd pass out straight away. The last time I saw Lola, she seemed out of control, hysterical even, and I couldn't be certain she wouldn't follow through with her actions. The truth is, I was pretty cruel. I said some things I shouldn't have done, and I regret that.'

'So you went to the river with the intention of reasoning with Lola?'

'Yes. After I made sure the girls were OK, and put on some warm clothes. It's a good twenty-five-minute trek from our place if I walk briskly, and I guess I reached there just before midnight. But no sooner had I reached there, I got another text from her a few minutes after, telling me to forget it, that she'd changed her mind and that I should just go home. She assured me I shouldn't worry about her killing herself anytime soon, or blabbing. I was a bit pissed off she wasted my time, to be honest. But also relieved.'

'I assume you deleted that message too?'

He nods meekly. 'Yes. I was worried Bianca might see it.'

'Damien, you must know this doesn't look good for you. Lola left the party around 11:40 p.m. so she would have reached the River Café around the time you were there.'

'Except I wasn't there when she reached the cafe! I'd already left!'

I keep going. 'Given your history, and the fact that you had a lot to lose if Lola made your kiss public, it wouldn't be unreasonable of me to think that there were no texts from Lola, and that you yourself perhaps engineered the meeting with the intention of murdering Lola?'

'No, no, that's not true,' Damien shakes his head vigorously.

'But you can't prove Lola sent you a message asking to meet, or a subsequent one cancelling your rendezvous. The truth is, with your wife telling everyone you were at home with the flu, looking after your children, no one would think to put you at the scene. But you made a mistake: you looked up at the camera, and we got you.'

'Jesus, you're twisting things! I looked up because I'm innocent. I wasn't thinking I mustn't get caught on CCTV because I'm about to commit murder. Besides, did you find any prints on Lola, any DNA?'

'We didn't, but that proves nothing. In this image, you're wearing gloves. It's clear that you were the last person to see her alive.'

'No, it's not, because she cancelled, like I said! I left just after midnight because she told me she wasn't coming. Check the CCTV.'

'We have, and there's nothing.'

Damien smacks his head in frustration. 'Fuck, that's because I took a cab back from outside Riverside Walk. It was late and I was worried about the girls.'

'Again, how convenient. Lucky to get a cab at that time of the night at the height of the party season too.'

'I know, it was, what can I say, God was looking down on me with the girls being home alone. But I did get a cab, I swear it's the truth.'

I shake my head. 'Damien, there are just too many conveniences cropping up here and not enough proof. You've been lying to me since we first met. The fact is, you kissed Lola, she became obsessed with you, and as far as I can tell you feared what she might do in terms of jeopardising your marriage and your father's business. Last Friday night was the perfect time for you to put an end to her obsessions. And it seems that's what you did, having been caught on CCTV less than twenty minutes before Lola's estimated time of death. This gives me reasonable grounds to search your property, your office, and bring you into the station for further questioning.'

'No, this is insane, you can't do that!' Damien rifles his hands through his hair again. 'It's Christmas. My girls, they'll be distraught.'

'I'm afraid I don't have a choice,' I say, getting up.

'But you do, Inspector.'

Caught off guard, I swivel around to see Bianca standing there. Her fiery gaze drilling through me. 'My husband is being framed, Inspector. And I think I know who's responsible.'

Chapter Thirty-Seven

Bianca

Before
Late September 2023

'Why have you called us all here, Dee? You didn't mention inviting Joy and Clarissa. I assumed it would just be me.'

It's 9 p.m. on a Tuesday evening. This morning Dee sent me a WhatsApp message saying she needed to speak to me urgently and that it was best I came over to hers. She said Stephen would be out, and so we'd be able to speak freely. Her tone worried me, but I couldn't think what it could be about. Having said that, she has been acting a bit strangely these past couple of weeks, and I wondered if she and Stephen were having problems again. I'm actually glad for the chance to escape the house. I feel like I'm living in a pressure cooker at the moment. I dread Damien coming home, can barely look him in the eye knowing he kissed that little slut. When I received the photo of them kissing, I wanted to be sick. I always knew he was an outrageous flirt, but I never believed he'd act on it. He claims it was just a kiss, but how do I know he's telling me the truth? How do I know he hasn't done the same with other women? When we sit down to have dinner together you could cut the air with a knife and I've found myself drinking more just to get through it. If our sex life was dry before, it's non-existent now. I can't bear the thought of him touching me, of his lips on mine. Lips that I know have kissed hers. And yet, I still love him. I will never stop loving him. That's why it hurts so much. And it's why I made the others swear they wouldn't speak to Lola from now on. That she would never again be included in our girls' nights, our spa days or our Friday coffee mornings. I told them to blank her in the playground too. I could just have it out with Lola face to face, I guess. Vent my anger, my rage. But for one, I don't want to cause a scene, and two, it's not enough. I want to punish her, make her sweat, and the most effective way to do that is through a team effort. The girls weren't keen, not at first. But then around ten days ago, it was like a switch had been flicked and they all started dancing to my fiddle. It gave me such a sweet sense of satisfaction seeing the humiliation on Lola's face when she tried to join in a conversation with Joy and Dee last Friday. They blanked her big-time, turned and walked away, her face instantly crestfallen. She deserves it, the little bitch. Hopefully it will all get too much for her. And before long, she'll pull Luca out of St Xavier's, and I'll never have to see her face again. That's the thing, you see. No matter, how hard I try to move on, every time I see her I feel nothing but pain and a blinding anger. The day I never have to cross paths with her again can't come too soon.

The four of us are gathered in Dee's living room. Clarissa, Joy and I all seated on one sofa, Deidre on a chair opposite.

'I also assumed it would just me here this evening,' Joy says.

'Likewise,' Clarissa confirms. 'In fact, you said not to tell the others, Dee. Very cryptic. What's going on?'

Dee draws her chair closer to the rest of us. 'Because I'm scared.'

'Scared? Why?' I ask.

'Because I think the same person who sent Bianca that photo of Lola and Damien kissing messaged me a fortnight ago, and I didn't want them thinking I called you all here to mine because I'm on to them.'

'On to them?' I glance at the others with a raised eyebrow, as if to say that's a tad dramatic, isn't it. But they don't look surprised by Dee's comment. If anything, they look worried, almost as if Dee's remark has hit home with them.

'Why do you say that?' I ask.

'What was the message about?' Joy questions nervously.

Dee looks at each of us in turn, her eyes filled with trepidation. 'Whoever it was, they claimed to know I was hiding something. A secret I can't afford to get out.'

I watch Clarissa's reaction. She looks nervous all of a sudden. Is quick to ask: 'What secret?'

'I can't say. It's something I'm deeply ashamed of, something that happened a long time ago. But most importantly, something I told Lola.'

'Lola!' I can't help exclaiming. 'Why on earth would you tell that little tramp a secret? She's the last person you can trust.'

Dee nods. 'Yes, I'm starting to think that.'

'What exactly did the text say?' I ask.

Dee picks up her mobile lying on the side table next to her. She goes to her messages, and starts reading.

> I know your secret, because Lola told me. She tells me everything. There's nothing you can hide from me. If you don't want it coming out, you'd be wise to do as I say. Cut all ties with Lola, and tell no one about this. Not your husband, and certainly not the police. If you do as I ask, your secret is safe. If not, then I'm afraid your days of hiding are over. It shouldn't be hard. After all, she kissed a married man, she doesn't deserve your friendship.

'Fuck, Dee, what the hell did you do?' I can't help blurting out.

Dee looks shattered, her face wan. I've never seen her like this; she's normally so together, so full of energy. Even when Stephen was playing around behind her back, she seemed more angry than anything. But now? Now I see genuine fear in her eyes.

'I can't say.'

'But you told Lola,' I bite back, even though I know that's not helpful. I just can't stand to think that she told that little vixen something so personal when she and I have been friends for over three years. As if it's not enough that she wheedled her way into my husband's affections, it seems she's managed to charm my friends too. I'm the only one who sees her for what she is.

'What made you tell her something so personal?' Joy says, voicing my thoughts.

'Is it something to do with that day we met up at yours?' Clarissa says. 'Back in February, just before half term. You both disappeared for some time, and then later, when we were all out having coffee and Bianca made some flippant remark about Lola's flat, you defended her and got really shirty with B when Lola was out of earshot.'

Clarissa's right. Dee really pissed me off that day. OK, so perhaps I shouldn't have poked fun, but the way Dee laid into me knocked me for six. It seemed so out of the blue and over the top. Clearly Lola had told her something about her past, but Dee refused to say what it was. Clarissa was convinced it was something to do with Luca's father, so I did some digging of my own. Found out that there were no fatal car accidents in Glasgow around the time Lola would have been pregnant with Luca. It just goes to show what a liar she is. I told Clarissa, and she became more and more convinced that Dee might have the answers. Are we finally going to get them?

Dee nods. 'Yes. Lola had been self-harming. I was concerned, and the only way I could get her to tell me why was if I told her something secret about me. It was the only way I could get her to trust me.'

'What was her secret?' Joy asks. 'Is it to do with Luca's father?'

Dee nods. 'Yes. But I can't tell you.'

At this, I can't help but erupt. 'Are you fucking kidding me? That tramp kissed my husband, and it seems she told some stranger whatever you're desperate to keep buried, and you feel loyalty to her!'

'B's right,' Joy says. 'You don't owe her anything.'

'Look, I gave her my word. What happened to her is bad. I'm a barrister, and I made an oath to protect my client's secrets.'

'Yes, but she's not your bloody client,' Clarissa says. 'She's a troublemaker, a fucking eavesdropper!'

We all immediately turn to Clarissa. 'What do you mean by that?' I ask.

She lets her gaze rest on me, and I think I know the answer to my own question. 'Are you talking about last Christmas?' I say. 'When you had us all round for dinner and got really drunk?'

'Yep.' Clarissa nods. She looks at Dee and Joy, both of whom are looking completely lost. Understandably so.

'You were really wasted that night,' Joy says, looking at Clarissa. 'More than that, you were clearly upset about something and then you and Bianca went to the kitchen and…'

'And Lola went to the bathroom,' Dee finishes her sentence for her.

'Look, girls, I can't tell you what B and I discussed,' Clarissa says. 'Like you, Dee, it's something from my past that I'd rather not get aired in public.'

'That's OK, I understand,' Dee says. 'We all do.'

Clarissa hesitates.

'What is it?' I urge.

She looks at Dee, her eyes harried. 'I also got a message the other week.'

'You did?' I say in astonishment. Until now, I thought Dee was perhaps being paranoid, trying to make a connection between the message I got and the one she received. Clutching at straws. But maybe there is something in it?

'It was clear this person knew my secret. In fact, they referred to specific details. Said they'd make sure everyone at school found out if I didn't do as they asked.'

'Which was?' Dee asks.

'Same as you. Steer clear of Lola, don't tell a soul about the message. I was too scared to trying calling the number or texting back.'

Dee nods. 'I also thought it best not to try and make contact, as much as I was tempted to give the fucker an earful. I suspect it wouldn't have done any good, anyway. I'm certain they would have used a burner. Like they did with B.'

'Fucking hell,' I say, 'this is scary shit. What the hell's going on?'

'Why have you two decided to own up about this?' Joy suddenly pipes up, looking at Dee and Clarissa in turn. Her eyes are somewhat fretful. 'I mean, whoever this person is, it's pretty obvious they mean business. What if they find out we've been talking?'

'They won't,' Dee says. 'Not if we make a pact to keep it to ourselves. I just felt like I was going mad. I needed to tell someone.'

I look at Joy and see that she's shaking. 'What is it, Joy?'

She doesn't respond.

'Joy?' Clarissa urges. 'What is it?'

Still nothing. Then a realisation hits me. 'Fuck. You got a message too.'

Finally, Joy looks up. I see the tears in her eyes. 'It's bad, really bad. What I did. But I'm not a bad person, you have to believe me. I had to protect...'

'Shush,' Dee says. 'Don't say any more – you don't have to explain yourself to us.'

'I told Lola,' she carries on, sobbing uncontrollably. 'I shouldn't have done, but it was something she said, when she came round to see me the day after I was discharged from the hospital. I was on heavy meds, I was emotional, and it all came out. Also, because of the loss she'd suffered, I guess. If I had known she was going to tell someone, some stranger who was going to blackmail me, I'd never have opened up to her, obviously. I feel so stupid, and I hate her for putting me in this position. Putting us all in this position. What the hell are we going to do, Dee?'

Dee has always been the strong, practical one. The one we automatically look to for a solution. But as I look into her eyes right now, for once she seems stumped.

'Nothing,' Clarissa says.

'Nothing?' I say.

'That's right.' She looks at Joy and Dee. 'We all agree we can't risk our secrets getting out, correct?'

They both nod.

'So, we do as this arsehole says, as much as I hate being at their mercy. Bianca already asked us to cut Lola off, and now we have added reason to do so. We don't know if she told this person out of spite, or because she's a blabbermouth. But whatever the case, she betrayed us, and I, for one, can't ever find it in myself to forgive her. Clearly this anonymous messenger has something against Lola themselves, or they wouldn't be asking us to blank her. They may just be a plain lunatic, or perhaps Lola betrayed them in some way. Whatever the case, it's none of our business. We keep quiet, do as they say, and give Lola no hint whatsoever as to why. Let her speculate, let her suffer. Because as far as I'm concerned that's what she deserves.'

'What about Simone?' Dee says. 'She's bound to ask what's going on?'

'If she does, we tell her to stay out of it,' I say. 'Make the point that if she wants her kids invited round for playdates and parties, she'd be wise to leave it be.'

'But that's not fair on Simi's kids,' Joy says.

I look at Joy with affection. She's always had such a soft heart. But it could also be our downfall. 'We have to make a choice, Joy. It's the only way to make Simone back off. OK?'

Thankfully, she seems to understand. Gives me a nod. As do the others.

'Right then, it's agreed,' I say. 'Let's not speak of this again.'

Chapter Thirty-Eight

Detective Inspector John Banner

Friday, 22nd December 2023

'So, you're saying the same person who sent you the photo of Damien and Lola kissing is blackmailing Clarissa, Deidre and Joy?'

Having heard Bianca out, my suspicions that her husband might have murdered Lola are starting to wane. Still, I just can't take her word for it. I need solid proof.

Bianca nods. 'Dee certainly seems to think so. It makes sense, doesn't it? I mean, the texts that she, Clarissa and Joy received all referred to Lola kissing a married man. I think Dee has her suspicions as to who might have sent them.'

'She does?' Damien says, looking hopeful. 'Well, why doesn't she say so? Clearly this person is dangerous. Isn't it looking more likely that they killed Lola?'

'Why would you say that?' I ask. In truth, I'm starting to think the same myself, but I want to hear Damien's explanation.

'Are you kidding?' Damien looks astonished I even asked the question. 'You don't think those texts are creepy? Bordering on psychotic? Clearly this person has something against Lola and wants to punish her, else they wouldn't have sent Bianca a photo of me and Lola kissing, or told Clarissa, Dee and Joy that Lola betrayed their confidences and that they should cut her out of their lives. It's obvious they wanted to paint her in a bad light.'

'I'm not sure that's the only reason for sending the messages,' Bianca says.

I look directly at her, can sense what she's thinking.

'What do you mean?' Damien asks Bianca.

'Well, in learning how we all gave Lola the silent treatment, because she did something to make us all hate her guts and want shot of her, it would naturally give Inspector Banner here good cause to think any of us might have murdered her, wouldn't it?'

Bianca's right. I think of the text I received on Wednesday morning, making me aware that Lola knew all these women's secrets. Secrets they'd do anything to keep buried. It cast suspicion on each of them with regards to her murder, as Bianca said. Could it be that this person has been playing us all? Counting on the fact that Dee, Joy and Clarissa would be too scared to tell me about the threatening texts they'd received because they were being blackmailed and couldn't afford to risk their secrets coming out, while also hoping that, having lured Damien to the river bank last Friday night, he'd subsequently be caught on CCTV in the vicinity were Lola was found dead, and this would therefore be enough to get him arrested for her murder?

Damien appears to read my mind. 'Obviously it wasn't Lola who texted me last Friday night! It was the psycho who sent Bianca and the others those anonymous messages. They were trying to frame me. But who the hell could it be? Clearly, it's someone Lola talks to a lot.

Perhaps she told them about the day she came to my office, when I shouted at her, threatened a restraining order.'

At this, Bianca turns her head sharply. 'She came to your office?'

Damien hangs his head. 'Yes, sorry, I didn't want to worry you.'

For a minute I think Bianca's going to explode, but she doesn't. She edges closer to Damien and places her hand on his shoulder. 'It's OK, I believe you.'

'Bianca,' I say, 'you said you thought Dee might know who sent the messages?' In my mind, I'm almost certain I know too. And yet, I have no way of proving it.

She nods. 'Yes, I think maybe Lola confided in her that same day Dee let Lola in on her secret.'

'OK, I'm going to speak to Dee,' I say. 'And Clarissa.'

'Clarissa?' Bianca looks at me in surprise.

I nod. 'Yes. I think she might know who's behind the messages too. Even if she doesn't realise it yet.'

Chapter Thirty-Nine

Lola

Before
14th December 2023

HERETOCHAT.ORG
Chat Now in confidence. We're here for each other

Lola: Tracy, are you there?

Tracy: Yes, I'm here.

Lola: Oh, thank goodness, I'm so relieved. I'm so sorry I've been so quiet. For a moment there, I was worried I'd lost you forever.

Tracy: No, you haven't. I could never abandon you, you must know that by now. I get why you've not replied to my messages, but I hoped that, with time, you would.

Lola: Thank you. You've helped me so much over the years, and I shouldn't have treated you like that. Do you forgive me?

Tracy: There's nothing to forgive. Like I said, I understand why you were upset. But please believe me when I say I was just worried about you. I can't bear the thought of you being upset or little Luca suffering. But I've also been thinking about things these past couple of weeks, and on reflection I think you should go to the party tomorrow.

Lola: You do?

Tracy: Yes. I mean, if you don't go, it means they've won. They've got what they wanted. Made you run away with your tail between your legs. You can't let these women win; you need to stand up to them. Stand up for yourself and Luca.

Lola: I don't know, I was thinking that maybe you were right about me not going. I mean, without Simone there, it's going to be awkward. So what's the point? It's not worth the stress.

Tracy: I get what you're saying. But then again, if you don't go, they'll think they can dictate your life, and bend you to their will. You need to prove them wrong, that you're stronger than they think you are. You've got how many more years left at this school? Six? If you don't make a stand, how are you going to survive?

Lola: I guess. And I suppose I can always leave if it gets uncomfortable.

Tracy: Absolutely. We can't let the bullies win, Lola. It's happened to the both of us once too often, and it's time we fought back.

Lola: You're right. OK, I'll go. Besides, the creepy messages have stopped, thank goodness.

Tracy: They have?

Lola: Yep. It makes me feel more comfortable about leaving Luca with my parents. Thinking about it, I don't think it was him who was sending the texts. I think it was perhaps one of them, the other mums. Just because of the way they've been treating me lately. Whether it's because they found out I kissed Damien, or it's something else they think I've done wrong, I don't know. But the last one I received sounded like one of them could be behind it.

Tracy: Why? What did it say?

Lola: It said: Everything was fine before you came along. Traitor. Temptress. Slut. Keep your mouth shut, or else…

Tracy: What the fuck?

Lola: I know.

Tracy: Clearly, this person knows about your kiss with Damien.

Lola: It would seem so. I just can't believe Bianca wouldn't have said something to my face by now. She's so hot-headed, you know how she can't resist blurting things out. Somehow this text feels too subtle for her.

Tracy: So maybe it's not her. Maybe it's one of the others. I mean, you know all their secrets. Perhaps one of them is worried you'll spill the beans.

Lola: But I've kept their secrets to myself this long. I've not told a soul.

Tracy: Yes, that's true. So maybe it's Damien?

Lola: Damien? No way, he wouldn't do such a thing.

Tracy: Wouldn't he? You did come over as obsessive. I mean, he blocked you after you texted him incessantly, and then he threatened to file a restraining order against you if you didn't back down. Maybe he's worried you'll tell his dad or his clients, so this is his way of scaring you off.

Lola: I hadn't thought of it like that. Still, I can't believe he'd be so cruel.

Tracy: You're too trusting, Lola. You see Damien through rose-tinted glasses. But I've come to realise you can't trust anyone in this world. And that includes the people closest to you. Even those you idolise and will do anything for.

Chapter Forty

Tracy

When I first signed up to Here to Chat, it wasn't my intention for things to get so out of hand. Certainly not for any of my victims to die as a result of my actions. I'm not a bad person, as such. At least, I don't think I am. I just have a few issues. Issues that predictably stem from my childhood. As cliched as that sounds. The fact that my father used to beat me, for example. The fact that he used to beat my mother too, when he thought neither my older sister, Jen, or I were around. When I was twelve, I found violent porn on his computer. One day he caught me looking at it. He was angry at first. Then he made me watch more of the same. Said it was best I started young and pick up some tips on how to handle women, just to put them in their place.

He never showed me any love. Not the way he showed Jen. She never saw that side to him, even though I tried to tell her what he was like. She could do no wrong in his eyes, which struck me as somewhat ironic. I mean, how could he treat her with such love and respect, but treat all other women, including his own wife, as if they were no better than the dirt beneath his feet. I resented her for that. It felt like he lived this double life. Having his cake and eating it. Growing up, my best friend was a girl called Becky. She was a good friend to me, but at the same time I envied her. She didn't have any siblings; she had her parents' love all to herself. Her home was a happy one, and I loved going round there, marvelling at the way her dad was so attentive towards her and her mother. Becky didn't realise how lucky she had it; she had no idea what it was like for me at home, playing second fiddle to my sister. More than anything, I wished I was an only child growing up, and I envied all my friends, like Becky, who were. Jen and I were never close, and it often felt like I didn't exist when she was around. As if she was my father's only child, who got special treatment, while I was made to feel like some kind of foster kid, over whose head he put a roof, but nothing more.

As I grew into my teens, I was desperate to show the bastard what I was made of. I studied day and night, hellbent on proving to him that I would make something of myself and earn a good living, command respect. I think somewhere in that cold heart of his he was proud when I achieved that, but he's never said so to my face.

I married a kind and beautiful woman, had two beautiful children, but it wasn't enough for the bastard. I just felt this anger, an anger I took out on my wife for some time because, like my mother, she was right there. An easy target, who I knew loved me with all her heart and would never leave me. It got to the point where I knew I had to stop hurting her, to release my anger in some other form. But I had to be clever about it, because I couldn't risk being caught. I had too much to lose.

I'm in the job I am because, let's face it, being a doctor you have the power of life and death at your fingertips, the ability to decide who lives and dies, ultimately. I suppose I could have used my position to release my anger. Abused the power I have. After all, it's rare anyone suspects a doctor. One of the most revered professions around. But it was too risky. And I'm not a cold-blooded murderer like some notorious criminals who've held respected positions like mine. So, I turned to the internet, like my father had back in the late nineties and early noughties. Only I was far cleverer about it. Because, let's face it, I'm so much smarter than him. I found a website where young, vulnerable women were looking to talk. About their fears, their troubles, their hang-ups. I developed a backstory of my own, of course, involving a history of panic attacks, an abusive partner and philanderer, a mum with cancer, but having got through those difficult times, citing how I wanted to help others like myself. Some people might consider it sick, but I genuinely believe I did some good. I helped them, after all. It was so exciting picking my targets. They couldn't be just anyone. It's why I never entertained picking some random victim off the street. Where was the thrill in that? They had to fit the right criteria: only children because I've always been jealous of them; they don't have to share their parents' love with anyone else. They get all the attention, attention I badly craved from my own father. Lola was so whiney when I think about it. Moaning about exam pressure when she had two loving parents who worshipped her. She was so easy to befriend. Easier than the others. As far as I could tell, she had nothing to complain about, and that made me resent her more. I urged her to study in the library at the same time, from 3-6 p.m., Monday to Friday. After all, I knew all about studying hard. How hard work paid off. I said that having a focus, a routine, would stop her from panicking about her exams. After about a month, it worked. Her panic attacks subsided, and

I knew that would be when she'd be the most vulnerable, simply because she was relaxed, in a happy place, and she wouldn't expect it. I told my wife I was going to Edinburgh for a medical conference, and like the trusting soul she is, she believed me. Why wouldn't she? I know raping the women I befriend online, and who selected me to be their "buddy" based on the fake profile I created for myself, is inherently evil, but it became an addiction that was hard to shake. I told myself I'd rather do that than take it out on my beautiful wife.

Lola wasn't my first conquest; there'd been several before, many more since. Although I of course made sure the attacks were well-spaced out and in various parts of the country to avoid a clear link being made. Most of them confided in me – as Tracy – after the attacks. That's how much they'd come to trust me, to value me and my counsel above anyone else's. Even their own loving parents'. From the outset, I made it clear that they should never mention me by name to anyone. Not so much as refer once to 'Tracy' or Here To Chat in any secret diary they might keep. I knew sufferers were prone to documenting their day-to-day lives, their relationships, their sufferings. To venting their thoughts and frustrations. And therefore should the police start investigating me, I couldn't take the chance of them making a link between 'Tracy' and the attacks. I'd tell my victims I was very particular about my anonymity because of the previous trauma I'd suffered, and couldn't risk my identity being revealed for that reason. Thankfully, they were fine with that. I guess they were just so grateful to have someone to talk to. Plus being vulnerable themselves, they would never dream of jeopardising the safety of the one person who was helping them. They'd always be distraught after

I had sex with them, of course; they'd tell me how their attacker had threatened their lives if they went to the police, how frightened they were of him following through. I always did my best to comfort them. I told them it would be OK, that they'd get through it. It made me feel better doing so. A sort of penance for the suffering I had caused them. A conscience cleanser, as it were. Although, I won't lie, in that it also gave me a bit of a thrill. Unlike most rapists, I got to see the effect my actions had on my victims. More importantly, I got to talk them through their inner turmoil, ease their sufferings. The way I get to cure my patients' ailments, like the good doctor I am. Of course, I'd make a point of saying it was too dangerous to go to the police, that they couldn't risk their loved one's lives, particularly as, by then, rather unfortunately, any physical evidence of the rape would be gone. It wasn't worth the risk, I'd say. *But you will get through this.*

To be honest, it didn't take too much convincing. And then, after a week or so had passed, I'd tell them that I was sorry but I needed to take a break from Here to Chat because something really big had come up and I needed to sort that out. It's what I told Dinah. Poor Dinah. I was genuinely saddened to hear she killed herself six months later. But it was always too risky continuing to chat with these women after I'd had my way with them. And besides, Dinah was already mixed up in the head – she lied to me for a start, going by a different name, claiming she was an only child and close to her parents. She brought it all on herself in my opinion, and I'm sure if it wasn't for me, something like this would have happened before too long. That's what I tell myself, anyway, even though it's sometimes hard looking Clarissa in the eye. I mean, what were the odds I'd meet one of my victim's sisters in person years later?

But when Lola told me she thought she might be pregnant, I knew I couldn't abandon her, the way I'd abandoned the others. Of course, I asked her several times if she was sure her attacker was the father, and she confirmed to me she was a hundred per cent certain. She said the timing fitted, and that she hadn't been with anyone else. I guess I shouldn't have been surprised at the time that this might happen one day. It was risky using the withdrawal method, even though I thought I'd perfected it to a tee. The risk was what excited me, plus it's never the same feeling with a condom.

How could I abandon her after that? Abandon our child. My wife and I had our little girl, and only that week we'd received confirmation we were having another. I'd tried my best to hide my disappointment, but it was hard. It was as if God had heard my prayers, with another shot at having a boy. A boy I would cherish, in contrast to the way my father had mistreated me. Lucky for me, Lola was very true to her faith, and I knew abortion wasn't an option for her. She said so herself in our chat. But at the same time, I could tell from what she wrote that she was beside herself not knowing what to do. *How will I explain this to my parents? How will I be able to raise a child at my age, with no money, no job? What will I tell people about the father?*

So, I devised a plan. A plan I hoped would help set Lola's mind at rest, and bring her and our child closer to me. In that way, I could watch over them. Protect them. For all my faults, I know I am a good father. I'm certain of it. I suggested she tell her parents that Luca's father was from Glasgow, who she met on a night out, but who died in a tragic car accident. I told her it was important they promised never to speak of it again, that they understood it was too painful for Lola to talk about. Of course, being who she was, she felt bad for lying to her parents, but I impressed upon her that it was for their own good and that she'd be protecting them by not telling them the horrible truth. I then encouraged her to change her name and move down south once the baby was born. I said I'd been doing some research on her behalf and that Kingston seemed like a nice option. With good schools, lots of stuff for kids to do, and big enough to avoid the undesirable gossip you'd get in a small town or village. Of course, she was so grateful to me for being such a good friend and going to so much trouble, and it only brought us closer. I warned her never to speak of the rape when she moved away, and that she'd be putting Luca's life in danger if she did. To ease her money worries, I set up a secret trust for Luca, for when he turns eighteen, using a law firm up in Scotland who owed me a duty of confidentiality and who I therefore knew would never disclose my identity to Lola or her parents. This niggled Lola, of course, not knowing the identity of Luca's benefactor, but I told her it had to be some higher being up there looking out for her, and that she deserved a bit of luck after all she'd been through, so she shouldn't knock it.

And for six years it all worked perfectly. I continued to befriend vulnerable female students on Here to Chat, only carrying out my attacks less frequently because I had my little boy to keep a watch over, something that for a time diverted my attention away from the urges I felt. But despite being overjoyed with having a little boy, it wasn't enough. I still felt this anger inside me. After all, it's not as if I could cuddle him, kick a ball around with him. Not until he started school, at least. I had to hear how he was doing through Lola, having encouraged her to open up to me about him because she didn't have many close friends to confide in, and I would occasionally watch them from a distance, just so I could get a glimpse of my son.

Of course, it was me, Tracy, who suggested St Xavier's to Lola, having claimed I'd done some thorough research into schools on her behalf. I knew with her strong Catholic leanings, if she and Luca attended its affiliated church regularly and ingratiated themselves with the vicar there, there was a strong chance Luca would get a place. A cynical tactic, perhaps, but one I knew many parents in the Surbiton/Kingston area at the time were guilty of. Again, she was so thankful, and finally, I got to meet my little boy, to have an excuse to spend time with him. I still remember the first time he came to our house for a sleepover a year ago. It was one of the best days of my life. Me and my mini me, my *wingman*.

But then things started to go wrong. Only a month before, a DCI in Oxford came up with his 'Campus Prowler' theory. It was rather flattering, I'll admit. And in many ways, I was desperate to tell my father; something along the lines of: *your son has made the national newspapers, aren't you proud, you arsehole?!* But I couldn't, of course. And I knew I had to stop the attacks, or risk being caught out and losing access to Luca. Losing my family, my status as a successful and respected family doctor, a model citizen; everything I had worked so hard to achieve. So I did stop. And things were fine for a while. Despite me losing my temper a few times with my wife. I felt terrible about that. But I knew she'd never tell on me. Let alone contemplate leaving me.

But then something unfortunate happened. I got sloppy and things got messy, and one thing led to another.

I regret Lola's death. She didn't deserve to die.

But I must protect my son. He's what matters most in this world to me.

I, Liam Loxley, won't allow anything or anyone to jeopardise that.

Chapter Forty-One

Detective Inspector John Banner

Friday, 22nd December 2023

'Why have you called us both here, Inspector? I don't understand.'

It's 9 p.m. I'm sitting in an interview room at the station, Deidre and Clarissa sitting opposite. They both look petrified, which is hardly surprising. I don't blame them for wondering why I invited them here rather than visit them in their homes. Making them feel like criminals, that they're under suspicion. They could have refused to come, of course, but I assured them both on the phone that I wasn't arresting them, I just needed their help, and what with it being late and the holidays I didn't want to upset their children's bedtime routines. They seemed content with that, but I guess once you're sitting in a dreary, soulless interview room, facing a senior police officer, it's pretty unnerving and you start to have your doubts.

I don't beat about the bush. 'I know about the messages you both received.'

Clarissa visibly tenses. Deidre does a better job of hiding her alarm. 'Messages. What messages?'

'Anonymous messages the both of you, and Joy Grainger, received, informing you that Lola had disclosed your secrets to the sender and ordering you to cut all ties with her if you didn't want your secrets coming out.'

'Who told you that?'

'Bianca Radcliffe.'

'Bianca?' Clarissa says. 'Why would she do that. We...'

'Made a pact not to tell anyone, yes, I know. To answer your question, she told me because I had reason to suspect her husband may have killed Lola and she wanted to draw my attention to another possibility.'

'Why would you suspect Damien?' Deidre asks.

I tell her.

'Shit.'

'Bianca said you didn't try calling or texting the number back. Is that correct?' I look at both women. Receive two nods of the head.

'I was too scared to,' Clarissa elaborates. 'It was clear they meant business, and I thought it best not to engage.'

'I also thought it was too risky,' Deidre says. 'No doubt they used a burner so we'd have no way of tracing it.'

I nod, feel certain that Deidre's right.

'You've asked both me and Clarissa here. But why haven't you asked Joy?' Deidre says.

'Because, unlike Joy, I think you both might be able to help me track down who sent those messages.'

'How's that?' Clarissa says, looking puzzled.

I catch the look on Deidre's face. She knows where I'm heading with this. Clarissa clearly hasn't connected the dots in her mind yet.

'You know, don't you Deidre.' I let my eyes rest on her.

She nods. Glances at Clarissa. 'I do.' Then she turns back to meet my gaze once more. 'Although I have no idea how you think Clarissa might be able to help. Lola only ever confided in me about Here to Chat.'

Clarissa's ears prick to attention. She turns her head sharply to look at Deidre. 'Here to Chat. You knew about that?'

Deidre nods. 'Lola told me last February, at my place. When we were all at mine and I took her upstairs to show her some of Oscar's old clothes.'

'You know the name of the person Lola spoke to, don't you, Deidre?' I say. 'Despite claiming Lola never told you.'

Another nod. Albeit slower this time. 'Yes. Tracy.'

Clarissa looks stunned. 'Am I therefore to assume that Lola also told you she was raped?' she says.

'Yes,' Deidre says, 'but how do you know?'

'Because I told Clarissa,' I interject.

Clarissa swallows hard. Then looks directly again at Deidre. 'My sister was raped seven and a half years ago. Six months after that, she committed suicide.'

Deidre's face is aghast. 'Oh, love, I had no idea. I'm so sorry.'

'Thank you. I don't like talking about it, as you can imagine. My mother had a nervous breakdown soon after Dinah died, and my dad, well, he retired from politics and now lives a solitary existence in Devon.'

'So not the US?' Deidre says.

'No.' Clarissa shakes her head. 'Bianca's the only one who knew. Or rather, she *was* the only one, until Lola overheard us in my kitchen last December when I had you all over for dinner. That's the secret I wanted to keep quiet, and which the scumbag who texted us all threatened to expose. Lola must have told him, else how would he have known?'

I explain to Deidre how I believe Dinah and Lola were both attacked by the same man and that Dinah had also been chatting to someone called 'Tracy' on Here to Chat around the same time.

'But this Tracy person stopped all communication with Dinah a month or so after she was raped,' Clarissa says. 'It devastated her. Why did she keep going with Lola? I mean, she must have done, because Lola told Deidre about her back in February.'

'Because I think Tracy forged a special connection with Lola,' I say.

'How do you mean?' Deidre says.

'I don't think Tracy is a woman.'

They look at me, confused. I carry on. 'I believe Tracy is a man masquerading as a woman. I think Tracy…'

'… is the man who raped Lola and Dinah. And is Luca's father,' Deidre finishes my sentence for me.

'Yes.' I nod.

Clarissa gasps out loud. 'And you think he's the one who messaged us all?'

'Yes.' I'm about to press them more on what both Dinah and Lola told them about Tracy, anything at all, however small or seemingly insignificant, that might help track this bastard down, when there's a knock on the door. It's Wild. I excuse myself, tell the women I shan't be long, then leave the room.

'What is it, Wild?' I say.

'Sir, DCI Kane just called.'

I feel the adrenaline pumping through my veins. 'Yes?'

'Since you spoke earlier, he's managed to speak with four of the victims who previously came forward.'

'Wow, that was quick. And?'

'And they all confirmed they subscribed to Here to Chat around the time they were raped. And, more importantly, confided in someone called Tracy.'

'Shit,' I whisper under my breath. 'It has to be the same individual.'

Wild nods. 'Not long after these four women were raped, Tracy told them she couldn't chat anymore, because she needed to deal with something big that had come up. She also made them promise not to mention the fact to anyone, on the basis that they could be placing her life in danger.'

'Twisted bastard. So, the pattern is established. Now we just need to find out his real identity. Whoever he is, he's smart, devious. He's tried to use everything Lola told him in confidence to shift suspicion onto Damien and the other women in her friendship group.'

'Yes, it seems so, sir. There's just something that puzzles me.'

'I know what you're going to say, Wild. Why kill Lola if she was the mother of his child?'

'Yes, although perhaps she found out his identity, and was going to expose him?' Wild offers.

I nod. 'Yes, that's something that's occurred to me. But neither the recent chat nor Lola's diary infers this. She was only talking to Tracy the day before she died. Was virtually begging for her forgiveness, in fact. No, I don't think it's that. But it is curious that Tracy went from telling Lola to ditch the party, to encouraging her to go. I thought it was because Tracy felt guilty for upsetting Lola, but now we know that can't be it. Something happened in those two weeks. Something that made Tracy, or whatever this arsehole is called, go from wanting to protect Lola to murdering her.'

I pause. My mind working overtime. I'm missing something. Something that's no doubt been staring me in the face. And then, just like that, it hits me. My expression must say it all, because Wild then says, 'What, sir, what is it?'

'The phone numbers, Wild. How would Tracy know the mobile numbers of Damien, Bianca, Clarissa, Deidre and Joy? Lola didn't disclose them in her chats with Tracy. Why would she have done? Neither does it seem feasible that Tracy would have been able to get hold of all five numbers from a simple google search or social media scroll. One or two perhaps, but surely not all five? It therefore stands to reason that Tracy is someone familiar to them all. But here's what's pivotal, Wild. Tracy texted me, as you know. But how? My mobile isn't listed anywhere. I've been racking my brains trying to come up with an explanation since Wednesday. But it seems the answer's been staring me in the face and that the reason I didn't pick up on it is because until now my mind has been focussed on Tracy being a woman.' I pause for breath, the full horror of what's suddenly dawning on me sinking in. Then I say: 'The only way anyone would know my number is if I gave them my card. Something I rarely do, as you know. And the last person I gave my card to, was Liam Loxley.'

Chapter Forty-Two

Liam

Saturday, 23rd December 2023

I loved spending time with my little boy on Wednesday. Simone wasn't feeling up to it, sadly, but secretly I was glad. It meant I got him all to myself. We played some football, then shifted to the playground where I pushed him on the swings, spun him on the roundabout for a while, before we left, stopping at a local café for a mug of hot chocolate. Poor boy was so quiet as we sat there. It's understandable, given he's just lost his mother. And what with Christmas just around the corner too. He started crying, which broke my heart. I lifted him onto my lap, hugged him tightly to my chest, stroked his hair, assured him his mummy was safe in heaven now, and that it was all going to be OK. Obviously, it's going to take some time for him to get over her death. But he will. Kids are so much more resilient than adults. And kindness counts for a lot. I just wish my father had been kind, the way I was to Luca.

When I look at him, it's like looking at my six-year-old self. Of course, he has Lola's eyes. But he has my dimples and full lips, I'm certain of it. Traits that are more often than not inherited from a child's father. I know this, of course, from my medical studies.

Although it pains me that Lola is dead, I'm going to try and make it up to her by being there for Luca. Of course, I've always been there for him financially. But now I can spend regular quality time with him. I mentioned to Elisa and Don that they should come to ours on Christmas Day, and they agreed. They need the company, to take their minds off their daughter. I've bought something special for Luca too. Something that will bring a smile to his face. A new bike and a football kit. West Ham, of course. The team I've supported since I was a kid. Dad has two season tickets, but he never took me to a game when I was a child; he said I had two left feet and took my sister instead. I really hated him for that. And her.

Little by little I'll make myself indispensable to Elisa and Don. I can already tell how much they like me. They told me how grateful they were for my kindness when I dropped Luca off on Wednesday. I think it helps being a GP. When you tell people you're a doctor, particularly a family one, it commands an automatic respect, a certain level of trust. With time, I hope Elisa and Don come to see me as a kind of surrogate father for Luca. They're good grandparents, but they can't do the things I can do with Luca. Like kicking a ball around, or taking him for long bike rides. Slowly but surely, I'll ingratiate myself into every area of Luca's life, and he will become a part of our family. He is the girls' half-brother, after all. He should be around them. And they around him.

Simone is a wonderful mother, so caring and kind, so I know she won't mind. That she'll be only too happy to go along with my plan. It killed her that she couldn't give me a boy. She knew how much I wanted a son, and how disappointed I was when she gave birth to a second girl.

Still, by then I knew I was having a boy, even though she was clueless.

I knew from the first moment I met Simone that she'd make a good mum. A trait in a woman that has always been so important to me. It's always been crucial that the mother of my children fulfil certain criteria. It's why none of my relationships before her lasted more than a month or so. Women who were either too ambitious or too lazy, too fickle, too self-centred, or not into babies or marriage; some were also way too headstrong for my liking. I need someone I can control, and it was obvious how smitten Simone was with me from our very first date. She was looking for a man to take care of her, be kind to her, the way her father hadn't. Her father wasn't abusive like my father was; he was simply cold. Simone worships me, and despite her really pissing me off lately, resulting in those ugly bruises on her neck and shoulders causing her to wear that unflattering turtleneck I hate, I have no doubt she'll help me take care of Luca as if he were her own son.

She'll do anything for me. Anything at all.

It's just on 8 p.m. and I'm sitting in our living room with a glass of red wine. Simone is upstairs taking a bath. She's not been herself since Lola's death. She'll come through it, though. Once the dust settles.

Just then, the doorbell goes. What the hell? It's probably carol singers, or some annoying charity do-gooder. Don't they know it's rude to knock on someone's door at this late hour? It's two days before Christmas, for pity's sake.

I rein in my anger, get up from the sofa and sprint to the front door, not wanting whoever it is to ring the bell again and wake the girls.

I first check through the spy hole. After all, you can never be too careful these days, it might be some psychopath. But it's not. To my surprise I see DI Banner and DC Wild standing there. My heart starts galloping. I can't imagine what they want at this late hour, and so near to Christmas. I've told Banner everything I know. Or rather, what I want him to think I know. Which is, of course, very different from the truth.

I take a deep breath, mindful of Simone in the bath upstairs. She's been so tense lately, understandably so, and I want her to relax, chill out for a bit. She'll have the radio on, so most likely won't have heard the doorbell. 'DI Banner, this is a surprise, is everything OK? I hadn't expected to see you at this time of night on a Saturday, so close to Christmas.' My voice is pleasant enough, but I want him to know I'm not happy with the intrusion.

He offers me a half-smile, as does DC Wild. 'Yes, I'm sorry to disturb you. Your girls are in bed, I presume. I hope I haven't woken them?'

I shake my head. 'No, you're fine, they were pretty tired this evening. Hopefully dead to the world. What can I help you with?'

'May we come in?'

'Yes, yes of course.' Grudgingly, I let them inside, then guide them straight through to the living room. Although I don't want to, I offer them both a drink out of politeness, which they thankfully decline. I may be imagining things, but their demeanour towards me feels different to the first time we met. Frostier, perhaps.

We all take a seat.

'Liam, there've been some developments in the hunt for Lola's murderer,' Banner says.

'Oh really, that's good,' I say, my heart thumping inside my chest in anticipation of what they're about to say. Hopefully that they've arrested Damien Radcliffe.

'At first, we thought perhaps Lola's falling out with the mums at school had led to her death in some way,' Banner explains. 'Perhaps revenge for her dalliance with Damien, or some such like.'

He said *at first*. That's good. It was always the intention to make them suspect the women initially, before spotting Damien on CCTV. I nod. 'Yes, that would make sense. Didn't you also tell Simone that Lola had disclosed some pretty dark secrets about them to some stranger she'd been talking to online, meaning they were perhaps worried about who else she might tell?'

'Yes, that's right.' Banner nods. 'And like I said, we did at first think there might be something in that.'

I feel the anticipation swelling inside my gut, waiting for Banner to break the news of Damien's arrest. I never liked that slimeball, and I'm really not sure what the hell Lola saw in him. The thought of him becoming a stepfather to Luca had made my stomach turn. 'But you don't anymore?' I say.

'No, we don't. As I told your wife, and as you pointed out, it's become clear that the person who messaged me is someone Lola had been chatting with online for the past seven years or so. On a forum called Here to Chat.'

Fuck. Not where I expected him to go next. I try to remain calm. 'Oh yes, she did mention the name.'

'It appears that the same person who messaged me messaged Clarissa, Deidre and Joy separately, telling them Lola had revealed each of their secrets to them, and blackmailing them into cutting all ties with Lola.'

I pretend to look shocked. 'Shit, you're kidding!'

'We also believe this same person sent Bianca the photo of Damien and Lola kissing.'

Damp patches of sweat have started to form under my armpits. Why hasn't he mentioned Damien being caught on CCTV yet? Still, I make a show of looking confused. 'Why would they do such a thing, if they were Lola's confidante and friend? I mean, granted, Lola shouldn't have disclosed her friends' secrets, or kissed Damien, but it seems like such a cruel thing to do.'

'Very cruel.' He nods his agreement. 'We believe this person, who we now know went by the name of Tracy, killed Lola. Not only that, Tracy is, in fact, a man, who raped Lola, along with a string of women, over the last seven years.'

I am literally on the verge of vomiting, but I think of my father, think of the disappointment on his face were I to buckle, and somehow, I manage to push the bile that's suddenly lodged in my throat back down.

'What?!' I express my alarm, widening my eyes as if to emphasise my shock.

Two pairs of eyes drill through me. Banner goes on. 'We believe that over the last seven years he befriended certain female university students on Here to Chat; women who fitted specific criteria. He came to know their routines, their whereabouts, their vulnerabilities. And then, when he felt the time was right, he went to those locations and raped them. Lola was attacked one night on her way back from the library to her digs at Edinburgh University. Attacked and raped.'

'Oh my God, poor Lola,' I say.

Banner remains poker-faced. 'You may have read articles about the Campus Prowler over the last year or so?'

I nod. While experiencing a fleeting sense of triumph, pride even. 'Yes, I do recall reading something about that. You think he's this Tracy person?'

Banner nods. 'We do. We know this because other victims have confirmed that they also corresponded with someone called Tracy on Here to Chat around the time they were raped.'

The air in the room has suddenly got thinner. I can barely breathe.

'What baffles me, Liam, is how this Tracy character got my phone number? My mobile isn't publicly available. Only someone I'd given my card to would have it. Something I do sparingly. As you can imagine, if I were to give it out freely, I'd be opening myself up to all sorts of nuisance calls.'

I give an uneasy smile, my insides churning. 'I'm not sure how I can help with that. Where exactly are you going with this?'

'The only two people who I've given my card to since Lola was murdered are Elisa Mosley…' He pauses, as if to exacerbate my discomfort. Then adds, 'And you.'

I feel dizzy, my brain manically trying to think up some clever response. But just then, Simone appears, dressed in jogging bottoms and a sweater. I can't help wondering how much of the conversation she heard. I fleetingly catch her eye, and can tell from her expression that she knows something is up.

'Inspector, sorry, I didn't realise you were here. I was taking a bath.'

I look at Banner. I had expected him to offer my wife a smile, at least. Thus far, he's been so compassionate with her. But he doesn't. It's obvious he thinks I killed Lola, but the fact is, he has no way of proving that. They won't have found my DNA or fingerprints at the scene, and they have no way of tracing Here to Chat to me because I was smart in using a virtual private network. Also, a burner phone was used to message those wretched women and Damien. There is nothing concrete to link me to her murder. Nothing. I know this for sure.

In that case, why is he here? Does he expect me to just come out with it and confess?

DI Banner relays everything he just told me to Simone. Including his point about only giving out his mobile phone number to Lola's mother and me.

Simone looks horrified. 'What are you insinuating, Inspector? Surely, you're not suggesting Liam killed Lola?'

DI Banner's eyes drill through hers. 'No, I'm not. I'm saying that you did, Simone.'

Chapter Forty-Three

Simone

Before
Friday, 25th August 2023

It's a little after 8 p.m. and Liam isn't home yet. It's unusual for him not to be back by now, and I can't help wondering what's keeping him. His surgery normally finishes by 7 p.m., with the practice where he works only a fifteen-minute drive away. The girls aren't in bed yet. They're in the living room watching Disney Plus. It's harder to get them down in the summer, when it's so light. But it's not a big deal. It's the holidays after all, and it's nice to have the company at least. Plus, they're generally so well behaved. No trouble at all, really. I can't help thinking how much harder a boy would have been to control. That's what I tell myself, anyway, to make myself feel better about the fact that I haven't been able to bear Liam a son.

I go to the kitchen and pour myself a second glass of wine. I shouldn't really, but it's so hot, and the prospect of chilled sauvignon blanc is just too tempting, especially with no other distractions to occupy me. I tell the girls I'm just going to sit outside on the terrace for a while, and enjoy my wine in the balmy evening air.

I sit at the table, take a sip from the glass, then place it down on the coaster in front of me. I smile to myself when

I think back to last night. When Liam and I made love. He'd been so tender, just like when we first started dating. Before we were married and the violence started. He's always been great at sex. Particularly make-up sex. That's how he'd apologise in the early days of our marriage, after hitting me. Especially if he saw me smile at another man and thought I wanted to sleep with him. Last night, he told me how much he loved me, and that made me feel so special. I know how sorry he is for his recent outbursts. He's nothing like his dad, really. What confuses me is that he hadn't been violent in some five years. Hadn't accused me of wanting to sleep with other men, or lost his temper at the drop of a hat. But then, last December, it started up again. He always apologises afterwards, insists he doesn't mean to get angry or violent, even though it's been going on for eight months now. I love him too much to leave him, and I could never break up our happy family. He is my addiction; he always will be. He cried when he saw the bruises on my arms the other week. Bruises I told Lola were the result of me taking kick boxing classes. She'd looked alarmed when she saw them, bless her. But I assured her it was fine, and all part and parcel of the sport and me getting better at it. I hope she believed me. I think she suspected something might be up between Liam and I back in June, at the school fair. It was my fault, really. I told her I thought Liam might be having an affair. I shouldn't have done; I was just so worked up that day because he'd had a lot of late nights at the surgery and Siobhan, his receptionist, is so hot. I was too frightened to ask him. I knew he wouldn't take it well. And, on reflection, I think it was just me being paranoid. Anyway, thank goodness I fobbed Lola off and we never spoke of it again. She's such a good friend, and sometimes

I'm desperate to tell her about Liam's other side. But I'm too scared. Too afraid he might find out. I don't want him to think I've betrayed him. Neither do I want Lola to go to the police about it. Even if she thinks she's protecting me. Besides, I think Lola's been hiding something from me too. I think it's got something to do with whatever she told Dee back in February. No doubt it's some sort of legal thing, so I don't feel too upset or hurt that she's kept it from me and confided in Dee. I just hope she's OK, because I care for her deeply. The way I know she cares deeply for me too.

Liam said it's the stress of work, of being responsible for a young family, that's taken its toll over the last year. Still, it's no excuse for him using me as a human punchbag; he admitted that himself. But I let it be, because I can't bear to lose him. It's why I take such good care of my face and my figure. I can't stand to think of him leaving me for someone more attractive. I did suggest that he go on a boys' trip, or take advantage of the next medical conference away, though. They always seem to relax him. Allow him to let off steam. He used to go on quite a lot of those work trips, but he said drug companies are cutting back, which is why he's not been away in nearly a year.

He hasn't hit me for a month or so now, so I'm hoping it was just a phase, and that he doesn't hate me because I've never been able to bear him a son. I know how badly he wants one, and I feel like such a failure having had two daughters and four miscarriages. But he assured me that's not the case. That he could never hate me. And that I'm a wonderful mother. It made me feel so much better when he said that.

Just then, my mobile rings. It's Liam. 'Simi, it's me.'
'Are you OK?'

'I'm fine. It's Mum.'

'What's wrong?'

'She had a fall this afternoon. I'm sorry I didn't have time to text until now, but I drove straight to Haslemere when Dad called. He wanted me to check her over.'

I smile at this, despite being concerned for his poor mother. Only because I know how it would have meant the world to Liam, knowing his dad wanted his opinion.

'Of course, no worries,' I say. 'Please give her my love. Will you sleep there? I mean, I'm fine with it; it's Saturday tomorrow, after all.'

'You sure? Maybe I will, then. Thanks, Princess. You really are one in a million.' His words make my heart sing.

'That's so sweet. Thank you. OK, so I'll see you tomorrow. Love you.'

'Love you too.' I end the call with a warm glow inside. He's so kind and caring, rushing to see his mum like that. It reassures me that him losing his rag is just a phase he's been going through. And that he'll come through it soon.

It's a little after 9:30 p.m. by the time the girls are settled in their bedrooms and asleep. I decide to be lazy and curl up in bed with my laptop and watch the latest romcom on Netflix. But when I open my machine, the screen is all fuzzy, like it's been infected with some sort of virus. Stuff like that always scares me, so I decide to switch the whole thing off. It's annoying. I had so set my heart on crawling under the duvet with a movie and another sneaky glass of wine.

It's then that I think of Liam's laptop, lying in his study. I could call him, ask for the passcode, but it seems a bit petty to ask for such a trivial thing when his mum's had a bad fall. I don't want to bother him. Or worse, anger him. It's a long shot, but maybe I can guess it. I go downstairs to Liam's study, switch on the desk light, then open up his laptop, a sliver of guilt rushing through me, just because of what I'm contemplating – cracking my husband's password. It's wrong, but it's not like my intentions are bad, I just want to watch a movie in bed. Would he be angry with that? I brush off the thought. No, why would he? OK, so there's no question I'd be upset if I found porn on Liam's laptop. But I can handle it, he's a man after all, and I know it's not uncommon, even though I can't imagine he'd look at that kind of thing. He's a family doctor with a reputation to protect. Surely it would be too risky?

I drum my fingers on the keypad. *What could the password be?* I try each of the girls' birthdays, but neither are correct. Two more attempts then I will be locked out. I try my birthday, but that doesn't work either. Then an idea hits me. The date and year West Ham last won a major tournament. I enter the relevant digits, and lo and behold I'm in!

Although I'm tempted, I don't look at his email, but go straight to the internet and Netflix. I find a film I want to watch, go back upstairs and spend the next two hours in bed glued to it. Once it's over, I'm about to close the laptop down and log out when a thought occurs to me: Liam will know I used his machine if he happens to check his history. Although I try to convince myself that he wouldn't get angry, I can't be sure. Why take a chance and upset how wonderful things have been between us lately? I go to his history tab, intending to delete the Netflix search when I see it: *Here to Chat*. Tons and tons of hits on the same website. I keep scrolling down, horrified. Has he been on some kind of sex chat forum? I feel nauseous at the thought. I scroll back up, and tentatively click on the first hit, frightened of what I might find. It goes straight to a password that appears to be autosaved. I click on ok and get an immediately greeting on the home screen – '*Welcome back Tracy.*' Tracy? I'm relieved it's not a sex line, but rather appears to be some kind of informal counselling website. But why is Liam calling himself Tracy? Is he depressed, I wonder? Is that why he's been so violent? Am I the cause of his depression? It would explain his outbursts. But why masquerade as someone called Tracy?

There's a drop-down menu to the left of the screen. One of the tabs says '*Your Private Messages*'. Tentatively, I click on it, afraid of what I might find. And then, having taken a few seconds to absorb what I'm looking at, I nearly pass out with shock.

Messages between Lola and Liam, only he's not Liam here, he's Tracy. Hundreds and hundreds of them, spanning months, years. I can't believe my eyes. Why would he do this? It takes me all night to go through most of it. Right back to when he first befriended her. When she wasn't Lola, but Elizabeth. To my horror, I learn that she was raped, how she told her parents her baby's father had died in a car accident up in Glasgow, how she decided to change her name and move down south once the baby was born – decisions Liam, as Tracy – practically made for her. I'm aghast to discover that he's been advising her on almost every aspect of her and Luca's lives for the last six or so years. And that she's told him things. Things she's learned about the others in our group at school. About Clarissa's sister being raped, about the others all keeping terrible secrets that could cost them their freedom. She also talked at length about her deep feelings for Damien. Curiously, when I look back, I see that Liam messaged Lola around a month after she was raped, saying he couldn't talk anymore, and giving some fabricated excuse. But then she got upset, told him she was pregnant and believed the father was her rapist. He asked her several times if she was certain her attacker was the father and she assured him he was. And then, just like that, he changed his mind. 'Tracy' told Lola she wasn't going anywhere.

Why? Why has Liam been masquerading as Tracy? And why is Lola so important to him?

I can barely press the keys, my hands are shaking so badly, as I go to Liam's One Drive, hoping to gain some clue. And that's when I find a folder, entitled *Luca*. I click on it, and it reveals various sub-headings. One of them is entitled *Trust Document*. I open it up and am shocked to see a copy of a trust set up for Luca Martinez by Liam, for Lola to use for Luca's education and general clothing and living expenses, and which Luca will get the benefit of when he turns eighteen.

Why would he do this? Sure, perhaps he felt sorry for Lola, but why go to such extremes, why give her money, provide for her son? Money that should be going to our girls? It's not fair, it's not right!

I look back at the chat again. Liam – as Tracy – insisted they could never meet in person, something Lola agreed to, making me certain she has no idea Liam is Tracy nor that he is Luca's secret benefactor.

And then a thought hits me. A thought so vile, so abhorrent, I can barely force myself to acknowledge it. It's clear from what Lola says that she was attacked in April 2017. Liam and I had just moved to Kingston. Penny was two. Liam went to a medical conference up in Scotland around that time. I remember because I was pregnant with Jess, and I was secretly upset with him for leaving me alone in a strange house. Looking back through the chat, I notice that at the end of April he told Lola he couldn't chat anymore. But the moment she said she was pregnant by the man who raped her, he changed his mind. Shortly after that, he encouraged her to move down south, saying he'd happened to find this great church school called St Xavier's. In every single message, he asks how Luca is, passively advises Lola on how to raise him. And, what's most telling, he repeatedly warns her not to tell anyone she was raped because it was too dangerous for her and for Luca. In fact, he got upset with her when she said she'd told Dee.

Liam was the one who raped Lola. It's the only explanation, the only thing that makes sense. And it explains why he's always so keen to have Luca over to ours, why he was so mad with Bianca when she had a go at Luca for pushing Summer over.

I rush to the toilet and throw up. I feel like I want to die. Luca is the son he never had. The son I could never give him.

I realise I have two options. I can confront Lola, tell her what I know, show her the chat and we go to the police together and Liam is locked away.

Or I take another route. A much darker route. A path I'm drawn to simply because I can't bear the thought of the shame this will bring on our family. What it will do to my girls. But mostly, because I can't bear the thought of life with no Liam in it.

I cannot lose him. But neither can I stand the idea that he might work his way into Lola's heart one day, so that he can be a proper father to Luca. I can't think that Lola would do that to me. Then again, I saw her kiss Damien Radcliffe in the park this afternoon. A married man. A man I warned her off. I couldn't help myself. I took a photo; I'm not sure why, really. I guess I half thought about showing it to her, asking her what the hell she thought she was playing at. But now I'm thinking it might come in useful.

Lola has proved she's not beyond the realms of adultery. And so, although I never thought I had it in me, and I might have gone slightly insane with jealousy, I know what I must do.

Chapter Forty-Four

Detective Inspector John Banner

Saturday, 23rd December 2023

'Are you serious? You think I killed Lola? My best friend.'

Simone's a good actress, I'll give her that. She's had me and everyone fooled this past week. I wonder if she fooled Liam too? Not that he's innocent in all this, not by any stretch of the imagination. Just being in the same room as him, I'm finding it hard to keep my cool. He stalked and groomed numerous women online, pretended to be their friend, to care about them, getting to know their likes and dislikes, their fears and insecurities, their everyday routines and whereabouts, all so he could sexually assault them. Ruin their lives forever.

'Lola was like a sister to me,' Simone goes on. 'Her death is something I will never get over.'

'Because you cared so much about her?' I say.

'Yes.'

'Or because of your guilt? A guilt that will wear you down like a ball and chain for the rest of your natural life.'

'What the hell is this about, Inspector!' Liam says angrily, although I suspect, knowing the kind of man he really is behind the saintly façade he portrays to the world, inside he's probably leaping for joy that my focus is no longer on him. Not for now, at least. 'You're bang out of order accusing Simone like that,' he continues. 'Where's all this coming from? Simone is the kindest soul I know. Why would she want to kill Lola? Like she said, Lola was her best friend. Surely, it's the likes of Bianca you should be looking at. Not to mention the others in her toxic clique. Simone was only ever a good friend to Lola. It's why Bianca never told Simone about the photo she received, isn't it? Because she knew Simone would go straight to Lola.'

'Yes, and I'm sure that's precisely what Simone here was banking on,' I say.

Liam frowns.

'Just as she was banking on me arresting Damien Radcliffe, after she sent him a text at 11:15 p.m. last Friday pretending to be Lola and asking him to meet her at the River Cafe just off the main Portsmouth Road at midnight, where she knew he'd be caught on CCTV.'

At this, Simone's eyes fill with alarm. 'You need to leave now, Inspector. You have no right to come here making such frightful accusations without any proof.'

I look at Wild. 'The envelope, please?'

'Yes, sir.' Wild opens his bag. Pulls out a brown envelope. Opens the flap and removes its contents. An A4-sized photograph. He hands it to me.

'What's that?' Simone asks, her expression still fretful, while I can practically see beads of sweat lining Liam's forehead. I thrust the photo in Simone's direction. 'You mean proof like this?'

She freezes. Her expression speaking volumes. I note the similarly horrified look on Liam's face. 'I'm guessing you weren't aware, at least not at the time, that there are a number of CCTV cameras in Canbury Gardens?'

Simone doesn't answer. 'One of them is located near the Boaters pub. This still is taken from footage captured on Friday, 25th August. The same day Lola kissed Damien outside the Boaters. After realising that Liam was the only person I've handed my personal card to in months, aside from Elisa Mosley, and which you therefore had access to, Simone, it made me suspect that one of you sent me that anonymous text message on Wednesday morning. A message in which you made it clear that I should perhaps be looking at Joy, Deidre and Clarissa as potential suspects in Lola's murder because she apparently hadn't kept quiet about some pretty devastating secrets they were hiding. Not only that, indicating that I should be wary of Damien Radcliffe. I therefore decided to look back at the CCTV footage near the Boaters that day, hoping to God I was wrong in suspecting one of you.'

I let that sink in, the air thick with tension. Then I continue. 'You know, if you look hard enough, it's amazing what you can spot on CCTV. This photo of you standing behind a tree near the Boaters, for example, where you appear to be taking a photograph of something close by with your mobile phone. And what do you know, as I continued to scan the footage, zooming out slightly, I noticed Lola and Damien sharing a kiss perhaps thirty feet away from where you had concealed yourself. Confirming without a shadow of a doubt that it was you who sent Bianca Radcliffe that photograph.'

Simone places her hand on the nearby sofa for support. 'Do you need to sit down, Simone?' I ask.

She doesn't answer. Liam is silent too, his handsome face drained of colour.

'A short time later, you sent Clarissa, Joy and Deidre anonymous text messages, letting them know Lola had divulged their secrets, thereby giving them extra impetus to cut Lola out of their lives. And to all intents and purposes behave cruelly towards her. You wanted to plant the seed of an idea in the head of any future officer investigating Lola's murder. That seed being that each of those women, along with Bianca and her husband, Damien, who you knew Lola had been harassing, had a motive to kill her. And with you being at home with your girls the night of the Christmas party, you had the perfect alibi. I'm guessing you texted Lola that evening, wanting to know her whereabouts, thereby giving you the opportunity to catch her unawares and kill her. As her best friend, someone who had urged her not to go to the party, but rather come and spend the night at yours, no one would suspect you, and all eyes would be on those with an obvious vendetta.'

Liam is still wearing a horror-struck expression. 'Inspector, I think you're letting your imagination run wild,' he says. 'Simone would never leave our kids alone at night. And just because she sent Bianca that photo, it doesn't mean she sent the other messages, or killed Lola. You have no proof. How on earth would she know about these women's secrets?'

I look directly at him. 'Oh, I don't know, perhaps that's something you can help me with. *Tracy.*'

Chapter Forty-Five

Simone

Before
15th December 2023

It's 11 p.m. and my insides are heaving, knowing there will be no turning back from what I am about to do. What I am contemplating is wicked, I accept that, but I just can't stomach the thought of losing Liam. He is my world, my reason for living aside from my girls, and with Lola alive there's always the possibility he will leave me. I see the way he dotes on Luca, how he loves spending time with him, and it makes me green with envy. After learning the truth, I realised why he was so keen to babysit Luca last December when Lola and I went to Clarissa's for dinner, why he's always offering to kick a ball around with him, do 'boys' stuff'. I'm not sure he's ever looked upon the girls in the same way. Or felt that kind of connection. I simply can't carry on like this, it's driving me insane. As is knowing he's been inside Lola. Every time I see her, it's all I can think about. Her face, her sheer presence is a constant reminder of what she means to Liam. That he impregnated her. But with her gone, she'll be out of sight, out of mind, and I won't have to think about that anymore. I can move on, forgive Liam. And we can be one big happy family, the way I always dreamed of us being.

Since discovering that behind closed doors my husband is an online predator and a rapist, the past few months have been torture. Having to pretend I remain in blissful ignorance, putting on a face for Liam, and for everyone. Swallowing down my disgust and jealousy. Allowing him to make love to me when all I can think about are the numerous women he's been inside. All those so-called medical conferences Liam attended over the years suddenly make more sense. At the time, I never doubted he was telling me the truth, because, like the naïve fool I am, I trusted him implicitly. But when I did some research and looked at articles online about the Campus Prowler, about some of the universities he targeted, I realised they were all based in towns or cities Liam had visited on his supposed conferences, in the timeframes those students claimed to have been raped. I also realised that he started hurting me again shortly after all this came out in the press. I'm guessing he knew he couldn't risk it anymore. And this had angered him. Causing him to seek an alternative way to expel his anger. Via someone easily accessible. Someone devoted to him, who would never talk. Never leave him.

Me.

As I said, I haven't told Liam I know the truth. Even when he's been violent with me and I've been so tempted to. He thinks I remain his feeble patsy. Has no idea of the plan I've been forging. I've allowed him to carry on chatting with Lola as Tracy. But whenever he's been at work or out with the kids, that's when I've caught up on their correspondence, always deleting the history, of course. Giving me ammunition, and allowing me to stay one step ahead of the game until the time is right to make my move, having sowed the seeds of doubt.

Sending Bianca that photograph was the first step. I knew it would turn her against Lola for good. Giving her a motive to want Lola gone. The next step was sending Clarissa, Joy and Dee separate messages insinuating that Lola had betrayed their secrets to a complete stranger. Of course, Lola never divulged in her chats with 'Tracy' what secrets Joy and Dee were actually keeping. But I didn't need to go into detail. All I needed to say was that I knew what they were hiding. Knowing it would be enough to scare them, anger them, cause them to cut Lola off completely, a fact I intend to make clear to the police over the coming days. I just haven't quite figured out how exactly I'm going to do that. I've also been sending Lola sporadic texts, threatening her and Luca's lives, in such a way as to make her wonder if any of the women could be behind them, as well as the possibility that it's her rapist back to make good on his threat from years ago. To my delight she's told 'Tracy' about these messages, something that I can tell has puzzled Liam and caused him sleepless nights.

But the text I'm about to send is the most important of all. I look over it one last time, then press send.

> Damien, it's Lola. I'm using my mum's phone because I lost mine yesterday. Tonight has been awful, I can't believe you didn't have the guts to show your face. I thought we could talk. Smooth things over. I hated how things ended last time in your office. Plus I think you know why the others have been treating me like shit, despite denying it. You have to meet with me this evening. If you don't, I'm going to send your father an email telling him about us. I'll make sure your clients know too. And then I'll swallow a bottle of pills, because I can't go on like this. Can't be rejected time and time again. Meet me at midnight by the River Café. I'm sure you don't want my blood on your hands. Or Luca losing his mother. And you certainly don't want your name being pulled through the mud. Lola x

I'm banking on him being too scared for his reputation not to do as she asks. There's a little slope going down to the River Café from the main Portsmouth Road, where I know there's a CCTV camera, and so I'm hoping that, before long, the police will spot him when they look back at the footage. It's just a matter of time.

I go to Liam's study where he keeps various medicines stashed in a cabinet – doctors are the worst for abusing their position and hoarding all kinds of medication – and remove the bottle of sevoflurane, placing it in my coat pocket, along with a tea towel and a pair of latex gloves. Then I fasten my hair in a tight low ponytail which I set with firm hairspray before placing the cheap black cap

I bought the other week from Amazon securely over my head, so as to ensure no hair of mine will be dislodged and found on or near Lola's body. My heart is thumping like crazy right now and I can hardly believe what I'm about to do – the monster I've become – in taking a mother away from her child. But I can't help myself. It's her or me who has to die, and my girls need me. I can't trust Liam to take care of them the way they deserve to be taken care of should he worm his way into Lola's affections in the event something happens to me.

Yesterday evening was the first communication I'd had with Lola with me playing the role of Tracy. Hopefully it will be the last. Liam flew to France for his medical conference – a real one for once – around 3 p.m., so I knew there was no chance of him walking in on me. I'd been a bit concerned because around a fortnight ago they fell out. 'Tracy' had told her not to go to the party, suggested she'd be better off hanging out with me that evening. It was clear Liam was worried about Luca. About the potential damage Lola's obsession with Damien would do to his son if she kept going on like this. I guess he was worried about Lola being forced out of the school by the likes of Bianca, the shame possibly causing her to move and our consequently losing contact with her and Luca. St Xavier's was Liam's way of establishing a connection with Luca, I see that now. It's why 'Tracy' recommended it to Lola as a possibility for Luca back when she was looking at schools.

Lola had become angry in their last exchange, and didn't reply to 'Tracy's' messages for nearly a fortnight. Causing Liam to take out his frustration on me on several occasions. I was on the brink of telling him I knew only too well why he was in such a bad mood, but I managed to

...in myself. And then, thankfully, yesterday around 5 ... Lola sent 'Tracy' a message apologising, and I was so ...ieved, because it was perfect timing. Liam was away by ...en, of course. I knew there was a chance he might log on from France and answer her. But somehow I doubted it. I think he feels safer conducting all his dirty work from the privacy of our house. It was still a risk pretending to be Tracy and messaging Lola, of course. But a risk I took nonetheless. I made a point of apologising to Lola, encouraging her to go to the party, to stand up to those bullies at school, no matter what 'Simone' said. Of course, I had previously and repeatedly asked her round to ours this evening, knowing I planned on encouraging her to do the exact opposite as Tracy. But in the end, I had faith that she would do as Tracy suggested. She always does, because she trusts her implicitly. I'm guessing she was a bit surprised at her confidante's change of heart, but I also think she was secretly glad. Because it gave her the perfect excuse to see Damien again. Thinking he'd be there. She's not unlike me in that sense. Obsessed with a bad guy. Still smitten despite the unkindness done to her.

After signing off, I deleted all her and 'Tracy's' chat, spanning seven-and-a-half years. Thankfully, there was a 'delete all' option, else it would have taken me all night to do so. I know it's possible the police will find out about Lola's time on Here to Chat – they will look over her devices and the means to recover the chat from Lola's end assuming she didn't use a VPN like Liam – but by then I'm hoping enough suspicion will have been laid on the other women. And Damien, of course. And that the police will simply think 'Tracy' got scared, and was worried she might be their next target.

Time is ticking, and now, glancing at my watch, I see that it's just on 11:15 p.m. I need to think about heading out. I don't want to leave things too late, even though I know Lola's still at the party because I'm registered with Celltrack, which allows you to trace someone's phone. There are so many things that could go wrong. For one, she might end up getting a cab rather than walk home. I deliberately advised her to pre-book one the other day, just to see what the chances of her walking home might be. To my delight, she said she'd play it by ear, see how the evening went, and that she was used to walking in any case so it wouldn't be the end of the world. It's fucking freezing and dark as hell out there, so I know for sure she'll regret her decision. But when she said all that, it was a struggle not to jump for joy. All I can do is bank on the fact that she'll never get a cab so late at this time of year. Also that, for obvious reasons, she'll be too nervous to ask anyone in our immediate circle if she can share a ride home with them. She barely talks to any of the parents outside our group so I'm also hoping she won't have the nerve to ask any of them either.

Still, she might prove me wrong and, like I said, there are a whole host of reasons why my plan could go awry. But I try not to dwell on them. If it doesn't work out today, I'll have to think up some other plan, when Liam is next away. It's frustrating, but not insurmountable. I quickly check on the girls. They're fast asleep. The Piriton syrup I gave them always does the trick. I say a silent prayer that they'll be safe, even though I know I don't deserve God's mercy.

I tuck my ponytail under my cap, sneak out the back door and double lock it, my eyes scanning my surroundings to make sure I've not been spotted. Then I start

g. Keeping my head down at all times. It's a twenty-
te fast walk to the river. I've memorised where all
CCTV cameras leading to it are located, and plan on
king them and taking as many side streets as possible
avoid being seen.

When it gets to 11:40 p.m. and I'm five minutes from
he river, I send Lola a text:

> Hey, honey, how's the party going? Hope it's been fun in the end and that Bianca's not been too much of a bitch. Let me know the goss when you can. Watching Love Actually for the millionth time, wish you were here, S xx

I keep walking, but get nothing back. What does that mean? She can't have not seen the message because she's too busy partying it up with the girls. They all hate her, I made sure of that. Unless she's made other friends? Or they've had it out, in some big heated argument? No, I don't think so. The others would have been too scared to tell Lola about the texts, because I made it clear their continued freedom depended on it.

I stop, check Celltrack again, see that Lola's left the hotel, and is walking along the main Portsmouth Road in the direction of her apartment in Riverside Walk. The same place I'm headed for, only from the other direction. That's good news, but I need to elicit a response from her, so I can show it to the police and make out that I was concerned. I pull out my burner phone and send another message. Only this time not from me, but from the person she thinks has been threatening her these past weeks. Hopefully she'll feel the urge to reply to me after that. To seek comfort from her best friend. It's only human nature.

> You think you can slink away like that, you filthy slut. Shy away from who you really are, from your past. You don't get to do that. I warned you not to talk, but you did. Even though you thought I wouldn't find out. Your son will be so much better off without you. You don't deserve Luca. Don't deserve to be a mother.

It works. Within five minutes I get a response on my regular phone. She tells me I was right and that she's left the party because it was a nightmare and that she had to get away. She explains she's walking home, taking a short cut along the river path because there are no cabs, and that, in any case, she doesn't mind so much as she prefers to walk. I could almost do a cartwheel. What a stroke of luck in there being no cabs available. Still, I feign my horror and I quickly text her back:

> WTF, are you fucking crazy?? I know you like walking, but it's pitch-black dark, it's not safe. Go back to the hotel now, I'll call you a cab. S x

There's a risk she'll do as I say but it's a chance I have to take. I need to convince the police I was looking out for her this evening. The only one of her mum friends to do so. The only one she trusted. But I'm also hoping the other message I sent her from my burner will give her the impetus to keep walking, because she's desperate to get back to Luca and can't waste time turning back in the hope of finding a cab.

To my relief, it does. She texts me back, thanks me for offering to get her a cab but explains that she needs to get back to Luca, and that she's nearly home anyway so it makes sense for her to keep on walking. I instantly message her back, tell her she's a nutter, but that she should text me as soon as she's home safe and sound. She promises me she'll do that, and I can't help but smile inside, once again feeling relieved that it's all going according to plan.

It's now a little after midnight and Damien should be waiting for Lola by the café. I need to get rid of him. I stop, pull out my burner and send him a text:

> I changed my mind, something's come up and I'm not coming anymore. You should go home to your kids. Don't worry, I'm not going to kill myself anytime soon. Or blab. You can rest easy. For now. Lola x

Fingers crossed he'll leave straight away, so there's no chance of him bumping into Lola, or spotting me. I carry on walking, being sure to keep my head down, the adrenaline pummelling through me as I cross over the pedestrian precinct to Riverside Walk where Lola lives. There are scores of late-night revellers about, what with it being the Christmas party season, and a popular area for drinking and dining. I walk fast to the main boardwalk, then make a left where there's a slight slope taking me down to the narrower, quieter river path, which Lola will have taken coming from the other direction. I move quickly, worried she might appear before I have time to hide myself. Even more fearful that Damien might still be there. But he's not, to my relief. And thankfully, there's no sign of Lola yet. I reach the café. It closes at 6 p.m., so there's no one about and, in any case, you'd be a fool to walk along here in this icy weather at gone midnight. I hide myself behind the cafe, my heart galloping. Then I douse the tea towel I brought with a good amount of sevoflurane. And that's when Luca's sweet face flashes through my mind, and I think about the first time I met Lola, what a good friend she's been to me, a friend I thought I had made for life, until that night I discovered what she and Luca meant to Liam. *Am I really going to do this?*

But then I think about the way Liam looks at Lola with Luca, the way he'd thrust himself into her, the possibility he might seduce her into his bed one of these days and ditch me, and it gives me the courage to see this through. I simply cannot bear to lose him, lose my family. It would kill me.

I hear the sound of heels approaching, a woman's frantic breathing, and I know it can only be Lola. She rushes past the café, not spotting me, and that's when I make my move, and pull out my burner phone and dial her number. She may not answer, of course, I just want to startle her, slow her down. It's my lucky night because she does answer, when I am less than three feet behind her.

And then I speak. 'I thought it only right you know the truth before you die, Lola. Liam is Tracy, Luca's father. The Campus Prowler. His secret benefactor. He brought you here to Kingston, has been manipulating you all this time. But he won't get to do that anymore. I'm here to make sure of that.'

Before she has the chance to react, I jump on her from behind, causing her to let go of her phone, which drops to the ground with a crash. I place the tea towel over her mouth and keep it there. Tight. She barely even struggles. I think she's too much in shock. Plus, she's such a slight thing. And then she collapses backwards into my arms. I pick up her phone, stuff it in my pocket, then drag her to the edge and waste no time in rolling her over onto the bank, my eyes darting left and right to make sure there's no one around. And then I place my gloved hands over her mouth. Depriving her of oxygen. Depriving her of life. Depriving her of Liam's love. Depriving Luca of his mother. She's so out of it, again she hardly puts up a fight. It's so easy, almost too easy in fact.

And then, just like that she is dead, her body limp. No pulse, no sign of her heart beating.

What the fuck have I done?

I don't dwell on that, though. I can't, for the sake of my girls. I must get back to them. I quickly stuff the tea towel back into my jacket pocket then scramble back up onto the pathway, before making my way towards Riverside Walk. But this time I don't walk through the piazza. I keep going, in the direction of Kingston Bridge. As I do, I send two messages from Lola's phone. One to her mother saying she'd decided to crash at a friend's house a short walk from the hotel, and so she shouldn't worry about waiting up for her, and that she'd call in the morning to say when she'd be coming home. Then, around five minutes later, as I take a right down a side street by The Bishop pub, where I know there is no CCTV, I send a message from Lola's phone to mine, confirming she'd reached home safely and would call me tomorrow.

Twenty minutes later, having taken a combination of smaller side streets, again with no CCTV, and thankfully passing no one on route, though I was alive to the fact I might be jumped on at any given moment, I'm standing outside my back door. I think I'm going to be sick as I open it and go inside. It's freezing outside, but I'm perspiring everywhere. The first thing I do is check on the girls. I'm relieved to see they are safe and sleeping soundly.

I then go back downstairs, fling off my cap, my forehead drenched with sweat, and pour myself a large whisky. Because I'm shaking. Not from the cold, but at the thought of what I've done. The risk I've just taken.

But Liam is worth the risk. Despite all he's done. I know that, deep down, he loves me. And now with Lola out of the picture he will stay with me forever. And together we can ingratiate ourselves into Luca's life, become surrogate parents to him. Elisa is fond of me, so it shouldn't be a problem getting her and Don to agree. They'll be glad of the help.

And it's for all these reasons that I find myself picking up my phone and dialling Liam's number. After five rings, he answers, sounding like he's half asleep. I guess it is nearly 2 a.m. in France.

'Simone, what's wrong?'

I waste no timing in dropping a bombshell he'd never in a million years expect. Not from me, his docile, sweet Simone.

'I know what you did. To her and to the others. *Tracy.* You need to come home asap so we can make plans for when the police come knocking on our door. We need to get our stories straight.'

He'll be angry at first. But then, when he really thinks about what I've done, and what I can do to him, it'll make him fear me forever.

The tables have turned, and I'm the one in control now.

Chapter Forty-Six

Detective Inspector John Banner

Tuesday, 2nd January 2024

It's my first day back at the station after nearly a week off. I was glad for the rest, to be honest. Not just because it allowed me to spend precious time with Jo and Mikey, but because the investigation into Lola's death really took its toll on me, both physically and mentally. It always does whenever kids are involved. Justice must be served, I know that, even if it means two innocent children end up having their parents taken away from them. But it pains me all the same, knowing that they will forever live under the shadow of their parents' crimes. Scarred for life. The only saving grace is that Simone's sister and her husband seem like good people, allowing me to take some comfort in their pledge to raise their nieces with the love and care they deserve, as if they were their own.

Despite both Simone and Liam continuing to proclaim their innocence, the CCTV footage of Simone photographing Bianca and Damien kissing in Canbury Gardens back in August was enough to give us reasonable grounds to believe she had committed an offence, thereby enabling us to search their house and seize anything we believed to be evidence of that offence and any further related crimes.

This included her and Liam's laptops, plus a number of unregistered phones concealed in a locked briefcase on the top shelf of a wardrobe in their spare room. And, more damningly, Lola's phone. It didn't take digital forensics long to access both, leading to Simone's and Liam's arrests. As if the Mosleys hadn't suffered enough, I then had to break the crushing news to them that Lola's killer was her best friend. Elisa collapsed, and the paramedics had to be called to the scene. Yesterday, Elisa's brother, Rafael, arrived from Spain to help Don care for Luca while Elisa recovers. It's all so sad, so tragic, and not for the first time it makes me wonder why such terrible things happen to the least deserving of people.

I guess I'll never know what secrets Deidre and Joy confided in Lola; that's something Lola went to her grave with. I just hope whatever they did, it is something they can live with, and make up for in their lives going forward, rather than let it eat them alive the way a guilty conscience often can. They, along with Clarissa, Bianca and Damien, were shocked to hear the news, of course. Simone and Liam had appeared to live the perfect life. Be the perfect couple. But I reminded them that perfect doesn't exist. That there's always darkness where there is light. And that all of us have flaws, secrets. Some darker than others.

I get a knock on my door. 'Come in.'

It's Wild. 'Sir, the DNA report came back on Liam Loxley. I thought you'd want to open it.'

'Thanks, Wild.' I take the envelope from him, open it up. Pull out the sheet of paper confirming Luca is Liam's son.

Only he isn't. It's not a match.

I sit back in my chair. Feel crushed by the cruel irony of it all.

Simone killed Lola for nothing.

Chapter Forty-Seven

Lola

Before
Early May 2017

I sit down resignedly on the toilet lid and wait for the three longest minutes of my life to pass. I can't bear to hold the pregnancy stick in my hand while I wait, it's too excruciating, even though I know I cannot delay the inevitable. I glance left, see it lying there on the side of the bath. Almost taunting me with its presence.

It's been nearly two weeks since that monster raped me. And in the last few days, I've started getting all kinds of weird feelings. My breasts have felt unusually tender, while the smell of coffee and tuna, normally two of my favourites, is making me want to gag. I've also been feeling nauseous, not to mention incredibly fatigued, but I guess those unpleasant symptoms could be the result of what happened to me. The fact that, psychologically, it's taken its toll, inducing all kinds of physical symptoms. That horrific night never leaves me. I think about it every second I am awake, and it plagues my dreams at night. I am broken. A different person. I can't face speaking to Mum and Dad. I keep telling them I'm too busy to chat, even though I've always been able to make time for them.

I've missed lectures, ditched my friends. But worst of all, I've been ignoring Sean's calls and messages. They have become increasingly frantic. Fuelling the guilt in me.

Sean. The guy I've been seeing for a few months. The guy who's stolen my heart. Who makes my heart flutter every time I'm in his presence. We met at a house party. Hit it off straight away. He's good-looking, smart, but most of all he's funny and caring and makes me feel special. Loved. Safe. I've not told Mum and Dad about him yet. I wanted to wait a while to see how things progressed. Neither have I mentioned him to Tracy. Only for different reasons. She's so wary of men, having just come out of a controlling relationship, and told me to steer clear of relationships while I focus on my finals. So I don't want to worry her. She's been so kind and helpful with the panic attacks I've been suffering from. Attacks I've been too embarrassed to tell Mum or Dad about. Sean too. I don't want to let my parents down, or for Sean to think any less of me.

He and I made love a week before that bastard attacked me. Shortly afterwards, he went on a ten-day field trip to Paris as part of his filmmaking course. We used a condom, of course. Like we always do, just because the pill has never agreed with me. He told me he loved me, that when we graduated, he wanted us to move to London together and share a flat. Like me, he has his heart set on making it in the big city – me pursuing a career in publishing, him in screenwriting. I love how creative he is, how we share similar interests, how at ease I feel in his company. I could see myself spending the rest of my life with him, and I had plans to introduce him to my parents the next time they visit.

But then, just like that, in the blink of an eye it seemed, my world changed. I feel so disgusted with myself, and I cannot bear to look Sean in the eye. I keeping blanking his calls, ignoring his texts. I feel so cruel in giving him no explanation, but I also feel too ashamed to tell him the truth. Neither can I bear to face the outside world, my attacker's parting threat before he left me in a crumpled heap in that wretched alleyway never leaving me. I so badly want to go to the police, but I'm too scared. Besides, any evidence is all but destroyed. Both inside me, and on the clothes I took to the local tip because I couldn't bear to have them in my student flat.

Three minutes is up. I feel sick as I raise myself up from the toilet lid and go over to the bath. Even without picking the test up I can see the result. Two blue lines. I collapse to the floor and weep.

As much as I'd like to believe the baby is Sean's, I know I am kidding myself. Condoms are over ninety per cent effective, and Sean would have noticed if it had split, I'm certain of that.

But that monster put his bare penis inside me. OK, so he withdrew before he ejaculated. I'm guessing that was part of the thrill for him, the sick bastard. But everyone knows it's a highly risky method. It has to be his, I can feel it in my bones. My life is over, and I have to end things permanently with Sean now, as much as it breaks my heart. It will be torture seeing him around campus, trying to avoid him this last month at uni. But somehow, I'll make it through. I don't have a choice. I at least need to finish my studies; I owe it to myself and to my parents. And then, when we graduate, I'll tell Sean never to contact me again, to pretend like I never existed. It will break his heart, but I don't have a choice, like I said. He'll get over me, find someone else, I know he will. I cannot kill this baby; it's against my faith, everything I believe in. But neither can I place such a burden on Sean. It wouldn't be fair.

I slowly get up. Feel a panic attack coming on. I need to talk to someone. Someone I can trust, who won't judge me. Who I know will offer me good advice and calm me down, make me see a way through this. And it's at this point that I realise my best option is Tracy. I'll go online, tell her what happened to me, and she will make me feel better, tell me it's going to be OK. I know she will.

With her help, I'll get through this.

I am so lucky to have found her.

I don't know what I'd do without her.

My friend, my lifeline.

Epilogue

Detective Inspector John Banner

Six Months Later
July 2024

It's good to see Luca running around again with a smile on his face. Equally heartening to see his devoted grandparents looking happier and healthier. Nothing will ever fill the horrendous void left by Lola's tragic death. But with time, it will get easier. Just like my mum used to say. Particularly now that they have Sean in their lives.

I watch him throw the frisbee back and forth with Luca, the son he only came to learn existed in January. After the DNA results revealed that Liam wasn't Luca's father, I became determined to find out who was. From the first, this case affected me deeper than most. I guess because Luca's around my son's age and the very thought of Mikey being left without a parent makes me sick to my stomach. After all the trauma Luca has suffered, he deserves some resemblance of a happy ending, even if it's a bittersweet one. And for me it became a mission of sorts to track down his real father. But initially, my efforts were in vain. It seemed that, since graduating, Lola had lost touch with everyone on her course and those she lived with in her student digs. Deliberately so. Which I suppose shouldn't have come as a surprise to me, knowing how determined she was to start over with a new name, a fresh start in life. I tracked down various individuals through records kept by Edinburgh University, but while a few of Lola's acquaintances remembered Lola had been seeing someone in her final year, and that he was called Sean, none of them could recall his surname, or the course he'd been studying. Apparently, they'd only been together a few months, and I'm guessing Lola was perhaps reticent about broadcasting the fact in case she jinxed things, as appeared to be in her nature. Having trawled through her chat with 'Tracy', it's clear Lola never mentioned Sean in any of their conversations, and so Liam would have had no reason to suspect Luca was anyone's child but his. But then, one day, when I was feeling frustrated at having turned up yet another dead end and had all but lost hope, Sean Emery walked into the station. I couldn't believe it when he told me who he was. It was as if my prayers had been answered, restoring in me some semblance of faith in a higher being. He'd read about Lola's death in the newspapers, had recognised her from a photo they'd printed, and was also aware she'd been a victim of Liam Loxley, the Campus Prowler in her final year at university. Shocked to discover this, he had wasted no time in coming to see me, seeking answers to the myriad of questions plaguing his mind.

Sean told me he'd never got over Lola, never understood why she'd ended things so abruptly, and without explanation. He'd been deeply hurt, but had always felt that, deep down, she'd been spooked by something. Or someone. And she had either been too afraid or too ashamed to tell Sean what it was.

And so, I told him. Told him every last little detail. It brought Sean to tears, and resulted in him taking a DNA test which delivered the joyous news that he was, in fact, Luca's biological father. The silver lining to a terrible tragedy.

Things could have been so different, and I know it's like a knife through Elisa's and Don's hearts when they think about what could have been. The fact that Lola and Sean could have lived a long and happy life together with Luca, their son.

Still, Luca has a father now. Flesh and blood to protect him the way Lola had done so fiercely.

He will be loved.

That's all that matters.